HEAVEN LIE ABOUT US

Eugene McCabe was born in Glasgow in 1930. His
works include the highly-acclaimed novel *Death and
Nightingales* and the trilogy of plays, *Victims*, one of
which, *Cancer*, won the Prague International Award. He
lives and works on a farm on the Monaghan/Fermanagh
border.

ALSO BY EUGENE McCABE

Prose:

Death and Nightingales
Tales from the Poorhouse
Heritage and Other Stories
Christ in the Fields
Cyril

Plays:

Pull Down a Horseman
Gale Day
King of the Castle

Eugene McCabe

HEAVEN LIES
ABOUT US

𝑉

VINTAGE

Published by Vintage 2006

2 4 6 8 10 9 7 5 3 1

First published in Great Britain in 2005 by
Jonathan Cape

Vintage
Random House, 20 Vauxhall Bridge Road,
London SW1V 2SA

Random House Australia (Pty) Limited
20 Alfred Street, Milsons Point, Sydney
New South Wales 2061, Australia

Random House New Zealand Limited
18 Poland Road, Glenfield, Auckland 10, New Zealand

Random House (Pty) Limited
Isle of Houghton, Corner of Boundary Road & Carse O'Gowrie,
Houghton 2198, South Africa

The Random House Group Limited Reg. No. 954009
www.randomhouse.co.uk/vintage

A CIP catalogue record for this book
is available from the British Library

ISBN 978 0099 470328 (from Jan 2007)

ISBN 0 099 47032 2

Papers used by Random House are natural, recyclable products made from wood grown in sustainable forests. The manufacturing processes conform to the environmental regulations of the country of origin

Printed and bound in Great Britain by
Cox & Wyman Limited, Reading, Berkshire

For Margot for a lifetime

Let's ignore the curlew's lament, nor mind
The brown hawk motionless above the wood
In broken light, the lake a silver blind
Below that single yew that's long withstood
The storms that hurl and howl from Lisnaroe
To strip the beech and fill the empty yard
With ghosts, invoicing us of what we owe
To time. Now Winter's marching round Drumard
We'll log up stoves against the coming cold
Much to live for, still more to remember
And never, ever talk of growing old.
Light can catch the glory in November
Of summers past and though God gives no sign
When love is all there is no final line.

CONTENTS

Heaven Lies About Us	1
Truth	35
Victorian Fields	45
Roma	57
Music at Annahullion	63
Cancer	75
Heritage	87
Victims	141
The Orphan	221
The Master	239
The Landlord	267
The Mother	295

If there is a sin against life, it is not perhaps so much to despair of life, as to hope for another life and to lose sight of the implacable grandeur of this one.

— Albert Camus

Heaven Lies About Us

HALF THINKING, HALF dreaming, she could make out from the cold light of her bedroom window Jesus sitting in the sun at the root of a great tree outside Nazareth or Jerusalem, where her mother had gone on her wedding holiday. Marion knew she had to be careful not to say honeymoon. It wasn't a bad word like the ones she heard at school, but her mother didn't say honeymoon. She said wedding holiday, explaining that wedding meant a solemn pledge or promise and holiday was really holy day and that marriage was a sacrament and that children were a gift from God.

All the children in the picture were loving Jesus and staring up at Him, holding on to His arms and legs. One of them was hanging round His neck. She could see that He was loving them. He was kissing the hair of one child's head, the little one on His knee.

In the margin of the framing at the top it said, "Suffer the little children to come unto Me."

Three years ago, when she was five, Uncle Felix had given her that for a birthday present. He was a priest in a monastery near Enniskillen, "not a *passionate* priest," her mother had corrected her. "It's Passionist, dear, as in the passion of Jesus," and Iggy would join their mother and say, "It's not the grand monastery either, it's the Graan monastery, and while we're at it, hospital is not hostipple, tomatoes are not bebomatos, they're tomatoes as in your big toe." That made her think of Iggy's big tommytoe and she wanted to keep that out of her head because it made her sick to think about it, and about him.

Yesterday Uncle Felix had given a one-day retreat for the boys in the Louis Convent primary. Today it was the girls' turn; midday Mass and sermon, confession and then another sermon, followed by Benediction of the Blessed Sacrament.

In the bottom margin of the picture there were three lines:

> Oh Jesus who for love of me
> Didst bear Thy cross to Calvary
> Grant to me to suffer and to die with Thee.

More than once her mother said, "That child on the Saviour's knee has golden hair like yours, Marion, and the same sky-blue eyes," but Uncle Felix said, "No, Marion's hair is more silver-blonde, more like white gold." That was hard to imagine. Gold was yellow, like a wedding ring. White was like the snowdrops all over the grounds and near the avenue gates, more like the white of her confirmation blouse with its blue shamrocks stitched on to the collar. She had said, "Blue is wrong, Mammy, shamrocks are green," but her mother said, "Blue, dear, is the colour of Our Lady's mantle, of the sea and of heaven; it wards off evil and impurity." When she thought about this, she asked, "How can you be certain if something you think or something you've done is bad?"

"For one thing, you're dedicated to Our Lady, you share her name as I do, and she'd never mislead you; also you've got a guardian angel and he *never* sleeps, and that is one example of the proper use of the word 'never' . . . it's a word people overuse all the time . . . *He* tells you what's right and wrong . . . your conscience really."

"In my dreams even?"

"Yes, even in your dreams, dear. Yes."

Some dreams were so real and so shameful she could cry now or any time thinking about them. Was it dreaming or not when Iggy came those nights when her mother was in Dublin for a fortnight's retreat at the Marie Reparatrix convent or Enniskillen for a weekend seminar with Uncle Felix at the Graan, and only Bridie in the maid's room at the back of the house with the separate staircase? He came and he did those things and it wasn't dreaming because each time when she wondered if it was a dream she found soiled knickers in the bedside cupboard next morning though she could not remember putting them there the night before. Two pairs she flung into the river below the grotto and the third she burned in the range when Bridie was up ironing in the old nursery. That time she wanted to go up and tell her but she didn't know how. She had a chance another time when Bridie asked about the blood on the sheets and she lied in fright, saying she'd cut herself.

"'Deed and you didn't cut yourself, love, blood is nothing to be afeared of, or ashamed of, it could be the start of your monthlies." As Bridie went on to explain, she kept thinking, I'll tell, I'll tell, I'll tell, but didn't, and heard Bridie say, "Don't let on I told you. Your mammy mightn't care about me tellin' before herself." And if she couldn't tell Bridie about Iggy, how could she ever tell her mother about how when she was very small he'd hold her up against his tommytoe till all the grey stuff came out, or the time in the bath he'd put the toothbrush into her bottom and then washed off the twotwos from the handle and from the little hole at the end and said with his Iggy smile, "Good as new." Or the other awful time he put it right up between her legs and it was so sore she screamed and bled and all he said was, "Crybaby, what's up with you?" and she'd said, "I hate this game, Iggy, and I'm going to tell Mammy when she gets back!"

"You will not – or you'll have us both in trouble. It's your fault as much as mine and *you* know that. *You* know that well."

He always said *we* and *us* till she shouted once, "It was *you*, Iggy, just *you* every time 'cause I was fast asleep."

"Go on," he'd said, "don't pretend. You like it as much as I do," and she'd said, "I hate it and I hate you."

All he did then was shrug and walk away.

Where was her guardian angel then? Did Iggy have a guardian angel? Who told him to do those things with the toothbrush and his finger and his tongue to make her head go all swimmy? Was it the Devil did that?

When those things came into her head she felt so soiled, so unhappy, she wanted to shout aloud all the ugly words she'd ever heard at school. Those feelings only came when they were kneeling at the Rosary in winter or down at the grotto in summer, or during the quiet belltime of the Mass when the church was silent and full, and the priest was turning the bread and wine into the body and blood of Christ and her head was so full of the foulness that she longed to shout out, and to stop herself from doing so made her tremble and sweat and feel sickish. She had to leave the church once, and another time bite her top lip so hard it all swoll up. Afterwards Bridie asked, "What happened to your lip, love?"

She had stared at Iggy eating his breakfast and he'd stared back at her as if he half knew what was in her head, daring her to speak, to say: "It's because of *him*, my brother of sixteen, who put his hand over my mouth the first time and the pain was terrible, a white burning pain and I was raw and bleeding after . . . *him*, Bridie, with the green eyes like Mammy and the reddish wavy hair, him always showing off his teeth, Captain of the Junior House at Mungret whose last report said, 'An exemplar to the whole school,' and Mammy reading it out so proud and telling everyone." How could she ever be told . . . ? She'd die of shame . . . So it's me has to die . . . every day and night, ashamed, ashamed, ashamed . . . and the secret hid, but how could you hide such things from God and His mother and all the angels and saints and the millions of dead souls looking down . . . seeing everything? Iggy didn't seem to care about any of that. Was his guardian angel a bad one pretending to be a good one? If she couldn't tell Bridie, she couldn't ever tell anyone except L, her teddy bear. And that was something else she didn't want to think about. So she thought, I'll think of Knockmacarooney in July. That was where Bridie lived in a mountainy area of Fermanagh under Carn rock. She always got those first two weeks off to help her mother and father at hay and in the bog. Last year Marion was allowed to go with her. They were the fourteen happiest days of her life so far, the hearth, and the bog and a horse pulling tumblers of hay in a steep meadow and neighbours being awful nice, "Who is this princess, Bridie?" and the ass and trap to Mass on Sunday. Not a single word about novenas and daily Masses and pilgrimages, and St. Joseph's Young Priests' Society and Lourdes and miracles and Uncle Ambrose in Rome and Uncle Felix in Enniskillen and special prayers for darkest Africa and the conversion of communist Russia and Iggy Iggy Iggy, Munster Captain of the junior tennis team and how the *Cork Examiner* said he was almost certain to be a member of the Davis Cup team before long, like his father before him, the late Philip Cantwell, MRCVS. One night when she asked Bridie's father why he called the boar he kept "de Valera," he laughed and spat in the fire and said, "Because he's a very long, very cute auld bollox, that's why."

Old Mrs. Rooney pretended to be cross and said, "It's not right, Dan, talkin' that way fornenst the child." Bridie laughed and said, "She knows far worse than that from school," to which Marion agreed and then said, "If he was my boar I wouldn't call him de Valera."

"Would you not now?"

"No, Mrs. Rooney."

"What name would you put on him so?"

"Iggy."

Bridie's parents did not understand. Bridie intervened and said, "She's bold as brass, this lassie. Her brother's name is Iggy . . . Ignatius."

4

"And why," Old Rooney persisted, "would you call a boar after your brother?"

"Because."

"Because what?"

"Just because."

"You wouldn't be that horrid fond of him?"

She had shrugged. Sensing that she would not tell, the talk went on to other things.

Apart from that fortnight with Bridie, daytime at school was the time she liked best. You could read, and learn and play, but not with the Culligan twins or any of the children who lived out the new line in Casement Park. This was not said but it was strongly implied. Her best friend, well, pal of sorts really, and warmly approved by her mother, was Martina Flanagan, who said most of the Casement Park crowd should have their mouths rinsed out with Jeyes Fluid and mustard. Martina's father gave you a pink drink to rinse out your mouth in his surgery. "All that rough talk," Martina said, "is what they hear in their own houses. It's not their fault, they can't help it really."

That was true, Marion thought, because one evening two years ago at homework she'd blobbed her ecker with a dip pen and said quietly to herself, "Ah, fuck me." Her mother was sitting at the fire crocheting the cuff of a surplice for the St. Joseph's Young Priests' Society. The crocheting stopped. When Marion looked up, her mother's face had gone very white and her one good eye looked round and staring.

"What did you say just now?"

"Nothing, Mammy."

"I can't quite believe what I think I heard."

Silence.

"It's only a word."

"Where did you hear it?"

"At school."

Infants!?

"In the playground mostly."

"What child uttered it?"

"Do I have to tell?"

"Yes."

"And will you tell Sister Dominic?"

"I don't like telltales but I do like to know."

Her mother was always saying things like that. How could she find out except from a telltale? But if you said the like of that to her she'd go into a huge huff. Marion went back to recopying her ecker, hoping her mother would forget. She never did.

"You're going to have to tell me, Marion."

"What do you want me to tell, Mammy?"

"What child or children use that ugly word?"

"Well . . . there's the Culligan twins for starters, and Sadie Caffrey and Josie McGuinness, they're the worst. But there's loads more. They just say it when there's no nuns about and no one passes any remarks on them."

After a long silence her mother said, "I don't ever want to hear that word on your tongue again . . . in my life. It's unspeakably coarse and those poor children who use it in common talk have no notion how much they're offending God and Our Lady. Do you understand me, Marion?"

"Yes, Mammy."

"Never in my life again . . . never on your tongue."

That was two nevers, and for the rest of that evening she worked out that you had to use your tongue for luck, tuck, duck and stuck, but fuck was just your top teeth on your lower lip and maybe the tiniest bit of your tongue away in the back of your mouth. And all the way up the thirty steps of the staircase to the landing she said fuck to herself at every step because it was nowhere near her tongue. When she knelt to say her prayers that night she asked God to forgive her for being bold. She knew well it was far from being bad.

Yesterday during the boys' retreat the Culligan twins were smoking cigarette butts behind the handball alleys and everyone said their skit was the best ever . . . or worst, all laughing, and laughing, and laughing, Martina Flanagan the loudest. They gave out the skit, every second line making big eyes and pursing their mouths up and making big eyes like Sister Emmanuel in pretended disapproval.

> Joseph and Mary went into the dairy
> Where Joseph showed Mary his hairy canary.

It went on, getting ruder, coarser and more detailed with every line. It took her breath away because it was exactly what Iggy had done to her, and the last two lines made her wonder with sudden fear:

> Oh Mary Macushla tell us quick and don't tease us,
> I was thinkin', says she, of callin' him Jesus.

Could a baby grow inside her from what Iggy did?

After the skit Martina said that if either of the Culligans died that night they'd go straight to Hell, straight down, definitely; and for certain sure. "*We'll* have to confess it, Marion, because we stayed and listened and laughed." Marion hadn't laughed once but didn't tell Martina that.

"It's spitting in God's face, you know, and that's blasphemy and nobody can forgive a person blasphemy bar the Pope himself, and he'd need to be in real good humour, and if he was in a pussy humour he'd put you straight out of his big confession box in St. Peter's."

"Why would he do that?"

"Because he's infallible, silly, and if he said no to the Culligans they'd go straight to Hell, straight down definitely, because it's a worse sin than . . . you know . . . the other!"

"What other, Martina?"

"Oh, sins of the flesh, Marion! Any old cod of a PP could forgive you those. Haven't you an uncle out in Rome?"

"Ambrose. My father's brother."

"A Jesuit, isn't he? They're ten times brainier than other priests. Our crowd here are 'poor types,' Daddy says, 'mostly bogmen in dog collars' . . . and listen, tell me, this uncle of yours, does he ever *see* the Pope in his white frock?"

"Every day walking in his garden."

"Ah, go to God, Marion, he does not."

"He does, Martina. He told me."

"And what does he *do* all day, your uncle?"

"He works in the radio."

"Vatican Radio . . . gody hymns and stuff like that?"

"No. He's in the news section."

"Posh just the same . . . Rome and the Pope's garden and all."

That was yesterday, a day like any other. It seemed now that she was half awake all night dreading this coming day, this last morning she would ever be with L, the teddy bear she got for her third birthday. Soon *he* would be six years old. As her mother had given him to her on that day, she'd said, "This is your Teddy, love, your own special little boy," and within hours she was calling him loveboy. For a day or two her mother had smiled and then said, "I don't think, dear, that Loveboy is all that suitable a name. Just call him L . . . would that be nice?"

And so he was called L and all those years he was by far her best friend. She could tell him anything and he'd listen. He was a bit of a stupoe at sums but if you gave him time, he could work things out, but mainly he was kind and patient and you could kiss him and kiss him and kiss him and not feel shy because he was a bit shy himself and no matter what, he always told the truth, not because he was a saint, but because, like her, he was no good at telling lies. If you thought about it, he was a kind of brown bear angel completely on your side, you could tell him very private things and be certain sure he'd never breathe a word to a living soul. He hated Iggy. Her mother had removed his black and yellow glass eyes. The hook things at the back could be, she said, dangerous. In their place she'd darned in pale blue woollen eyes that gave him a purblind look. Any sort of hitting or punching terrified him and if you wanted to be unkind you could call him a coward, but she knew that, like herself, he was timid but brave.

One evening last week when her mother was reading a life of the Little Flower, she suddenly said, out of nowhere, "I've been thinking, dear, about L, your little teddy friend, and wondering if perhaps it's time he went."

Went!!! She'd been unable to think at first, too startled and disbelieving to grasp what her mother was suggesting.

"But I'll never see him again."

"You exaggerate, dear . . . and I'm tired of telling you about the word 'never'. If he goes to some deserving child, most likely you'll see him from time to time . . . if you want."

Now sick with shock and anger she asked, "Why should he go?"

"Because you're almost nine, big for your age. You put him sitting on that table and whisper to him during your homework . . . and that's all right because your marks are good enough . . . but taking him to school in your schoolbag and talking to him in the school toilets is another matter."

"I don't . . ."

"Now *don't* lie to me. You've been overheard . . . it's too much . . . it's not healthy."

Martina Flanagan, she thought. Her mother most likely: telltales.

"Why is it not healthy?"

"Because it's unnatural, that's why."

"How?"

"Don't get clever, Marion. Don't argue with me. It's unhealthy and it's unnatural, believe me."

Mary Cantwell did not hear her daughter mutter, "If it was Iggy's he'd be let keep it."

"I didn't hear that but I wish you wouldn't call your brother Iggy. You know I dislike it."

Marion did not respond. She'd heard her mother say another time, "It's better than Naasi, with its hint of nasty and Nazi. But only just. Your brother's name is Ignatius Loyola, like the founder of the Jesuits."

And she thought, I know what his name is. I know too much about him. Aloud she said, "I think it's a horrible name."

Mary Cantwell put down the biography of the Little Flower, anger growing, and looked intently at her daughter.

"It's sad to think of you as an ungiving child, Marion."

"I'm not giving you L."

"Are you not? Then I'm confiscating him."

During the silence that followed Marion thought she would cry, managed not to, and said quietly, "If Ignatius died I'd *never* see him again, would I?"

After a startled silence Mary Cantwell said, "That's a very odd example. But . . . yes and no, because we're only on this earth a brief while and when we go to Heaven, please God, we'll see your daddy and my mama and papa and Ignatius *if*, God forbid, God should decide to call him . . . but . . ."

I'll just tell her now, Marion thought, and her breathing became suddenly so shallow she knew she would hardly be able to utter, so she said, in a sort of choked whisper, "I wouldn't care if he was dead . . ."

Her mother's good eye began to pulsate.

"You don't mean that, Marion. You can't."

"I do . . . and I hope he goes to Hell."

For a moment it seemed as though Mary Cantwell might strike her daughter.

"That is the most vicious thing I've ever heard any sister wish on any brother, let alone her only brother. How could you utter such a monstrous wish?"

"Because."

"Because what, child?"

"Because."

"Is it because you've become jealous of the only boy ever in the Junior House in the history of Mungret to get the Best All-rounder medal . . . and don't smirk in that silly, vixenish way. I'm ashamed any child of mine could be so begrudging, so *mean*-spirited. What *is* wrong with you, child? You've become so unkind and remote, and Bridie thinks the same and so does Sister Dominic."

Marion looked away and said nothing. Neither broke a protracted silence till her mother spoke . . . slowly and carefully.

"I'm not trying to spite you, dear. I'm doing this for your own good because I love you and because the carry-on with L has become . . ."

"*What* carry-on?"

"The make-believe in the school toilet . . . it's too much . . . it's . . ."

"Is Santa Claus unhealthy, unnatural?"

Silence.

"Is God a bit like Santa Claus?"

"Go to your bed, Marion. You've gone too far!"

That night she made a mound of her knees and sat L in the hollow of her lap and looked at him and told him that most likely he would be going away forever but not to be lonely or afraid because most likely he would be well looked after. She was, she said, almost certain of that. But then he asked in a very small voice could she not hide him somewhere? There were dozens of places. There was a huge attic, three lofted yards, there was the little play cave at the back of the grotto which they called Heaven, a secret place where they had often played for hours long ago and told each other secrets. There was underneath the floor of the tennis house, the willow house beside the river . . . or even up one of the lime trees that lined the haggard field . . . you couldn't see into lime trees even in the middle of winter . . .

It broke her heart to say, "L, they'd see me going to visit you, no matter where, and there would be a terrible row. I could drown you in the river but I couldn't watch you sinking. I'd want to be with you . . . but I'd rather drown you than think of you with some cruel child who didn't care." And he said, "I'd rather be drownded, gone and forgotten than be abused, and that's a fact."

"And you'd be right," she said. "Don't you worry, L. I'll be with you."

Driving back that morning from her weekly voluntary one-hour vigil and six o'clock Mass at the Convent of the Marie Reparatrix, Mary Cantwell drove with extreme caution. The smooth tarmac looked dangerous and she could see that the grass verge was frozen, a thing unusual eight miles inland.

The radio weatherman did mention a cold snap and the possibility of snow later.

She had valid reasons for that caution.

Almost nine years ago, on the second of February, a skid outside Dundalk had altered her life unimaginably. She was eight months pregnant, Ignatius was six, and she and her husband, Philip Cantwell, had left the hotel and the annual veterinary dinner earlier than most. Philip was driving fast. During dinner, across the table Jack Moriarty, three-quarters drunk, had asked Philip if PV stood for paper vet. Through the laughter she had seen the cruelty of the question strike home. She knew from the way he blinked and the way he drank thereafter. Working out of Salmon in a busy, well-established practice, he had inoculated fifty-seven cattle in one day on eight or nine farms within a radius of thirty miles – all from one veterinary-size pack of inoculant. The following day they were all dead, a lethal accident in every sense. Tests proved that the blackleg virus was live. The Swiss pharmaceutical company blamed storage, and although the Veterinary Association fought on his side, it was three years before the farmers got compensation. Meantime most of them shook their heads and said, "A bad mistake, surely." They tended to use the word mistake in place of accident, implying a degree of incompetence, more damaging even – they were wary about employing anyone with an aura of ill luck. He had been forced to join the Department, where in fact he seemed to be working quite happily as a "paper vet," but clearly regarded himself as a failure. And what she knew must be especially galling for him was that he came first or second all the way through college to his finals. Moriarty boozed, womanized, repeated, cogged and scraped his way through, but now ran one of the most successful veterinary practices in the whole country, north or south.

She had thought Philip was driving safely but a little fast, and was about to suggest a decrease in speed, when suddenly there it was, an ass plodding down the centre of the road, head down, blinded by the headlights. He jerked the wheel suddenly, missed the ass and went into a fast spin, a sense of tumbling, then impact, and she knew as she went through the windscreen that her face was torn terribly, and she thought, my baby's dead. Eight days later she woke up to find herself a widow, blind in one eye, with eighty-four stitches in her face and a baby girl of four pounds in an incubator.

Unconscious when Philip was buried, many colleagues came for the month's mind, including Moriarty. When he put his hand towards her outside the church, she ignored it. Drunk before the meal had started that night, he was talking in the bar about "the blight of grotty grottoes all over the country, all from the hallucinations of a pubic girl. I've been to Lourdes . . . thousands of crutches in that cave and not one wooden leg. It's another God Almighty rotten Roman racket . . . Popes, saints and Mafia all tied up with Hairy Ned!" A lot of his colleagues and their wives seemed to think he was hilarious. She had asked, quietly but firmly, "What about the terminally ill, Jack, the suicidally depressed, the maimed, the blind, the crippled in wheelchairs . . . what would you say to them?"

"I'd say, 'Stay at home and get drunk.' Or better still, 'Go to the sun and get drunk.' Do them far more good."

She did not reveal at the inquest that Philip had swerved to avoid an ass. It seemed a ludicrous, almost farcical way for a young man to lose his life. As time passed she began to think about his death, and all the obvious things that people tended to say seemed nonetheless true. There is "a divinity that shapes our ends." God does have His own agenda, His divine plan which must have included the time and manner of Philip's death, the loss of her eye and Marion's birth. All were threads woven into the great weave of Christ's loom. Time would unravel their meaning, their truth and their beauty. Meantime, like St. Peter, she in a sense had denied Christ by omitting to mention the ass at the inquest. An ass had carried Mary to Bethelehem, an ass had carried Christ in triumph into Jerusalem. There were those very beautiful lines of Chesterton's that caused pins and needles from her neck to her spine every time she read them or heard them – "There was a shout about my ears, and palms before my feet."

She bought books and articles about bereavement, attended retreats and lectures dealing with loss and resignation. Every now and then she dreamt about those few seconds before that swerve and the sick, fast spin on that dark road northwards, the ass always in the dream, plodding, Christ astride, or the pregnant Virgin, both in a splendour of light, and sometimes she herself was the Virgin and sometimes Christ was poor Philip with death in his eyes.

Her rule on arriving home after her Wednesday vigil was to drink a glass of water, go to bed and then breakfast about ten. She did not see Marion leave for school on the vigil mornings, which was why she chose this morning to subtract the contentious teddy. Less fuss and unpleasantness. Confiscate – far too strong a word . . . but she must do what she said she would do. For such a quiet child Marion had become obdurate and cheeky, seriously cheeky.

She looked down at the floodlit grotto built by her mother in 1922 to celebrate the foundation of the state. It lay halfway between the front of the house and the river, encircled by a birch copse more striking now in winter, the white Carrara marble beautiful against the black limestone, the Virgin ever smiling down, Bernadette Soubirous ever kneeling and staring up in open-mouthed wonder. There were a number of raised sandstone slabs facing the grotto where people could kneel or sit and pray. In good weather there was always somebody there and that was wonderful too, the aura of sanctity.

Was it sometime last May, that Kensington couple, heading for Connemara, said they were related? Descendants? I didn't bother listening . . . something to Richard Atkinson, they said, who'd built Salmon House in the eighteenth century. It was continuously occupied, they said, by their family till 1883. Was Thomas Love, the Newry cattle-dealer, by any chance any connection? Yes. He was my grandfather. "How very fascinating . . ." Could they see around grounds and garden? They looked to be in good order.

"Yes," she'd said, "there was money in pigs. My father, Laurence Love, started a bacon factory here near the town. It's still in the family."

"Ah!"

"And he bought back the land sold off bit by bit by your people, but the salmon fishing rights were of course still more valuable than the land on either side of the river."

"And you *do* charge for that?"

"It's expensive to fish here but costly to have it watched night and day. Poaching is a way of life."

But the grounds were no longer private. They were open to the public all the year round, free of charge.

"You couldn't very well levy people who wanted to pray, could you?" she'd said.

"Not nowadays," he smiled. Meaning what? Given half a chance would they still be Paddy-whacking and priest-hunting?

She had walked with them as far as the grotto, catching what she imagined to be a look or half-smile flit between them, nothing as ill-bred as a smirk, but it was something. About the grotto itself they said not a single word. Just looked impassive. Then both exclaimed at the back, "Oh! Ah!" and "How very charming."

Sometime in the thirties Harry Greenan, an architect friend, had designed a children's play area incorporating the back of the grotto, slotting in sandstone shelves, a small hide-and-seek play cave, stone troughs and concealed soil pockets spilling Our Lady's colours – white and blue aubretia. There was a sandpit, a seesaw and a swing, all set in the circle of birch.

"If you don't mind my saying so, I prefer the backside of your grotto to the front."

And before she could think of a reply, his wife or mistress said, "It's very imaginative . . . must be a children's paradise." Pagans. They missed the whole point. Supposing she'd said, "Yes, I do mind what you've implied and would you both please leave now." But of course it's afterwards in an access of anger you think of these things to do and say. Deliberately insulting, the almost blasphemous use of the word "backside" . . . more subtle of course than old Dixon in the gatelodge who snarled "Rubbish" every time he heard the Angelus on Radio Eireann. *They'd* no children. He'd be the last of the old "occupiers" anywhere near the place. Protestants. Lower or upper class, they seemed contemptuous both of the Virgin as God's mother and of virginity itself. They would pay for their contempt hereafter. God's mother is not easily sneered at.

She unpinned the black Clones lace mantilla she sometimes wore to Mass, the same mantilla she had worn for the semi-private audience with Pope Pius XII. There was a silver-framed photograph of this moment on the desk in the window. She was on her knees kissing his hand. Philip's brother, Ambrose, had arranged that. It was beyond all doubt the greatest moment of her life, like being in the presence of God, like kissing the hand of God Himself . . . and every time she looked at the photograph, something of the overwhelming emotion of the moment came back to her.

She took off her day clothes, put on a nightdress, dressing gown and slippers, and as she bathed her glass eye in a saline solution, the optician's waiting room at Enniskillen last November came back to her like a coarse shout on a quiet, beautiful night.

She had picked up the feature section of a London quality Sunday showing a large, full-length photograph of Pius XII, with the headline THE SILENT CRIMINAL? Underneath it said, "Not the evil he did, the evil he did nothing about." Inside she read and half read, skipping and rejecting and then going back to see if she'd misread, headings and sentences so startling that she put the paper down with shocked disbelief, then picked it up again. The words jumped off the page:

"If there was any justice in the world they should be talking about his criminalization, not his beatification . . .

". . . the man should be dug up, strung up and burned as a Nazi collaborator.

"His knowledge total, his silence absolute, his crime unforgivable.

". . . this cold-hearted Roman aristo watching and praying a long way from Gethsemane . . ."

Too dazed to read on steadily, she went to the last sentence.

". . . past masters at ignoring the brutality of truth, at washing their blood-stained linen in secrecy and silence . . ."

After the opticians she'd gone straight out to Felix at the Graan. He read the feature, frowning: "It's . . . very biased."

"Is it true?"

"It's garbage. Garbage sells."

"It doesn't read like garbage."

"What could any journalist know about a man like Pius? Ignore it."

Was it because he was her younger brother or because she knew too much about him that she seldom found his answers satisfactory?

Two months later, collecting Ignatius from Mungret for the Christmas holiday, her brother-in-law, Ambrose, had brought them both into the book-lined library. Like Philip, but six inches taller − "It's the Norman blood," he said, "we Kilkenny Cantwells came here with Richard the Second" − he was in charge of the English-speaking section of Vatican Radio. He had an accentless voice, narrow, fine-skinned face, gold-rimmed glasses and a gold-filled eyetooth when he smiled. He was here on a break of sorts. He had homework, a bulky file about the Catholic Croats bulldozing orthodox Christian Serbs into Catholicism *or* into mass graves during the war, some hundreds of thousands of them! Accusations too absurd, too monstrous to answer.

When she'd mentioned Pius XII and the Holocaust, he said, "Every day in every part of the world the Church is vilified. If it's filth or lies, we ignore it; like Christ we remain silent because truth will out in God's own time . . . and yes, the Holocaust was an *appalling* crime, but to vilify Christ's representative on earth is to mock at Christ Himself . . . and God, as we well know, will not be mocked."

He went on to talk about "the new man," John XXIII, "not very well equipped intellectually," he thought, "and clearly fond of his food and drink. The late Pius spoke twelve languages beautifully . . . he had such grace, such elegant manners. This new man has Italian only, but a good man nonetheless, and after all, St. Peter had only one language. And we must remember that God had a hand in his election and God does not make mistakes. When we think He does, there is a purpose." Restrained, balanced, persuasive, a classical scholar with six modern languages.

Ignatius had asked a couple of shrewd questions – you could see they liked and respected each other, uncle and nephew, men's men both, good scholars and sportsmen. She was not all that surprised on the way home in the car to hear him talk of joining the Order . . . make a good Jesuit, something fastidious about him, secretive almost. Ignatius Cantwell SJ. Would he end up like Ambrose, regarded by his peers as one of the cleverest men in the world? You could see from his report that he was especially gifted at languages. She'd mentioned this to Felix. He ignored the possibility of Ignatius joining the Society of Jesus and just said, "You can have a hundred languages and be a bloody bore in every one of them. So Shaw says, and he's right."

Levitical jealousy? Certainly Marion is intensely jealous of Ignatius. Do I talk about him as much as I think about him? Maybe girls are more emotional, more spiteful than boys? Bitchy really is the word . . . vixenish I called her, and jealous, but dear God, to wish him dead and in Hell and not care . . . and not allude to it or withdraw one word of it in over a week . . . and Felix pooh-poohing it last night with talk of phases and the moon and changes . . . and utter nonsense . . . and going on to ask about the fishing season.

"Felix," I said, "I think this is serious," and he said, "I wanted to kill you often as a child, Mary. You used to punch hell out of me if you didn't get your own way."

"Did I?"

"You did, and you know you did."

"That was different."

"Why?"

"You didn't mean it."

"I probably did."

"Felix, if you'd heard her, if you'd seen her face . . ."

"Her face is about the loveliest face I've ever seen on any child . . . and some lucky beggar is going to get her all to himself. It's a phase, Mary . . . she's growing up."

Was he implying, like Bridie the other morning: "Could it be the start of her monthlies, ma'am?" in a loud voice, and Dermy Dolan polishing shoes in the scullery? The best-hearted girl in the world, but ignorant, no tact, no sense of decorum whatsoever. Girls of nine do not bleed. Utter nonsense. I didn't answer her. I must get that pamphlet in Veritas by Sister Ita Magdalen . . . Ita handles the whole thing with great delicacy.

She switched off the grotto light and made her way towards Marion's room. She would send Dermy Dolan with the teddy to the dry cleaners, collect it later herself before she got back from school. The trouble is she's refusing to grow up, so growing up will have to be imposed on her. Yes, she'll be moody for a week or two but that will pass. Loss and grief were two emotions Mary Cantwell understood. No need to tiptoe down the landing to avoid creaking boards. The child was always deep asleep . . . sometimes almost impossible to waken. The bedside lamp did indeed show her in profound sleep, mouth slightly ajar. She *was* an extraordinarily beautiful child, as everyone kept saying, but even sleeping beauties can seem far from ideal when you see them open-mouthed, frowning, and lying all crunched up with that lump again in the middle of the bed. Mary Cantwell felt slightly embarrassed as she pulled back the bedclothes because there it was, the wretched teddy, pushed and held down between her daughter's legs, innocently of course in her sleep . . . but so unseemly.

As she began to remove the teddy, Marion's grip tightened. She pushed harder against her crotch, her eyes opening and staring up in something akin to terror.

"It's all right, dear, it's all right. Let go."

Not yet awake, Marion still clutched tightly.

"Let it go, Marion! It's all right. Don't fight me, like a good girl. Let it go!"

Suddenly, awake and abashed, she relaxed her grip and sat up, pulling her nightdress down, aware with a hollow feeling of what was taking place. Her mother was "confiscating" L, making him into an orphan, giving him away "to some deserving child." She heard her own voice wheedling like a three-year-old's.

"No, Mammy, no! Oh, please, Mammy."

"We've been through this, dear. Don't argue with me."

"But I love him. He's my only friend and you're giving him away to someone who might hate him."

"If you could hear yourself. Crying like a baby."

And although she knew she was doing the right thing, it was with a heavy heart and tears in her eyes that Mary Cantwell left her daughter's room and went back to her own room to try and sleep. She put the teddy bear in a drawer.

Bridie had the main lights and wall lights on in the basement kitchen. Outside the sky was dark with sleet or snow. She was riddling the woodstove when Marion came into the kitchen.

"Would you look at the sour puss on the lovely girl. What's wrong now?"

When Bridie saw that Marion was too choked up to answer, she closed the draught of the woodstove and went over. Bridie was a big-bottomed woman in her thirties, with a soft, freckled face and a softer Fermanagh accent.

"What is it, love?"

When Marion covered her face and cried inwardly, Bridie put her arms around her.

"Gawdy, gawdy, gawdy . . . whisht, lassie . . . it can't be all that bad," and as a sob escaped, she said, "You'll wake the mistress and her up half the night praying for us sinners."

"She's giving L away, Bridie."

"I know."

"Confiscating him."

"Ah now, you made that up, Marion."

"I did not."

18

"You made her say it so. You back-answered her."

Silence.

"Only a small bit."

"What did you say?"

"I've forgotten."

"You've no wit, love. You don't argy with the like of your mother. You'll not best her . . . and maybe she knows best anyway."

"Who'd want him, Bridie? It's cruel. She hates him."

"Where did you get *that* notion?"

"She only loves God and Our Lady and Iggy."

"Now quit that wild class of talk."

"But I love him more than anything in the world. He's my best friend."

"Oh is he now!"

"Don't tease, Bridie. You know you are too. Oh God, what am I going to do? I think I'll die."

"Well before you do that, would you think of a word with your Uncle Felix . . ."

"Do you think?"

"Nothin' bates tryin'."

Suddenly Bridie put her hand on her breastbone and uttered, "Jesus Christ!"

Standing outside in the recess of the basement window a tall, capped figure stared out of brown spaniel eyes, smiling through yellowed gapped teeth, a week's stubble on his gaunt face.

Marion waved out at him and laughed and said, "It's Wishy Harte."

"Thanks be to God somethin' can make you laugh."

"Oh, let him in. Bridie, he looks famished."

"Are you mad in the head? He'll have the whole house hoppin' with fleas."

"The scullery so."

Lifting her plate of porridge and mug of tea, Marion followed Bridie out to the scullery and to the back door, where she was letting Wishy in and half giving out, half greeting him warmly.

"Wishy Harte, you put the heart crossways in me, staring in that way like a ghost. Why don't you knock or ring like any other Christian body?"

The answers, when they came at all, were twenty or thirty seconds after the query, monosyllabic, apologetic, accompanied by a smile or nod.

"Sit down there and eat that porridge and we'll get you a wedge of soda. Where have you been all summer and half the winter?"

"Here and there, Bridie."

"Where mostly?"

"The west."

"At what? Still the horses, is it?"

"Aye."

"Fair to fair . . . ten horses trotting behind you . . . forty miles a day for next to nothin', for what wouldn't get you a bed for the night! Bad rogues them dealers and knackers. You'll catch your death, so you will, out in all weathers."

"We'll all catch that, Bridie."

"That's for sure."

Marion watched him eat, fascinated by his scarecrow gauntness, his oddness, his slowness, his disconnection from ordinary life, his extraordinary gentleness.

Cycling home one evening through Casement Park she had come across a screeching gang of brats, chanting again and again as he passed, smiling uncertainly:

> Wishy Harte
> Let a fart
> That cracked the roof
> Of the butter mart.

Enraged by the smiling, they began throwing a bric-a-brac of rubbish, tins, sticks, turnips, bottles and stones, till something sharp cut his neck. She could tell from the way his head jerked and saw blood come through his fingers. He looked at his bloody hand and then at the children, without anger, his eyes dazed and hurt. The taunting stopped. In the silence she heard herself shout as loud as she could, "Ye striggs of Felon . . . ye rotten, rotten cowards!"

"Striggs of Felon" was how Bridie's father described the foul pus that came out of a cow's infected quarter. She had memorized it for future use. Going over she tugged the cuff of his jacket and led him out on the road to Salmon, where Mary washed the wound, called a GP for stitches and took him over – not only cutting his fingernails but bathing his feet in hot water and Dettol, cutting his toenails and giving him a pair of Philip's good working boots. Again and again she said, "He could be Christ." To herself she said, "In a sense he *is* Christ."

Marion delayed cycling to school without L in her schoolbag. She watched Wishy eating so slowly, delicately, almost absentmindedly. She found it hard to believe that anything about him could be the same as Iggy. Like L he probably had no tommytoe.

"What do you think of all day long, Wishy?"

"Things."

"What things?"

For a couple of minutes she thought he wouldn't or couldn't answer. Then he said, "If I was a bird, I'd fly."

"Where to?"

"Heaven."

"So would I, Wishy."

Bridie called from the kitchen, "Marion, you'll be late. Go."

She was glad it was retreat day. Every year they had a different Order of priests – Franciscans from Rossnowla, Passionists from Enniskillen, White Fathers from Cootehill, Oblate Fathers and Dominicans from Dublin, none of Uncle Ambrose's Order, Jesuits. They only gave retreats to the Marie Reparatrix nuns or Louis nuns, and her mother thought it unsuitable for a priest to be staying in a convent, and of course there was no hotel "remotely civilized enough to cater for such men." So they all stayed at Salmon, where they loved the tennis and the croquet and the bridge and the musical evenings and every one of them blessed the house. "The most blessed house in Ireland," Mary Cantwell often said. "The Atkinsons by now are well exorcized, thanks be to God and the Jesuits."

This was the first time Marion would hear her Uncle Felix on his home ground. From yesterday the boys reported him to be "great craic and lots of scary bits." The morning session was mostly stories, a few jokes, some questions and answers followed by Mass. Afternoon was very different. He seemed like somebody else, staring up at the stained-glass window of St. Patrick banishing the snakes from Ireland. When there was utter silence, he began:

"St. Matthew tells us, 'It were better for that man, that woman, that boy or that girl, that a millstone be placed around their necks and that they be cast into the depths of the sea.' "

He paused and lowered his voice.

"Down down down as deep as the sky is high. Down down down to that undiscovered underworld where sightless monsters of the deep cruise in everlasting darkness and loneliness. And who are these tragic creatures plummeting to perdition? And why!? I will tell you girls what St. Matthew tells us. 'They are those who lead astray these my little ones.' And what does he mean by 'astray'? I will tell you what he means."

Felix continued in this manner, giving examples of what to do, how to be aware of the wiles and guiles of the Devil. "Girls, put on the armour of Jesus Christ, and for God's sake and your own, guard your tongue and your soul night and day against the snares of Satan."

As he continued, one of the Culligan twins whispered to the other, "Your bum and your hole."

From where she was sitting Marion could see the Culligans and a group around them giggling.

Felix stopped and stared down at the group. All stopped except the Culligans, who were now out of control. She could see their shoulders going like jelly. Felix waited and waited, looked up at St. Patrick, then down at the Donegal altar carpet specially commissioned and presented by his mother, Helen, to celebrate the Eucharistic Congress of 1932, gold chalice and white Eucharist set on a beech-green base edged by an intertwining Celtic pattern.

Slowly he raised, pointed and held his left arm in the direction of the Culligans and said so slowly it could scarcely be heard: "There are two girls on the outside of the sixth row who look like twins, and those two girls are . . ."

He paused and uttered a great shout: ". . . sniggering and giggling in the presence of Almighty God." The Culligans for all their bravado got quite a fright. Josie went white and Breede went red. Outside, recovered, they said to Marion, "A noisy auld shite, that uncle of yours." They refused to confess to him despite Sister Louis Mary's threats and urgings. As the other girls queued obediently, Louis Mary came over.

"If you don't want to confess to Father Felix, Marion, that's perfectly understandable."

"I don't mind," Marion said.

She didn't. She was fond of her Uncle Felix . . . more than fond . . . loved.

Lying reading behind a couch one night she overheard her mother telling Iggy, "He hasn't caught one salmon on our stretch or any other for thirty years."

"You're not serious!"

"I am. A duffer at golf, worse at tennis or croquet, but as a fisherman – hopeless." She dropped her voice. "A few years back the Prior of the Graan phoned to thank me for the two beautiful salmon Felix had caught and presented to the community from our stretch. 'We're all grateful and impressed, Mary,' he said."

"You mean . . ."

"Bought them up the town in McElwee's fish shop."

"Good God! Did you tell the Prior?"

"Of course not."

"You should have, Mother. That's not sport – it's cheating. He's a chancer, old Felix."

"But harmless, Ignatius, surely."

"I'm not so sure."

She missed what they said next. Heard only laughing, and remembered thinking, "I hate them, both of them." She had gone fishing the previous summer with Felix. He seemed to fumble, get overexcited and lose a lot of baits in trees and river weeds, while other men on that same day on the other side of the river caught good fish. Clearly it upset him. He talked to her about the light, and being on the wrong bank, and being out of casting practice. "My casting is gone to hell. It really is damnable." In his room in the Graan she had noticed a whole shelf of fishing books, well used, and knowing what she knew, she felt terribly sorry for him for being so unlucky and loved him all the more for it, unlike Iggy and Ambrose who almost always caught something, and praised each other's skill as fishermen, all-rounders, exemplars.

In the confession box immediately after, she'd said, "Bless me, Father, for I have sinned." Felix looked through the grid at her and said, "Marion, sweetheart, how are you?" He was the only person who called her "sweetheart" quite naturally.

"I'm fine, Uncle."

"Are you going to frighten me with your terrible sins?"

For about ten seconds she didn't know how to answer and then heard him say, "No place for banter, eh. On you go. How long since your last confession?"

She told him, and then trotted out disobedience, laziness and lies about her eckers being done when they weren't.

"Anything else?"

She took a deep breath and said, "Sometimes very bad words come into my head."

"Yes?"

"At Mass and at the Rosary, and I want to shout them out."

"Words like what?"

She knew fuck, shite, bugger, prick, cunt, bollox, arsehole, and hoor. Tommytoe she knew was only a pet word for a boy's thing and fanny for a girl's. They weren't really bad words. She heard herself say, "Hoor."

Felix repeated the word and made it sound like door.

"Do you know what it means?"

"Yes, Uncle."

"And why do you feel you have to shout out such words?"

"Because I hate Iggy."

"You do?"

"Yes, Uncle."

"And why is that now?"

"Because . . ."

"Hate is a much stronger word than whore or any of the other words that come into your head, far stronger. It is a terrible word, and a terrible thing. I don't think you hate Ignatius, Marion. I won't believe it."

"I do."

"Why?"

She began and told him everything. When she stopped, she wondered if he'd gone to sleep, so long was the silence.

"Are you asleep, Uncle Felix?"

"Very far from sleep, very far." Then he asked her, "Did he penetrate you?"

Not quite certain of the word, she hesitated. He clarified, "Put his organ into your body."

"Yes, Uncle."

She could see him put both hands up to his head. His voice had become odd.

"And did you not cry out?"

"Mammy was always away . . . and he put his hand over my mouth."

24

She heard Felix mutter, "Jesus God. So no one knows."

"No."

"Or guesses."

"Well . . . Bridie was on a night off and Mammy'd gone to a Vincent de Paul meeting. She'd forgot something halfway down the avenue and walked back. There was no car noise. Iggy was in my bed and when he heard the front door he got out and sat on the side of the bed and said, 'If you open your mouth, I'll kill you. You're no innocent.' When Mammy came in I thought, 'I'm all right. She'll know. She'll guess. She'll save me,' and she said to Iggy, 'What are you doing, Ignatius, in Marion's room?' and he stared back at her and said, '*Talking. What* did you think I was doing?' and she got all flustered and left. But I think she guessed."

"You must tell her."

"I can't."

"You must."

"She won't believe me, Uncle."

"Of course she'll believe you."

"She won't."

"I believe you, sweetheart. Of course she'll believe you."

"She won't. I know she won't. Can't you tell her for me, Uncle? She'll believe you."

"Not from confession I can't. Tell me again at Salmon – this evening – and then I'll tell her."

He gave her absolution and then for a penance: "A few Hail Marys for the very troubled Marys in our family. Stay brave, Marion, stay brave," and blessed her.

Parking her bicycle in the coach house she could see her mother across the yard. The duckhouse door was open and Wishy Harte was sitting on a stool, looking down at the top of her head. She was on her knees, bathing his feet and cutting his toenails. Her face was very close to his feet because of her single eye.

Wishy looked over and responded to Marion with a slow uplift of his left hand, something between a salute and a blessing.

In the warm kitchen she knew from Bridie's face.

"I don't know, love . . . honestly."

"You do, Bridie."

"True as God. All I know is Dermy took him to the dry cleaners."

"The what!"

"The dry cleaners . . . and your mother was to pick him up later. That's all I know. I didn't ask."

"Oh God, Bridie . . . the dry cleaners."

"I know. I know, love."

"Where *is* he . . ."

"You'll have to ask her yourself."

From the kitchen window Marion watched her mother crossing the cobbled yard, a towel over her forearm, soap, Dettol, nailclippers and nailscrubber in a copper basin. Like a one-eyed altar server.

As Mary Cantwell approached the outside basement door she could read unmistakable hatred in her daughter's face. She did not want a scene in the kitchen in front of Bridie, sensing her tendency to softness and to side with the child. Without looking at Marion she said, "Go up to the living room, Marion. I'll be up in a minute."

When she heard Marion's footsteps going up the sandstone staircase, Bridie said, "She's not just in a quare state, ma'am, she's in a fury, so she is. I never seen her as wicked cross."

"I can sense that, Bridie . . . It'll be all right."

"God and I hope you're right, ma'am."

As Mary Cantwell followed her daughter up the staircase, Bridie sat heavily in a kitchen chair, fumbling for her Gold Flake cigarettes and matches. She closed the kitchen door, not wanting to hear the altercation.

Marion was looking out the living room window, watching a heron gliding downriver towards the sea, when she heard her mother's voice.

"It's rude to talk with your back to somebody."

"It's cruel to give things away that don't belong to you and are precious to *other* people. Cruel."

"You think I'm cruel, Marion? Turn round, child. Answer me."

Marion turned and looked down at her mother's rubber overshoes. They were standing very close together. She wanted to say, "I hate your old galoshes and I hate you."

She said nothing.

"Look at me, dear."

Mary Cantwell mollified her voice to a pleading note.

"I love you, Marion, as much as any mother can love a daughter. I did what I thought was right and I did it for your sake. Do you believe me?"

"Yes."

"Well then, can we just get back to normality and . . ."

"I've something to tell you."

"Very well."

"It's very bad . . . it's about Iggy. Ignatius. He did things to me in the bath when I was small . . . and times when you were away. He penetrated me between my legs . . . and . . ."

She did not see the open-handed slap, so hard it not only knocked her down to the parquetry surround but blinded her with pain and tears and took her breath away, blood spilling down on to the blouse of her uniform. She could not see or make sense of the falsetto scream of words, like separate smarting blows, spitting from her mother's mouth till they settled into a trembling voice saying. "How dare you utter such filth about Ignatius when I know and you know it's a monstrous lie."

Then all she could half see was the raging mouth because of a blur in her eyes, a nightmare mouth. It must be a nightmare mouth because her mother had never in her life struck her in the face before, and as the ringing in her ears began to ease, she could now see her mother's face twisting in anguish, tears pouring out of the good eye, and then she was kneeling on the floor with her arms around her, sobbing and saying, "Oh, my lovely lovely daughter, you must be unwell to say such things. Jealousy is bad enough, but to lie like that is a grievous . . . grievous mortal sin. Do you not understand that?"

Marion managed to nod.

"Tell me you're lying, dear, and we won't ever mention it again in our lives. You *were* lying, weren't you? Tell me the truth now, Marion, you were lying just now about your brother, weren't you? Don't be afraid. Tell the truth."

Marion could feel her head nodding again.

"Oh, I knew it. I knew it absolutely. Thank God and His Virgin Mother you came out clean with the truth. That's all that counts, dear, the truth. Oh my God, my poor child. Let me wipe your poor nose. Oh, look at that dreadful welt on your face. Did I do that to you? Can you forgive me, Marion, my beautiful, beautiful daughter? Can you forgive me?"

And again Marion nodded and thought: "I will never talk to her in my life again, never . . . ever . . ."

"Oh, thank God, thank God, thank God." Mary Cantwell had stopped sobbing and was now hugging and kissing and saying, "A little cup of cocoa, dear, would that be nice? A little cup each. Just the two of us and we'll forget the whole thing. Every last bit of it. It never happened, clean slate, new beginnings. But silly me, what did I do but give all our milk to Wishy Harte . . . poor Wishy, he loves milk. I can send Bridie . . . no, Bridie has ironing to catch up on. I'll . . ."

Mary's face was very close to Marion's. They were almost nose to nose. "I know. We'll send you out for a drop to Mahoneys. They'll be started evening milking by now. Slip on your coat . . . the two-pint can, your bicycle lamp and you'll be back here in two shakes. Won't you, dear?"

Marion nodded again, got into her school uniform coat, put the small copper can on the spring carrier of the bicycle, her mother following, talking talking talking, touching, hugging, crying, laughing, blowing her nose, and to every direct question her daughter answered with a nod, until finally she got on to her bicycle and set out for Mahoneys of Longfield on the other side of the town. It was the first farm beyond Casement Park. Cantwells had been getting milk from John and Vera Mahoney for over a quarter of a century. Mary Cantwell did not trust pasteurized milk.

There was a hasky wind blowing off the sea as she cycled, her mind unable to cope with what had happened. Or what might yet happen. She would never again speak to her mother – that much was simple and certain. The sky was a darker grey than the grey of the Louis Convent. Even the snowdrops all over God's acre looked cold. The streetlights came on as she approached Casement Park, very few people about.

John and Vera Mahoney were brother and sister in their fifties. Vera kept homemade fudge for children callers in a cupboard in the dairy. From August on there were apples as well. Both were hand-milking when she arrived, shorthorn cows in a clean whitewashed byre, lit by two long neon lights. Both greeted her warmly. As Vera dipped with a porringer into a ten-gallon churn, she said, "What happened to your face, Marion?" Unready for the question, she had no answer. Vera suggested, "Trouble at school?"

She nodded.

"That big Dominic nun, was it?"

Marion agreed, unthinking.

From under a cow John Mahoney was peering out, a bucket between his knees. "Boys adear, if she done that to you, she should be horsewhipped, so she should."

And Marion was thinking, why do the answers and the questions seem so
– nothing?

"Do you know what I'm goin' to tell you, John?"

"What is that, Vera?"

"This child is in shock. She's not fit to talk. You'll take the van out now
and you'll run her home, so you will."

"I will, I will man surely."

"You'll leave your bike here, Marion. John'll run you home."

As in a dream she heard herself say emphatically, "No, no, no. You're
awful good. But no, no. I'll cycle home. I want to cycle home."

"You're sure?"

"I'm sure."

As they watched her leave, John Mahoney said, "Thon's a holy fright,
whoever done it. We should've kept her, Vera, till she was at herself."

"Agin her will? We couldn't. God help her . . . cratur . . . growin' up can
be hard too."

"Hard as growin' old, Vera."

"Harder, John, harder."

There was a flurry or two of snow as she cycled back. Uncle Felix would
be there. Would he see her face and know what had happened? "I can tell
him in private, then he would tell her and she wouldn't hit him and scream
her head off or howl lies lies at him the way she did at me and she won't say
sorry to me "cause I won't be there to hear her . . . I'll be gone somewhere
and she can make cocoa and talk to Iggy for the rest of her life."

Halfway through Casement Park she saw a familiar shape lying facedown
in the gutter. With a heart-twist of grief and disbelief, she got off her bicycle,
milk spilling from the can on the carrier as she ran towards the shape.

Before she picked him up she knew unmistakably, and when she saw that
he was now blind, his woollen eyes cut out, his stomach ripped open spilling
fibre, an arm and a leg torn off, it was like a terrible punch in the stomach, so
winding her she felt unable to scream out her sorrow and rage. It was
directly outside Culligans and Caffreys. There was a dark entry between the
two houses. She wanted to knock on Culligans' door and tear their eyes out
and shout, "Give me back his eyes, his arm, his leg." But she knew they
would look at her and at each other and shrug. That would be worse.

There was nobody anywhere about on the street. She went to the dark of
the entry and sobbed there till she could sob no longer, talking and

whispering to him all the time, kissing his blind sockets, poking back the fibre into his stomach and putting him carefully under her cardigan and then buttoning up her coat, his face resting against her breast so that he would know again that he was loved deeply and truly, and that no one would ever confiscate him again and that no mad dog foul-mouthed Culligans would ever rip and tear at him again . . . never . . . never . . . because he was the only one in the world who knew what happened that terrible third time when he had been so brave and tried to save her when she was fast asleep. She had held him down then between her legs and Iggy just said, "What are you at? Let go . . ." and when she wouldn't, the side of his hand came down on the back of her fingers with such sudden force that she could remember afterwards only the way he was chucked and the sad look on his face as he tumbled and tumbled through the air to land upside down on her dressing table.

One thing was certain, she would not go home. She could go on down this entry to the wicket gate that gave on to a lane that led to an old coach road, grown in now, that would bring her out on this side of the river to the cattleyard and stables that lay outside the grounds and garden of Salmon House.

It was growing darker and colder, the snow had settled and was now falling continuously, lightly, on the street and rooftops and all over the adjoining countryside. Snow made no difference. They could go on blindfolded to where they were going. We'll be happy there, just you and me. Wishy might be sleeping on a hayloft. She might talk to him. She might not. There would be shelter and time to think, to make plans.

The phone rang from the six o'clock news item until midnight; old friends, new friends, forgotten friends and acquaintances, the factory manager and factory employees, people from all over the Island, and almost non-stop the media and gardai. Both Mahoneys had arrived, almost incoherent with worry and guilt. Felix talked to them all. Mary and Bridie were too distraught to talk. It was on every news bulletin till closedown. They knew it off by heart . . . name, age, appearance, last seen, how dressed, the abandoned bicycle and the spilled milk, the green Vauxhall car that a child was seen getting into, Leitrim registration. It turned out to be a Ballyshannon man collecting his daughter from a music lesson. The gardai were no longer following "a definite line of enquiry."

All night they prayed, mostly in the bay window of the bedroom looking down on the floodlit grotto; mostly the Rosary. At 5:30 Mary asked Felix to celebrate Mass.

"I will say Mass, Mary, for all of us." His voice sounded distant, his manner unlike himself. Was he so overwhelmed that he seemed unlistening every time she began to talk? Even more extraordinary, when grief took hold of herself and Bridie, the comfort of his arm went round the maidservant's shoulders. And have I lost that too, no brother comfort, the only pure and perfect love, brother for sister, sister for brother? And then she thought again how she'd told . . . no . . . said, half said I suppose, how I'd lost my head and struck with sudden temper for the first and last time in my life, but deservedly, if you'd been here, Felix, known her moods, her cheek, her lies and this nonsense of a teddy bear in the school toilets and lies about Ignatius, too shameful to repeat. And all that time he was looking past my face, his head nodding or shaking, saying *nothing*, not one single, solitary word of comfort, and when he did look into my poor eye his two were full of accusation, or is that the doubt and terror in my own heart? Is there no comfort so? Here on earth? Or in Heaven? And she prayed in a whisper, Oh God you have left me half-blind and husbandless, will You now take my beautiful, my only daughter from me . . . I don't know what to think or how to pray . . . and Felix is cold and so unlike himself, and God must hate me too, but if He takes her He's hateful and I'll hate Him. Oh, God in Heaven, protect the child, let me die . . . don't take her, she's innocent, I'm the guilty one. Take my body and soul, not my daughter.

Aloud she began to pray, "Remember, oh most glorious and loving Virgin Mary, that never was it known that anyone who implored Thy assistance, fled to Thy protection or sought Thy intercession was left unaided. Remember, remember, remember."

The snow had piled high against the back of the grotto, leaving the front almost snowfree. When Felix heard about the Ballyshannon man he phoned the local Superintendent, who came to the house immediately. Alone with him downstairs, Felix said he was fairly certain his niece was in shock. He was not at liberty to say why, but perhaps they should start thinking along other lines.

"Not an abduction?"

"I think not."

"You're talking about garda divers, Father? Dragging equipment?"

"Yes."

As light broke slowly they saw Wishy Harte walking like a scarecrow Christ towards the grotto. He sat on a stone seat, took a crust out of his pocket and began to eat. The gardai had questioned him at great length and, Felix thought, with unusual tact. Yes, he had seen her for "a small time. Then she left." Again and again they asked what she had said. "Going home," he said. "Going home." They had searched and double-searched every outbuilding, loft and shed . . . no trace of her whatsoever. There seemed nothing else they could do till daylight, when local volunteer search parties, extra gardai and troops promised from Finner Camp would widen and intensify the search.

"Poor Wishy," Bridie said.

"You should bring him down something hot," Mary said.

"We should all go out for air," Felix said.

They arrived together at the grotto, Bridie carrying a tray with porridge, bread and tea. It was Wishy who spoke first.

"No . . . word . . . of . . . Marion?"

"No, Wishy, no word."

All three watched him eating his porridge very slowly till he looked up to answer Bridie's question.

"How long was she with you, Wishy?"

"A small time."

"But how long. A minute? Two? Three? Four?"

He looked away, thinking, and said again, "A small time, Bridie."

"And what did she say?"

"Goin' home."

"That's all?"

"Aye. 'Goin' home' she said."

None of the three dared look at each other or at the blackness of the river flowing between the white banks, aware that Marion could be somewhere down there on her way to the sea. It was too terrible an image to contemplate. Then Mary picked up on something Wishy muttered that sounded like "Heaven."

"What did you say?" she asked with such intensity that it startled him.

"I mind now," he said very slowly. " 'I'm goin' home,' she said, 'to Heaven.' "

At first Felix could not understand why his sister and Bridie looked at each other and began screaming and running to the back of the grotto, both scooping armfuls of snow frenziedly from the area directly in front of the playcave. Both saw at the same time the buckled shoes and white stockings. It was Bridie who pulled her out to reveal the reality of rigor mortis, L in a vice grip against her breast like a blind infant. Felix could see at once that nothing looked so utterly dead as his dead niece, nor had he ever heard a cry so inhuman as the cry that seemed to come savagely from his sister's lungs.

Wishy Harte had come round, and was standing, holding his mug of tea, when Mary slapped it suddenly from his hand and began to pummel his shoulders and chest, shrieking, "Christ, oh Christ, if you said 'Heaven' last night, we could have saved her. Fool . . . we could have saved her. Fool . . . fool . . . idiot. Half-wit. You let her die. Oh, Jesus Christ."

Felix pulled her away roughly, saying loudly, "Stop that, Mary. He's a simpleton."

Wishy stood blinking, frightened, his arms up protectively, watching as Mary in frenzy snatched Marion from Bridie, kissing her and whimpering and stumbling with grief to the front of the grotto, where she staggered and slipped against the statue of Bernadette Soubirous. It tipped over, struck a stone seat, and as the head snapped off Mary held her child up to Our Lady of Lourdes and howled: "How could you let your Son do that to her? Let her die like that. How? How? How? Were you deaf, dumb, blind to her sorrow? Oh, my Marion, Marion, my only beautiful beloved daughter, Marion," and it was then that Felix covered his face for the first time, his other arm around Bridie. Wishy Harte, arms still outstretched, stared unsmiling from desolate, uncomprehending eyes. The marble face of the Virgin Mary did not respond to Mary Cantwell's anguish. It continued to look down, smiling.

Truth

HE COULD SEE THROUGH the glass door of the living room. The brass hood was bright over the coal fire. Nellie bent down in the hall, her mouth to his ear, and whispered:

"The minute your mother says, come back out to the kitchen." His father and the two priests were drinking out of the special glasses and smiling. One was small and grey and the other heavy, red and fat. He had to shake hands with both as his mother said their names.

"A dead ringer for you, Eddie," one said.

The other said: "Yes, a replica. . . ."

Then the questions: "Is this the youngest? What age? . . . What class, who is your teacher? Do you like school?" and they always let on to be shocked when he said "No" and they would ask "Why?," but when they asked: "Which do you like best, Scotland or Ireland?" that was a trap, so he said now, "I don't know."

"You don't know?" the big priest asked. "No flies on that boy!"

"Not from the dew of the grass he gets that," the small priest said.

His father laughed: "You'd think butter wouldn't melt in his mouth, but he's a rogue you know, a trickster, you wouldn't have a notion what goes on in his head."

Frank could feel himself blushing. Sometimes things did go on in his head that he'd never say to anyone, and he did have a secret with Nellie. His father was joking about being a trickster, it was a thing to say for the visitors, like the priest saying about no flies. It was the way grown up people talked to children, they didn't really mean what they said. Once Nellie said: "I could eat you," but she only meant she could give him a kiss and a hug. Sometimes her sister Maggie came at night, when his mother and father were out.

Maggie brought lemonade and chocolate biscuits, and sometimes toffee apples – that was a secret. She didn't live in Rutherglen, she lived in the

35

middle of Glasgow. She wasn't well; you could tell from her face. His mother had a softer voice than either Nellie or Maggie and could play the piano for a long time without stopping. Everyone clapped and said: "That's beautiful, Angela," and asked her to play again. Then they would all look at the ceiling and listen. When his mother played the piano his father kept tapping with his fingers on the side of the chair. He liked people to sing and recite. He sang "The Pale Moon Was Rising Above the Green Mountains." Tonight there would be no singing or piano, they were going out to Paisley somewhere, where his Uncle Petey kept a ham and egg shop. Uncle Petey said everyone who worked in the shop stole things from him, he said you couldn't trust anyone any more – take the garters off the Virgin. Once a month Uncle Petey had to have a man nurse in the house, or he would break all the furniture and all the windows, and Frank often heard his father say it was because he married such a stupid woman; that was Aunt Molly. She wrote stories for Holy magazines. You could buy them in the church at Rutherglen. Every story had a miracle. His father was pouring more whiskey into all the glasses, and one of the priests was trying to stop him. His father said: "We're going to a dry house." Then his mother called him over and said:

"Out to Nellie now, love, and then bed."

"Are you going to cards?"

"Yes, say goodbye to Father Moore and Father Duffy." He said what he was told to say always:

"Good night everybody."

And they all said together, "Good night Frank."

"A dead ringer," he heard the big priest say.

Nellie must have known his parents were going out. She was sitting at the kitchen table eating her tea. It was near dark outside. He could see the concrete yard from the street lights and across the road the high wall that went around Dr. Slowey's place, and the high railings round Queen's Park. There were fields round Dr. Slowey's, and cows. And old man called Ferguson came to milk the cows night and morning.

Every day in the year Nellie took him for a walk in the park. There were owls and squirrels there, and a rockery, and some of the stones in the rockery were faces. In a hollow there was a bandstand like a stage, and a round iron tent and you could sit there in the summer and listen to music. The men wore costumes. There was a place for playing too, swings, see-saws and skip-arounds, and in the middle of the park, a fat lady sat on a chair under a sort of small bandstand. "The old Queen," Nellie said, "she's dead now." Once he heard his father say, "If the Sloweys had their way they'd sooner kneel to that fat old bitch than go to Mass."

Dr. Slowey's wife wore very big hats, and the Slowey boys were a good bit older. They went to school in England. They talked a different way. There was a tall flagpole near Slowey's house. It was higher than the trees round the house. On special days they put up a flag, and they were the days his father got angry. "Irish my arse," he would say, and his mother said, "Hush, Eddie." She didn't like words like arse. Frank had been in Slowey's surgery twice. It was old, faded and dark, just as everything in their own house was new, shiny and bright. He asked his mother why.

"Truth is they have no money, love."

"No money?"

"Not *real* money."

It was hard to understand why his father got angry, and even though his mother didn't use words like his father, he could tell she didn't like the Sloweys either, even though he was the family doctor. What was hard to understand was how people without money could have a cow and a man to milk it, and a man in the garden, and a special man to drive the car, even though it was the oldest car in Glasgow. The car had no roof. "All show," his father said, "their auld fella was a drunken tailor from Tyrone and a bad one at that." It was hard to know the truth about a lot of things.

"Sit down, love," Nellie said.

She put a plate of beans on the table. His mother came in and told Nellie she would be late and left a telephone number. Every time she was going out she stood in the middle of the kitchen under the electric light in her furry coat with a basket of mending showing Nellie the different things to mend, and talking about phone calls, and fireguards and keeping the chain on the door, and how there was a murder every week in Glasgow, and sometimes two or three. She said the same things to Nellie every time and Nellie said: "Yes Mam . . . I know Mam . . . I will Mam. I'll phone if there's anything . . . goodbye Mam." There never was anything; nothing ever happened. It meant he could stay up late, and watch Nellie sewing or look at comics. Then his mother was kissing him, then she was gone.

Through the kitchen window Nellie watched the car reversing out of the garage. It turned right and went out by Cathkin. Then he was standing on a chair in the scullery helping her to dry dishes. Even so she was still a good bit bigger. The phone rang and she went out and talked a long time to her sister Maggie. When she came back to the sink she stood looking a long time and thinking.

"Would you like a wee journey, Frank?"

"Where?"

"To see Maggie."

"In a tram?"

"If you want."

"Would it be dark?"

"It's dark now."

"Is it a long way to Maggie?"

"About half an hour."

"That's a long way."

"Get your coat, hurry."

Walking down Mill Street to Rutherglen Nellie asked:

"Can you keep a secret, Frank?"

"You know I can."

"No matter what?"

"I wouldn't tell on you, Nellie."

"I don't think you would, well this is a secret."

"What is?"

"Going to see Maggie."

"Why?"

"It just is, very secret."

"Why, Nellie?"

She didn't answer so he asked again.

"Because you should be in your bed, and I should be mending. If your mother found out she'd ate the face off me."

That was true all right. Once his mother came back early with a headache and was very cross with Nellie because he was still up. He was very sorry for Nellie that night, it was really his fault.

The tram was full downstairs. They went upstairs. He sat on Nellie's lap to make room for a lady. Cars, coloured lights, traffic lights, lorries, taxis, big advertisements outside picture houses, the noise of engines and horns humming and booming, mixed with the sound of rain, and water running down the glass of the tram window, and the tram full of smoke and people coughing. They got off near the river. They walked along for a while. He could not see over the wall to the river.

"Is it far where we're going, Nellie?"

"A brave wee bit, are you tired?"

"No."

They went down dark streets. The rain had stopped. The pavements were wet. They passed close after close, some lit, some black. In the black ones he could make out white faces, sometimes a woman's, sometimes boys'. From a close a boy shouted something, a very bad word. Nellie didn't look back or say anything.

"Why did they shout that, Nellie?"

"They know no better, pass no remarks."

The close they turned into had no light on the staircase. He held Nellie's hand as they went up, his other hand against the tiled wall. It was wet. There were a lot of tiles cracked or missing. There was an odd smell like the dark pit under the garage. They went up a lot of stairs. Then they came to a door and Nellie knocked. A man opened it. He had fuzzy reddish hair and glasses. He was wearing braces over his shirt. He had no collar. Sometimes his father shaved like that. The man with the glasses hadn't shaved for two days or maybe three. When he saw it was Nellie, he didn't say "hello," or kiss or shake hands, he just said:

"She's not here."

They were standing in a narrow hall. There was nothing in the hall. Nellie walked past the man and went through the door. From the room she called:

"Come on, Frank."

He passed the man and went into a square room. There was a black range, a sink full of washing, and beside it clothes drying on a rack, a double bed in the corner and dirty dishes everyway on a draining board. There were two children asleep on a mattress in another corner. There was a table with a shiny cloth and four chairs round the table. One of the chairs had no back. The smell in the room was worse than the smell in the hall, like when a person got sick, but different. There was one window, and no other door out of the room.

"Where is she?" Nellie asked.

"Out."

For a while they looked at each other and said nothing. The man was blinking behind his glasses. Nellie said:

"Sit there at the table, love, and look at your comic."

He went to the table and opened his comic. He tried to look at the funny pictures. Nellie was talking in a low voice, almost a whisper. He couldn't hear anything, she seemed upset. The man wasn't bothered. He stood and looked at her. Then he was startled to hear Nellie say:

"Your fault, you lazy, drunken blackguard. Your fault, not hers."

The man said:

"Shut your mouth or I'll break your back."

That was a terrible thing to say. If you broke a person's back they would never walk again. Frank looked up at the man's face. He did not look angry.

"She's my sister."

"She's a born bitch, she'd do it for nothing."

"Liar, you make her," Nellie was screaming. She came to the table and put her hands on it. Frank kept looking at his comic, but he could feel the table with Nellie's hands on it like when you touched the fridge, a kind of shiver. Then the outside door opened.

"That's her now," the man said.

And Maggie came in. She looked awful tired. When she saw Nellie she began to cry. Then they were all talking in very loud voices, and he couldn't understand what happened, but the man was pulling at Maggie's handbag, and Maggie wouldn't let it go. When the man got it he emptied it upside-down on the table. Bits of things came out, coins and lipstick rolled over his comic and off the table. Then the man was pulling at Maggie's clothes, it was terrible. He pulled off her coat, and put his hands in the pockets, then he pulled at her dress. When the dress tore, she had nothing on under the dress and she was screaming. Then Nellie was screaming and trying to stop him. The man pushed Nellie away with his elbow, and knocked down Maggie. Then he was kicking Maggie on her stomach, and between her legs, and the children on the mattress were screaming, and Frank was so frightened he couldn't move. Then he saw Nellie on the floor, with her arms round the man's legs to stop him from kicking Maggie. That made the man begin to fall. For a moment he knew the man would fall towards him. He tried to get off the chair; something hit the side of his head.

Back now in bed in his own room, his father and Dr. Slowey were staring out the window, looking towards Queen's Park and Cathkin. They were talking in low voices. His face was swollen out. His mother sat on his bed. She asked again:

"How did it happen, Frank?"

"I don't know."

"Why don't you know?"

"I forget."

Dr. Slowey looked over from the window; he had a white face like the statue of the Sacred Heart on the landing, but no beard. He said:

"You must tell your mother how it happened." Frank thought for a moment and said:

"What does Nellie say?"

There was a long silence, and then Dr. Slowey said:

"Nellie says she doesn't know how you got such a bump."

"I fell downstairs."

"When?"

"Last night."

"How?"

"I was going for a drink of water and I fell." There was another very long silence. Up to this they had only asked questions, now his mother said:

"You are not telling the truth, Frank."

She nodded towards his father. His father left the room and came back with Nellie. Her face looked very odd, you'd know she'd been crying a lot.

"Frank says he fell downstairs, Nellie."

"True as God, Mam, I don't know what happened to the child."

Again there was a silence. Nellie had told a lie; he too to save her, he would have to stick to it no matter what. She often told small lies, but this was a very big one. His mother said:

"Frank, we know you're lying, dear, why can't you tell us?"

"It's the truth, Mama."

"You're telling lies, you were seen, both of you, going down Mill Street after we left last night, and you were seen again at the tram stop in Rutherglen."

He looked from face to face. They knew that; that was true. Nellie seemed lost and frightened. He said:

"I didn't tell, Nellie, I didn't say anything." Then Nellie began to cry. It was awful because none of the others said anything, so Frank said:

"It wasn't Nellie's fault, she was just trying to stop the man kicking Maggie on the floor."

That seemed to make things worse. Nellie left and then they all went out and he was alone. It was coming on dark again. His mother brought up tea and he had to tell about the tram, the walk along the river, the dark streets, the man and Maggie, the children and the mattress. Some parts he left out, like the words the boy shouted. He had to say about the fight. He knew from the way·his mother nodded that she believed him. He was almost asleep when Nellie came in and told him she was going back to Ireland.

"Why, Nellie?"

"I have to."

"I didn't tell."

"I know, love – not your fault."

Frank said: "It's the bad man's fault, the kicking man."

"He's not bad, he drinks too much, that's all – like your Uncle Petey."

Her voice sounded odd.

"I must go, love."

She gave him a kiss and went out of the room. For a long time that night he tried to understand what the truth was. Was it true what she said, that the kicking man was not bad? It was terrible what he was doing, but then his Uncle Petey smashed every window in his own house, but that was just silly, not the same as kicking a woman on the floor. If that wasn't bad, then what was? Did Nellie just say he wasn't bad because he was Maggie's husband, a kind of brother? Why did she not tell the truth? His father could visit his brother Petey, why could Nellie not visit her sister Maggie? Why was it secret? And when Maggie came at night, why did that have to be secret? And why was Nellie going now so sudden? He couldn't understand any of it.

Next morning Nellie was gone. He asked his mother and was told, "She got the Belfast boat." He felt suddenly very unhappy. She had said last night she was going back to Ireland, but he knew now he would never see her again. Where was she now? In Belfast somewhere, or getting a bus back to Strabane. Maybe he would write to her. That evening his father came in and talked a while. He asked his father about Nellie.

"Sad business," he said.

"Did she have to go?"

"Yes."

His father refused to talk any more about it. When he was almost asleep he heard his mother saying:

"I wouldn't mind the headscarves or the cutlery or the bits and pieces from the fridge, the rashers and God knows what, but taking a child that age into the middle of the Gorbals . . ."

There was a silence.

"If they take anything, they'll take everything. Dr. Slowey's right, they're all the same: they lie as they breathe. Truth is you can't trust them, any of them."

Victorian Fields

PETTY SESSIONS (IRELAND)
ACT 1851 14 & 15 Vict. Cap. 93
FORM A.a: INFORMATION

May 10th, 1872

STATEMENT BY ALICE DUFFY who saith on her oath: I remember
yesterday morning the 9th day of the present month. I was in my house at
Drumbane about ten o'clock in the morning. I'd come in from milking the
four cows. My husband James Duffy was in the bed. His brother Oweny
lives with us now close on a year. He was putting herrings on the pan. The
half of them was scattered on the fire. He is seprate this past three years from
his wife Lizzie who lives in the townland of Arasala. He told me once she
was a mad whore like most women. Like all the Duffys he is a bit touched
himself. This brother Oweny has a great spite on me. It's my belief he made
my husband more bitter than he was. I know the reason. One night when he
was a short time here he came back from Ballybay with drink taken. My
husband was playing cards at a neighbour's house. Up to this time I was very
civil with Oweny. I asked him that night would he like a bite to eat. "I
know what I'd like" he said "and I know what you'd like." He was fornenst
me at the fire and exposed himself. "Don't do a thing like that Oweny" I
said, "It's a mistake, you've too much taken." "Damn the mistake" he said
"Did you ever see the like of that?" "Shame on you Oweny" I said "I'm
your brother's wife." "And your child's not his" he said "and well you know
it." I said if he didn't make himself decent I'd go straight for Sergeant Reilly.
I know well that he's a coward. He talks loud and has a name for showing
himself to women and is the laugh of the country. I told him to have more
wit. I wasn't afraid of him or any man. He got up then and tried to assault me
indecently. I pushed him away.

From that night he behaves bitter towards me and my husband is worse in his manner. He wouldn't believe my story. He told me that I had tempted his brother Oweny. I asked him how. No decent man he said would talk of what I'd done. On my oath this is lies. My husband has a grudge on account of the land. He brought £60 the day we married. The land and the four cows is mine. At the start he tried to get the land in his own name. I put him off. He took this bad and nothing I done after was any good in his eyes. Five years back when we first married he abused me so much I went to the priest in Ballybay Fr. Alex McMahon. The Priest's housekeeper Bridget Hanley closed the door in my face and said the likes of me should not be let next or near a priest. She left me standing in the street. I know now for sure my husband turned the priest against me because when the priest came out to talk to me he wouldn't let me tell my story but let a shout at me and said I was a disgrace and a scandal to the whole country and the Catholic faith and that only a saint could put up with me. I said "God help me father what have I done." "What have you not done woman," he shouted, "the devil's work."

My husband took the notion that the child I was carrying was not his. On account of this he abused me day in, day out, and started into drink, telling the clergy and the whole country a dose of lies about me and my brother Michael. He's still bitter about the land.

Yesterday morning when I came in from milking, I saw the herrings scattered in the fire, I got fire tongs to take out the herrings.

"Don't mind them," Oweny said.

"I'm only giving you a hand," I said.

"I don't want your hand," he said and pushed me away from the fire. I told him not to do that again or I'd break a crock across his skull. He then let a roar and told me to get to hell out of the house while he was at his breakfast. I told him to talk quiet and think again. I told him it was my house and my food. He was living on my charity and if he was any kind of man it was himself would get out of my house and go back to his own woman Lizzie and show her the scenery he showed me one night at the fire. I know it was a mistake to say that, but I couldn't stop myself. He then struck me on the mouth with a fish. I cried and said "Don't do that with the herrings I bought dear for my own child" and he shouted "To hell with you and your bastard you whore you" and he caught hold of me and pushed me out the door and gave me a kick with the toe of his boot. The pain of that went up through me and I fell holding my stomach. He then gave me a box of his clenched fist in my left eye when I was kneeling. I screamed at him that I was carrying a child. "It's no Duffy," he shouted. "Take care or I'll kick you and it in a bog-hole."

In all this commotion my husband was upstairs in bed. I don't know if he heard. To my knowledge he never got up before mid-day. Most days it's nearer one o'clock.

After I was abused by Oweny I went up to a neighbour's house: Pat Ward. His sister Mary bathed my face and told me to go and see Sergeant Reilly at Ballybay and make a complaint.

SIGNED: ALICE DUFFY

PETTY SESSIONS (IRELAND)
Act 1851 14 & 15 Vict. Cap. 93
FORM A.a.: INFORMATION

Today at Hollands Forge I Cautioned Owen Duffy of Drumbane and late of Arasala. When I served A Summons he shouted abuse about his sister-in-law and asked me to take the following Information.

SIGNED: SGT. HUGH REILLY

STATEMENT BY OWEN DUFFY WHO SAITH ON HIS OATH:
When I first came to my brother's house about a year ago I noticed my sister-in-law Alice Duffy strange in her mind. She would shout that all about the place would be taken from her. One day she had stones in her hand to throw at whoever came. One day she asked me to look about the house and yard for her brother Michael McKenna and herself began to look, talking and crying. Her brother Michael is in America this six years. Sometimes she is troubled beyond what a man can understand. Nobody she says can do any work right about the place only herself, and she is all the time complaining about the work she has to do. I have my own opinion of that work. She's a great one for travelling through the country looking for a stray calf or a lost hen and this takes her to strange townlands and men. I believe myself she is a woman of low character.

My brother James has great patience. This last while she has been trying to run away. Yesterday she flung a scald of spud water at the two of us and said she would drown herself and her child in a bog-hole. She buys herrings and the like and forgets about them till they smell the house. The day before yesterday when I went to cook a herring she went out of her mind. I believe my sister-in-law Alice Duffy is a dangerous lunatic and I pray she may be committed to Monaghan asylum.

May 12th:

ADDITIONAL INFORMATION OF ALICE DUFFY WHO SAITH ON HER OATH:
When my husband James Duffy found out I went to Sgt. Reilly he began to call me a "whore out of hell" a "bitch to end all bitches" I said nothing. I am well used to that class of talk so he come up close to me and said . . . "You're a cunt woman nothing more or less than a cunt" I scratched his face and pulled out a go of his whiskers. He then pushed me away and took a plough reins from the dresser. He thrashed me about the kitchen with the reins until I was not fit to scream. When my child Andy tried to stop him he cuffed him and knocked him down. Every time he cut me with the reins he said, "Where's Sgt. Reilly now?" Then he put my child out of the house and told me I'd get the rope proper. He said he would hang me. I was afraid and took the child and slept in Pat Ward's kitchen. My back and stomach still have the marks of the reins. I showed them to Dr. MacAllister. I am in fear and dread of my husband and my brother-in-law and will not go next or near the house until they have been charged and locked away.

May 13th:

INFORMATION OF JAMES DUFFY WHO SAITH ON HIS OATH:
I believe my wife Alice Duffy has been deranged in her mind since I married her six years ago. The truth is I married a bad one. She's an unnatural woman. She was two months gone with child when we married. I asked her to name the father. She would not say. I spoke strong. I stayed at her night and day till I got it from her. She screeched at me that the father was her brother Michael from Lisaduff. When I heard this from her own mouth it sickened my stomach. I walked to her brother's farm four miles. I faced him in his own yard:

"Your sister says you made a whore out of her and that the cub is yours."
"She's sick then," he said.
"Is she a liar," I asked him.

"No man would do the like with his sister." So I asked him who it was and he said, "No woman could be watched." A month after I spoke to him he sold his land and left for America.

That same day I went back to Drumbane. My wife was in the haggard behind the house milking. I went up to her and told her what her brother had said. She began to shiver and cry. I told her to quit whining, and tell the truth. After a while she said there was no woman in the whole country as unhappy as herself. So I said, "What about me?" As God's my judge she stared up at me her face all twisted and said, "I don't give a snotter for you or any Duffy. I never did nor I never will. There's only one man I care about." I said he didn't care much about her. She screamed, "I was ignorant and knew nothing." I said I understood well that she was an unnatural woman. From that day out I hardly spoke to her. I worked anywhere but Drumbane.

This last while she is a brave bit worse and talks a lot to herself. She will not talk to me or my brother but she told a neighbour Mary Ward that when she tries to pray her head is full of cursing and black notions and death.

Three days ago she screamed and shouted for twenty minutes that a devil was in the house and after that she threw boiling water at my brother and myself. Later in the day she took a turn and said she would be a stiff corpse before long and that something terrible would happen. I sent my brother Oweny for Canon Hackett. She told the Canon in front of us that we would not let her out of the house. That we kicked her and cuffed her and that she was worked to death, that both of us hated herself and her child and that we wanted her locked up to get our hands on the bit of land. She said we would starve her child to death. The Canon then took her down to the low room and she quieted a little. Later at black dark she got out a window with the child and made off across the fields. I followed her with Oweny for fear she would do harm to herself. She stayed that night at Ward's house and has been there since. I know she has made statements to the Constabulary. I would say they are a string of lies. I don't know what she said about my brother and myself but the whole country knows the truth about herself and her brother Michael. I believe my wife Alice is now a dangerous lunatic. I pray she may be arrested and committed to Monaghan asylum.

I swear this statement is true.

SIGNED: JAMES DUFFY

Roma

MARIA CAME OUT of the kitchen with a fish supper. "It's here, Mickey, on the counter."

Wiping the mock terrazzo he thanked her from his knees, no press stud in his cap, the peak almost level with his foggy glasses. He seemed blind. She sat at a formica-topped table near the jukebox, opened a magazine and watched him get up. Not his fault the way he looked, yellow teeth in red gums, the face white like a monk's. That was why kids chucked things as he pulled his barrow through streets, women giggling in doorways when their men tonguefarted or used the Holy Name. A bit of crack, they thought, to see him drop the handcart and bless himself. Of course he was odd, out praying like that from house to house, and when he wasn't carting brock or clearing dumps he sat in the loft he shared with Joe the Bush down their yard. Joe was part-time beggar, full-time drunk. One day she asked Joe what Mickey did in the loft.

"Never done cuttin' slips from wee Holy Books and stickin' them in copy books with Holy pictures . . . the kind of thing an auld nun puts in her time at." Holy Mickey, mad Mickey, Mickey the mutter, Mickey the Brock, Mickey Longford, he had nicknames enough to do ten townlands. She had never really bothered much with him till yesterday when Connolly took him away to load pigs. He had left the garden in a hurry, his jacket bunched in the fork of a tree. Hanging clothes on the line she could see a wad of stuff in the breast pocket. There was no one about. Under an apple tree she went through the wad, bits of paper, clippings, mostly hand-printed with different coloured biros.

She read:

> c/o Digacimo
> Cafe Roma
> The Diamond
> The World is Dying
> The Town is Dying.
> A Cure for the World

Shut the Pubs
Shut the Dance Halls
Shut the Picture Houses
Put cars off the roads
More Penance
Live Modest
Think on death day and night,
Bad thoughts make bad Talk
Makes man do bad things
After that the head goes
Burn Dirty Books, Papers and Pictures
Pray for my father in the mental, keep him from Hell
Pray for my Mother in her grave at Knockatallon
Pray for Annie and Josie who have forgot me
Pray for Joe the Bush who sins every night
Pray for people who shout at me and childer who mock me
Pray for Mr. and Mrs. Digacimo, and M
Above all things keep M pure

Cellotaped to a piece of cardboard was a picture of the Virgin waistdeep in cotton wool. Printed carefully underneath:

MARIA

May God scatter over her path the Flower of His Divine Benediction

She began to feel she had encroached and fumbled the wad. Medals, scapulars, notes and letters fell on the grass. As she gathered them one caught her eye. It began with her name:

Maria I must tell you things   The truth   In the yard at night I often stand under your room   I would like to be the light in your room   I could see you then and give light for your homework   I would stay awake all night watching you breathe   that's all   Odd times too I would like to be slippers you wear about the house and cafe or the sheets in your bed or your comb in the streets I am crying to myself because of you my life is terrible and there is nothing I can do   the squeal of pigs I hate and

the smell of them makes me sick   every day I see little pigs sucking out of
big ones and the big ones breed like rats   acres of them out at clonfad   a
town of pigs beside the town   when they are fat for the factory I help
load them on the lorries   the smell is awful on a hot day blood and
squeeling in the factory yard   do they know   I often wonder   most
people eat sausages   even you   I don't   it makes me sick   everything
does in this world except you   I can't explain it   nothing is new to me
before I sleep   you are my gate to heaven   when I wake you are my
morning star and the truth is the heart is broke inside me because of how I
feel and I can never tell you or give you this letter   I write this because it
is the truth maybe I'll give it to you sometime but I don't think so

Guilty, she had gathered the stuff and put it back in the wad. All that evening
she felt disturbed. It broke her sleep and this morning she woke early. All day
it had been with her and now near the jukebox she waited, watching him
begin to eat.

He could feel her eyes. Sometimes of a Saturday when the cafe was closed
she came in like this and sat looking through a magazine, an overall over her
school uniform. Odd times she'd play a record on the machine or move
about by herself, making noises with her fingers. Other times she'd join her
mother and father in the kitchen. They sat there most Saturday nights when
the place was shut, reading out of foreign papers, hard workers who kept to
themselves. No friends; much like myself.

"How old are you, Mickey?"

She was looking at him very straight, eyes in her head like no other girl or
woman body he ever knew.

"Is that a cheeky thing to ask?"

"I'm six and thirty."

She went back to her magazine. He looked up at the panel above the steel
chipper, painted in shopgloss by Murray the decorator; Pope John smiling
before Saint Peter's, hand upraised in blessing; beside him President
Kennedy smiling before the White House, hands in jacket pocket addressing
the world through a megaphone. He put a chip in his mouth.

"Why are you so grey?"

"The breed of me, nature I suppose."

"Are you long left home?"

"I quit home when my mother died. I was glad to quit."

"But you're from this country?"

"I'm a Longford man, here this brave while. I mind when you were born, people sayin' 'them Italians have a daughter.' "

"You were here then, Mickey?"

"About the town."

"Working?"

"When I could."

"At what?"

"Anything."

"And your people; what did they do?"

"The auld fellow was a blacksmith when he was sober . . . he drank wild."

"Is he dead too?"

"In the Mental, below in Mullingar: God blacked his mind, he broke my mother's heart, let the roof fall in, and the whole place go to rack. I couldn't stop him. I've two sisters married in England."

"You see them?"

"No."

"Do they write?"

"No."

"Don't you?"

"Not this brave while."

"They have fambleys of their own, it's natural."

He couldn't keep looking in her eyes so he looked away. She put money in the machine and played a record. It made a noise like pigs being castrated to the sound of drums; when it stopped she asked:

"Do you ever see him, your father?"

"He didn't know me last time, and let a shout: 'I have no son, I'm the Holy Ghost, I have no son.' Then he started in to laugh and giggle and wink and said all classes of bad things. It's on account of his rotten life. God's punishment for the dark things he had done when he was drunk."

"What things? Was he bad?"

"I'd call him bad."

"What did he do?"

"He was bad."

"Papa says you shouldn't be sleeping down the yard with Joe or carting brock about the streets. He says it's a great pity of you, that you're a strange person."

"Every man has some oddness."

She had never talked close before. He felt clumsy. He moved his knife about the table. .

"Am I annoying you?"

"No."

"If I didn't ask you'd say nothing. Sometimes you go a month without saying a word. Why?"

"No call to . . . anyway . . ."

"Yes?"

"You're too young."

"For what?"

"To know."

"What?"

"Maria! Maria!" Mrs. Digacimo's voice called high in the house.

"Si, Mama?"

The voice said something in their speech. As she got up to leave she said: "You'll have to tell me what I don't know. I'll be back."

He watched her walk up the terrazzo floor under the fluorescent lighting past Pope John and President Kennedy, past the glossy murals of old buildings and bridges falling down across fields, past the tower going sideways and streets full of boats, and through the beaded string opening that led to the house.

What was it he couldn't tell her? There were things a grown man couldn't tell a growing girl, specially her. He couldn't say the loft he shared with Joe the Bush faced a pub entry and how night about he could hear the pissing and puking, the gropes and groans of men and women, or of how he saw his auld fellow drunk once in a shed, or remark on how Joe the Bush abused himself night after night. Even tonight when he came in to wash the floor Cissy Caffery and young Mulligan sat on facing each other. Mulligan had his hand up Cissy's skirt and she not fifteen and the two of them talking and laughing with no trace of shame. Course they were young. You had to allow for that. Maybe God would look gentle on hot blood, but there were other things so bad you couldn't scour them from your mind. The world was sick and the more he saw the worse it got. Sometimes it seemed God was deaf or blind or gone asleep. Sometimes it seemed there was no cure.

The lights in the cafe went out and the hood of the chipper caught the street lighting, and made the two Johns a pair of grinning ghosts. He heard someone again on the staircase.

Maria came into the cafe and made her way through the dark tables to where she had left her magazine. Still there; alone. The street lights made him seem unreal, like the morning early she looked down from her window to the yard. He was standing against the gable of the coach house, grey face and head, arms outstretched. She had put on her dressing gown and watched. Holy Mickey, Mickey the mutter, Mickey Longford. What she had read in the wallet was so strange, somehow private, she meant to keep to herself, but today when Ursula Brogan began boasting again about that old Ward man who always stopped her and held her hand she found herself talking about Mickey. Ursula listened and said:

"Ah God, that's awful, I'd straighten him out, Maria, honest to God I would."

"It's nice someway."

"The Blessed Virgin . . . It's pukey!"

"But I am a virgin."

"Not the Blessed Virgin. It's not right. I'd tell him if I were you."

"Tell him what?"

He moved in the chair as she approached. She could just make him out.

"Did we leave you in the dark again, Mickey?"

"No odds. I'm for bed."

She moved to see him better and said:

"What am I too young to know?"

Mickey heard her voice but didn't know what she had asked. It was darkness all round but where she stood it seemed light. For a moment he thought he'd like to go down on his knees and kiss her hands and feet.

"Pardon, Miss."

"What am I too young to know?"

"The world is bad, Miss."

"Sure I know that."

"And this town is rotten like the bad end of a city."

"Ah come off it, Mickey, how do you know?"

"I hear it and see it."

"Where?"

"Down the yard, round the town, out the country, everywhere. No one thinks of God or dying or what comes after."

She looked out towards the street. She was holding the magazine against her breast, exactly as the Virgin held the child in a picture he had, but much younger, more beautiful. He wanted to say he'd die to keep her the way she was, clear of the Mulligans and Joe the Bush, the pubs, the drunks, the women in the doorways, the pigs and the dance-halls, the brock, all the ugliness of life. She was like a sloping field one spring day he remembered long ago in Longford, high high hedges that hid houses, roads, lanes. You could see nothing but sky. Just grass, thorn blossom and the sky. It was so beautiful he felt that it would blind him. He wanted to sleep and never wake. That was what she was like looking out in the street. He had the same feeling now that he got in the field, but how did you say a thing like that? Then he heard himself say:

"You're like a field."

"A field?"

Did she give a little giggle? He wasn't sure.

"At home near Knockatallon. It had high hedges."

He knew he couldn't say the thing he thought.

"A field in May . . . thorn ditches . . . there was a power of blossom."

For quite a time neither said anything. Then Maria said:

"I'm not like that; I know what you mean but I'm not like that. When you said a field I nearly laughed because I was in a field last week with Ursula Brogan behind the football pitch. We followed Cissy Caffery there and two boys from the secondary. She's a wagon. She did it with them one after the other, and we watched."

The street lights went out. The silence was odd. She felt she must go on talking:

"I wouldn't do that but if I loved a fellow I'd lie with him and make him happy. That's the truth about me. Are you there, Mickey?"

"Yes."

"You heard what I said?"

"Why did you say it?"

"It's true."

"You shouldn't."

"Have watched or told you?"

He didn't answer. His chair scraped and she saw him move towards the kitchen.

"Mickey!"

He went through the kitchen out the back door down the yard. She could feel heat in her face and an odd beat in her heart. It had seemed right to tell him, but as she spoke it sounded blunt, ugly and final as though she were deliberately destroying something; false too because she'd been disgusted and didn't say so. "But I didn't mean anything," she thought. What made her say it when she knew what he'd written and how he thought about her, it was like mocking a cripple or putting poison in a baby's bottle.

She went down the yard and looked up at the loft; no light. Even if she did see him how could she unsay what she had said. She felt now she was worse than Cissy Caffery, that she had done something very stupid and very wrong and there was no way she could undo it.

"I'm sorry, Mickey. Honestly I'm sorry."

He sat in the loft on the iron frame bed. Twice Joe the Bush said something to him. Mickey heard words but couldn't give them meaning.

"Are you deaf, man?"

"What?"

"Why don't you spake?"

"What?"

"Arra God!"

Mickey lay back on the bed dressed and looked through the skylight at the stars. Joe the Bush began to shift about, abusing himself as he did most nights. The springs skreeked and the broken castor scraped on the wormy boards. Mickey listened.

"God sees you, Joe."

"For Christ's sake shut up, you eejit. They'll lock you up like your father."

Then Joe was snoring and Mickey was counting hours from the Church. Again and again he scoured his mind with prayer, but he could see her eyes seeing what she said she'd seen, her mouth telling nakedness and sin and for an instant he saw her lying with Joe the Bush and he woke startled and sweating. Why had she said such things? Would she earn Hell too with filthy hags, a hag herself, her mouth black and screaming, damned? What was happening to the world? Men, women and children walking to damnation. The stars were mostly gone when he found himself saying: "House of Gold,

Arch of the Covenant, Gate of Heaven, Morning Star, Morning Star, Morning Star." Winter and there were stars over the frosted field and he was kneeling on hard ground waiting for the Mother of God, Christ born again in this field at Knockatallon. He'd be there and the world saved. An ass carrying a small cloaked figure came through the frozen gap. A hatted man behind kept prodding. He could see it all very clearly, even the mincing trot of the ass, its tail wagging . . . It was Saint Joseph and the Virgin Mary. The ass came up the field to where he was kneeling. Mary dismounted and began opening a pack. He could tell she was very young, a girl. Saint Joseph made an arch of blackened ash rods and pulled a tat of bags across it. He lit a fire at the opening of the tent and sat. The Virgin took something out of the pack and crept over beside him. He saw then it was Maria and Joe the Bush and she had a bottle of whiskey and they were swigging it now and laughing and after a while Joe whispered something. She smiled, and put her head in his lap. Mickey closed his eyes. There was a terrible noise of animals and humans squealing, shrieking together like the pigs at Clonfad and something in his head was saying: Help of the weak, Refuge of Sinners, Comforter of the Afflicted, but the noise got louder and above it clearly he could see her beautiful head in Joe's lap and Joe was holding it when suddenly Joe was shouting: "Christ" and then "Oh Christ, Christ, Christ, Christ" and pushed her from him. She spat, picked up the bottle of whiskey and drank till it was empty. She looked round and at him with lost eyes, a sag in her mouth, her face blotched, her hair a dirty frizz like old Maggie Greggan of the Gullet. There was a smell from them like the smell in Connolly's boar sty, so strong he could hardly breathe. He tried to get up. He couldn't. The smell got worse and began to smell like corruption and death and he couldn't breathe now at all because the smell was so bad and he was retching and then he was sitting up in bed choking and crying.

The stars were gone. In the corner of the loft Joe the Bush was asleep, his mouth open like a black hole in a grey stubble. It made him feel sick to look at Joe. He thought for a while, got up and strapped what he had into a blanket, emptied a box of clippings into a cardboard bin and went down the ladder. Grey light in the flagged yard. The slates of a disused bakery showed rain; church, houses, streets and fields seemed huddled, condemned. He washed at a tap in the yard. The water splashed on pocked cement and ran away down a blind gully that went under the dripping apple trees. He carried the cardboard box to a bare patch beside a plum tree and set fire to it.

As it burned he dropped everything from the wad keeping only his Mother's memorial card. He watched the flames twist and warp and said aloud, "I'd like to be dead and buried, yes that's a fact." When the papers were ash he went back to the yard and looked up at the stucco house and read the words on the wall:

CAFE ROMA
Snacks, Fish Suppers, Accommodation.

A black plastic sewage pipe came down the middle of the house, past her open window with its blue curtains.

"I'll not think," he said, "I'll go."

Then he turned to climb the pipe. It was wet and slippery. He went down the stone staircase to the basement and got in the scullery window. Up then to the street hall with the arched doorway, big photographs, the table and two chairs. Up again the rubbernosed staircase to the upper landing with its one high window looking north. There was brown lino on the floor, a big green plant in a brass pot. Five doors. That was hers, open. He could see the blue curtains, her school uniform on a chair. He went in. She was deep asleep, breathing easy, beautiful as any picture he ever saw:

"Impure."

Her eyes opened:

"Impure," he shouted, "dirty."

She got up on her elbows. He could hear himself but wasn't sure what he was saying. Then he was trembling and crying and muttering. Maria was startled. She felt no fear just pity, and shame.

"Mickey, I'm sorry. Please. Don't. You're shouting, you'll wake them. Please go, please."

"Impure, dirty, dirty, dirty."

Then Mr. Digacimo was standing in the room in pyjamas, the hair he combed carefully across his pate hanging down over one ear. Mickey was muttering:

"God Almighty's Mother, a bitch fit for any mongrel, dirty, impure."

Mr. Digacimo took his arm.

Maria said:

"Please Papa, he means nothing, he's upset."

Mickey pulled away and left the room. He saw Mrs. Digacimo on the landing in an overcoat. He heard her say something that sounded like Police. He went out the back door to the yard, put the strapped blanket on the handcart and pushed it up the entry to the street.

"I'll not think, I'll go."

He went out the west road heading for Leitrim. He heard a man say once there was nothing left in Leitrim now but bare mountains, empty houses and the bones of sheep. The hedges gave way to a straggle of whins. He looked back and down. The town was gone in a smore of rain. She too would die in his mind and be forgot, like when a body died. Later there were cars, trucks and vans; children on a school bus looked out pointing and laughing. He went up a branch road. He would find his way through side roads and lanes. There was no going back. Tired he sat on a ditch and looked at the country, the sun lost in clouds, thousands of crows flying somewhere, over dark lakes, November again, a thin wind, and the fields sodden.

An old man came up the road driving two bony cows. He had a fag-coloured stubble and smoky eyes, a withered face like his father's:

"Where are you going with the handcart, son?"

"Leitrim."

"Where to?"

"I don't know."

The old man stared. Mickey got up and said, "I must go." The old man said nothing, then spat and called:

"Good luck to you, son, and Leitrim."

Later he would pray when he could think easy. As long as you had God and his Blessed Mother it was no odds where you were going, or when you got there. He must keep to that and burn all else from his mind: that was truth. Then he said aloud:

"My heart is broken, that's the truth; my love is dead, that's a fact."

Music at Annahullion

SHE PUT HER bike in the shed and filled a basket of turf. Curtains still pulled across Teddy's window. Some morning the gable'd fall, and he'd wake sudden. Course you had to pretend to Liam Annahullion was very special. "See the depth of them walls" . . . "Look at that door; they don't use timber like that now" and "feel that staircase, solid, made to last." Bit of a dose the way he went on; sure what was it only a mud and stone lofted cottage, half thatched, half slated, with a leaning chimney and a cracked gable.

"The finest view in Ireland," Liam said a hundred times a year. High to the north by Carn rock it was fine in spring and summer, very fine, but all you ever saw from this door in winter was the hammered out barrels on the hayshed, the rutted lane and a bottom of rushes so high you'd be hard put at times to find the five cows. Liam went on about "the orchard" at the front put down by their grandfather Matt Grue: a few scabby trees in the ground hoked useless by sows, a half acre of a midden, but you couldn't say that to his face.

One night Teddy said, "Carried away auld cod: it's because he owns it."

"Shush," Annie said, pointing upstairs.

"A rotten stable, it'll fall before we're much older."

"We grew up here, Teddy."

"Signs on it we'll all die here. They'll plant it with trees when we're gone."

"It's home."

"Aye."

Teddy talked like that when he came in late. He drank too much. His fingers were tarry black from fags, the eyes burned out of his head. Even so you could look into his eyes, you could have a laugh with Teddy. She called up the stairs as she closed the kitchen door.

"Teddy, it's half-eleven."

"Right."

He gave a brattle of a cough and then five minutes later shouted down: "Is there a shirt?"

"Where it's always."

"It's not."

"Look again."

She listened.

"Get it? In the low drawer?"

"It was under a sheet."

"But you've got it?"

"I got it."

"Thanks very much," Annie said to herself. She hooked a griddle over the glow of sods to warm a few wheaten scones. She could maybe mention it quiet like, give it time to sink. He might rise to it after a while maybe, or again he might know what she was up to and say nothing. He was always low over winter, got it tight to pay Liam the three quid a week for board and keep. In the summer he had cash to spare, on hire through the country with a 1946 Petrol Ferguson, cutting meadows, moulding spuds, buckraking, drawing corn shigs to the thrasher. Sometimes he was gone a week.

"Knows all the bad weemen in the country," Liam once said. "Got a lot to answer for, that bucko."

Teddy came down and sat at the north window under an empty birdcage, his elbows on the oilcloth. A tall stooped frame. He ate very little very slowly, put her in mind often of some great grey bird; a bite, a look out the window, another bite. "You were up at Reilly's?"

"We'd no butter."

"Who was there?"

"George McAloon."

"Wee blind George?"

"He's not that blind."

Teddy lit a cigarette and looked out. He could see Liam stepping from ridge to ridge in the sloping haggard. The field had earthy welts running angle ways, like the ribs in a man's chest, hadn't felt the plough since the Famine or before.

"Anyone else?"

"Only Petey Mulligan the shopboy. He kep' sayin' 'Jasus' every minute to see poor George nod and bless himself, and then he winked at me, much as to say 'mad frigger, but we're wise' . . . too old-fashioned by half."

Teddy was quiet for a minute and then said: "Religion puts people mad."

"No religion puts them madder."

He thought about this. He hadn't confessed for near forty years, lay in bed of a Sunday with rubbishy papers Liam wouldn't use to light fires. Sometimes they had bitter arguments about religion and the clergy. Liam and Annie never missed Mass.

"It's a big question," Teddy said.

Annie filled a tin basin from the kettle.

"I saw a piana at Foster's."

"Aye?"

"In the long shed at the back of the garden."

"What's it doin' there?"

"They've put a lot of stuff out."

"What kind?"

"Horsetedder, cart wheels, pig troughs, beehives, auld churns, a grass harrow, stuff like that."

"Useless?"

"Less or more."

"Over from the auction."

"Must be."

"Odd place to leave a piana."

"The very thing I thought."

After a moment she said, "It looks very good, shiny with two brass candlesticks, like the one in the photo."

"Auld I'd say?"

"Must be."

"The guts of fifty years."

"And maybe fifty along with that."

Teddy went to the door and looked out. Annie said to his back, "Pity to see a thing like that going to rack and loss."

"If it's worth money," Teddy said, "some fly boy goin' the road'll cob it . . . maybe it's got no insides or it's rusted or seized up some way, must be something wrong with it or it would have gone in the auction."

"If it come out of Foster's it's good, and it could come at handy money."

Teddy looked round at her. "Who'd want it?"

Annie shrugged.

"You want it, Annie?"

"A nice thing, a piana."

"Everyone wants things."

Teddy looked through stark apple trees towards the wet rushy bottom and the swollen river; rain again today.

"Who'd play it?"

"A body can pick out tunes with one finger, the odd visitor maybe, and you could put flowers on top of it, light candles at special times."

Teddy was picking at his teeth with a tarry thumb: "When one of us dies Annie?"

"Christmas, Easter, times like that."

He went on picking his teeth with the tarry thumb.

"It's a bit daft, Annie."

"Is it?"

There was a silence and Teddy looked round; when he saw her face he said, "Don't go by me, but it's a dud I'd swear."

"I'd say you're right."

He took his cap from the top of the wireless.

"I'll see if there's letters."

"Tell Liam there's tay."

Annie saw him cross the yard, a scarecrow of a man, arms hung below his knees. Teddy wouldn't bother anyway. A Scotch collie bitch circled round him, yapping and bellycrawling. Guinea hens flapped to the roof of a piggery. She could see Liam blinding potholes in the rutted lane. Even in winter scutch grass clung to the middle ridge. Teddy stopped for a word; hadn't much to say to each other that pair, more like cold neighbours than brothers. Teddy went on down the road. Two years back Liam had put the post box on an ash tree near the gate . . . "to keep Elliot the Postman away from about the place."

"What's wrong with him?" Teddy had asked.

"Bad auld article," Liam said.

"What way?"

"Handles weemen, or tries to, in near every house he goes to, anyway he's black Protestant."

Teddy let on he didn't understand. "Handles weemen? What weemen?"

Liam got redder.

"He'll not put a foot about this place."

Annie thought about Joe Elliot, a rumpledy wee fellow, with a bate-in face, doggy eyes and a squeaky voice. No woman in her right mind could let him next or near her without a fit of the giggles, but there was no arguing with Liam. He was proud and very private. Four or five signs about the farm forbade this and that. A "Land Poisoned" sign had been kept up though there hadn't been sheep about Annahullion for twenty years. When stray hounds crossed the farm Liam fired at them. Every year in the *Anglo-Celt* he put a Notice prohibiting anyone from shooting or hunting.

"Jasus," Teddy said, "thirty wet sour acres and maybe a dozen starved snipe, who's he stopping? Who'd want to hunt or shoot about here? There's nothin' only us."

Near the bridge there was a notice "Fishing Strictly Forbidden." The river was ten feet wide, the notice nailed to an alder in a scrub of stunted blackthorn that grew three yards out from the river bank. When the water was low barbed-wire under the bridge trapped the odd carcass of dog and badger; sometimes you could see pram wheels, bicycle frames, tins and bottles Liam once hooked a pike on a nightline. She had cooked it in milk. It tasted strong, oily, Teddy wouldn't touch it:

"I'd as lief ate sick scaldcrows, them auld river pike ates rats and all kinds of rubbish."

Annie found it hard to stomach her portion. She fed the leftovers to the cat. Teddy swore later he saw the cat puke. Liam was dour for days. She heard him crossing the yard now and began pouring his tea; he blessed himself as he came across the floor, pulling off the cap.

"Half-eleven I'd say?"

"Nearer twelve," Annie said.

Liam nodded and sucked at his tea.

"You could say mid-day."

"Next or near, you could say that."

Liam shook his head. Every day or so they had this exchange about Teddy.

"I'm never done tryin' to tell him," Annie said. "I get sick hearin' myself."

"It's a pity of any man, he couldn't be tould often enough or strong enough."

"True for you," Annie said, and thought how neither of them ever dared a word, let alone hint. Teddy was his own man, paid steady for his room, helped about the yard or farm when he felt like it. Liam sucked his teeth. They were big and a bad fit, put you in mind of a horse scobing into a sour apple. He was squatter than Teddy, sturdier, slate-coloured eyes and tight reddish skin. He smiled seldom and no one had ever heard him laugh. Sometimes Annie heard him laugh alone about the yard and fields.

"Same as the Uncle Eddie," Liam said, "lazy and pagan and you know how he ended. In a bog-hole . . . drunk . . . drownded."

Crabbed this morning, better leave it till evening. "Teddy said you remarked a piana at Foster's."

Oh God, Annie thought and said, "I saw it from the road."

Liam ate another scone before he said, "Scrap."

"I'd say."

"Whole place was red out at the sale. Piana must have been lyin' about in a pig house or some of them auld rotten lofts."

"That's what Teddy said, a dud."

"He's right about that anyway."

And that's that, Annie thought. Soon they'd all be pensioned, maybe then she could buy the odd thing. It was put up to her to run the house on the milk cheque. It could be a very small one in winter. She made up by crocheting, anything but approach Liam. All afternoon she thought of the piano. In the end she found herself crying as she kneaded bread. "Yerra God," she thought, "I'm goin' astray in the head . . . an auld scrap piana, an' not a body in the house fit to play, and here I am all snivels over the head of it." She blew her nose and put it out of her mind.

It was dark when Teddy got back. He smelled of whiskey and fags and his eyes looked bright. Liam didn't look up from the *Anglo-Celt*.

"Your dinner's all dried up," Annie said.

"No odds," Teddy said.

Liam switched on the wireless for the news. They all listened. When it was over Teddy said: "I saw your piana, I made a dale for it."

"Ah you're coddin', Teddy!"

"It's out of tune."

"That's aisy fixed."

"Woodworm in the back."

"You can cure that too."

"There's a pedal off."

68

"What odds."

From the way Liam held the paper she could tell he was cut. God's sake couldn't he let on for once in his life, his way of showing he kept the deeds. Teddy winked.

"Who sould it?" Liam asked.

"Wright, the Auctioneer. It was forgot at the sale, hid under a heap of bags in the coach house."

"Cute boy, Wright."

"He's all that."

"How much?"

"Two notes, he give it away."

"You paid him?"

"He's paid."

"That's all right," Liam said and went out.

They heard him rattling buckets in the boiler house.

"Pass no remarks," Teddy said. "If you want a thing, get it. What's he bought here all his years but two ton weight of the *Anglo-Celt*, one second-hand birdcage that no bird ever sang in and a dose of holy pictures."

"Horrid good of you, Teddy," Annie said.

"Ah!"

"No, it was," Annie said. "If you'd waited to chaw it over with Liam you'd be that sick hearin' about it you'd as lief burn it as have it."

"Liam's a cautious man."

Next day Teddy took the tractor out and went off about three o'clock. Annie lit a fire in the parlour. It led off the kitchen at the end of the staircase. It was a long, narrow room smelling of turpentine, damp and coats of polish on the parquetry lino. The white-painted boards, ceiling and wainscoting was yellow and spotty. Like the kitchen it had two windows at either end, a black horsehair chaise lounge in one, a small table with a red chenille cover and potplant in the other. Two stiff armchairs faced the painted slate fireplace. On the mantelshelf there was a clock stopped since 1929, a china dog, and a cracked Infant of Prague. Annie looked at the photograph over the shelf: Teddy with a hoop, Liam wearing a cap and buttoned britches. Her mother had on a rucked blouse, a long skirt with pintucks at the bottom, high boots and gloves, and that was her with a blind doll on her mother's knee. Their father stood behind looking sideways. At the bottom of the photograph "McEniff, Photographer, Dublin Road, Monaghan

1914" . . . some fairday long ago, no memory of it now. The rough-faced man and the soft young woman buried. She was now twenty years older than her mother was then, and she thought now how her mother in her last sickness had kept raving: "the childer, the childer, where are my childer?" She remembered saying, "This is me; Annie, one of your childer." Her mother had looked at her steady for a minute, then shook her head. Course she was old, dying of old age.

It was dark when they sat down to tea and Liam said, "Long as he's not drunk . . . and lyin' in some ditch under the piana. That would be a square snippet for the *Celt*."

"He'll be all right," Annie said.

No noise for an hour but wind in the chimney, the hiss of thornlogs through turf and the crackle of Liam's paper. She began to worry. Supposing he did cross a ditch, get buried or worse over the head of it. Then she heard the tractor, and went to the door. A single light was pulsing on the bonnet of the old Ferguson as it came into the yard. Teddy reversed to the front door and let the buck-rake gently to the ground. He untied the ropes and put the tractor away. Annie tested the keyboard in the dark windy yard. There was an odd note dumb. Guinea hens cackled and the collie bitch barked. Liam was watching from the door.

"What's wrong with them?"

"Damp," Annie said. "Nothing a good fire won't mend." It was heavy, the castors seized or rusted.

"Like a coffin full of rocks," Liam said.

"Time enough," Teddy said. "No hurry."

They had a lot of bother getting it into the kitchen, Liam wouldn't let Annie help.

"Stand back woman, we're well fit."

It seemed very big in the kitchen. Teddy sat down and lit a cigarette. Annie took down the Tilley lamp and went round the piano. Made from that thin shaved timber; damp had unstuck some of it. That could be fixed. The keys had gone yellow but the candlesticks were very nice and the music stand was carved. God, it was lovely. She lifted the top lid and looked down into the frame. She could see something . . . a newspaper? She pulled it out, faded and flittered by mice. Liam came over.

"That's an auld one," Teddy said from the hearth.

"The 7th November, 1936," Liam read.

"The weight of forty years," Annie said.

From where he was sitting Teddy could read an ad:

WHAT

LIES

AHEAD

FOR

YOU

Why not make the future certain?

"What's in it?"

Liam had put on his glasses . . . "A Cavan man hung himself in an outhouse."

"Aye?"

"Last thing he said to his wife was 'Will I go to Matt Smith's or get the spade shafted?' . . . and the wife said 'Damn the hair I care but the childer have wet feet . . . don't come back without boots.' "

Liam looked up. "Then he hung himself."

"God help her," Annie said. "Women have a hard life."

"God help *him*," Liam said.

"Safer lave God out of it," Teddy said.

"I must have bought that paper and read that maybe ten times . . . and it's all gone . . . forgot . . . Do *you* mind it, Annie?"

"No."

"You, Ted?"

"It's like a lot of things you read, you couldn't mind them all."

Liam put the paper aside. "Better get this thing out of the way."

He went to the parlour door, looked at it and looked at the piano. The two last steps of the staircase jutted across the parlour door. It was made from two heavy planks, each step dowelled into place. The whole frame was clamped to the wall with four iron arms. "None of your fibby boxed in jobs," Liam often said. "That's solid, made to last." He went to the dresser, got a ruler, measured, folded the ruler and said: "Won't fit."

"It'll be got in some way," Annie said.

"How?"

"Let's try and we'll know."

"If it doesn't fit, it doesn't fit. Damn thing's too big."

Teddy took the rule and measured.

"We might jiggle it in," he said, "it's worth a try."

"Won't fit," Liam said.

Annie made tea and watched for an hour, measuring, lifting, forcing, levering, straining, Liam getting angrier and redder.

"For Christ's sake, don't pull agin me."

"Where are you goin' now, up the friggin' stairs?"

"What in the name of Jasus are you at now?"

Finally he shouted, "Have you no wit at all, the bloody thing's too big, the door's too small, the staircase is in the way, it won't fit or less you rip down them stairs."

Annie tried not to listen. Teddy kept his voice low, but he was vexed and lit one fag off the other.

"Maybe we could strip her down," he said, "and lift in the insides, build her up again in the room."

"Maybe we could toss the sidewall of the house," Liam said, "and drag her through, that's the only way."

They said nothing for a while and then Annie said, "I suppose it'll have to go out again?"

"Where else?" Liam said.

They got it out the door again and half lifted, half dragged it to the turf shed. Two castors broke off. The thrumming and jumble of notes set the guinea hens clucking and flapping in the apple trees.

Liam went to bed early. Teddy sat at the hearth with Annie and drank more tea.

"It's only a couple of quid, Annie."

"No odds," she said.

He looked at her. He felt a bit of an eejit; maybe she did too.

"What odds what people say."

"I don't give tuppence what people say . . . never wanted a thing so bad, dunno why, and to have it in the house."

"If you're that strong for a piana, we'll get one, the same brass candlesticks, one that fits."

"No."

Teddy looked at her again. If she'd come out straight and say what was in her head; women never did. They never knew rightly what was in their heads.

"Two quid is nothing, Annie."

"I told you, it's not the money."

Teddy sat a while at the fire.

"I'll go up."

He paused halfway up the stairs. "It's only scrap, Annie, means nothin'."

"I know."

Annie dreamed that night that Liam had hung himself in the turf shed. Teddy cut him down and they laid him out in the parlour. She looked at the awful face on the piano, and then the face of the little boy in the photograph, and knelt. She felt her heart was breaking, she wanted to pray but all she could do was cry. "What are you cryin' for, Annie?" Teddy was standing in the parlour door. "Everything . . . all of us . . . I wish to God we were never born."

When she woke up it was dark. She lit a candle, and prayed for a while. It was almost light again when she fell asleep. That morning she covered the piano with plastic fertiliser bags. The guinea hens roosted on it all winter. Near dark one evening in February she saw a sick rat squeeze in where the pedal had broken off. By April varnish was peeling off the side. One wet day in July Teddy unscrewed the brass candlesticks. On and off she dreamed about it, strange dreams that made her unhappy. It was winter again and one evening she said, "I'm sick to death lookin' at that thing in the turf shed. For God's sake get shut of it."

She watched Teddy smash it with an axe. In ten minutes the rusted steel frame lay in the hen mess of the yard like the carcass of a skinned animal. Teddy slipped the buck-rake under it and drew it out of the yard. From under the empty birdcage Liam watched through the kitchen window. "No wit, that man," he said. "Always bought foolish. His uncle Eddie was identical."

Cancer

TODAY THERE WAS an old Anglia and five bicycles outside the cottage. Boyle parked near the bridge. As he locked the car Dinny came through a gap in the ditch: "Busy?"

"From the back of Carn Rock and beyont: it's like a wake inside."

For a living corpse Boyle thought.

"How is he?"

"Never better."

"No pain?"

"Not a twitch . . . ates rings round me and snores the night long." Boyle imagined Joady on the low stool by the hearth in the hot, crowded kitchen, his face like turf ash. Everyone knew he was dying. Women from townlands about had offered to cook and wash. Both brothers had refused. "Odd wee men," the women said. "Course they'd have no sheets, and the blankets must be black." "And why not," another said, "no woman body ever stood in aither room this forty years." At which another giggled and said, "Or lay." And they all laughed because Dinny and Joady were under-sized. And then they were ashamed of laughing and said "poor Joady cratur" and "poor Dinny he'll be left: that's worse." And people kept bringing things: bacon and chicken, whiskey and stout, seed cake, fresh-laid eggs, wholemeal bread; Christmas in February.

In all his years Joady had never slept away from the cottage so that when people called now he talked about the hospital, the operation, the men who died in the ward. In particular he talked about the shattered bodies brought to the hospital morgue from the explosion near Trillick. When he went on about this, Protestant neighbours kept silent. Joady noticed and said: "A bad doin, Albert, surely, there could be no luck after thon." To Catholic neighbours he said: "Done it their selves to throw blame on us" and spat in the fire.

It was growing dark at the bridge, crows winging over from Annahullion to roost in the fibrous trees about the disused Spade Mill.

"A week to the day we went up to Enniskillen," Dinny said.

"That long."

"A week to the day, you might say to the hour. Do you mind the helicopter?" He pointed up. "It near sat on that tree."

Boyle remembered very clearly. It had seemed to come from a quarry of whins, dropping as it crossed Gawley's flat. Like today he had driven across this border bridge and stopped at McMahon's iron-roofed cottage. Without looking up, he could sense the machine chopping its way up from the Spade Mill. He left the car engine running. Dinny came out clutching a bottle of something. The helicopter hung directly over a dead alder in a scrub of egg bushes between the cottage and the river. Dinny turned and flourished the bottle upwards shouting above the noise: "I hope to Jasus yis are blown to shit." He grinned and waved the bottle again. Boyle looked up. Behind the curved, bullet-proof shield two pale urban faces stared down, impassive.

"Come on, Dinny, get in."

He waved again: a bottle of Lucozade.

Boyle put the car in gear and drove North. They could hear the machine overhead. Dinny kept twisting about in the front seat trying to see up.

"The whores," he screeched, "they're trackin' us."

On a long stretch of road the helicopter swooped ahead and dropped to within a yard of the road. It turned slowly and moved towards them, a gigantic insect with revolving swords. Five yards from the car it stopped. The two faces were now very clear: guns, uniform, apparatus, one man had earphones. He seemed to be reading in a notebook. He looked at the registration number of Boyle's car and said something. The helicopter tilted sharply and rose clapping its way towards Armagh across the sour divide of fields and crooked ditches. Boyle remained parked in the middle of the road, until he could hear nothing. His heart was pumping strongly: "What the hell was all that?"

"They could see we had Catholic faces," Dinny said and winked. There was a twist in his left eye. "The mouth" McMahon neighbours called him, pike lips set in a bulbous face, a cap glued to his skull. Boyle opened a window. The fumes of porter were just stronger than the hum of turf smoke and a strong personal pong.

"It's on account of Trillick," Boyle said, "they'll be very active for a day or two."

"You'll get the news now."

Boyle switched on the car radio and a voice was saying: "Five men in a Land Rover on a track leading to a television transmitter station on Brougher Mountain near Trillick between Enniskillen and Omagh. Two BBC officials and three workers lost their lives. An Army spokesman said that the booby trap blew a six-foot-deep crater in the mountainside and lifted the Land Rover twenty yards into a bog. The bodies of the five men were scattered over an area of 400 square yards. The area has been sealed off."

Boyle switched off the radio and said: "Dear God."

The passed a barn-like church set in four acres of graveyard. Dinny tipped his cap to the dead; McCaffreys, Boyles, Grues, Gunns, McMahons, Courtneys, Mulligans; names and bones from a hundred townlands.

"I cut a bit out of the *Anglo-Celt* once," Dinny said, "about our crowd, the McMahons."

"Yes?"

"Kings about Monaghan for near a thousand years, butchered, and driv' north to these bitter hills, that's what it said, and the scholar that wrote it up maintained you'll get better bred men in the cabins of Fermanagh than you'll find in many's a big house."

Boyle thumbed up at the graveyard: "One thing we're sure of, Dinny, we'll add our bit."

"Blood tells," Dinny said, "it tells in the end."

A few miles on they passed a waterworks. There was a soldier pacing the floodlit jetty.

"Wouldn't care for his job, he'll go up with it some night."

"Unless there's changes," Boyle said.

"Changes! What changes. Look in your neighbour's face; damn little change you'll see there. I wrought four days with Gilbert Wilson before Christmas, baggin' turf beyont Doon, and when the job was done we dropped into Corranny pub, and talked land, and benty turf, and the forestry takin' over and the way people are leavin' for factories, the pension scheme for hill farmers and a dose of things: no side in any of it, not one word of politics or religion, and then all of a shot he leans over to me and says: 'Fact is, Dinny, the time I like you best, I could cut your throat.' A quare slap in the mouth, but I didn't rise to it; I just said: 'I'd as lief not hear the like, Gilbert.' 'You,' says he, 'and all your kind, it must be said.' 'It's a mistake, Gilbert, to say the like, or think it.' 'Truth,' he said, 'and you mind it, Dinny'."

He looked at Boyle: "What do you think of that for a spake?"

They came to the main road and Moorlough: "Are them geese or swans?" Dinny was pointing. He wound down his window and stared out. On the Loughside field there seemed to be fifty or sixty swans, very white against the black water. Boyle slowed for the trunk road, put on his headlights.

"Hard to say."

"Swans," Dinny said.

"You're sure?"

"Certain sure."

"So far from water?"

"I seen it before on this very lake in the twenties, bad sign."

"Of what?"

"Trouble."

The lake was half a mile long and at the far end of it there was a military checkpoint. An officer came over with a boy soldier and said, "Out, please." Two other soldiers began searching the car.

"Name?"

"Boyle, James."

"Occupation?"

"Teacher."

"Address?"

"Tiernahinch, Kilrooskey, Fermanagh."

"And this gentleman?"

Boyle looked away. Dinny said nothing. The officer said again: "Name?"

"Denis McMahon, Gawley's Bridge, Fermanagh."

"Occupation?"

"I'm on the national health."

The boy beside the officer was writing in a notebook. A cold wind blowing from the lake chopped at the water, churning up angry flecks. The officer had no expression in his face. His voice seemed bored and flat.

"Going where?"

"Enniskillen," Boyle said.

"Purpose?"

"To visit this man's brother, he's had an operation."

"He's lying under a surgeont," Dinny said.

The officer nodded.

"And your brother's name?"

"Joady, Joseph, I'm next of kin."

The boy with the notebook went over to a radio jeep. The officer walked away a few paces. They watched. Boyle thought he should say aloud what they were all thinking, then decided not to; then heard himself say: "Awful business at Trillick."

The officer turned, looked at him steadily for a moment and nodded. There was another silence until Dinny said: "Trillick is claner nor a man kicked to death by savages fornenst his childer."

The officer did not look round. The boy soldier came back from the jeep and said everything was correct, Sir. The officer nodded again, walked away and stood looking at the lake.

Dinny dryspat towards the military back as they drove off. " 'And this gentleman!' Smart bugger, see the way he looked at me like I was sprung from a cage."

"His job, Dinny!"

"To make you feel like an animal! 'Occupation' is right!"

Near Lisnaskea Dinny said: "Cancer, that's what we're all afraid of, one touch of it and you're a dead man. My auld fella died from a rare breed of it. If he went out in the light, the skin would rot from his face and hands, so he put in the latter end of his life in a dark room, or walkin' about the roads at night. In the end it killed him. He hadn't seen the sun for years."

He lit a cigarette butt.

"A doctor tould me once it could be in the blood fifty years, and then all of a shot it boils up and you're a gonner."

For miles after this they said nothing, then Dinny said: "Lisbellaw for wappin' straw, / Maguiresbridge for brandy. / Lisnaskea for drinkin' tay. / But Clones town is dandy . . . that's a quare auld one?"

He winked with his good eye.

"You want a jigger, Dinny?"

"I'll not say no."

Smoke, coughing, the reek of a diesel stove and porter met them with silence and watching. Dinny whispered: "U.D.R., wrong shop."

Twenty or more, a clutch of uniformed farmers, faces hardened by wind, rutted from bog, rock and rain, all staring, invincible, suspicious.

"Wrong shop," Dinny whispered again.

"I know," Boyle said, "we can't leave now."

Near a partition there was a space beside a big man. As Boyle moved towards it a woman bartender said: "Yes?"

"Two halfs, please."

"What kind?"

"Irish."

"What kind of Irish?"

"Any kind."

Big enough to pull a bullock from a shuck on his own Boyle thought as the big man spat at the doosy floor and turned away. Dinny nudged Boyle and winked up at a notice pinned to a pillar. Boyle read:

> Linaskea and District Development Association
> Extermination of Vermin
> 1/- for each magpie killed.
> 2/- for each grey crow killed.
> 10/- for each grey squirrel killed.
> £1 for each fox killed.

Underneath someone had printed with a biro:

> For every Fenian Fucker: one old penny.

As the woman measured the whiskies a glass smashed in the snug at the counter end. A voice jumped the frosted glass: "Wilson was a fly boy, and this Heath man's no better, all them Tories is tricky whores, dale with Micks and Papes and lave us here to rot. Well, by Christ, they'll come no Pope to the townland of Invercloon, I'll not be blown up or burned out, I'll fight to the last ditch."

All listening in the outer bar, faces, secret and serious, uncomfortable now as other voices joined: "You're right, George."

"Sit down, man, you'll toss the table."

"Let him say out what's in his head."

"They'll not blow me across no bog; if it's blood they want then, by Jasus, they'll get it, all they want, gallons of it, wagons, shiploads."

"Now you're talking, George."

The big man looked at the woman. She went to the hatch, pushed it and said something into the snug. The loudness stopped. A red-axe face stared out, no focus in the eyes. Someone snapped the hatch shut. Silence. The big man spat again and Dinny said: "I'd as lief drink with pigs."

He held his glass of whiskey across the counter, poured it into the bar sink and walked out. Boyle finished his whiskey and followed.

In the car again, the words came jerking from Dinny's mouth: "Choke and gut their own childer. Feed them to rats."

He held up a black-rimmed nail to the windscreen.

"Before they'd give us *that*!"

"It's very sad," Boyle said. "I see no answer."

"I know the answer, cut the bastards down, every last one of them and it'll come to that, them or us. They got it with guns, kep' it with guns, and guns'll put them from it."

"Blood's not the way," Boyle said.

"There's no other."

At Eniskillen they went by the low end of the town, passed armoured cars, and the shattered Crown buildings. Outside the hospital there were four rows of cars, two police cars and a military lorry. Joady's ward was on the ground floor. He was in a corner near a window facing an old man with bad colour and a caved-in mouth. In over thirty years Boyle had never seen Joady without his cap. Sitting up now in bed like an old woman, with a white domed head and drained face, he looked like Dinny's ghost shaved and shrunk in regulation pyjamas. He shook hands with Boyle and pointed at Dinny's bottle: "What's in that?"

"Lucozade," Dinny said.

"Poison."

"It's recommended for a sick body."

"Rots the insides: you can drop it out the windy."

"I'll keep it," Dinny said, "I can use it."

Boyle could see that Dinny was offended, and remembered his aunt's anger one Christmas long ago. She had knit a pair of wool socks for Joady and asked him about them.

"Bad wool, Miss," he said, "out through the heel in a week, I dropped them in the fire."

She was near tears as she told his mother: "Ungrateful, lazy, spiteful little men, small wonder Protestants despise them and us, and the smell in that house . . . you'd think with nothing else to do but draw the dole and sit by the fire the least they could do is wash themselves: as for religion, no Mass, no altar, nothing ever, they'll burn, they really will, and someone should tell them. God knows you don't want thanks, but to have it flung back in your teeth like that it's . . ."

"It's very trying, Annie," his mother said.

And Boyle wanted to say to his aunt: "No light, no water, no work, no money, nothing all their days, but the dole, fire poking, neighbour baiting, and the odd skite on porter, retched off that night in a ditch."

"Communists," his aunt mocked Joady, "I know what real Communists would do with those boyos, what Hitler did with the Jews."

"Annie, that's an awful thing to say."

There was silence and then his aunt said: "God forgive me, it is, but . . ." and then she wept.

"Because she never married, and the age she's at," his mother said afterwards.

Joady was pointing across a square of winter lawn to the hospital entrance: "Fornenst them cars," he said, "the morgue." His eyes swivelled round the ward. "I heard nurses talk about it in the corridor, brought them here in plastic bags from Trillick, laid them out on slabs in a go of sawdust on account of the blood. That's what they're at now, Army doctors tryin' to put the bits together, so's their people can recognise them, and box them proper."

The old man opposite groaned and shifted. Joady's voice dropped still lower: "They say one man's head couldn't be got high or low, they're still tramping the mountain with searchlights."

"Dear God," Boyle said.

"A fox could nip off with a man's head handy enough."

"If it came down from a height it could bury itself in that auld spongy heather and they'd never find it or less they tripped over it."

"Bloodhound dogs could smell it out."

"They wouldn't use bloodhound dogs on a job like that, wouldn't be proper."

"Better nor lavin' it to rot in a bog, course they'd use dogs, they'd have to."

"Stop!"

Across the ward the old man was trying to elbow himself up. The air was wheezing in and out of his lungs, he seemed to be choking: "Stop! Oh God, God, please, I must go . . . I must . . ."

Boyle stood up and pressed the bell near Joady's bed. Visitors round other beds stopped talking. The wheezing got louder, more irregular, and a voice said: "Someone do something."

Another said: "Get a doctor."

Boyle said: "I've rung."

A male nurse came and pulled a curtain round the bed. When a doctor came the man was dead. He was pushed away on a trolley covered with a white sheet. Gradually people round other beds began to talk. A young girl looking sick was led out by a woman.

"That's the third carted off since I come down here."

"Who was he?" Boyle asked.

"John Willie Foster, a bread server from beyont Fivemiletown, started in to wet the bed like a child over a year back, they couldn't care for him at home, so they put him to 'Silver Springs,' the auld people's home, but he got worse there so they packed him off here."

"Age," Dinny said, "the heart gave up."

"The heart broke," Joady said, "no one come to see him, bar one neighbour man. He was tould he could get home for a day or two at Christmas, no one come, he wouldn't spake with no one, couldn't quit cryin'; the man's heart was broke."

"Them Probsbyterians is a hard bunch, cauld, no nature."

There was a silence.

"Did he say what about you Joady? . . . the surgeon?"

"No."

"You asked?"

" 'A deep operation,' he said, 'very deep, an obstruction,' so I said 'Is there somethin' rotten, Sir, I want to know, I want to be ready?' 'Ready for what,' says he and smiles, but you can't tell what's at the back of a smile like that. 'Just ready,' I said.

" 'You could live longer nor me,' says he."

"He hasn't come next nor near me since I've come down here to the ground . . . did he tell yous anythin'?"

"Dam' to the thing," Dinny said.

And Boyle noticed that Joady's eyes were glassy.

There was a newspaper open on the bed. It showed the Duke of Kent beside an armoured car at a shattered customs post. On the top of the photograph the name of the post read "Kilclean." Boyle picked up the newspaper, opened it and saw headlines: "Significance of bank raids"; "Arms for Bogsiders'; "Failure to track murderer"; "Arms role of I.R.A."

He read, skipping half, half listening to the brothers.

"In so far as ordinary secret service work is concerned, could be relied on and trusted . . . under the control of certain Ministers. Reliable personnel . . . co-operation between Army intelligence and civilian intelligence . . . no question of collusion."

"Lies," Joady said to Dinny, "you don't know who to believe." His voice was odd and his hand was trembling on the bedspread. Boyle didn't want to look at his face and thought, probably has it and knows. Dinny was looking at the floor.

"Lies," Joady said again. And this time his voice sounded better. Boyle put down the paper and said: "I hear you got blood, Joady."

"Who tould you that?"

"One of my past pupils, a nurse here."

"Three pints," Joady said.

Boyle winked and said: "Black blood, she told me you got Paisley's blood."

Joady began shaking, his mouth opened and he seemed to be dry-retching. The laughter when it came was pitched and hoarse. He put a hand on his stitches and stopped, his breathing shallow, his head going like a picaninny on a mission box.

"Paisley's blood, she said that?"

"She did."

"That's tarror," he said, but was careful not to laugh again. Boyle stood up and squeezed his arm: "We'll have to go, Joady, next time can we bring you something you need?"

"Nothin'," Joady said, "I need nothin'."

Walking the glass-walled, rubber corridor Boyle said: "I'll wait in the car, Dinny."

Dinny stopped and looked at the bottle of Lucozade: "We could see him together."

"If you want."

The surgeon detached a sheet of paper from a file, he faced them across a steel-framed table: "In your brother's case," he was saying to Dinny, "it's late, much, much, too late." He paused, no one said anything and then the surgeon said: "I'm afraid so."

"Dying?"

"It's terminal."

"He's not in pain," Boyle said.

"And may have none for quite a while, when the stitches come out he'll be much better at home."

"He doesn't know," Dinny said.

"No, I didn't tell him yet."

"He wants to know."

The surgeon nodded and made a note on a sheet of paper. Dinny asked: "How long has he got, Sir?"

The surgeon looked at the sheet of paper as though the death date were inscribed: "Sometime this year . . . yes, I'm afraid so."

The Anglia and bicycles were gone now. It had grown dark about the bridge and along the river. Boyle was cold sitting on the wall. Dinny had been talking for half an hour: "He was never sick a day, and five times I've been opened, lay a full year with a bad lung above at Killadeas; he doesn't know what it is to be sick."

Raucous crow noise carried up from the trees around the Spade Mill, cawing, cawing, cawing, blindflapping in the dark. They looked down, listening, waiting, it ceased. "He knows about dying," Boyle said.

"That's what I'm comin' at, he's dyin' and sleeps twelve hours of the twenty-four, ates, smokes, walks, and for a man used never talk much, he talks the hind leg off a pot now, make your head light to hear him."

He took out a glass phial: "I take two of them sleeping caps every night since he come home, and never close an eye. I can't keep nothin' on my stomach, and my skin itches all over; I sweat night and day. I'll tell you what I think: livin's worse nor dyin', and that's a fact."

"It's upsetting, Dinny."

It was dark in the kitchen: Joady gave Boyle a stool, accepted a cigarette and lit it from the paraffin lamp, his face sharp and withered: a frosted crab.

"Where's the other fella gone?"

"I'm not sure," Boyle said, "he went down the river somewhere."

Joady sucked on the cigarette: "McCaffreys, he's gone to McCaffreys, very neighbourly these times, he'll be there until twelve or after."

He thrust at a blazing sod with a one-pronged pitch fork: "Same every night since I come home, away from the house every chance he gets."

"All the visitors you have, Joady, and he's worried."

"Dam' the worry, whingin' and whinin', to every slob that passes the road about *me* snorin' the night long, didn't I hear him with my own ears . . ."

He spat, his eyes twisting: "It's *him* that snores not *me*, him: it's *me* that's dyin', *me*, not him . . . Christ's sake . . . couldn't he take a back sate until I'm buried."

He got up and looked out the small back window at the night, at nothing: "What would you call it, when your own brother goes contrary, and the ground hungry for you . . . eh! Rotten, that's what I'd call it, rotten."

Heritage

HE STEPPED BACK AS the pigeon shattered through the dairy window. For an instant he saw the brown outstretched wings of the hawk, the yellow flouted eyes. It swerved sharply left with a screech, cutting under the archway, up over the beech copse in line with the orchard towards the border river. He was holding the dead pigeon as his mother and Maggie Reilly crossed from the porch, his mother's mouth a question mark, Maggie's face fat, flat and curious.

"There was a hawk after it," he said.

"God help it," his mother said with pitying eyes.

He left it on the dairy window.

"God made it."

"Poor hunted cratur," Maggie said.

His mother touched the plumage. "These days every sound fright's me."

She had a grey dress on for service. Maggie had green Sunday buttons sewn on her Monday coat, a floppy brown woollen that covered her fourteen stone.

"I'll have your milk in ten minutes Maggie, I've cans to collect."

"No hurry, Eric."

Blister, his father's mongrel hound, appeared from somewhere and ran from the yard, the pigeon in its mouth.

"Nature's cruel too," Maggie said.

Eric watched them walk towards the house. Maggie had two children by different men, and lived in the office section of a disused creamery.

"A proper Papist hedge whore," George said often to his mother. "You should get shut of her, Sarah."

"Indeed I should," his mother said.

Maggie worked at other farms and helped out odd times with house parties at Inver Hall. Apart from harmless news his mother liked to hear, she was a good worker and likeable.

He went out under the stone archway. The rutted laneway, dry now in summer, had a thick tuft of scutch down its spine. On a stricken ash in the middle of the orchard the hawk perched in rigid silence. Eric stood and looked. It stared back sullen. He clapped his hands sharply. It fell from the branch, swooped across the lane, upwards from the rolling fields and stout ditches of Drumbowl.

He followed its flight towards Shannock and Carn Rock, a dim, hidden country, crooked scrub ditches of whin and thorns stunted in sour putty land; bare, spade-ribbed fields, rusted tin roofed cabins, housing a stony-faced people living from rangy cattle and Welfare handouts. From their gaunt lands they looked down on the green border country below watching, waiting. To them a hundred years was yesterday, two hundred the day before.

"A rotten race," George said, "good for nothin' but malice and murder; the like of Hitler would put them through a burnhouse and spread them on their sour bogs and he'd be right, it's all they're fit for."

The lane sloped steeply to the country road. He walked by the orchard and beech copse planted by his grandfather in 1921 to block off the view of the Fenian South. He could see through the grey-lichened trunks the slate-coloured river winding through thick rushy bottoms past Inver Hall and Church towards Lough Erne. A week ago he had watched a gun fight between British soldiers and gunmen across the river in the Republic. He saw one gunman hit and dragged away by two others. His mouth was dry for hours after. Every other day this last few years their windows rattled from explosions in nearby towns and villages. Now since he had joined the U.D.R. the thing had got ugly. Three men he knew were dead, two U.D.R., one Catholic policeman. Tonight when he put on his uniform his mother would be near tears. Every day when they talked about land, neighbours or cattle prices, they were thinking something else. He was a big target. He could be got handy. Death spitting from a gap or bog, a sharp bend in the road, a cattle mart or shop counter, a booby-trapped pad between townlands, or blown asunder on the tractor drawing turf from Doon forest, where it seemed dark now in July. Anywhere, anytime, a clash to the head or body, brain shattered, his name in a news-reader's mouth:

"This evening in South Fermanagh, Eric O'Neill, twenty-one, a part time member of the U.D.R."

Where and how it happened, along with oil shortages, strikes and rumours of revolution. TV coverage, a vast Protestant attendance. The *Impartial Reporter* would give it two full pages with photographs, his father, George, Sam and Joe Robinson carrying the coffin, his mother supported by neighbours at the graveside. More hatred but he'd be gone from it. Forgot in a week except for Rachel and the family.

As he approached the milk stand he could see a label tied to the can handle. A reject? Then he noticed the envelope, black edged. Inside printed with red marker pen he read:

ERIC O'NEILL U.D.R. DRUMHOWL
BORN 1952
DIED?
GET OUT . . . OR BE GOT LIKE CROZIER
R.I.P.

He felt more anger than fear. Even now as he stood they could be watching ten fields away or further, in a hedge, up a tree. He put the note in his pocket, grasped the churns, jumped the low ditch and walked up the back of the hedge, keeping out of sight of the road, through the orchard into the yard. He brought the cans straight to the dairy. As he loosened the lids to let air circulate, he noticed his hands were shaking like an old man's. He was sweating. "I'm a coward," he thought. He took out the note and read it again. "R.I.P." A sick, cruel touch that. One by one he thought of his Catholic neighbours from Drumhowl to Carn Rock, tried to imagine them writing this . . . all hard-working people. Martin Cassidy the only active man in politics, a Civil Rights man; open and manly, respected by both sides.

Maggie came across the yard pushing her bicycle, a milk-can in one hand for two pints of milk, part payment for the work she did. She followed him into the byre.

"You tend them well, Eric, great cows God bless them."

She said this every day, or something like it. She understood the work that went into the feeding, cleaning and milking of twenty-three cows, the awkward calvings, calf scours, sudden deaths. She looked at him now with clear kind eyes, but of another race and creed, who might by now have decided on the time and place of his death. Eric hunkered to attach a milk cluster.

"You can't tell what they're thinking," George said "never, ever."

Straightening, he looked down at the four claws of the machine, the milk pulsing into the bucket.

"You're not talking to the people this morning, Eric."

"Sorry, Maggie."

He looked round. It was almost as if she knew. When she dropped her voice he listened carefully, looking straight into her eyes.

"Something to tell you, Eric," she was saying.

"Yes?"

"A neighbour man." She stopped and looked at the bright cobbled yard. "This neighbour man, he told me he heard three men in a pub in Arva."

"Yes?"

"Talkin' quiet. They had a list of names at a table."

Colour had come into her face. She was finding this hard to say. He looked away, Maggie went on:

"From where he stood this neighbour man, he saw your name."

"What sort of list?"

"I don't know . . . he said they were young men, not country boys." She stopped again. "Could be another Eric O'Neill."

"Me all right . . . maybe your neighbour left this for me."

As she read the note her eyes filled; Eric watched. "What neighbour man, Maggie?"

"A good man, wouldn't say a cross word to a dog."

"Would he know the men with the list?"

"Never seen them in his life . . . he said they sounded like Tyrone."

"The publican must know them?"

"I wouldn't know that, son."

"How do they get names? How do they know when I come and go?"

He could hear a sharpness in his voice. She was staring with dilated eyes.

"They'll shoot postmen next."

"Get out, son."

"Maggie, I was in uniform, that's enough."

He had known her since he was a child and had never seen her look frightened. She knew a man who knew men who carried guns and were prepared to kill. He was on their list and she had warned.

"I'd as lief die myself, Eric, as see you harmed."

"I know that, Maggie."

"Honest to God, I . . ."

"My worry, not yours . . . it's a bloody mess."

Outside under the winch-gibbet on the byre gable he tapped two pints of milk from the cooler.

"What'll you do, son?"

She didn't hear him say "I'm still alive" because of their old Bedford revving in the lane as it approached the arched entry. He watched it bounce over the stone gulley into the sunlit yard. His father reversed into the open turf-shed, cut the engine and opened a newspaper. Before he could think to stop her Maggie was moving towards the van. She talked with his father through the side window. When she left, his father got out of the van. He stood looking towards the byre, then walked towards the back porch of the house. One way or another they'd have heard. Notes like this had to be shown to Dixon the Commandant; sooner or later they'd all know. Twenty-five U.D.R. men shot since he had joined, buried in parish graveyards, skulls and bodies smashed, married or single, in or out of uniform. He felt again a hatred for these hidden killers, the hatred he felt for rats; everywhere watching, waiting, in walls and ditches, dung heaps and gullies, following old ruts and runs, half blind, grubbing on filth, smelling out the weak, the crippled and the cowardly. Trap, cage, shoot, or poison, hunt them with terriers, ferrets or starving cats, and a month later they were back, scraping, clawing, gorging, no ridding the world of them.

"Thinking like George now," he thought. "Beginning to hate them, *all* of them." Maggie? Sam's wife Maisie?

He tried not to think, finished the milking and crossed to the house. Pulling off his rubber boots in the glass porch he could see the kitchen door slightly open, voices loud inside; his mother's shrill. Silence for a few seconds. He pushed the hall door open a little. Sunlight from the kitchen window on the freshly polished linoleum, handmade rugs, two stiff chairs and a hallstand, photographs of his O'Neill grandparents, an embroidered sampler and a mahogany wall clock above the wainscotting.

"You pushed him in, woman, get him out now."

"Cruel to say the like of that."

"True: a death warrant, and you might as well have signed it, you and your brother George."

His father's voice was quiet. It seldom changed tone. His mother said: "He asked to join."

"Made to feel a coward if he didn't; a gun, a uniform and the money's good, that's what you said . . . what he's got for himself won't bury him. Half his pay it took to put lino on that hall."

"He gave that to me."

"And you look down on Maggie Reilly."

"You talk to me of her."

"She loves her bastard sons, you've driv one away, and set the other up for a cock-shot . . . my sons."

In the silence that followed Eric could feel his heart knocking strongly at his ribcage.

"It's me you hate, you've hated me for years."

"I'd rather be dead than talk like this."

"Better dead, a coward like all your people."

When he heard his mother cry he pulled on his rubber boots, went out to the yard and stood at the gable of the house. Worse than fear, hearing them like that. The voices had stopped.

"Get out," Sam said when he was leaving four years back.

"It's home," Eric remembered saying.

Sam said, "This place! It's a prison, worse; no drink, no smoke, no dance, no love, nothing but work, work, work and the Rev. Plumm every Sunday. Trouble or no trouble, no man could live in this house and stay sane."

He heard the porch door open, saw his father cross the yard.

"Eric."

He moved from the gable. "Here."

His father moved to join him; taller, leaner, a lined face under a weathered hat, deepset eyes, a huntsman, farmer and tradesman who could read the time on the Post Office clock from the far end of the street in Five-miletown. He looked now at Eric very directly.

"Maggie told me."

"Aye."

"Your mother knows."

"She'd have heard."

"She'll go off her head."

"Been off it since Sam married and before."

Eric looked away, his father said: "You could leave till things quieten."

"In a hundred years? I'd as lief take my chance."

"You'll be got if you stay."

"Someone has to . . ."

"I don't want to bury you, son."

"Someone must fight."

"Who? Every second neighbour? American money? Gangs of street savages. There's a reason for all that and they can't all be locked up, hung or shot, they'll come again, and again, and again till they get what they want, or most of it, the same the world over."

Eric was tempted to say "Like rats" but didn't.

"I should have stood my ground that night, put George out and sent her to bed and said No. I should have took a stand. Show us the note."

He watched his father read. Two days of stubble seemed greyer.

"The whole thing makes me sick."

He handed back the note: "We'd best go in."

At the table his mother sat, hair knotted up, scared eyes, her face white as eggshell. When Eric looked up she was staring straight at him, porridge and wheaten bread on the deal boards, silence but for the wall clock in the hall. Then his mother said:

"You blame me both of you."

Eric said: "I blame no one."

"Whispering outside."

"Talking," his father said, "we'll say it again if you want."

"Men tortured in back streets, butchered fornenst their wives and childer, all of us awake when a car stops at night or the dog barks, and you blame me 'cause you think someone should take a stand."

"What's he fighting for, woman, God and country? The Queen? I'll tell you what he's fighting for . . . the big boys who splash more on weekends whoring than he'll make in a lifetime, and good luck to their whoring I say, if there's goms who'll die to keep them at it; that's your cause, son, the one true God, pound notes, millions of them; and the men who have them don't care a tinker's curse who kills who as long as they keep their grip, and if that's a coward's talk, I'll stay one."

"That's something you read in your trashy paper."

"It's the truth, woman."

"From a liar . . . and a hypocrite."

"Take care."

"You'll take what you get from Papist or Protestant . . . you don't care, and never will . . . tip your cap to money like anyone else and I'll not hear speeches 'bout big men and their rotten lives, when there's little men twice as rotten."

"Like George?"

"He's not cruel to his own kin . . . you said things to me just now, John Willie, no man who calls himself a man should say to any woman, let alone his wife, things I'll not forget the longest day I live."

His father was looking fixedly at a point on the kitchen floor, his face rigid. He said quiet and cold:

"You'll live to know worse days, woman."

"God forgive you."

"And you."

She was beginning to break. "The child is frightened."

"I'm no child, Mother."

"You didn't know what you were doing."

His father said blunt, "You did, George did. He signed, took the oath, money, what odds who's wrong or right, we've been over this a hundred times."

"You don't care."

"If one neighbour in ten thousand wants to kill me or mine, I'll not hate them all for that one, and I don't hate someone I've never met."

"Please, Da."

"Maisie, your own daughter-in-law."

"Please."

He understood what his father was saying, he knew what his mother was feeling.

"You don't know right from wrong, woman, good from bad."

"You're one to talk."

"Say what you like to your brother and his Christian friends, I'll not hear it in my house."

"A sad day I ever stood inside it."

"Damn little you've ever done in it, but gripe and whine."

She left the table stumbling as she went up the stairs, her bowl of porridge untouched. When they heard the bedroom door close, his father said:

"Day's I'd pay to be shot by anyone, dead and done with this crabbed life."

"You shouldn't, Da."

"What?"

"Talk so hard."

"I have reason . . . take a drink, crack a joke and it's the end of the world, never heard her laugh right in thirty years, and never seen her body and won't or less she dies first and I'm at the laying out."

"Don't."

"True . . . I had land, a stone built house, after you two were born she'd all she wanted from me . . . hates bodies, her own and mine . . . even food, hates that, won't eat fornenst strange eyes . . . the other end of stooping, and that's shameful. She could live on black bread, water, the Bible and hating Catholics; that's enough to keep her happy, makes me sick. If I could pray to God odd times it's not her blind God or George's. He's got a lot to answer for."

Eric could not eat. His father did not look up when he said:

"I'll change."

Passing his mother's room he could hear crying. He knocked.

"Yes."

"Me." He went in.

"Close the door, son." Eric did as he was told.

"The cruel things that man says to me with his quiet voice. I'd as lief he'd shout or hit me."

"We all say hard things be times."

"He meant every word, God in Heaven, how could he say such things, let alone think them. I told Sam before he married her I wouldn't meet that girl or let her cross the door. I won't pretend about Papists, he hates me 'cause I tell the truth, he's afraid of that."

Eric had heard this so often it was difficult for him to reply. If he disagreed she wept; if he seemed to agree even by silence she used this against his father . . . "Eric agrees with me."

"Am I speaking the truth, son, answer me?"

He picked his words carefully. "You believe what you say is true, Mother."

"I tell no lies."

"I know."

"Say what's in your head."

"You're distressed, that bothers me more nor the note I got."

She kissed his hand. "I'll die if anything happens to you, Eric, and he'll blame me, we should leave, all of us."

"How?"

"Just go."

"Where?"

"Away from here, anywhere, if we go he'll have to go."

"Sell out?"

"Yes."

"He won't."

"You were whispering out in the yard."

"Mother, I'll go if you want but . . ."

"If you go, we all go, for good. I'll not stay and hear a son of mine called 'coward.' God I hate this house, these blind bitter fields."

"We'll talk again."

He kissed her forehead, went to his room and changed. When he came down to the kitchen his father was staring out of the window, the *Sunday People* open on the table. He picked up the paper and nodded at the door. As they crossed the yard his father asked:

"What's she on about?"

"The same."

"Maisie?"

As they neared the turf shed the bedroom window went up with a snap. They stopped. Eric turned.

"Say it loud, John Willie."

His father kept his back to the house.

"You'll die, man, I'll die, and the only son we can call our own will be murdered if we don't go!"

His father turned and said looking at the ground: "If you want to go, woman, go, I'm staying."

"And do what, man?"

"What you want."

"Cook and scrub, is it? Wash and scald? I worked all my days for you, for next nothin' and when I ask one thing for myself, for your son, you say 'no.'"

"You've got *two* sons."

96

His father dropped his voice and asked Eric: "You want me to sell or go?"
"No."

"Don't whisper," his mother screamed, "talk loud."

"All right I'll talk loud . . . I was born here, I'll die here."

"Keep your fifty rotten acres, bury yourself in them and your son, and don't blame me."

Then the squeal of the window pulleys as the window snapped shut. Father and son stood in the sunlit yard looking at the ground.

"One thing to be said for the grave, you lie on your lone in a box; small wonder men die young, it's a wonder to Christ more don't hang themselves or walk out. What'll she pray about this morning in Church eh? 'Love thy neighbour' is it?"

Blister came bounding round the side of the barn. John Willie opened the door of the old Bedford. The mongrel jumped into the back.

"I'm taking the van," he said. "You'll have to walk."

Eric went back through the glass porch and stood listening in the long narrow hall. The wall clock, a tap turned in the bathroom, a helicopter somewhere far north. There was a smell of polish and paraffin oil. He opened the front door. July sunlight and the rich odour of cut grass. He looked at his pocketwatch, went back to the hallstand and took two hymnals.

"Mother."

"Yes."

"The van's gone."

"I heard, what's the time?"

"Quarter to."

Waiting at the hallstand he read the glazed and framed sampler stitched by his mother in memory of her own mother.

FOR ABIGAIL HAWTHORNE. 1874–1938
STRENGTH AND BEAUTY ARE HER CLOTHING AND SHE
SHALL LAUGH IN THE LATTER DAY. THE LAW OF
CLEMENCY IS ON HER TONGUE. HER CHILDREN HAVE
RISEN UP AND CALLED HER BLESSED . . . HER HUSBAND
AND THEY HAVE PRAISED HER. FAVOUR IS DECEITFUL
AND BEAUTY VAIN. THE WOMAN THAT FEARETH THE
LORD? SHE SHALL BE PRAISED

Between a sundial and a floral corner her signature stitched over in black thread:

Sarah Hawthorne
October 1941

She came round the bend of the staircase white with anger in her good Sunday coat and hat.

"Away with his filthy paper. Hunt . . . and stupid beer talk, anything but Church . . . Where's he gone?"

"He didn't say."

"Some Papist hovel up by Carn, thinks they like him, 'cause he can patch their slates and fix guttering, they'd knife him quick as they'd look at him, he'll find that out yet."

She was so angry, so used to Eric's silence that they walked by a farm pass to the back of Inver Church, without exchanging another word. Eric was grateful for the silence. July meadows baled or ensiled, pale or dark green, uncut meadows on rising land a light fawn colour, cows and dry stock content on good pasture. Over by Cavan and the Cuilca Mountains the sky was a darkish blue, but clear over the rock. It would be a good bright windy day.

Inver Church came into view as they topped a low drumlin, a small Romanesque block all spikes and parapets with one sharp spire to the front in two acres of burial ground, the family church of the Armstrongs, their mausoleum massive and dominating amongst plain weathered stones. Here his O'Neill grandparents were buried in the unkept grave. The Hawthornes' grave, his mother's people, had heavy protective railings around it forged by George. Even now in summer George kept it trim and neat with hedge clippers, particular, like his sister, to show evidence of Protestant order and privacy. He was waiting now at the stile in a dark suit topped by a white face and grey hair, uneasy, his head at an angle, a restive scaldcrow.

"Well?"

It was a rebuke and a question. Sarah answered: "He took the van."

George shrugged and sucked at his teeth: "How's Eric?"

"Alive, George."

His uncle's limestone eyes stared from under shag-black eyebrows, both stood aside to let his mother through the stile. George followed listening as his mother told about the note Eric dropped back. Twice George looked around with bleak concern. He tended the collection plate: there would be no time for talking until after the service. They went up the left aisle and sat in a pew near the baptistry under a white marble plaque, shaped like a shield. At the eagle lectern the Rev. John Plumm was reading from the Bible:

"And there is no remembrance now of former things nor indeed of those things which hereafter are to come."

He paused and looked down at the half-full Church.

"All things in this time are mingled together, blood theft, murder, dissimulation, corruption and unfaithfulness, and men keep watches of madness in the night."

In front of the lectern on the outside of the front pew sat Colonel Norbert Armstrong, erect and grey alongside his wife. Behind him a fine-skinned American with steel-rimmed glasses wearing a Norfolk jacket. Both pews were filled with the house party from Inver Hall. His father said often:

"They go for curiosity, to hear ould Plumm rave on, they believe in nothin' but land, stocks and shares, and keepin' things the way they are."

Years ago he said he had seen a party of them bathing nude by moonlight in the shallow artificial lake fed from the border river. "Blind drunk," he said, "leppin' on each other, men and women, squealing like cut pigs, a wonder to God the half of them weren't drowned."

A week ago some Fenian wag hung a dated tourist poster on the main gates:

COME TO ULSTER FOR
YOUR SHOOTING HOLIDAYS

and smeared across it in green paint:

UP THE PROVOS

There was a rumour once that the Colonel had interfered with the game-keeper's son, and squashed a case with money. His father half believed the rumour, his mother rejected it as:

"Foul Papist lies. It's what they want to believe about all our kind."

Every now and then the Colonel fired off letters to the *Irish Times* and the

Belfast Telegraph about Law, Order, Violence and the lunacy of Paisleyism. George bought the *Protestant Telegraph* and liked Paisley.

"The I.R.A. wouldn't waste a bullet on the Colonel," he said once, but he tipped his cap as reverently as the next, and shod their hunters when requested at the Estate forge. The Rev. Plumm looked at the empty gallery on either side:

"If thou shall see the oppression of the poor, and violent judgements, and justice prevented in the province, wonder not at this matter, for he that is high hath another higher, and there are others still higher than these." Eric watched George across the aisle, a daw listening for worms.

"All human things are liable to perpetual change. We are to rest on God's providence and cast away fruitless cares. I said in my heart concerning the sons of men, that God would prove them, and show them to be like beasts. Therefore the death of man, and of beasts is one; and the conditions of them both is equal; as man dieth, so they also die, all things breathe alike; and man hath nothing more than beast; all things are subject to vanity. And all things go to one place; of earth they are made and into earth they return together."

The Rev. Plumm turned from the lectern. George got up and moved for the collection plate. All stood to sing, Miss Pritchard fingering the introductory phrases of Psalm three:

> Oh Lord, how are my foes increased!
> Against me many rise.
> Many say of my soul, for him
> In God no succour lies
> Yet thou my shield and glory art,
> The uplifter of mine head.
> I cried and from His Holy hill
> The Lord me answer made,
> I laid me down and slept, I waked;
> For God sustained me
> I will not fear though thousands ten
> Set round against me be
> Arise, O Lord; Save me, my God
> For Thou has struck my foes
> Upon the cheek; the wicked's teeth
> Hast broken by Thy blows

Salvation surely doth belong
Unto the Lord alone;
Thy blessing, Lord, for ever more
Thy people is upon.

Service over, the Rev. Plumm walked into the presbytery. The Colonel stood in the aisle to allow his guests out first, English mostly, Eric thought, over with a pack of otter hounds he had seen yesterday from the haggard, a mahogany trailer towed by a yellow Land Rover. When the house party had filed out the Colonel walked down the aisle glancing and nodding here and there. Tom and Ruth Robinson followed with Joe and the rest of the congregation. Rachel remained seated. Eric smiled at Tom Robinson, an arthritic old farmer with a strong face. He winked at Joe who scarcely nodded back. When the church was empty Rachel looked around. Eric went into the baptistry; she followed. Through the high Gothic window they could see the sunlit graveyard, George and his mother talking with Rachel's parents, Joe sitting by himself on a tomb slab smoking a cigarette. A fine-boned narrow face like Rachel's, which seldom showed colour or emotion, the same cool eyes, hair like bleached deal, Joe's ruffled at the nape, his skin coarsened by work and weather. Miss Pritchard was playing something complicated. It was hard to talk with the sound of the organ. Rachel took his hand and said:

"I've got 'till tomorrow, night duty next week. Were you talking to Joe?"

"He looked worried."

She hesitated. "Last night they stopped me near Maguiresbridge, three of them in tunics and berets."

She was looking out at the graveyard.

"When they found I was Joe Robinson's sister one of them said, 'We should eff her arseways, only she might like it,' another showed me a pistol and said, 'See this you black bitch, I'll ram it between your legs next time you, your brother or any of his like puts a hand on any of ours, and tell him from us we'll blow his effing brains out first chance we get.' "

The words, and the quiet way she told it, startled him more than if it had been screamed. The note in his pocket now seemed trivial; he could feel blood coming into his face. He said:

"They mean it."

"I know. I begged Joe all night to get out, he won't listen, will you talk to him, Eric?"

He shrugged.

"You can try."

"Your auld fellow's not fit to work, your place'd go to rack without Joe, even if he did get out what would he do? Where would he go?"

"Dig tunnels in Britain, anything; at least we could sleep at night."

"I'm not leaving, and I got a note tied to a can this morning."

"A note?"

"A warning."

"From them?"

"Who else?"

"Oh God."

The organ was pumping so loudly they were almost lip-reading. They waited for the passage of music to stop. On the baptistry wall on a large sheet of rectangular bronze, there was an engraved account of the Armstrong family, their arrival with King William, battles, sieges, glory, death and reference to the "disaffected Irish." In this marble font under this window both had been baptised in Christ to serve God and love neighbours. All round the church walls heraldic inscriptions, faded flags, sculptured guns, flutes, pipes, bayonets and loving tributes to violent death in Gallipoli, Flanders, Germany, North Africa.

"Catholics kneel under plaster saints," his father remarked once, "we sit with Christ under guns and swords."

The Rev. Plumm came down the aisle dispensing a nod towards the baptistry.

"Why do we come here?"

"It marks the week."

When the Rev. Plumm was gone Rachel said: "Let's go out."

From the arched entrance they saw groups of neighbours standing about exchanging news and views, George mouthing strongly with his mother and the Robinsons, an old forge bellows, the hiss of iron in the cooling tub. As Rachel moved into the sunlight to join them, Eric said:

"I want a word with Joe."

He went over, handed him the note and said: "Rachel told me about last night."

Joe read the note and handed it back without a word. He was looking across the river at the lime-washed Catholic church half a mile away, a plain stucco barnlike building, with a separate belfry, a white Madonna in a cave between the church and the curate's bungalow, a full congregation funnelling through the square porch spreading through their graveyard.

"Bees from a hive," Eric said.

"Wasps," Joe said.

"Any notion who stopped her?"

Joe shook his head.

"All Fenians round here, could be any of them."

"You believe that?"

"What odds what I believe or you . . . they'll choose the time and place, pick us off, no chance to fight back."

"Unless we go."

"I can't."

"Nor me."

"Do your people know?"

"What?"

"About last night; Rachel?"

Joe shook his head. "They're worried enough."

Cars were beginning to move from the Catholic church park down to the border bridge, the sun throwing flashes of hostile light from windscreens as they turned up for Carn. Joe jerked his head towards the gaunt uplands.

"It's a jungle from here to the rock; they don't need phones, radios or helicopters; sneeze at the back of a ditch, they know who it was and why he was there; they know every move, we don't stand a chance."

True. It was what Eric had told Maggie two hours ago. A lot of men got notes and were still alive. There was no point in further talk. Eric asked:

"You goin' to the hunt?"

"What hunt?"

"Otter, some pack from across, come last night to the Inver crowd. My auld fella's goin'."

"In our house they're death on doing anything of a Sunday."

"So's my mother and George, we might as well walk after dogs as sit and worry."

"What time?"

"Three, at the Hall."

"I'll come if I can."

"Bring Rachel."

"She hates huntin'."

"Ask her anyway."

Eric went over to join the others. Old Tom Robinson was looking at the gravel, squat in his late sixties, his wife Ruth, a tall thin woman with a forlorn face, blinking against the light, watching Eric approach. His mother was touching her upper lip nervously, upset by what George was saying. Eric heard him rasp:

"If we don't do it to them, they'll do it to us, and that's the story to the bitter end."

Old Tom looked embarrassed. George looked at Eric: "Any man tries to slide out is no man."

"I'm not sliding out George."

His mother said: "He's not your son, George . . ."

"More to me nor his own father. When it comes to the bit I can depend on him."

Old Tom said, "I'll run you up, Sarah."

"It's only ten minutes," his mother protested.

"Take the lift, mam," Eric said. "I'll walk."

He nodded at the Robinsons and Rachel and moved away.

George called, "Hould on, son, hould on."

Eric slowed, waiting.

"What's your hurry?"

Eric was tempted to say, "I don't want to listen to you George." He said nothing. Afraid of George, of his mother, afraid to pick between his mother and his father, afraid of Catholics, afraid to hate or love. It was from George as a child that he first heard about Catholics in the forge at Oakfield:

"I'll shoe no Catholic ass, my boot in his hole."

And some of the Protestant men in the forge took out their pipes and laughed. Others said: "You're an awful man, George."

But even as a child he knew they agreed with George. When a Catholic did bring work he was greeted with "Well?" or "What's wrong now?" or "What are you trickin' at this weather?" With Protestant neighbours he was courteous and helpful. "How's all the care, Bob?" No Catholics had come near his forge now for three years. He jerked his head towards the lime-washed church across the river.

"I'll say one thing for them, they're animals with balls, our side whines like Ruth Robinson . . . what's the end of it to be at all, at all, at all. Whiners get their teeth kicked down their throats."

George slashed at a nettle on a neglected grave with his blackthorn.

"Have you lost your tongue?"

"You have all the questions and answers, George."

"I know my mind, son, and you know yours if you were let, your father doesn't give a damn, and your mother wants you out, am I right?"

"Out where? I took an oath George, I'll stick by it."

"Now you're talkin'."

From the stile, across a narrow humped field of thistle and ragwort lay George's forge, a low squat crypt separate from the slated house, three fine oak trees at the back, proof to passing poverty in secondhand cars that Oakfield could grow sound hardwood.

"Come on up a while, we'll brew tay and talk."

Eric wanted to refuse but had no ready excuse. He nodded assent. Every day of childhood, summer and winter, on his way home from school he had called with George, running messages across the spongy river bottoms to Johnson's border shop, black green rushes so high he sometimes lost his way, always a reward for his trouble, a slice of bread and butter sprinkled with caster sugar. In this world of small fields and bogland he had loved and still did, this coarse bigoted man with his rasping voice. No matter how he spewed blind hatred, it was difficult to disengage from the past, to scrap old memories. The lane they walked on now was rutted by a thousand carts, the bramble shoots reaching halfway across as they did every summer.

"A good straight man," his mother said. "The best blacksmith in Ulster, afraid of nothing and no one."

"You're wrong," his father said, "he's afeered of everyone and everything, drinks every penny he gets and too mean to marry, and all that loud rough talk; thinks he hates Catholics, it's himself he hates, and I wouldn't fault him for that."

In the sepia light of the kitchen George wet strong tea from the black range. They faced each other across the blue checkered oil-cloth; on the wall smokey portraits of the Queen, Carson and Paisley, a row of faded sashes, a large drum sitting beside a disused dash-churn in one corner, alongside it a thick pile of *Protestant Telegraphs*. As a child the sound of the drum frightened Eric so much that he crept to his mother's bed at night.

"It's only Uncle George with his drum," she whispered, "nothin' to be afeered of."

This last few nights ten townlands could hear him thumping at the dusk beside the iron scrap heap behind the forge. Next Thursday on the Twelfth at Fivemiletown, he would make it reverberate to the whole mountain. He took a sip of tea now from his mug and stared out the window, a welt on his left cheek where a mare had lashed it twenty years ago.

"Any man drives off a Sunday and leaves his wife walk to Service is a poor breed of man."

"He had cause maybe, in his own mind."

"What cause? What's he ever done for her or you?"

"Pay bills."

"Ten pound a week this thirty years, what's that now, only for you son the farm would have been sold off long ago; you know that, I know that."

"He works, George."

"Not real work, not like you or me."

"He helps, when he's home."

"When's that? Tinker, footer, travel, talk? Drink in Papist houses, and doesn't give an ass's fart when his firstborn marries one of *them*, went to the weddin' in *their* church, and your mother at home near astray in the head, what sort of man's that?"

Eric moved from the table. "I'd as lief you didn't talk this way George."

"Afeered of the truth, son?"

"He's my father."

"And Sam's?" George paused and added quietly, "And more."

Eric said nothing for a moment and then: "You better say what you mean, George."

"She's been abused, your mother, that's what I mean."

Odd times, maybe twice a year, his father went on three-day benders. Twice in the last six months Eric had collected him, once from a pub in Blayney, and last time from a boarding house in Armagh. George drank every day. He despised men who couldn't hold their drink, and keep their feet.

"Don't you want to hear, son?"

Eric stared, he wanted to say yes and no.

"It's time you heard."

The limestone eyes jerked round from the window: "That eegit son of Maggie Reilly's, that's your half-brother . . . true."

It was like a sharp slap on the face from a cold heavy hand.

"You know what you're saying, George."

"I do. From his own mouth I got it eighteen years back, after the fair at 'Skea. We both had a drop taken, I put it to him square, and he didn't deny it. I tould him then if I ever got hint of the like again I'd kill him stone dead and I meant it. That's why he hates me."

Maggie had been working at Drumhowl since he was born, and every week since he could remember. Eric tried to shape the question in his mind; George answered it before he could ask.

"Every man and woman for miles around knows, bar you, Sam and your mother, and she must half know, that's what has her the way she is."

Eric went to the small back window that looked north. He could see Robinson's Vauxhall coming down the steep lane from Drumhowl. Joe and Rachel? The whole country?

"You shouldn't have said that, George."

"Time you heard, son."

"Why tell it?"

"Cause you don't back her. Now you know what she suffered, still suffers, that fat sow waddling up every mornin' for her milk, workin' around the house, twice a week, sickens me to my stomach to think of it."

George got up and poured himself a measure of Bushmills whiskey.

"Don't take it too hard."

"I don't believe it, George."

There was a pause. The side of George's mouth went down a little. For a moment he seemed almost angry, then he turned with a shrug.

"Would I lie about a thing like that? Ask him, your father, tell him what I said, see what he says."

In the half circle of gravel before Inver Hall he could see about a dozen cars including their old Bedford. A speedboat bounced on the water about a hundred yards from the shore, two skiers making a pattern behind it. After dinner with his mother, he was evasive about checking a heifer. From her eyes he could feel she suspected. Had he said he was going to join the hunt at Inver she would have asked him not to go, and he would have agreed. Because of what George had told him this mild deception cut sharply. Her face was still in his mind. As he walked through the parkland he could see his father clearly now with local huntsmen and farmers on the stretch of lawn between the eighteenth-century house and the lake, wee Willy Reilly amongst them, wearing the silly knitted cap like a tea cosy he wore summer and winter. The stables and yard were separate from the house, the otter pack whimpering, scraping at the wrought-iron gates, like big rough-haired foxhounds.

Two-stepping down the granite steps in black Aran sweater, grey flannels and shabby tennis shoes, Colonel Armstrong came clapping his hands for attention, directing his voice to the local huntsmen:

"Sherry, tea and seed cake inside before we start, the hunt begins at three sharp."

The voice across the lawn seemed to cut the outboard to silence, the two skiers skimming ropeless towards the shallow gravel. There was hesitation for a moment, then simultaneous mutters.

"Dammit, that's nice?"

"Aye."

"Why not, sir?"

"That's a dacent notion."

Of the dozen local huntsmen three were Catholics including Willie Reilly. The Colonel said: "Dogs not of the pack should, I think, be kept on leash, or tied until we see how they behave."

More muttered agreement. Small boys and youths were left in charge of the dogs. The huntsmen moved towards the house, his father talking easily with the Colonel. He had the casual self-respect of a farmer tradesman working over thirty years through the country; tinker or gentry, Papist or postman, he was the same with them all, a man seemingly without worries. Robinson's Vauxhall was not among the cars. His father seeing Eric approach put up a long arm and pointed towards the house. Eric signalled back, but decided to wait for Joe. He watched the skiers tinkering at the outboard motor, till he heard the car. He was surprised and pleased to see Rachel beside Joe. She wound down the side window.

"Might as well see an otter killed before one of you get it."

"Is your father here?" Joe asked.

Eric nodded to the house. "Inside."

"Posh," Rachel said.

"Sherry, tea and seed cake."

108

"Parlour or pantry?" Rachel asked.

Eric shrugged and smiled. She seemed petulant, looking at the skiers and the lake.

"Do we have to go in?"

"Unmannerly not to."

"Would they notice or care?"

"We'll go in," Joe said, getting out. "I like to hear them talk."

He walked towards the steps.

"Can't stand her," Rachel said.

"Who?"

"The Colonel's wife . . . They'll put us down in some poke with a bottle of cooking sherry."

"They're all right," Eric said.

"With two thousand acres they'd need to be."

He had helped here at threshing as a boy. Armstrongs' arrogance was natural. It was the way they were bred, and the Colonel had obliged him in different ways, loaning him farm machinery and a Friesian bull. The flagged hall went the length of the house, a wide slow-raked staircase, walls hung with military portraits, and strong faced women; couches, odd shaped chairs and garden furniture round the walls, a central refectory table, decanters of sherry, teacups and a canteen-type teapot with two handles. There were about thirty people in all, locals grouped separately in a corner baiting Willie Reilly. Joe had joined them. Eric could hear his father laughing. He paused with Rachel at a games table midway between the local group and some of the house party. The American with the steel-rimmed glasses was talking to the Colonel's daughter, beside them the Packmaster. He looked a bit like Harold Wilson. Then he saw Maggie Reilly coming out behind the staircase with a steaming steel container. As she walked to the table his father leaned towards her and said something. Maggie smiled. Eric felt suddenly embarrassed and uncomfortable. His father's voice was easy and teasing at Willie Reilly:

"Thon wee brown bitch of yours, Willie, what happened her ear?"

"I et it," Willie said.

There was a burst of laughter. With his slightly mongoloid face, the stutter and blue knit beret, he was a natural target for yeomanry unease in gentry surroundings:

"What odds about her ear, she's got the best nose in the country."

Someone said: "She's very small, Willie, very small."

"Hardy, well bred and fast, and she'll stick to the river, just you watch, not like some big auld mongrels I'll not mention."

Another said: "If an otter got a good grip on her, Willie, he'd pull her under."

"Would you think that, Petey?"

"I would, Willie."

"That big dog of yours John, what do you call him?"

"Blister."

"Aye . . . Blister . . . pity he's blind."

The laughter turned from Willie. Eric heard his father chuckle.

"He can see a mile off, Willie, and he can smell further."

"But will he hunt with the pack, John?"

"Ahead of them, Willie."

There was a slight burr in his father's voice. He had spent the morning in a pub somewhere. Eric felt a revulsion now he had not thought possible.

The Colonel was going around with a tray of sherries and a decanter, his wife following with a plate of cut seed cake. The Colonel asked Rachel: "Sherry or tea, dear?"

"Sherry, please."

"Eric?"

"Tea, please."

The Colonel called over: "Tea here, Maggie."

Mrs. Armstrong held out a plate of seed cake. She looked at Eric with unfocused, brown eyes and smiled as he took a slice of cake, then moved on to Rachel. Maggie came waddling over and filled Eric's tea cup. There was a slight tremor in his hand.

"You look awful worried, Eric?"

Rachel said: "He got a love letter this morning Maggie."

Maggie frowned and said: "Some playboy sent that, pass no remarks."

When Maggie moved away Rachel asked: "Are you all right?"

"Yes."

"What's wrong? Do you want to go out?"

"No."

Gradually the quickness of his heart slowed. The people in the hall seemed glazed. He sat on the side of an armchair, his teacup on the games table. Rachel leaned towards him and said quietly:

"I love you."

He looked at her and said: "And I you . . . something come over me, I'm sorry."

"What?"

"Nothing, I'll tell you after."

The American was saying to the Colonel's wife: "Yes but the kill is a fact of nature, Harriet, and nature plays sick jokes on all of us, like blindness, right? Old age? War? Death?"

"Brother Rat St. Francis said, likewise Brother Otter." She smiled oddly.

"Was he sane?"

"The greatest human being since Christ. Have you read Chekhov's *Ward No. 6*?"

"No."

"About a doctor in an asylum who realises as he goes mad that sanity is locked away and lunatics outside run the world . . ."

"Odd notion!"

"Probably true."

"You're joking, Harriet!"

"If they were in charge history might make more sense!"

"History would end!"

"A consummation devoutly to be wished."

The American laughed. The Colonel was amongst the locals again, refilling proffered glasses. He dropped his voice and said to Eric's father:

"This Packmaster isn't over keen on local hounds joining the pack; if dogs get out of hand some of you may have to put them on leash or withdraw them, you understand."

"Aye surely, Colonel."

"That makes sense."

"We're not here to spoil the sport," his father said.

Willie Reilly stuttered, "My wee bitch will hunt with any pack, she'll stick with the best of them Colonel."

"I hope she does, Willie."

"She's killed otters, and foxes and hares, and an auld badger dog, big as a boar, that's what happened her ear."

"There must be a drop of the tiger in her, Willie."

Laughter caused all heads to turn in the direction of the locals.

"Yes'll not laugh when ye see her workin'."

The Colonel moved towards the Packmaster and had a word with him. He looked at his wrist watch and said:

"We'll have to make a start."

Locals and guests followed him towards the big double door. Only the Colonel's wife remained. She stood at the refectory table, with the same odd smile.

The iron gates of the yard were opened. The otter hounds came whimpering and whining on to the sloping lawn, smelling and snarling round local hounds. Blister stood rigid as the pack nosed warily round him. The Packmaster shouted something, the Whipmaster cracked his whip for order. As Rachel and Eric walked across the gravel to the lawn, Rachel asked:

"Do you want to tell me what got you inside?"

Eric was watching the dogs. "The auld fellow and Maggie Reilly."

There was a ten second silence before she said: "That's a long way back."

"How long have you known?"

"School, I didn't rightly believe it till I heard them at home one night." She paused and looked up at him. "You never guessed?"

"Nothin' till George this morning."

"So?"

"My mother, she must know, and that one up every day about our place."

Rachel stepped up on to the grass and moved ahead of him. She turned. "Could happen to me."

"Could it?"

"Any woman . . . or you, like your father."

Eric shook his head. Willie Reilly was laughing and yapping with excitement. He had unleashed his wee brown bitch. She was making circles in a small area wagging her tail between her legs. The Packmaster was saying something to Willie.

"Because she's Catholic?"

"Maybe. I don't want to think about it."

"Don't, it's history now."

John Willie came over smiling, his hat cocked well back.

"Are you childer goin' to talk or walk?"

Rachel asked: "Will we see any otters killed John?"

"You'll not see an otter, let alone a kill."

The horn sounded and John Willie moved away, the Whipmaster in the middle of the dogs, the Packmaster walking ahead with a steel-shod stave, the countrymen with ashpoles, in their dark clothes and caps, coats tied with twine across their shoulders, the house party in colourful gear with an assortment of blackthorn and racing sticks. Now and then the Whipmaster called a dog by name . . . Elvis, Togo, Billy . . . all fanning out, the dogs setting a sharp walking pace. Where the lake narrowed to the river the hunt spread to both banks, the Packleader midstream wading haunch-deep, the Whipper on the northern bank, the otter hounds swimming, plunging, lapping water, testing otter holts, running up and down shallow drains. Where the lake ended, the river went in a slow curve for half a mile. All land north of this was Armstrong land, reclaimed and in good heart, a deep bog loam, rye grass with tufts of coxfoot, laid out in ten-acre divisions, a herd of over eighty cows grazing in one division, a Friesian bull walking alert through them. Wee Willie's brown bitch had left the river following a hare scent. The bull came trotting towards her, head lowered. She came back cowering to Willie's heels.

"That wee bitch of yours, Willie, she'll kill a bull before the day's out."

General laughter from the locals as Willie said: "The day's not done yet."

He kicked his dog sharply in the ribs. She ran off yelping. The hunt paused to watch Willie running up a ditch after her. Someone said:

"Between them they'll kill a hedgehog!"

The flat land sloped upwards, loamy hillock country, rising sharply thereafter to the gaunt highlands left of Carn Rock, thousands of acres planted with larch and Sitka spruce. Eric saw the American looking up and heard him say to the Colonel:

"It's Greek."

"It can be beautiful."

"How far does Inver go?"

"To the forest, ten townlands, but there's shooting rights for some hundreds, some I've never stood in."

Rachel said to Eric: "Let's cross."

The river was knee-deep. They crossed to the southern bank. The sun was high and hot. From this first bend the narrow tributary of the Finn changed character, snaking through boggy rush land, long weedy tendrils waving in the brackish water, broken sedge and froth, tins and plastic bags dammed by a rusting barbed-wire fence from bank to bank, the bric-a-brac of a river dump used by the Grues of Annahullion, Catholics. The dogs swam under the wire. The hunters got out of the river to bypass. The banks were now so steep they had to stay in the river bed or walk the high verge watching from a height. Rachel and Eric kept to the bank. A crane hidden in an area of sedge and bulrushes flapped slowly out, rising gradually, as though in slow motion towards a scrub of alder and stunted thorn. Midstream, John Willie waded alongside the Whipmaster. His eyes did not follow the crane. He was watching Blister who seemed to keep separate and now broke away swimming strongly across a deep dark pool, towards a big leaning forked ash tree cloaked with ivy. At the opening of the fork he gave a screeching yowl partly dispersed by water in his mouth. The otter hounds immediately gave tongue. The horn sounded, all dogs swimming towards the fork, scrabbling to get a grip on the bare tentacles of ash root. The Whipmaster hunkered, slipping sideways down the northern slope, thrusting himself towards the tree, a terrier yapping at his heels. When he reached the trunk he grabbed a root with one hand, the terrier by the scruff of the neck and thrust it into the opening with some rough word of encouragement that sounded like "g'winn, g'inn." The terrier went into the hole. All stood, the hounds frustrated at the opening were scrambling up again. The Packmaster followed by John Willie waded chest-deep to the opening and listened, examining the earth for tracks.

The Master shouted: "One here or was!"

All waited, watching. Nothing. The Whipmaster got up on the tree trunk, held a branch of ash and jumped up and down on the sloping earth as best he could. Still nothing. Blister had left the pack and gone down the river hunting alone. The American's voice came from the far bank.

"Scent is an astonishing sense."

The terrier appeared at the opening, shaking a glossy river rat. Rachel giggled with relief. The rat went floating slowly down stream, twitching. Most faces registered disappointment.

"Not quite a trophy," said the American.

"There was an otter here," the Packmaster called up.

"Could be a quarter of a mile away by now," the Colonel said.

"I hope it's at Lough Erne," Rachel whispered and asked: "Why do they hunt them?"

"They eat trout."

"So do we. Have you seen one ever?"

"Twice."

"Killed?"

"No."

"What are they like?"

"Big water squirrels, brown fluffy fellows, whiskery, with big tails."

"They sound nice."

"They are."

"Timid?"

"They'll fight if they have to, a whole pack, so they say."

Unseen by Pack- or Whipmasters Blister had worked his way out of sight round another bend. John Willie knew this but did not draw attention to it. The hunt proceeded slowly. There were a lot of holts in this deep section, men and hounds working back and across from one holt to another.

Down river Blister gave tongue. There was a look between Pack- and Whipmaster. The hounds replied, scrambling out of the river, bypassing a hundred yards' stretch towards Blister's call. All running now, men, women, huntsmen towards the bend. When they got there it was an arched bridge, a car parked on it. A small round man standing on the parapet waving his cap and shouting something. All running now towards the bridge. The man on the bridge was pointing down towards the pond of a disused scutch mill. House party and hunters crossed the bridge and got down into the shallow water underneath. The man was saying:

"A big otter dog, by Christ he must weigh thirty pounds or more, thon big hound dog of John Willie's near caught him."

At the bridge the water was two feet deep, deepening gradually as the pond widened. It was deeply ringed with bulrushes, sedge and reeds. Anything moving would be spotted. The mill-race was dammed by three old railway sleepers, the end of the pond a limestone wall. The mill itself had been shattered last year by the I.R.A., U.D.A. or British Army; no one quite knew or at the moment cared. Under the bridge ten men had now formed an underwater barricade of legs by standing close together, moving slowly down the pond prodding ahead with their ashpoles and iron-shod staves. About half the otter hounds were in the pond swimming, the other half hunting the fifty-yard stretch of bank and sedge on either side. With a sudden heart stop Eric saw a small brown head emerge in the sedge on the left bank. He was about to shout. Instead he nudged Rachel and pointed with a jerk of his head. Her mouth opened in wonder and pity; she whispered:

"Don't, Eric! Don't! Let it live, let it live."

As they watched the brown head submerged again. No one else had noticed.

From the cottage above the mill a small hunched figure came down towards the pond, through a half acre of flowering potatoes. Rachel asked:

"Who's he?"

"Dinny McMahon."

"He has a gun."

"I can see that."

"What's he doing?"

"Dunno."

They watched the figure pushing through the thorn ditch, stumping across a waste of egg-bushes, boortrees and brambles to the clearing at the edge of the pond where the dogs worked and the men and women watched. No one looked round until he aimed his gun at the water and splayed a blast of pellets through the swimming dogs. There were shouts from the men, screams from the women, yelps from a dog. All turned to look at the small man. He split his smoking shotgun, dropped the empty cartridge, put his hand in his pocket and inserted another cartridge. In the silence everyone could hear the click of the hammer going back. The Colonel walked out of the river to face the gunman. Only Eric and Rachel could see the two figures outside the cottage.

"Yes!?" His military voice, a rifle report.

"No," the little man said, his voice a hard Fermanagh rasp.

"What do you mean? No."

"That's what I mane, NO . . . Sorr. Colonel . . . I mane go back to the bridge and round the other side."

"Who are you?"

"Here a thousand years, and the same again, McMahon, Daniel and this mill-pad is mine, it's my land you stand on, and I say 'No' to you, and all like you, and to any of my own race down there in that shuegh with you, none while I breathe is goin' to go down this pad, no means no, and that's that."

"I see."

"I'm glad you're not blind, Sorr, I can see rightly too and I want to see you walk back that pad while I stand here."

An otter hound was whimpering on the bank licking at his flank which seemed bloody and shattered.

"Did you have to fire on the dog?"

"Ah Jasus, is it the poor cratur of a dog, slaverin' to rip a wee otter dog half its size?! Shite talk, Sorr, keep it for your guests at mess in the Hall."

The hounds had stopped hunting aware of human tension. The chain in the river had slackened. The four women present looked frightened. The Colonel unruffled, his voice iron hard asked:

"Is this the townland of Shanroe?"

"You're on it, Sorr, my part of it, all three acres."

"I have hunting and shooting rights for this townland and all the townlands from Inver to Corrawhinny."

"Is that a fact?"

"It is."

"Well I have shooting rights here in my two hands, that's how you got yours, and if you want now I'll show you how it works."

He raised his gun and aimed it directly at the Colonel's head. John Willie came up from behind the Colonel both arms outstretched, stepping between the Colonel and the gun.

"Ah now, Dinny, for Christ's sake!"

"Go back, John."

"Dinny, please listen . . ."

"You listen . . . John, go back, I'm tellin' you."

Eric felt a contraction in his stomach. The little man said:

"I've nothing against you or yours, John, I only want you and this man to get back to the bridge, and go down the far bank. From there on you can hunt to Enniskillen, you can kill all the otters in Ulster for all I care. What I say is plain and I mane it, and you better tell your friend, the Colonel, that."

John Willie turned and had a quick-whispered word with the Colonel. The Colonel said to McMahon:

"Do you understand what you are doing now?"

"Do I look a fool?"

The Colonel said nothing to this.

"If I were you, Sorr, I wouldn't think about police let alone mention them. It'd take one of her Majesty's buggerin' Regiments to shift me, you can go in God's good time, or now; if you don't I'll blow the head clane off your shoulders."

Again John Willie said something to the Colonel. For ten seconds that seemed like a minute the Colonel stared coldly back at the two-barrelled gun, and the ugly hunched little man with one eye closed. When he turned to go back the chain in the river broke, going different ways to the southern bank. The Colonel walked slowly towards the bridge, his face impassive as a boot.

The Colonel's daughter looked very white and shaken. She took his hand. He let her hold it for a moment. As he moved towards the American he passed Sam Heuston who had left the river and was walking towards McMahon.

"I wouldn't," the Colonel warned.

"I will," Heuston said and then shouted suddenly at McMahon: "There's one not afeered; I'll walk this river bank and you'll shoot me dead before I quit: bluff!"

For a moment McMahon stared then spat: "Scaldcrows, weasels aye, and river rats, I'll honour *them* with this." He tapped the barrel of his gun: "Not *you* . . . let the Colonel try again or the dogs and you'll see how I bluff."

At the bridge the American said to the Colonel: "Interesting."

The Colonel asked John Willie: "Do you know him, John?"

"Dinny McMahon, I do Sir, he's half-odd."

"A lunatic," the Colonel said. "We've hunted this stretch before."

"Before 'sixty-nine," Courtney said.

Tony Courtney was a Catholic who trained gun dogs for the Colonel. There was a long pause and then the Colonel said:

"Yes."

All faces fixed in suppressed anger or embarrassment watched the small hunched figure, ignoring Heuston's taunts, walk back through the potato patch towards the cottage. The Colonel asked:

"Whose dog is grained?"

The Whipmaster said: "One of the pack."

"Better take it to the vet . . . whose car is this?"

The man who waved on the bridge said: "I'll take the dog, Sir."

The dog's leg was badly shattered. The Whipmaster lifted the dog into the back seat of the car and got in beside it. The car drove off. The rest of the pack were walking about the bridge, some still shivering with excitement, others looking intently up at the human faces. From a mass of bulrushes near the mill-race there was a brown splashy leap, a quick scrabble and the otter was over the rotting sleepers and swimming down the mill-race towards the steel structure of the wheel. In a few seconds it would be in open river again and away. If anyone noticed apart from Eric they made no mention. The Colonel said:

"No point in standing about."

The Packmaster said: "Can't we walk down the left bank and hunt on?"

The Colonel said bluntly: "No. We'll go back, trailer the dogs and hunt Mullivam."

There were general murmurs:

"You're right, Colonel."

"Wouldn't plaze him."

Sam Heuston back from his confrontation said: "If I had my way I'd bury him alive and hunt on."

"I don't want talk like that . . ." the Colonel said.

"I don't want talk either," Heuston said, "I'd do it."

"Trivial . . ." the Colonel said . . . "we'll forget all this and go."

"I'll not forget it . . ." Heuston said.

Courtney and the other Catholic farmers looked very tense.

"I'm sorry," the Colonel said to Courtney.

With a glance he included the other Catholic huntsmen. Heuston said: "I'm not sorry."

The Colonel said: "I'm not afraid to use a gun, Sam, or face one, but I reject that sort of thinking."

He jerked his head towards the McMahon cottage: "You're talking his language."

Heuston said: "And look where it's got them, look where it's left us, twenty men on a bridge afeered to cross because of a wee man with a gun, afeered to tell police, for fear we'd be blown up or burnt out . . . you think about that, Colonel, hard, 'cause you'll have to sooner than you think."

He snapped his fingers, and walked off, followed by a mongrel hound. Joe said quietly to Eric:

"He'd get on well with your Uncle George."

Eric said: "They drink together."

John Willie came over and Rachel said: "For a moment I thought he was going to shoot."

John Willie shook his head and smiled.

"He's waited years for that, and he'll put in the rest of his life telling about it."

Rachel said: "It didn't look that funny from here."

"You two coming to Mullivam?"

Before Eric could answer Rachel said: "No."

Joe said as he left with John: "See you tonight, Eric."

"Right."

From the bridge they watched the hunt spread back up the river till it went out of sight. Rachel took the ash rod Eric had broken off on his way down the river and threw it into the water. They watched it float down and stop against the dam. Rachel said:

"Let's go home by the fields."

From Shanroe bridge to Tattnagolan was about four miles as the crow flies. They climbed across a wooden bridge into Sam Foster's farm, unreclaimed bottom land, sprit, rushes and rough tussocks growing them a heavy morass, snipe twisting and wheeling away as they walked, white clouds drifting north towards the fields under Carn Rock. They stopped at Foster's well, a clean stone arched well, white-washed with a glitter of gravel in the bottom, so clear they could see spiders and tiny creatures walking on the surface. As they were about to drink they paused and turned to look. From half a mile they could hear the great wing beats. Two swans came down the river from Inver, flying low over the mill, heads craned for Lough Erne. They stared as though they had never seen swans fly before.

"So beautiful," Rachel said, then added, "but so ugly . . . the world."

"You're not."

"How I feel is . . . the hunt, and that little man, a thing like that, I get sick with hate, fear or both."

They drank from a tin porringer, chained by its handle to the wall of the well. For minutes they sat in silence looking. Then Rachel said:

"At home I listened . . . I thought they're wrong my parents, because we had Catholic neighbours. I didn't want to hate them, and I didn't, but in the delivery ward in April some time they were mostly Catholics. I heard them talk, so coarse and stupid, holy magazines and rosaries and this fuzzy-headed priest going about blessing their labours and their babies, and the horrid way they sucked up to him." She paused: "Even I didn't hear what I heard at home, I couldn't live with them or work with them because . . ." She paused again and shrugged . . . "Last night those animals . . . their husbands . . . sons, brothers, cousins; they do hate us, you can feel it."

For a moment Eric was silent and then: "I've seen them look at me in streets, marts, I don't want to hate or kill any of them, but a body must do something when the thing's gone the way it has."

"Get out."

"I can't."

"If you don't, you'll . . ."

"We can't run out, we're farmers. I love these fields."

"More than me?"

"We *made* this country, they *are* this country and know it, they won't rest till they bury us or make us part of themselves. Like you I don't want that, maybe that's why I joined, though I'm not sure now."

"We didn't ask to be born here, I don't want to stay here now."

"Nor me."

"Can I tell you something?"

"Anything."

"It's ugly."

"If it's about you it's not."

"It's ugly . . . I was on night duty a month ago, infant wards, all Catholics, in the middle of the night I thought . . ."

"Go on . . ."

"I thought if I set fire to it they'd all be burned, about thirty less of them."

There was quite a silence before Eric asked: "Dreamt or thought?"

"Thought Eric, thought. I was tired, I wouldn't do it in a million years, but I did think about it, how I'd start the fire, make it seem accidental, and when I knew what I was thinking, I got so frightened I almost got sick. That's why I'm leaving after midwifery. We're sick Eric, they're sick, and we don't know what to do, I want to believe in God, I can't, I want to be happy, I can't . . . Look around, look, Eric, it's beautiful . . . you are too . . . you are!"

She looked intently at the nail of her left thumb and said: "You've never touched me ever, why?"

He was so startled when he realised what she meant, that he said without thinking: "It's wrongful."

"Yourself, have you touched yourself, ever?"

He heard himself mutter: "Of course."

He knew, without looking at her face, that her heart was thumping.

"Me too, more wrongful that, when we love each other."

He glanced up; her face was tense: "No, don't look away, Eric. I'm shy too. Along the river I thought, I'll talk today, say what's in my head, ask him, tell him, and . . ."

"I know."

"You don't because . . ."

"Yes I do . . ."

She stopped suddenly. The questions had come cramped and awkward from her mouth that always had two answers where he could seldom stammer one. Her mind, quick and contrary seemed more frightening to him than her body, untouchable in the old Bedford smelling of pigs, or cinemas reeking of perfumed Jeyes Fluid. He had hardly ever kissed her without embarrassment and awkwardness, believing what his mother told him often.

"You say so little, Eric, I don't rightly know what you think."

"I don't rightly know myself."

"Then I'll ask again; you've never touched me, why?"

"It's for begetting. I believe that."

"And love?"

"In wedlock."

She shrugged and stood suddenly. "Let's walk."

He followed, angry with her, with himself. You could read up about politics, farming and veterinary, learn from experience and mistakes. What book could explain this girl to him or his mother. She was ahead of him, alongside a ditch of foxgloves and double-combed bracken, walking soft as a cat, her jeans clinging from ankle to knee. She turned and said:

"I shouldn't talk that way, it's too forward."

"Better than treacle talk, but I don't want to feel stupid: I want to understand."

"Only for you I'd hate men . . . all men, you make me feel special."

"You are."

"Far from it."

"To me, you are."

She was staring at him. Then she was crying. She took his hands and put them to her face. He could feel her kissing his hands.

"Why are you crying, Rachel?"

"I don't know."

The brindle heifer was not with the cows nor in the beech copse. He went to the Fortfield, three stripgrazed acres topped by a circle of ash, thorn and hazel. The heifer was on her side pressing in a mass of nettles and docks, the forelegs and nose of the calf protruding. He spoke to her gently strapping his belt round the slimy forelegs. With a foot on her hinchbone he pulled steady for five minutes. The head slipped, coming inch by inch, tongue out. He rested, his body wet from tension. Another five minutes and the shoulders were clear, then the whole calf, slurping out. He slapped it sharply on the ribs, cleared its throat with his forefinger and stood it on splayed shaky legs. Then the heifer was on her feet, spilling afterbirth. He sat on stone, and watched the calf nosing round till it found the warm udder, a teat to suckle. He wiped his hands with dockleaves. Birthsmell, rich warm and milky mixed with rank odour of nettles: and man hath nothing more than beasts All things go to one place: of earth they are made; to earth they return together. But they knew nothing of love or hate, tithes or time, the packer's knife, the knacker's lorry. And what did he fear? Death? What differ when the body chilled, now of a sudden or slowly in a cockloft fifty years from now? And what did he think she had asked. Not much of this life as he knew it, less of what comes after. Afraid more of living than dying. A coward's mind? Rightly or wrongly it was what he thought. And love? The warm secrets of her body which he feared to touch would cool to clods with bones and rusted mountings; her children, and her children's children walking the same pad.

He left the calf suckling and walked the cows from the river bottoms round the lower end of the house field, approaching the yard from the front of the house. His mother came out in wellingtons to open the gate. She would see his pants were wet from the river and ask. Should he lie or tell? The truth would hurt; the lie more deeply if she heard later.

"Were you in the sheugh, son?"

"I followed dogs with Joe and Rachel."

"A hunt?"

"Yes."

She helped him tie the cows.

"Was your father there?"

"Yes."

"Where is he now?"

"Up Mullivam way; we left after an hour."

She said nothing and went back to the house. Spooning an egg at table he caught her eye.

"You said you were going to check the heifer."

"I was, she's calved, a white-head bull."

"You knew about the hunt, that's the same as a lie."

"Is it?"

"He's always lying. I don't believe a word comes from his mouth and that hurts; you don't lie to someone you feel for."

"No but . . ."

"Do you, son?"

"No."

"I'd as lief you wouldn't hunt God's creatures of a Sunday or any day, but I wouldn't interfere, would I?"

"No," he lied and finished his egg in silence.

"Why don't you talk, son?"

"Thinking."

" 'Bout what?"

"What you said."

"Lies?"

"Aye, and Sunday . . . God's creatures."

He couldn't say what he thought. By ten-thirty he had to be in uniform, then drive with George to the U.D.R. Headquarters at Lisnaskea. They would be stopping and searching cars till four in the morning. He drank his tea and looked out at the slow twilight:

"You think I am a hypocrite?"

"What?"

"You heard."

"Yes I heard, Mother."

"Because I pray but won't see her, Sam's," she paused dropping her voice before she said, "wife."

Eric shrugged. She went on:

"It's wrongful I know, and I've prayed God to help me but . . . the children of my firstborn . . . Papists . . . and Maggie Reilly pleased to tell me there's another coming . . . God help him . . . I shouldn't say this but I think it . . . I'd sooner he was dead."

"You don't mean that, Mother?"

"There are things you don't know, son: the joke now is a good person . . . the world's gone bad . . . we should beget as God intended, work hard and pray . . . that's what I was taught: I believe it, I abide by it."

Eric found the contradiction painful. Very quietly he said: "And love our neighbour?"

"Those who murder! . . . Only Christ himself could do that . . . other ways I try to be honest . . . kept my marriage vows, reared you boys and run this house for a man who used me unnatural from the start . . . and false from the start."

It was time to go. Eric stood. When he had kissed his mother she said:

"I don't want to be the way I was this morning. Ever . . . because I love you, son, and your father, as much as he hates me."

"He doesn't hate you."

"Worse . . . he doesn't care."

It was near dark at Oakfield when George came out in uniform. He slumped in the front seat of the Bedford, thrusting a rifle between the seats. Eric put on parking lights and drove the twisting hump-backed lane towards the county road. In the soft, grey dusk there was a herd of cows on the road, Willie Reilly in front with a torch. He pretended not to recognise Eric's van. As the cows passed the man at the back moved towards the car. Cassidy. Eric wound down the window.

"Eric."

"Martin."

"How's George?"

"I know how I am and how *you* are!"

McMahon's stand at Shamroe bridge was already local legend. Eric could see Cassidy smiling in the faint light of the dash.

"I hear Willie's wee bitch disgraced him today?"

"Reilly's dog wasn't the only thing happened today," George said.

There was a moment of silence and then Cassidy said: "There's a bomb scare in 'Skea."

"How do you know that?" George asked.

"Radio."

"We'd better move son."

As they drove away George said: "A cog in the murder gang, one of your Yankee mafia, I mind him barefoot, his auld fella out for hire, tricked his way into Protestant land."

"You don't know that, George."

"Catholic and Civil Rights, isn't he? . . . Seen him two years ago on the platform in Derry with that wee whore Devlin. See the way he smiled. He's laughin' at us; every bomb that goes off, every man that's maimed or murdered, laughin' 'cause they think we're afeered. No balls, that's what they say to themselves. He knows who sent that note, knows where, when and how you'll be got, it's all linked: Rome, politics, America, gunmen. In Christ's name how did he get money to buy Protestant land and pay two prices for it, a back-hander to a crooked solicitor and some lundy to bid; and them cows! The whole shute must come to near £30,000!"

"Borrowed, he works hard, George."

"Murder money; they're diggin' graves for us night and day and we're standin' lookin' at them like the Jews in Europe; they've got their score to settle and they mean to settle once and for all; if we let them."

A scaldcrow feeding on the carcass of a run-over dog flapped away as they passed in the growing dark.

"We bate them before: we'll bate them again."

Two miles from Lisnaskea they could see flames and ragged smoke over the town.

"Cassidy's bomb," George said.

A British Army patrol stopped them. They showed their papers, a soldier said:

"One of your mates got it an hour ago."

"Where?"

The soldier called back to the radio jeep: "Where were the father and son got?"

A voice called back: "Tatnagone."

Eric's heart stopped. There were only three families in the townland of Tatnagone.

"Name?"

"Robinson."

Eric heard himself ask: "How?"

"Gunned in a car at the house; the son's dead."

Eric could feel his body shaking. He drove slowly into Lisnaskea past a burning supermarket, two fire brigades, black helmeted figures, the garish street, Saracens and shattered glass, debris, soldiers, a siren moaning, huddled groups in the doorways; people sweeping up glass, a draper's dummy headless in a shop window. George said:

"Someone must pay."

There were about a dozen cars at Robinsons', two black R.U.C. patrol cars, a U.D.R. jeep and overhead a helicopter with a powerful beam scanning fields and ditches. As he got out of the van George said loudly:

"Mick Cunningham's car! What's he here for?"

"He lives two fields away," Eric said.

"What's he here for?"

"It's no time for shouting, George."

Dixon the Commandant said: "George, we don't want guns in a dead house, leave it in the van."

George made a kind of whining noise: "For Christ's sake what are guns for?"

Dixon said: "You take no gun, you can stand out here with your gun if you want!"

George handed his gun to another U.D.R. man. Dixon answered Eric quietly:

"About an hour ago Cunningham heard the shot and got on the phone, we were here in ten minutes."

"Old Tom?"

"In the head, unconscious; poor chance. Joe died outright."

Eric had seen this kitchen often in a dream, the black police uniforms, British soldiers, Ruth Robinson on a chair by the stove delirious with grief, two other neighbour women trying to comfort her, a superintendent taking notes. In a corner Mick Cunningham, a tall balding Catholic with a heron's neck and the eyes of a rabbit. Eric had bought a suck calf off him two years ago, a big, harmless fellow with a shrill voice. From where he stood Eric could see into the parlour, Joe's boots level with a pot plant in the window, Bryson the undertaker measuring. As he moved towards the parlour door he saw George edge like a coiled spring towards Cunningham. Whatever he said it was as though he had struck him in the mouth. Cunningham jerked a nod and moved sideways towards the front door. Eric paused to let Bryson out.

The body was sheeted, Rachel sitting on a stiff parlour chair at Joe's head, no expression on her face. She turned as he came in. He put a hand on her shoulder. He could feel her trembling. Say something he thought, "What?" "Your trouble?" Pray! Kneel! He heard himself say:

"Where?"

"What?"

He nodded at the body.

"Nothing, doesn't matter."

"Where was he hit?"

She indicated the covered face and said: "You won't know him."

He knelt. No prayer came to mind. He knew only that he was alive and that Joe was dead, and was so ashamed of thinking this he said quietly:

"I'm sorry, Rachel."

Then George was standing opposite. He lifted the sheet and Eric saw Joe's face, a mass of congested blood, unrecognisable. From Joe's dead face he looked up at George and said:

"Cover him, for Christ's sake cover him."

He felt Rachel leaning against him. George stood and stared. Eric was trying to hold and lift Rachel and pull the cover.

"For pity's sake, George."

"For pity's sake, I want to see this proper, and I want to mind it."

Rachel had fainted. There was a door off the parlour, a bedroom probably. He got it opened and managed to get the switch. Striped pink and white paper, a deal floor, brass bed, a corner wash stand. He placed her on the bed.

Her face was so cold that he put his hand to her mouth; breathing all right. Her hands seemed grey. He took them in his own. When her eyes opened she stared at the electric bulb, frightened animal eyes that slowly swivelled and then there was such pain and anguish and ravaged incomprehension that it cut more deeply than Joe's awful face in the next room. If there was a living man could speak now, what words would he use? Christ in Heaven, what were they, who could speak? Say what? Joe, her father, the awful choking sound of the mother two rooms away, George staring stupidly, what words? And because her face was still and her eyes pouring over, it was worse because she made no sound. If she cried out he could say "Don't Rachel" or "Please" or some word of solace, but there was no word or words, and he knew it and she knew it, and he knew he was cold and factual: "Word has just come in now that Tom Robinson, father of Joe Robinson the part time U.D.R. man who was shot earlier this evening, has also died."

The voice went on about oil shortages and President Nixon. In the turf shed Eric saw the machine-gunned Vauxhall, Army ballistic experts examining it with a powerful torch. He could see blood splattered on the windscreen. More cars had arrived, military, police and private cars, neighbours standing about in groups, not wanting to go in, knowing they must. He saw a British Army officer walking towards the door with a priest. When the priest went into Robinsons, one of the women began to scream something; it sounded like "Fenian Bastards, Murderers!" he was glad George was in the van and not in the house. He started the engine and drove slowly through the lighted yard and the uniformed figures, towards the main road.

"Left, take the low road," George said.

For a moment Eric hesitated; it was two miles longer, but he was not going to argue. He turned left. For miles not a word was said. They were stopped twice at Army checkpoints and quickly cleared. At Latgallon quarries, George said:

"Pull in here."

"What?"

"I have to stoop."

Eric drew in behind a gravel dumper. Midway in the cratered quarry of crags, rock face, and jutting limestone rose the black scaffold of a grading machine, topped by a hut. Beyond it and below five acres of worked over quarry and rock pools, the fields sloped upwards towards Latgallon. George got out and went over behind the dumper. Eric checked that both rifles were still in the car. A dog barked somewhere, a military convoy passed. George was taking his time. When the windscreen got muggy, Eric got out and saw the figure of a man against the sky at the far end of the quarry. The figure was clear of the quarry, and moving in an upland field towards Latgallon. "Oh God no," Eric thought, and then called "George, George!" He cupped his hands and shouted louder "George!" The figure went out of sight. Eric began to run, tripping over the ragged surface. He fell, cutting both hands and a knee. He got up, aware of blood dripping from his left hand. He put his left hand in his pocket and kept running. There was a rough staircase of stone hacked out of the quarry face. He went up them two and three at a time. From the quarry top the fields switchbacked up towards Cassidy's. No sign of George, should he call again? Some neighbour, drunk, or courting couple might hear. He was running as in a dream. Two fields from where he was he could see high hedges. He crossed a gate into the lane. He could then see the lights in Cassidy's yard, the reconstructed cottage, the new barns, byres and silo pit.

As he approached the familiar hum of an Alfa-Laval milking pump, the smell of fermenting silage. No sign of George. He kept running till he came to a padlocked gate. He clambered across it. The lane forked two ways, one to the house in darkness, the other to the lighted yard. He could see cows tied in cudding in the herringbone parlour. At the yard entry between two outhouses, he saw what looked like two sacks of meal lying sideways on top of each other. As he neared, with a sudden sick shock, he saw Willie Reilly humped across a bag of dairy nuts, sprawled as though copulating in an obscene posture of death, mouth and eyes open, tongue out. In the yard, he saw George from the back, driving a graip into what looked like a dungheap; again and again and again, and again.

"George!"

Under the 200-watt bulb his uncle's face looked back in knotted fury, his mouth drooping. He flung the graip towards the middle of the yard. It spun bouncing and ringing off the concrete, blood on the prongs. Eric saw that it was a man's body facedown in the dungheap. George walked to meet him. Eric tried to say something, his voice made no sound.

"Your bastard brother's in the entry, and that's Cassidy . . . two for two and no shot fired, let them equal that and don't stand there like a gom, the job's done."

Then George was walking out of the yard and down the dark laneway towards the padlocked gate. The body on the dungheap twitched. Eric's heart was pumping so fast he found it difficult to breathe. He moved towards the body. Cassidy's profile all right, bloody lacerations on his neck and back. He turned away retching.

In the kitchen at Oakfield George filled two mugs with Bushmills whiskey. He drank his own, filled it again, and pointed at Eric's.

"Drink up, son."

"I don't drink."

"Time you started."

The yellow liquid in the cracked mug was the colour of the manure effluent on Cassidy's face. Eric put his hands on the table to stop them trembling. His left hand was badly cut and swollen. He was aware that

George had hung his coat behind the door and was examining it, groping in pockets. He then looked down at his boots, examined the soles, first one, then the other. Black, dry and shining, a little mud on the toe-caps. The limestone eyes stared straight. He came to the table to fill his mug again.

"What are you afeered of?"

He picked up the bottle of whiskey and held it. "No shake in that hand; my heart's steady as a rock, and my head; I'd do the same tomorrow or next week. They'll all make noises, but our side'll be glad some men had guts to act; blood for blood, this is a celebration son. They won't know it was me, but vengeance is done, the job's a good one."

Eric stared. He was insane. The country was full of savage talkers on both sides. He had always thought talk was only talk, and that the men of blood were cold, stupid and silent, hired by men too clever to take risks.

"Say what's in your head."

"They didn't do it, George."

"Cassidy knows who done it, not just by name, he knows them, he could hand you a list from here to Portadown of all their murdering heroes, age, rank, how many jobs they done, *he knows*: that's enough for me."

"Willie; you knew he'd be there?"

"Luck of the draw."

"Could have been anyone?"

"I'm not in the dock, son."

"You are!"

George smashed his mug on the black stove and began quietly, his back to Eric:

"I do solemnly swear support for King William the Third Prince of Orange and all heirs of the Crown so long as they support the Protestant religion and Ascendancy and I do further swear, I was not, I am not, nor ever will be a United Irishman nor took oath of secrecy to that Society and on no account will I admit a Roman Catholic and I am now become an Orangeman without fear of bribery or corruption and I will keep a brother's secrets as my own."

He had turned from the stove. Eric said without looking up: "Unless in cases of treason or murder."

"You goin' to whine, go to that Papish Inspector, fall on your knees, tell him it was your Uncle George! That what you're going to do?"

"I'll not do that, George."

"Then for Christ's sake stop niggling, the job's done; we done it well."

Eric heard the incredulous pitch of his own voice: "Ah Christ, George, quit!"

"What?"

"We! We! I'm not stupid; you tricked me."

"I what?"

"Tricked, tricked."

"Say your say, go on, say it."

"Dirty . . . yes, dirty, you're bad as the worst of them, you done a rotten thing, and you clean your hands on me."

"Did I ask you to folly me, one single word, to witness what was done? You follied, you saw, you're not fit to stomach what you saw let alone do it, so now you whine 'tricked' . . . you don't know you own mind . . . I do."

He was at the bottle again. Eric noticed a slight tremor in the pouring hand.

"They're lucky."

"Who?"

"Joe, Tom, Cassidy and Willie, the dead ones. I'm going."

Eric began moving towards the door.

"Wait son, stay awhile."

"For what?"

"Stay, please."

That long white face pleading. He had never heard that mouth say "please." Nausea gave way to a moment of pity:

"For what, George?"

"Don't cry, Eric, Jesus son, don't cry."

George put a hand on his shoulder and made him sit on a chair.

"Look at me, son, you know me, don't shake your head like that, speak boy, open your mouth, you sat on my knee in this kitchen and . . . ."

"George, that's nothing got to do with what we know."

"We marched together, made hay, cut turf together we . . . I'm George, your mother's brother, your uncle, your friend, you know me, Eric."

"I thought I did."

"My life, have you thought on that, no woman, no brother, no close friend ever, wrought on my lone all my days, for what? I have nothin' but this house and forge, a few acres and a stretch of bog but *that* is somethin', land that is somethin' and I've somethin' to tell you."

"I know too much, George, I don't want to hear any more."

"Listen son, old Tom's dead, Joe's dead, Rachel and Ruth, think of them, their men gone."

"I don't want to hear, George."

"There had to be a reckoning."

George held the glass of whiskey towards Eric and said: "Drink, son, you're like a ghost."

"I don't want to drink or talk of Robinsons, or Cassidys or Catholics or Protestants, or what's goin' to happen or what's not goin' to happen."

There was a long silence and then George said: "I'll tell you what's in my head, been meanin' to tell you this long while, no odds about me, I'm for the suit of boards and the clay. I've no money much, but there is this place, and the bog at Kilcrin; it's all yours."

Eric looked out the window at the dark fields.

"Land's gone mad everywhere, even round here they'll pay three prices for it . . . all yours, from this night on."

Land, earth, spades, gravediggers, varnished boxes, women stumbling with grief, men crying. The day after tomorrow four burials between the two churches that faced each other across the river. Machines still on the cows at Cassidy's, kicked off by now. Tomorrow some neighbour or the postman would find them in the yard.

"All yours, eight generations of Hawthornes, yours, I mane it."

Eric did not look at the white blurred face as he said: "I don't want it."

"Take care what you say, son."

"I said it with care, George, I don't want it. Put it on the collection plate, I don't want it."

"You don't talk to me like that."

"How should I talk, what's in our heads now? When we wake; when we meet tomorrow; next day; next week? We won't want to meet. I won't want to work this land, any land about here, ever."

"You're a coward, boy."

"Yes."

"You are . . ."

"Yes, all my life, afraid of you, George, afraid to pick between my mother and father, afraid of God, afraid of Catholics, afraid of dark and dreams, afraid to hate or love . . . I'm tired of being afraid . . . but if you're brave George, then I'm a coward like my father and I'll stay one."

George stood suddenly. "Your father's son. O'Neill treacherous bloody Irish at the back of it, begrudgers, traitors, turn your back when I need you most."

George was whining now, mumbling drunk. Eric said:

"I dunno why I'm in this uniform, who I'm fighting, or what the fight's about, and when it blows by I'll be elsewhere, anywhere, I'll do anything, but I'll not go through another night like this, I'd as lief be dead."

George suddenly shouted: "You're nothin' to me . . . nothin', on you go, empty dustbins in Hammersmith, join your brother Sam and his whorey Papish wife, that's your future if you lave here."

Eric felt anger rising: "And yours, George?"

He left him standing in the kitchen and went out to the van. Then he was aware of George stumbling across the yard towards the driver's window. Eric wound it down.

"Hand back your gun, son, and get to hell out of this country, you're nothin' to me now, do you hear me, nothin'.'"

"We're both dead, George, when you're sober you'll see that."

As he drove down the lane, he could see George in the rear mirror standing swaying against the squat black outline of the forge.

His mother had been crying, his father's face like ash. Both seemed very shaken. His mother said:

"Could have been you, son, and your father, whoever done it, I hope . . ." Her voice choked off in a sort of noise. "God help Ruth and Rachel; what are we goin' to do John?"

"Go to Robinsons'," his father said.

His mother said: "Tell me, son."

"Nothin' to tell, Joe's dead and old Tom, it's an awful house, they don't know what they're doing, you'd best go and help whatever way you can."

"Your hands are cut, son, and your knee."

"I fell."

"You've been crying, the boy's terrified, John."

"Not now."

His father said: "We'd best go."

"God help us all."

"George?"

"Home."

"You saw him home?"

"That's where I left him."

Eric knew they were looking at him closely. His mother said: "The boy's shocked."

As he looked in his mother's eyes Eric thought: what if I said, I saw your brother up at Cassidy's, he's murdered Martin Cassidy and Willie Reilly, and if you go out to the haggard and look down you'll see the lights are still on about Latgallon, and they'll be on all night. I never want to see your brother George again, or hear stupid quarrels in this house, or hear the news on telly, or see daylight, and if you go up to oakfield now you'll find George three quarters drunk and half mad, and maybe he'll tell you the story himself. His mother came very close to him.

"Are you all right, son?"

"I'm all right mother, I'll wash my hand and put a cloth on it."

His father said: "We'll go."

His mother went up to put on her coat. His father stood and stared at the floor.

"The best people you could meet in a year's travel Joe and Tom Robinson, I've thought some bitter thoughts this last hour. A time like this you start to think, maybe George and your mother are . . ."

He paused, as Eric said sharply: "They're not right!"

"I wasn't goin' to say that, son, but it's a low thing a killing like that, unmanly, father and son trapped in a car, like rats burned in a cage. I've thought and thought of every Catholic man I know, I can't see one, not one, would do such a thing, then bit by bit I start to doubt, maybe Dinny McMahon, maybe if he had drink taken, then you begin to doubt them all, hate them all, that's what's happening, men who don't want to hate are pushed to it, that's what I was goin' to say."

When they were gone Eric washed his hand at the kitchen sink, went to his bedroom, took off his uniform, and lay on the bed in his underclothes. An army helicopter moved up from Robinsons', its searchlight scanning the fields between Robinsons' and Cassidy's, probing ditches, hollows, scrub and gap. Could be they'd find Cassidy and Willie before morning. He switched on the transistor waiting for the next bulletin. When it came in ten minutes there was no mention. His mother and father would be back in an hour or less. He couldn't face any more talk about Robinsons'. He tried to lie still and close his eyes. They were pulsing under the lids. His body was trembling. With an effort of will he could stop it, but moments later it would start again. From where he lay he could see the winch gibbet on the gable wall of the byre where he had talked today with Maggie . . . a hundred years ago. When he closed his eyes he could see Willie Reilly across the bag, his tongue out, George like a clip from an old film, ramming away with a steel fork, the crowded kitchen, Rachel's eyes pouring over. All this was more frightening when he closed his eyes. He kept them open and looked out the window again. Then the board ceiling lit up and he heard the engine of the old Bedford, the squeal of the back springs as it crossed the gulley. Silence. Two doors closing, his mother and father talking in the kitchen, then his mother.

"Eric."

He replied, his voice strange. They were at his door. As the door opened he said: "Don't put on the light."

His father came into the room, his mother stood at the doorway. Even from the low light in the hallway he could see how drawn she was. His father said:

"You go on, Sarah."

To Eric she said: "Good night, son."

His father moved to the window: "The world's a midden, a bloody midden . . . birds are lucky and trees."

"You were a brave while."

"We came back by George's."

He knows, Eric thought, and asked quietly: "How was he?"

"On the floor in his own vomit. I put him to bed, your mother cleaned up."

"Did he say much?"

"Raved, something about 'Christ in the fields.' "

"What?"

"Christ in the fields . . . raving."

His father moved from the window, sat on the side of Eric's bed and lit a cigarette. "Sam's well away from it all."

"Yes."

"Dead, you're good for nothin' but the ground; I think you should go, son."

"I will."

"When?"

"Tomorrow."

"Where?"

"Across the water, anywhere."

"You might have to stay a brave while."

"No odds, I saw and heard enough today, to keep me away a brave while."

"You're right, try and sleep."

"And you, Da!"

Two hours till daylight. He closed his eyes and turned from the window. A helicopter like a gigantic hawk whirled silently over the beech copse, a searchlight moving from tree to tree. Birds in outline perched in stuffed stillness on black branches. The pelts of badger, fox and otter, battened to trunks. Soldiers and masked men moved in shadows outside the copse. The searchlight moved to the centre of the clearing. From a gibbet over a huge stone hung a cage full of men and women, fear and hatred in their faces. Beside the stone the Rev. John Plumm read soundlessly, solemnly from the Bible. Below him Maggie Reilly, sow-like, confessed to the anus of a curate listening to her leering between his legs, his father behind Maggie on all fours about to mount. The helicopter ascended slowly, the beam of the searchlight widening. Then Cassidy came into the clearing with a Civil Rights banner carrying a statue of Christ with a bleeding heart, Willie Reilly walking behind him in his blue knitted cap. George, crouching behind the stone altar with a long narrow root scobed out as a collection box flailed at Cassidy, smashing his skull, driving the other end of the shaft through Willie's heart. A young British soldier walked into the clearing with a girl. The girl had rosary beads around her neck. They lay down. The soldier began kissing between her legs. She took a Webley from her handbag and shot him three times in the head. Paratroopers directed by a tall British officer ran from skeletal bushes into the clearing. One of them opened the cage hanging from the gibbet. As the men and women came out they were machine-gunned, bodies falling screaming, coughing, spluttering blood. Rachel in nurse's uniform watched, a hand on her groin, her face blank and crying. Sam and Maisie followed by small children approached his mother. His mother's face was white with hatred. She ripped open Maisie's stomach with a bread knife, pulled out a bloody child and smashed its head against the lectern, screaming "Papist murderers . . . bastards." Then a great noise of birds, animals and humans, a noise like a gathering storm, and Eric shouting.

And he was sitting up unable to shout, a retching in his throat, the sky livid behind the black winch gibbet on the byre gable. For a minute he sat, his heart jumping in his chest like a caged animal. The house still. Had he shouted or dreamt he shouted? He looked at his pocket-watch, 6:28, two minutes till the news. He closed his mind against what he knew. A summer dawn like any other, sitting on the side of the bed trying not to think of Tatnagone, Oakfield and Latgallon, looking out beyond the byre to the haggard field, cows cudding ignorant under hedges, swallows skimming low over the humps and hollows of the house field, rain today with that red sky, hay-rot for small upland farmers, growth for lowland silage makers. It must break soon. Police, questioning, back-tracking, threads of uniform on barbed wire and thorn bush, fingerprints on graip and gates, tractor loads of evidence . . .

"George," he said to himself quietly. "Oh Jesus, George . . ."

Lying in a stupor in the cockloft or maybe having his first whiskey to greet the coming day. The voice came low on the transistor: "Miners, Robinsons, a soldier shot dead in Belfast, two bombs in Lurgan, Nixon, nothing." He dressed quickly and went out to the hallway in his bare feet, avoiding boards that creaked, his father deep asleep, a grey faced, open-mouthed corpse. His mother's door closed. Would she wake and call? Silence but for the wall clock in the lower hall beside his grandparents. He stood in the glass porch listening, the tiles cold under his feet, looking at the sloping yard, the out-buildings stepping down. Always this way. It would stay this way for a hundred years or more when he was gone and all forgotten. He felt pity for the two people asleep upstairs in their separate rooms, Rachel sitting at Joe's side with her mother, and along with pity, shame. No fear; there was nothing left to fear.

The van was facing the entry. He let off the hand-brake. It rolled across the dry yard, bounced over the gulley with a squeal and down by the orchard. Well past the beech copse he let it slip into gear. The engine jolted to life. There would be military checkpoints every few miles, soldiers watchful and jumpy. This was it, a dull red glow in the east, the small odd-shaped fields, bushes, rushes, his heart pumping steadily. Desertion? The coward's way? Maybe, who'd know: George?

Christ! He came on them so suddenly he almost braked, two Saracens across the road, about a dozen soldiers, one of them waving him down from a hundred yards or more. His right foot hovered over the brake, the soldiers grouped round the big rubber wheels, all moving now. He could see their faces, the waving soldier moving backwards.

Now! He put his foot on the accelerator, saw them move apart, some go behind the Saracen, others falling on their stomachs. A flash came from the left ditch, glass shattering; pain, and the old Bedford skidding sideways before it lurched tumbling across the ditch, his lungs bursting, dying, yes, dying, blood in mouth and eyes, done, yes, over, and then as the Fermanagh uplands dimmed he heard Yorkshire voices far away, one saying:

"Christ knows, he's Irish, mate; they're all fucking mad over here; shoot first, ask after."

Victims

LEONARD WAS LEANING on the rail of the jumping enclosure watching the entrance. Music had been coming from the speakers since he arrived – "Land of Hope and Glory" – now competing with the staccato of cantering, jumping horses, the bawling of show cattle, megaphoned instructions from stewards, the squealing of pigs, sudden bursts of applause, the continuous hubbub of talk within and without the licensed marquee.

On a pole above the marquee a Union Jack flapped in the south wind. From it triangular bunting in red, white and blue stretched round the enclosure taking in the judges' platform and a small committee tent. Across the entrance from the road an embroidered cloth read:

WELCOME TO INVER SHOW

GOD SAVE OUR QUEEN

Dark-suited countrymen in hats, caps and boots, their wives in capacious summer wear and strong shoes examined pens of sheep, pigs and fowl, inspected and criticised glossy, prize-winning show cattle, walked through covered stalls of garden and domestic produce, argued cheerfully with salesmen about the merits and defects of gleaming new tractor models and agricultural machinery, or sat about in family groups eating sandwiches, whip-ices or drinking beer in the August sun.

Here and there, jodhpurs, tweed and blatant voice, or casual urban wear allied with a Yorkshire accent marked the presence of gentry, their guests and British soldiers on unobtrusive day-leave from barracks at Lisnaskea or Roslea.

Nothing much had happened. A horse had broken its leg. Leonard had heard the vet say quietly to the owner:

"It'll have to be destroyed."

As the last horse cleared the jumps he kept watching the entrance with his good eye. Beyond the show-ground the sloping meadows of after-grass gave way to the grey-brown brooding of Fermanagh uplands. In the long view detail seemed blurred. In the enclosure a fresh crop of dandelions crocheted in the green sward pulsed with a violence that forced him to look away. He covered his eye with a scarred hand, took out a scrap of paper, read the coded message without expression, put a match to it and dropped the blackened ash.

When he looked up she was in the entrance, waiting, a smallish madonna, composed, with cool all-seeing eyes, her face set in a medieval mould. He waited till she moved, then left the railing and went towards her. Unsmiling, Lynam watched him approach. He had grown a beard which hid the aggressive jut of his lower lip. They did not shake hands as she said:

"It's you."

"Yes."

"That much I was told."

A city girl dressed for summer streets, leather shoulder bag and sandals. From a battery-powered megaphone a steward announced twice: "All winning competitors in the beef section to the judges' stand."

Leonard guided her through the crowd past farmers urging a nervous Friesian bull up the ramp of a trailer, down a grass alley-way of farm produce and display stands towards an open space at the rail of the jumping enclosure directly opposite the judges' platform. He reached in the pocket of his denim jacket for cigarettes. When they were both lit his silence forced her to speak.

"For a friend you are not saying much."

"Nor you."

"I know nothing except . . ."

She paused for the megaphoned voice to announce: "Armstrong Memorial Award for the best beef bull: Samuel Foster of Mullinahone."

When the ragged applause faded she said: "A car called at four, an Army Council note, I was to go where I was taken, didn't say where . . . under your command . . . Burke's hand . . . and the driver said nothing between here and Dublin. That's all I know."

After another announcement she said: "I was very frightened . . . still am."

"Of what?"

"A final journey."

"Nothing like that."

"You've been briefed, warned, something."

"I don't believe all I hear."

"You take orders."

"Don't you?"

She paused before asking: "What orders?"

Another announcement greeted with back-slapping and laughter, a popular winner.

"Big house," Leonard said. "We hold some gentlefolk till they bring us Quinn, McIntyre, and Fanin from Long Kesh."

"What big house?"

"Inver Hall, two miles from here . . . that's him," Leonard said, with a jerk of his head towards the judges' platform. "I don't want to point, the tall one, jodhpurs and cloth cap."

"Who's he?"

"No one . . . the young one's his son-in-law. Secretary, Foreign Office."

As Lynam shrugged Leonard added: "Also he's an English lord."

Lynam stared across the enclosure: "When?"

"Tonight."

There were three more announcements before she spoke: "They won't release them."

"They'll think about it."

"And if not?"

"We keep our word."

"How?"

"Does it matter?"

"Will that involve me?"

"You'll be there."

The spikey growth of bladed grass at her feet seemed terrifying in the golden light. She could feel sweat going down her back.

"And if they bring them?"

"We leave."

"With the gentry?"

"Till we're clear."

"Where to?"

"That's fixed."

"And if they refuse?"

"I've said it."

For a moment she hesitated before saying: "Kill them?"

"Execute."

"Then what?"

"We fight."

"It's suicidal."

"Simple and works elsewhere."

She paused to ensure that her voice would not betray what she felt.

"I didn't volunteer for active service, why me?"

Leonard shrugged.

"Policy?"

"He, they . . . someone wants rid of me . . . you . . . have you thought of that?"

"Like?"

"Burke."

Leonard thought about this then shook his head.

Lynam asked: "And if I refuse now?"

Leonard dropped his cigarette on the grass and covered it with his foot, and asked with more concern than threat: "Can you?"

When Lynam did not reply Leonard asked: "Drink?"

"No."

"Sandwich?"

She shook her head.

"Tea?"

"No . . . thanks."

"Ice?"

To stop the persistent questions, sort out the awfulness of what he had just told her and steady the unnatural racing of her heart she nodded assent.

She followed him as he made his way towards the whipped ice machine. A woman in charge was adjusting something at the back.

"Two please," Leonard said.

"In a minute," the woman said.

Leonard nodded and moved away a few yards. As they waited Lynam looked at him properly for the first time.

"What happened to your eye?"

"Accident."

"On a job?"

"Yes."

"Can you see with it?"

"No."

"I'm sorry."

He nodded and said: "And me . . . for your trouble."

Her face gave nothing away. "Not much you don't hear."

When he made a gesture she said: "Abortion is the word."

Her mind, he thought again, a clenched fist against pity, maidenhood, motherhood or anything denoting feminine softness. She had climbed fast and high, in a movement dominated by power-hungry men, unafraid of violence and now unsure of her motives. Some felt she secretly despised them and the cause. Drunk once in a Rathmines flat Burke had told him:

"She knows too many dodgy Press boys and politicians . . . calculating as a cat . . . makes love with her eyes open . . . Christ knows what she thinks or believes . . . not in me . . . not in God . . . I've even wondered if she's Special Branch, but I think not."

At the time Leonard was amused at Burke aligning himself with God, but felt the assessment of Lynam was fairly accurate. He was tempted now to say something unkind. He said:

"It's a bleak word."

She looked at him steadily for a moment. Like other Northerners she'd met, close; spare with words.

"Almost," Burke had said, "as clever as me."

The reply in her mind did not reach her mouth. She looked over at the woman filling cones and said:

"Your whips are ready."

A blond man, almost albino, with a tall limber Negro, both in vivid shirts and jeans, approached the ice-cream stand unaware of Leonard. The Negro spoke:

"Can you give us two love?"

The woman said, nodding towards Lynam and Leonard, "These were here first."

The Negro turned: "Sorry mate."

"That's OK," Leonard said.

As they walked away Lynam asked the question with her eyes. Leonard nodded.

"What does he think of it over here?"

"Who?"

"The Negro."

"He doesn't, he reads the gutter press."

A tinker woman carrying an infant wrapped in a rug blocked their path. She had reddish hair, bad teeth, glazed eyes, and looked years beyond child-bearing.

"God bless you Sir, Miss, can you spare a copper for a poor baba?"

The child, Lynam thought, looked pallid and sick. As Leonard groped for a coin she asked: "What age is your baby?"

"Near three month Miss."

The Colonel approached from the right, and said to her: "You're welcome my dear but I've already told you twice . . . you must not beg from people."

"Yes, your Honour."

As she moved away the Colonel said to Leonard: "Not charity to give when she spends it all in there."

He nodded towards the licensed marquee. The Colonel looked directly into Leonard's face then into Lynam's eyes. As he moved off he said: "Lovely day."

"It is," Leonard said.

As they watched him walk away Lynam asked: "Do you want to kill him?"

"You know the answer, why ask?"

They walked in silence to the enclosure where Lynam asked: "Deadline?"

"Tomorrow midday."

"If they refuse . . . what?"

She stopped, unable to frame the question. Leonard answered: "One on the hour . . . then one every six hours."

Lynam looked at the whipped ice. A squirt of liquid raspberry on top had run down the cone onto her fingers. She had not tasted it and looked at it now with revulsion.

"How many?"

"Six or eight most nights to dinner."

"I don't want this."

Leonard took her whipped ice . . . Everywhere farmers were loading livestock onto trailers and lorries. The Show was over but the presentation of rosettes continued at the judges' platform, punctuated by announcements and scattered clapping. From the speaker the melody of "The Eton Boating Song" was drowned by the sudden slash of horse-piss on grass as a brown gelding straddled comfortably about ten yards from where they stood. Lynam asked:

"Must we endure this?"

"We can go any time."

Making their way towards the entrance they passed stalls of garden and domestic produce flanking the marquee. A tall woman with a well-structured face and beautiful limbs surrounded by farmers' wives was saying with careful articulation:

"My mother used to add lemon verbena to crabapple jelly; gives it a wonderfully subtle flavour."

Leonard said quietly, "His wife."

"Whose?"

"Colonel's."

"She'll be there tonight."

Leonard nodded and Lynam said: "She reminds me of someone."

They walked out of the show-ground, got into a black beetle Volkswagen and drove south towards the border.

The Colonel had shaken many hands, dispensed rosettes, certificates, trophies, Perpetual Cups and Medals of Merit. As he moved towards Alex Boyd-Crawford, George Hawthorne, blacksmith and small farmer, approached:

"George?"

"A word Sir."

George was serious. He had been questioned, the Colonel knew, by the R.U.C. in connection with a double murder three miles from Inver. His nephew Eric O'Neill, a boy of twenty-three and part-time soldier in the U.D.R., had been accidentally shot at an Army checkpoint; suicide it was rumoured.

Glazed by grief and whiskey the eyes that stared from that anvil-grey face looked someway blind. The Colonel was prepared to listen briefly:

"Something over here I want you to see," George was saying and began to walk.

"Yes?"

He was pointing a callused finger at the dry closet left of the entrance with "Gentlemen" printed over the door.

The Colonel stopped:

"Can't you tell me George . . . some obscenity?"

"I'll say it straight Sir . . . one of our 'patrons' shit on the floor and writ above it, 'That's what we think of the Brits and their Army . . . up the I.R.A.' "

The Colonel's expression did not change.

"Words."

"Animals . . . turn your stomach."

"Words, George."

The Colonel looked away to a helicopter hovering over the field and forest uplands of Roslea:

"People are being murdered every day."

"*You* tell me that Sir . . . then I'll tell you . . ."

Harriet's nervous laugh came across the enclosure. She had been to the licensed tent before midday. Dinner would be awkward again this evening. He missed what George was saying, then heard:

"O'Donnell from the Show committee . . . he's one of them . . . and they're all like that . . ." he clenched his fist, "agin us."

The Colonel looked into George's eyes. The fist gesture was both ridiculous and menacing. Aiden O'Donnell, a solitary Catholic on the Inver Show committee, was an English-schooled, weekend farmer, and a full-time barrister, his Jesuit brother on the teaching staff of Stonyhurst, another brother director with a Belfast merchant bank. O'Donnell had once said, "I must argue for justice in a system I think unjust. Most of the time I feel hypocritical." A disloyal statement? From a Northern Irish Catholic warmed by liberal wine, a predictable one. The Colonel understood both George's demand and O'Donnell's dilemma.

"George, you must understand . . ."

"O'Donnell goes or I quit . . . and you'll find another to shoe your horses."

The Colonel shook his head. As he tried to find a moderate reply, George turned and walked away. The Colonel watched him go. In comparison with such complexities war was a simple discipline, no weak links in the chain of command, deserters shot, the enemy destroyed, no confusing allegiances, no references to root causes, no twingings of conscience. In an unsubtle way

George was right. O'Donnell had refused the bench. He would never truck with violence, but his ambivalence was as insidious as George's cast-iron bigotry, a subject in the old days for patrician table talk. "Keep them hostile," a powerful, landed neighbour had said with a bark-like chuckle, "but not too hostile." Now that this hostility had turned to rank hatred and daily murder, bigotry was no longer amusing. There seemed no solution. He moved towards the judges' stand. Alex was sitting on a low step of the platform, reading *The Belfast News Letter*, a cigar in his mouth; an ageing wrinkled primate in baggy suit, tartan shirt and horn-rimmed glasses, a hearing-aid clipped to his jacket. Harriet's ex-lover.

"Trouble, Nobby?"

"Nothing, where's Stuart?"

Alex pointed across the enclosure. Canon Plumm with rotund gravitas was talking to Professor Stuart Caldwell, the Canon gesticulating, Caldwell listening, the sun bright on his steel-framed glasses, a spare, almost boyish figure, clean and narrow as a sword. Alex folded the *News Letter* and thrust it into his jacket.

"It's the end, Nobby, the whole Show's folding . . . matter of months, less."

"Saying that all your life Alex."

"This time it really is, 'course I've nothing to lose, you stand to lose a lot."

"Smallish crowd this year, not bad considering."

"In the old days I used to sit up trees at night with Basil watching out for Fenians or Germans . . . they never came . . . once I shot a rabbit . . ."

Alex paused. Unlistening, the Colonel scanned the grounds as Alex asked, "Who's the enemy now, can you tell me that Nobby?"

"Harriet," the Colonel said quietly. "She's drinking a lot."

A man with a silver trophy walked past leading a Charolais bull with a rosette on its forehead. He saluted the Colonel who said, "Fine animal, Sam, well done."

"Foreign, Sir, the ould breeds is dying out."

"True."

They watched the great golden bull pad towards a loading ramp.

"Never understood the cattle business," Alex said. "Lost a fortune trying to."

The Colonel said again: "Harriet, Alex, she's drinking a lot."

Alex paused before saying: "She dislikes the American."

"Did she say so?"

"Can't you tell?"

Alex stood, brushing and blowing cigar ash from his jacket. "Imagine spending eternity with old Plumm!"

"With anyone . . . can you speak to her?"

Alex shook his head. "She's out of reach . . . and why die sober if you can afford to die drunk?"

"She's killing herself and you're facetious!"

"People get drunk to forget they're alive Nobby; happiness is under ground."

The Colonel pondered this for a moment and said, with edge: "That's heartless and rather stupid."

As the Colonel moved to join the Canon and Caldwell, Alex muttered to himself: "Suppose it is . . . but then I'm bankrupt every way."

He took out another cigar and lit it. A group of farmers nearby smiled indulgently. They could not hear what Alex muttered as he lit his cigar, but they knew he was Alex Boyd-Crawford, an oddity, something of a drinker and womaniser, a wise fool who would probably be the last of the Boyd-Crawfords, his estate depleted, a widower, his only son a drop-out, inheritor of one of the oldest names in Ulster.

Alex looked at his pocket-watch and muttered: "Show's folding, time for a drink."

He moved towards the marquee to extract Harriet without fuss.

"That," he muttered, "is one thing I can do better than Nobby."

Leonard had driven about five miles on winding by-roads, through rolling drumlin countryside, up a dirt lane with high hedges to the front of a small two-storeyed farmhouse, painted tin over thatch, a byre adjoining, and beside it a small square concrete house with a rain-water tank above. There was a blue Cortina parked in an empty turf shed.

"Where is this?" Lynam said.

"Mid-Monaghan. Townland of Drumgrone."

"Is there a bathroom?"

He pointed to the small concrete building and said: "A jacks."

"Can I wash?"

"There's a tap in the backyard."

She hesitated. Leonard added: "There's a river at the bottom of the garden."

"When do we leave?"

He looked at his wristwatch: "Eight-thirty."

Leonard left her, went into the kitchen and directed his voice to someone behind the *Northern Standard*. "Where are the boys?"

From behind the *Northern Standard* a voice said: "Watching with Mother."

"We have a guest, Jack."

"Yes?"

The paper did not come down.

"She'll be at the river in five minutes or less . . . keep her in sight and stay out of sight."

"She?"

"I'll tell you later; go out the back."

Jack Gallagher went out the scullery door, round behind the barn, and keeping to the fields walked alongside the wild garden.

Lynam went to the concrete toilet, then round to a tap dripping into a sandstone trough. A scullery window looked directly out. She left the yard walking through the haggard, past an empty haybarn into an overgrown garden, dense with nettles, docks and some kind of wild rhubarb, rank and gross-smelling, that reached the lower branches of a dozen tortured apple trees.

There was a trodden path from house to river. She could hear water. The bank was steeper than she expected, bracken fronds fringing both sides at the roots of alder, ash and thorn. Water flowed clear over the rust-coloured bed. She sat on a dry stone by the edge of the water, took out a small wash-bag, mirror and makeup. Wet from tension, the cool air felt good. When she took off her blouse she noticed damp sweat patches, and realised she was more frightened now than she had been on the silent journey from Dublin. In an hour or less she would be facing, maybe talking with, those two people she had seen in the show-ground, and very possibly present when they were shot. Round a table or from a platform it was easy to talk and propagate the merits of violence as she had done for two years. Different now that it had prowled to her side, the bloody midwife of regeneration, a ruthless animal with dripping mouth and glassy merciless eyes. She took off her sandals, put her feet and hands in the water. In the snug of a bar in Dorset Street, when she had told Burke how she had ended the pregnancy, the gravel-voiced arbiter of life and death was so stunned he could scarcely reply.

"Why do that?" he had asked.

"It had no future."

"Why that?" he had repeated almost stupidly.

Was he so puerile that he saw her as a mere seed bed for his image? Why now without warning had he drafted her to possible martyrdom under Leonard? Pressures from others on the Army Council who disliked her bluntness? His wife's threat of suicide, or simply a cold, subtle move? Leonard, as yet publicly unknown, was privately spoken of North and South with a respect approaching awe which Burke must have noticed. And why had she joined? She tried to recall now her student impatience, bordering on hatred, for the congenital Irish condition, drunken meaningless talk breeding more drunken meaningless talk; an inability to think clearly and act coldly, "like the British" Burke said with irony. Once in, men who seemed complex became commonplace creatures jostling for power, a mix of waffling left-wingers, and old-fashioned Catholics led by Burke, who believed, she was certain, in nothing much but power for himself.

What now, sitting on a stone at a river's edge in Co. Monaghan, did she believe on this August evening? Aloud to the water she said: "I don't know."

Before Birmingham she could have walked across this river through a series of hump-backed fields to the nearest village, phoned a taxi and caught the Larne ferry to oblivion, like others unsure, frightened or disillusioned.

Somewhere up the river she heard the liquid bleat of a curlew. The gable of her grandmother's house faced the sea. At night the curlews swept up the stony inlet past Coolfada to Dungarvan. Coolfada, thatched roof roped against storm, mud floor, white-wash gone brown, smoke-yellowed glass, hens, dogs, cats, meal bags, a Pierce bellows and the leather-faced old woman, blood of her blood muttering Gaelic crossly to the animals, soda bread and sweet tea from a tin porringer in the morning, at night deep sleep in a settle bed in sheets stitched from flour bags, and God was the tide and all things related; people, fields, sea, sky, life and death, the immemorial land of childhood; lost.

It called again nearer. She looked up into the lowering sun as it winged closer. When she looked back to the river there was something floating downstream; rushes? A Moses' basket? The curlew wheeled calling again overhead and she thought, "I'm hallucinating." Then she saw clearly a fawn shopping bag in rushwork design. It drifted past spinning in the shallows and on into a deep pool round the bend; plastic, illusive, childless. She had sacrificed the blood of her blood for what? A dream? Nothing, she thought, as fusty and narrow as nationalism or the dead sentimental drag of Coolfada. "No," she said aloud. She had chosen freely the waking nightmare of action, the comradeship of men whose vivid words, aims and violence seemed more attractive, honest and hopeful than the hollow crafty manoeuvrings of politicians like her father grinding out their mean, greedy lives towards anonymous death. For these reasons and others complex and unclear she had joined. Trapped now, frightened and betrayed, it was weak to say, "I don't know," but thinking ahead she was not only sickened by violence but terrified at the idea of staring in its awful face. "Oh God," she muttered, but knowing she did not believe in God she accepted now her cowardice as natural. No option; she had chosen: so be it.

Dressed, she felt cool and fresh. She scrutinised her face in the small mirror. Who stared back? If she could fully understand the mind behind that mask she might begin to understand others a little and the world.

As she made up her face she became suddenly aware of something, a presence? She looked around sharply. Thirty yards downstream a young man was sitting at the edge of the river, his head just visible above the grass and bracken, a white fish-belly face that often goes with vivid red hair, no Monaghan farm boy. He was smiling and the effect was both attractive and repellent. She put the mirror away in her handbag, anger growing. How long had he been there? More shameful, more revealing that he should see her search in her mirror than see her wash. The soul more private than the body. Had he heard her speak aloud? He was moving towards her, still smiling, medium build, regulation jeans, polo, jerkin and desert boots.

"What are you grinning at?"

"Not much."

"Did Leonard send you to watch?"

"You sound Dublin."

"You sound pure Fermanagh."

"Derry, love, and you're shivering . . . you'll catch your death."

"Some day, and you?"

He was amused by her anger. "Don't let on you're ashamed by a man's eyes; what do they call you?"

"*La belle dame sans merci.*"

The smile evaporated slowly; she waited for him to speak.

"I'm Jack Gallagher and I've notched five men in four years, three Brits, one R.U.C., one U.D.R., blown up three barracks and left over a hundred bombs all over this province and when I ask a civil question I expect a civil answer."

She smiled up at him and said:

"Je m'appelle Isabel Lynam, et je voudrais changer les choses telles qu'elles soient, sans des salopards comme toi, mais la cause a besoin de toi, comme les champs ont besoin du fumier des cochons."

There was something in his expression that seemed almost subtle. She out-stared him, sure of her ground, till he turned and walked away from the river into the blind garden. Insulting and stupid of Leonard to have her watched like that. She picked up her handbag, momentarily aware that anger was more tolerable than fear, and that both were more tolerable than despair.

When Gallagher came into the yard Leonard could tell that he was tense.

"If I'm pig dung," he said, "she's sparrow shit. Bella Lynam, Christ man you're close, you could have warned me . . . why all the mystery . . . ?"

"You saw her?"

"And heard . . . smiling in my face she called me thug in French, that means you too boy, all of us."

"I said to keep out of sight."

"I was down river, she turned and saw me . . . is she with us tonight?" Leonard nodded.

"She's suspect."

"We're all suspect."

When they heard Lynam padding up the yard, Leonard put a forefinger to his lips and made a small gesture commanding silence. When she came round the gable of the concrete toilet her face was inscrutable. Leonard smiled uneasily.

"Bella this is Jack Gallagher."

"We've met," Gallagher said without looking up.

She looked directly at Gallagher and said: "Yes, I know him."

Leonard opened the door of the house to let her in. The kitchen was startling, green, white and gold boldly used on walls, ceiling and lino, gleaming Formica-top table, chrome kitchen chairs with leatherette seats. Above the stove an enormous oleograph of the Sacred Heart, between a butcher's calendar and the two Johns, Kennedy and Roncali, framed in smiling profile. All other available shelf and wall space was taken up with clocks, grandmother, grandfather, a dozen wall clocks, wag-o-the-walls, cuckoo clocks, shelves of ticking alarm and marble, clocks from railway stations and reading rooms, and one very impressive piece cast in iron from a big house yard or stable. The room itself seemed a clicking mechanism. As she took this in she heard Leonard say:

"Pacelli."

"Sorry?" she questioned.

Leonard repeated:

"Pacelli."

"Pius the thirteenth," Gallagher said.

A smallish youth approached her, a long almost monk-like face under crow black hair, with guileless eyes. A gunman? Incredulous, she took his hand as Leonard introduced her.

"Isabel Lynam."

"Bella," she said.

"We've heard plenty about you," Pacelli said. The voice had a sharp Monaghan edge, and the smile was disconcerting, both mocking and reassuring; he was older than he appeared.

"Pacelli what?" she asked.

"McAleer," he said.

"Touched like all the Monaghan McAleers," Gallagher said.

"He means we believe in God, he lets on he doesn't."

A replica of Pacelli came round the staircase and Pacelli said: "This is Pascal the brother . . . Bella Lynam."

As she shook hands she wondered if they were twins.

"How can I tell you apart?" she asked.

"Pascal has a bigger pendulum," Gallagher said.

Leonard smiled and Pascal said: "Jack's full of crack."

"But sour like a crab."

"Pay no heed."

"Pass no remarks."

"It's the kind of him."

"He can't help it."

"You'll get used to that," Gallagher said. "One goes tick the other goes tock."

Pascal pointed a forefinger at Gallagher, cocked up his thumb, closed one eye and said: "You'll mock once too often boy."

"I leave that to God," Gallagher said.

There was a short silence. It was clear to Lynam that the McAleer brothers did not approve of Gallagher's blasphemy. Seeing Gallagher close she noticed that his eyes were green, the whites blood-shot. His presence conveyed a tension you could almost touch. Because she knew he was a killer and enjoyed killing? Then Pascal said:

"You come on the express Bella?"

"By car."

Pacelli smiled:

> The Boyne at Slane, Ardee in rain
> North to Carrickmacross
> It's there the fields stare back and say
> Eternity will be no loss

"What do you think of our little hills?"

"Pleasing."

"General Owen Roe marched through this townland in 1646."

"He did?"

"Retreated half dead from syphilis," Gallagher muttered.

"From what?" Pascal asked.

"Camp fever," Leonard said.

"Lovers' plague, Pascal . . . won't bother you," Gallagher explained.

"What's he at Martin?" Pacelli asked.

Leonard shrugged. "We betray ourselves and are betrayed, and so we've lost time and again."

"*Not* what I meant," Gallagher said . . . "Owen Roe tried and lost . . . we'll win or die trying."

"Fair enough," Pascal said.

"I'm with you there," Pacelli added.

Gallagher looked at Lynam. "What do you say Mademoiselle?"

For five seconds Lynam stared back, before saying: "Little men who sneer at giants are ludicrous."

Leonard turned away so that Gallagher would not see him smile. Pascal, aware of increasing tension, intervened backed by Pacelli.

"The Mammy wants to meet you."

"She's above in the bed."

"An invalid."

"Bed-ridden this five years, arthritis and a dose of other things."

"She'll tell you herself."

"Likes to talk."

Leonard indicated to Lynam that she would have to do as requested. She followed Pascal across the gleaming green lino then up the narrow staircase. He opened a bedroom door.

"Bella Lynam from Dublin, Mammy, you've heerd tell of her."

A deep woman's voice uttered something in the room. Pascal smiled as she went in, closing himself out. Mrs. McAleer was enormous, an Irish Queen Victoria, with de Valera's nose and Churchill's mouth, all chin and breast, her stomach making a tent of the patchwork quilt, plaited hair bunned up behind, and lenses so powerful that her eyes peered out in huge and permanent astonishment. She looked as though she could deliver Pascal and Pacelli fully grown. As Lynam approached Mrs. McAleer held out a plump, regal hand. Lynam took it. It was clammy, the arthritic fingers rigid. The room had a personal fishy smell, mixed with Lysol and deodorant. Above a bedside commode a frail madonna stared upwards in tears, her heart transfixed by a sword. Beside the madonna, a calendar print of Padraig Pearse, his head in a halo of flames. Underneath someone had printed in red biro, his poem, "The Mother." Mrs. McAleer said:

"You don't look twenty, I thought you'd be older."

"I feel like a thousand."

"You'll be with them tonight?"

"Yes."

"Are you afraid daughter?"

"Of course."

"It's a joy we can still breed your likes."

The fishmonger smell was oppressive. Lynam moved to a partially opened window and looked at the August landscape and the evening. Mrs. McAleer patted the patchwork quilt and said:

"You can sit here by me."

"The view is beautiful," Lynam said.

"It is, it is, a wonder and a pity when you think of the men and women who died for them crooked hedges, ditches and lanes, the blood, the hunger, the burials, the old sorrow. I've suffered too all my life. Hughie my husband, that's him in the snap, used to say to me, 'Listen Rosie don't argue with God's will, he knows best,' a religious man, a feeling man, couldn't get doctors enough for me, London, Belfast, Dublin, no solution. They got him in '57 with a gun near Armagh, tortured and locked him away five years, then let him out to die. In this his deathbed he said to the boys, 'I'm broke lads, finished, but you have a score to settle,' and them only half reared, and me half crippled. Sometimes I think life's a bigger tragedy nor death. The Dublin Doctor Fagan said to me, 'Mrs. McAleer,' he said, 'there's nothing for it only aspirins and patience.' To myself I thought, 'Patience unto death.' "

She paused to take a breath and change gear. "What do you think of my boys, daughter?"

"They seem nice."

"Small, like Hugh, but big hearts and clean living, and they've got nerve, don't smoke, don't drink, don't interfere with girls like that Gallagher, and they can take down any clock in the world and put it up again, and bombs . . . ! Not a one in this country to touch them . . . Mr. Burke told me himself, 'You should be proud Mrs. McAleer, proud, they'll get their reward and so will you.' Every day I thank God for my three green fields and my two brave sons."

She sighed. Lynam was about to say something when Mrs. McAleer continued:

"I was once a slip of a girl like you would you believe that? And look at me now. Only for my two boys I'd be lost entirely, and I could lose them any time, some day, some night, like tonight, they'll go off, and the neighbour woman that cares me will come in some morning and say: 'I'm afeered Mrs. McAleer I've bad news for you,' and I'll say: 'My boys is it, both?' And she'll nod."

Mrs. McAleer bowed her head and quoted:

> "Lord thou art hard on mothers,
> We suffer in their coming and their going,
> And though I grudge them not, I weary, weary
> Of the long sorrow, and yet I have my joy,
> My sons were faithful and they fought."

Mrs. McAleer looked up. "I wouldn't be the first nor the last, it's the price of freedom; you're too young to understand the dread, your own flesh and blood dead in the cold earth."

"I understand."

"Young girls like you shouldn't be in danger . . . war is men's work, if them Brits or black Protestants got hands on you, you'd never stand up to them . . . what made you join, daughter?"

"That you wouldn't understand."

"Why not?"

"Because . . ." Lynam paused, aware of the great devouring eyes, and said: "I don't understand myself."

"To free Ireland, it's simple."

"For what?"

"Us."

"From what?"

"Them."

"We are them . . . now."

The blancmange cheeks trembled till the mouth uttered: "Never . . . despise us, always did, always will."

From the window Lynam saw Gallagher cross the yard and place a canvas bag in the boot of the blue Cortina. She said quietly: "We died long ago with our language."

"What are you saying girl?"

"Win or lose nothing changes, because men don't nor women . . . even the blind know that light leads on to darkness."

In the silence that followed, they could hear the ticking of innumerable clocks from the kitchen below. Mrs. McAleer opened her mouth to say something, hesitated, then said, almost tenderly:

"You sound honest, do you pray daughter?"

"When I'm frightened."

"Do you believe in God?"

"Not yours."

"Jesus Christ?"

"Not yours."

The great face darkened again. On the edge of anger she said loudly. "There's only one Jesus Christ."

"Dozens Mrs. Mac., and they hate each other."

There was a heavy silence punctuated by a sudden storm of cuckoo clocks and a dozen reverberating gongs in the kitchen.

"Are you a Communist, child?"

"I'm twenty-three. Arts graduate, only child of Willie Lynam, publican, Dáil Deputy and drunkard, separated from his wife, my mother, who devotes herself to poodles and Jesuits, and soon I will be in jail, exiled or dead."

Lynam paused and turned from the window. "What I am or think doesn't matter, but I'm glad we've met."

In silence Mrs. McAleer pointed a crooked finger to a chest of drawers facing the bed.

"Left-hand drawer, open it."

Lynam did as she was asked. There was a cardboard box, a large plastic bottle and dozens of empty aspirin bottles filled with transparent liquid.

"Open the box."

Lynam took off the cardboard lid and saw a hoard of miraculous medals and chains.

"Take one and a small bottle."

Lynam felt absurd but knew refusal would give serious offence.

"Here daughter . . . sit."

Mrs. McAleer put the medal over Lynam's head and poked it under her blouse. Lynam slipped the aspirin bottle into her bag.

"You know what that is?"

"Holy water?"

"Better again, Lourdes water; she believes in you girl, and you mind that."

Mrs. McAleer was holding her with a crab-like grip between rigid thumb and forefinger. Close up the two great floating eyes in that flaccid face had the impact of a Hogarth cartoon.

"Always wanted a daughter . . . if I had one she wouldn't be troubled like you . . . too much learnin' is the ruination of the world, all a body needs is faith in God, his Blessed Mother, faith in your people and faith in your country."

"Goodbye Mrs. McAleer."

"God go with you child."

Lynam closed the door quietly and stood dazed in the narrow upstairs hall. Mrs. McAleer was a rural, Republican edition of her genteel mother who fed anzaks and coffee to rotating Jesuits in return for vapid spiritual consolation. In every part of this island she had met men and women unreal beyond description. A race of inbred lunatics? Sometimes it seemed frighteningly like that.

She could hear Leonard talking below. When she rounded the bottom of the staircase he had his finger on a map or drawing. As she moved towards the table Gallagher came in the front door, his cold face fixed in amused contempt. Without irony Pascal asked:

"You got your medal Bella?"

"Yes."

And Pacelli added: "Your wee bottle?"

Lynam nodded.

"Pre-war," Gallagher said. "Drink it and you'll get typhoid."

Pascal and Pacelli said almost together:

"Don't mind him."

"He's bred that way."

Gallagher smiled and said: "Tick tock, tick tock."

"Can we keep to this?" Leonard asked, his finger on a drawing. To Lynam he added: "You'll be with me, I'll gen you up on the way."

"Can I come and watch?" Gallagher asked.

For a moment it seemed as though Leonard would reply. It was Pacelli who spoke. "No call for talk like that."

"Like what?"

"Bad talk," Pacelli said.

"What the fuck did I say?"

Lynam moved away. In the silence that followed she read the legend on a butcher's calendar, her back to the table. Pascal said:

"That's too much, no man should talk like that fornenst wemen."

"She doesn't give a shit about you boy, me, any of us."

"You can tell?" Leonard asked.

"I can tell," Gallagher said.

Her back to them Lynam said: "Let him fuck all he likes if it makes him feel manly."

"Not you," Gallagher said. "I don't pick over garbage."

The McAleer brothers were very uncomfortable. Leonard said quietly: "Jack please."

Lynam looked around. Leonard was white. A nerve twitched under his blind eye. She looked at the green lino, aware of a sudden release of adrenalin. As always when tense she smiled. In the silence that followed the clocks seemed suddenly hysterical. Without opening his mouth Gallagher said:

"Bloody women, muck everything."

Leonard was aware that this was mostly his fault. Burke's cryptic coded note had advised him to watch her. The river thing was unfortunate. Either of the McAleers would have been more discreet, and Gallagher would have been more careful had he known who she was. To Gallagher all females were for screwing in ditches or cars. He boasted his prowess as lover and killer, how the girls whimpered, how his targets spun, stumbled and fell, date, street and townland, all carefully reported back to Dublin: History. An epileptic, a sick aura of success hung about him, the black flag of violence and death. In the further silence Leonard looked from face to face, Gallagher's rigid, the McAleer brothers' aware of unseemliness. Lynam kept her head bowed. Was she smiling? With emphasis now he said:

"That's it."

"Come off it Martin."

Gallagher pointed a trigger finger at Lynam. "We know about her, Bella Donna, Burke calls her, she's poisonous, maybe Special Branch, Dublin or London, both the one . . . you're doing the Belfast gent and she's laughing at you . . . all of us . . . look at her, we're a joke."

They all looked at Lynam. She lifted her head and stared back, her face indecipherable. Leonard paused for control. As he was about to speak a bell sounded upstairs.

"Mother Lourdes on the line," Gallagher said.

Both McAleers moved for the staircase. Leonard looked at his watch.

"Five minutes, boys, make your farewells . . ." To Gallagher he said: "You'd better say your bit and be done with this."

Gallagher said: "Thios ansin ag an abhainn thug tu cailleach orm sul a rachaimid ait ar bit anois gabhfaidh tu mo leath sgeala.'*

Lynam was startled. In the silence which followed a faint colour came into her narrow cheek bones. She said, nodding towards Leonard: "I was angry with him not you."

"Mea culpa, it was stupid of me."

---

* "Down at the river you called me a thug . . . before we go anywhere you'll apologise."

"I'll drink to that," Gallagher said, and moved towards a cupboard beside the range. He took out a bottle of Powers Gold Label and half-filled three plain tumblers. He topped up with water from a jug, handed a glass to Leonard and Lynam, raised his own and said:

"To Ireland free."

"Whatever that means," Lynam muttered.

Gallagher lowered his tumbler. "From the centre to the sea, girl, that's what it means." He paused, looking intently into her face, and said: "And no deals, no compromise ever, no Catholic gents on horseback telling us what to think, no Murphys in a wig locking us away because they're afraid, no po-faced Prods whipping us for white nigger trash, no smug clergy hiding behind props and property, and whining about violence, no jet-set, pin-stripes buying up half the country; that's what it means Lynam." He jiggled his glass. "And death to all traitors . . . you'll drink to that? . . ."

"I'll drink to that."

"You believe it?"

"I'll drink to it."

She was startled, not so much by what he said but by the articulate intensity, the twisting mouth and bloodshot eyes, the low key fury as words came jerking out with barely controlled violence . . . Had she misjudged him at the river as a boastful moron? This he was, but more. Could Leonard, anyone, control such a creature? The cold whiskey burned its way down, spreading a warm blurring numbness in her empty stomach. I'll be drunk in five minutes she thought, maybe dead by Monday. Gallagher added now:

"And success to the job."

"I'll be big," Leonard said, raising his glass and lowering his voice. "The world," he said, "and the socialist future."

"Does it have one?" Lynam asked.

"Can you let nothing by?" Gallagher asked.

"What the fight's about partly," Leonard intervened.

They drank and Gallagher looked at Lynam. "Now your dream?"

There was quite a pause till she said with an odd smile: "Life and death."

They hesitated.

"Whose death?" Gallagher asked.

"Peace," she said.

"That's better," Leonard said, and realised that she knew clearly as he did what they were venturing . . . Two Army Council meetings had been, he was told, entirely taken up with "The Inver Move." The first vote went against, the second in favour. He had spent three long days and sleepless nights being briefed in Dublin. At the time Burke had said that he might send extra help, but had given him no hint that it would be Lynam. Since then Leonard had thought of nothing else night and day, trying to justify in advance, to cancel fear and doubt. The wealth and privilege of the Armstrongs in these islands and Europe had been gained by force and fraud, sanctioned and maintained by Church and Law for centuries. This he told himself again and again. If London refused to negotiate they would have to kill and be killed. The clamorous condemnations that would follow were nothing; they would be at peace. He had shot one soldier near Strabane two years ago and one bomb he had placed had killed a mother and child. It was painful to see images in newspapers and read accounts. Sometimes he heard screaming in his sleep and woke sweating. Unlike Gallagher he had never seen, nor wanted to, the face of a victim. This time they would be face to face in one room for eighteen hours or more. As the McAleers came down the staircase Leonard asked:

"Time?"

Pascal and Pacelli looked at their wristwatches, smiled at the clocks round the walls and said:

"Eight twenty-five."

"Dead on."

Gallagher and Leonard adjusted their watches fractionally and Leonard said: "We leave in five minutes."

Pascal and Pacelli came up to Leonard and shook his hand in solemn ritual. They then turned to Lynam. She was about to offer her hand when Pascal kissed her on one cheek, Pacelli on the other. Both had the same joyous, guileful smiles, at variance with their guileless eyes. Gallagher watched them go out the door, followed, turned and said:

"Slán."

"Slán," Leonard and Lynam said simultaneously.

"Have they killed?" she asked.

"Yes."

"Both?"

"Yes."

"And you?"

"Yes."

"All but me."

"You might have to."

"I know."

"You have a weapon?"

"No."

Leonard put his glass down. She noticed he had scarcely touched it. He went to the built-in cupboard where Gallagher had found the whiskey, took out two shelves, removed a loose board from the back and put his hand into a cavity. He took out a small pistol.

As he explained how it worked his voice seemed far away. She could see his scarred thumb pressing the catch, his forefinger curling round the trigger: then words: "Dead simple, safety catch, gentle pressure, flick this here, can't miss, hold the shooting wrist with your hand, like this." Gallagher's measure of whiskey seemed to heighten the gleaming phallic awfulness in Leonard's hands. He undid the catch of her bag, and thrust in the pistol. If he had unzipped his fly, peeled off a used condom and dropped it in her bag, she would have been less shocked. He was aware of her silence.

"All right?"

"Fine."

As he held the front door open he called out: "Monday night late Mrs. Mac."

The deep voice above sent down a sepulchral blessing.

The Cortina went first, Pascal driving, Gallagher in front, Pacelli in the back. After ten minutes scudding along a by-road into the gathering dusk they passed a sign which said: "UNAPPROVED ROAD."

From the back seat Pacelli grinned and gave the thumbs-up sign. Leonard nodded and thumbed back at him.

"This is it," he said.

Lynam did not answer. After a mile she said: "We're dead."

"Every time I think that and I'm still alive."

"This is different."

"More difficult . . . if it wasn't it wouldn't be worth doing."

"Suppose we're stopped on the way by police or Army?"

"We won't be."

"Suppose?"

"This road's checked out, and all by-roads."

"How?"

"Friends."

The Cortina slowed, turned left up a by-road; as Leonard slowed to follow he said: "Clumsy . . . the river thing, I'm sorry."

Lynam said nothing for a minute, then asked: "Where did he get French?"

"Brittany, Breton Freedom Fighter."

"Will he do what you say?"

"Jack? I think so."

"Think?"

"I'm sure."

"He's paranoid, schizoid."

"Epileptic."

"I could sense something, the sick colour and the raving."

"If it comes to killing he won't waste words."

"Or pity?"

"No," Leonard said, "he's dedicated and deadly."

"What did Burke tell you?"

"If it was serious you wouldn't be here."

"Tell me."

Leonard hesitated before saying: "Anyone who can wreck two marriages and arrange three press leaks in one year should be in advertising or a brothel."

"He's lying . . . reptile."

"All of us, if you believe the Press, Churches and politicians."

In a few sentences Leonard outlined what she would have to do. He asked if she was clear. She said yes she was. They were now in forest twilight away from the small drumlin fields with their ditches of thorn and thwarted ash. They sped past a limestone baronial gatelodge with conifers crowding and stretching back into the embracing dark. A hundred yards further on there was an obelisk in a circular clearing, its base engraved in gold lettering. Leonard said, nodding at it:

"The dead of two world wars."

"Is this Inver?"

Leonard nodded. The Cortina had stopped a hundred yards from the monument where the high estate wall had been smashed by a falling tree. Gallagher and Pascal had gone through. Pacelli took the canvas bag from the boot and followed. Leonard drew in behind the Cortina and cut his engine.

As Lynam stepped over the rubble of the wall she saw below a long stretch of lake and meadowland and, beyond the lake, bunched in trees and shrubbery, the outline of a tall Tudor house.

Millicent left the tray on the pantry table, plugged in the coffee percolator and watched her father decanting port, waiting for him to say something.

"I've spoken to her."

"When?"

"Before dinner."

The Colonel inserted a cork firmly into the empty bottle of port as his daughter said: "Her blouse is buttoned the wrong way, and out at the back, and she's been like a zombie all through dinner."

"Worse when she talks."

"It's awful to say this, Father, but I'll leave on Monday if she doesn't . . . I can understand today at the Show, but other days where does she get it?"

"The staff are 'loyal'."

"Why is she so unhappy?"

"Why does winter come?"

"She fell in the marquee when Alex went to . . ."

"Yes I heard."

"Such a mockery of a man."

"He's kindly, reads a lot, they share that."

"Don't you care?"

The Colonel had moved towards the heavy, panelled self-closing door that gave to the living-room. If he said yes it would be short of honest. No, and it would seem that he did not love or cherish his wife, her mother, when in truth he had connived at the affair through guilt. He looked at the decanter of port and said:

"Yes and no."

"That's not an answer."

"The best I can give."

Because they were only six the hunting table was opened before the Adam grate in the long high-ceilinged living room cleared now except for two ashtrays, port glasses, and some cut-glass tumblers. Harriet was sitting at the head of the table facing the high, wide, bay window that looked south-west across the lake. All through dinner she had been watching a dark red sun go down behind the forest lands of Inver and Shannock, leaving the lake a blooded gash in the quiet landscape. Now, as she watched, the blood congealed to a blackish navy blue, as lake, field and forest merged into night.

Caldwell had been talking and getting attention through dinner. Harriet lit her last cigarette, watching the moving lips, hating the intelligent blue eyes behind those steel frames, the sickening drawl, the elegant brown safari-type jacket, and creamy silk shirt that seemed to blend with his feminine skin. Alex was nodding, bored, she thought. Canon Plumm seemed attentive. Suddenly the Canon's face broadened. He gave a short avuncular laugh. Caldwell smiling touched the tip of his fine-boned nose with a long left forefinger. Harriet noticed the perfectly groomed nails. Some rhyming joke? She had missed it. In the momentary pause that followed she said with unusual loudness:

"Very stupid of me but I seem to have missed the point."

The Colonel was at the other end of the table. As he sat and placed the decanter of port he said with quiet hardness: "Possibly you weren't listening my love."

Caldwell said: "It's nothing."

"But Canon Plumm laughed," Harriet said. "It must be amusing."

There was a longer pause. Harriet looked from face to face and then began:

"Sitting snugly at his fire William Wordsworth said to Charles Lamb, 'I could write plays like Shakespeare if I'd a mind to,' and Lamb replied, 'Nothing lacking Willie, but the mind.' "

Alex Boyd-Crawford smiled; he had heard it before. No one else responded. Harriet went on:

"Oscar Wilde envied that reply, did you know that Professor?"

"I did not."

"Shy man Lamb, devoted to his sister, charming essays."

Harriet could see the knuckles of her husband's hands go white as both fists closed. Surely he wasn't going to bang the table? She kept her eyes down and heard Caldwell say:

"More sick than funny I suppose."

"What?" Harriet asked.

Canon Plumm explained. "Professor Caldwell was telling us about some grave inscriptions in eighteenth-century Virginia."

"Which Virginia?"

"United States."

"Grave inscriptions?"

"Yes."

"Funny ones, Professor?"

"Odd ones," Caldwell said.

"In our graveyard here," Canon Plumm ventured, when Harriet cut in suddenly.

"Hideous subject, utterly."

She searched the ornate Italian frieze for a word, found it and uttered emphatically:

"Horrendous . . . numbing . . . if you ponder it . . . thy kingdom dumb . . . terrifying . . . ." She paused. "But life itself, now there's true comedy, because people do the strangest, the most anguish-making, cruelly funny things . . . friends, neighbours, nations . . . when I think of the things we all do to each other in the course of living, in the mill of history, I laugh and laugh till the tears come."

Harriet bowed her head. She was trembling, forgot what she was saying and why, aware only that Milly had placed a tray with coffee cups and percolator on the table and was now sitting down.

"What was I saying Alex?"

"Something about life dear."

"Ah yes, some burial joke that Dr. Caldwell made . . . I missed the point, and that is a defect, not to respond to the niceties of civilised necrophilia."

The Colonel said coldly: "Harriet."

"Yes my love?"

"Would you like to pour coffee?"

"I'll pour," Millicent said.

They watched as she poured, each responding when she asked about sugar and cream.

"Some graves," Alex said vaguely, "are self-dug."

"Indeed," the Colonel said, looking directly at his wife. Behind those eyes, she thought, a mind foreign as his locked study. The charm was for others, that tilt of the head as though he could listen forever. Long since he had stopped hearing unless she screamed. What had she loved or thought she loved? The soldierly bearing, the graceful manners, the family accumulations, in Tudor mellowness. He knew about everything in the house, who bought it, where, when, why, how much it was insured for. Yes. He understood about insurance. "Any policy, Nobby, for a withering heart?" He had smiled that night as though she had asked a silly question, the smile he used when talking with her gifted unpredictable father whose money had helped finance the expensive yards, the milking merry-go-round, the yards full of cows and bawling bullocks. Some time near dawn she had smashed three plates of value against the door of his study. He did not refer to the gesture at the time or since. The armour of infinite politeness, behind it something callous; inhuman.

Aloud she said, "Inhuman."

No one seemed to hear. The talk now had shifted to employment, the E.E.C. and agriculture. Agriculture. His real devotion since the war; his hobbies, military and local history: "The Armstrongs in Ulster: The intruders who contributed."

In the functions room of an Armagh hotel his paper was well received by the Clogher Historical Society, Catholics and Protestants, mostly teachers and clergy. She had read it in advance and thought it dull and tendentious. When he spoke it standing upright in that warm level voice, it sounded humane, conscientious, liberal. Everyone likes him for some reason, she thought . . . perhaps I'm jealous . . . Yes. All that correspondence with Denis Brogan which she had resented till they met at Cambridge, an Irish-Scot professor, with a port-wine face, startling white hair and a mind so complex and comprehensive that his tongue stumbled after, a soul more alive to poetry and philosophy than the brutal facts and farce of war. In comparison Caldwell was an intellectual eunuch, a beautiful, polished New England eunuch. She was aware now that they were all looking at Alex. Watching his pursed mouth she forced herself to understand what he was saying. He paused, shrugged and continued:

"We never employed Papists, family tradition, they all cheat, lie and thieve, dirty, careless, superstitious, stupid; when you hear this from the nursery onwards, right or wrong it tends to stick."

"Fact, Sir," Canon Plumm said gravely. "They've a lower I.Q. than Negroes, an American professor has proven this, am I right Dr. Caldwell?"

Caldwell considered a moment and said: "That study is controversial, Canon."

"To the Irish, no one else; what they've done down there in sixty years is not in doubt, ruined Dublin, painted pillar boxes green, and produced more lunatics and alcoholics per square mile than any other country in the world. This is proven fact."

Harriet finished her glass of wine, wiped her mouth with a napkin.

"Did you not say, Milly, that this lovely county of ours has the worst housing problem in these islands?"

"It has," Millicent said.

"Papist housing you'll find," the Canon said, "won't avail of grants, they're shiftless and Rome's responsible."

"Rome?" Harriet asked.

The Canon smiled and shook his head patiently as he muttered: "Italy, Spain, Portugal, Latin America."

He opened his hands and pursed his lips. The target was so enormous he did not know quite where to aim. Suddenly he struck. "Take Plunkett, the rebel priest, hung as Crown traitor. This year they plan to canonise him."

He paused, staring from face to face. "Here their Bishops preach against violence while the Pope in Rome aligns himself with I.R.A. bombers and murderers."

He paused again. "This is not just mischievous; it's political, criminal."

There was an embarrassed pause, until Harriet said: "We did burn Joan of Arc, Canon . . . they made her a saint."

"Different."

"Is it? Of course I don't understand politics; Nobby does and Professor Caldwell is an expert. How does it strike you, Professor, as an outsider? Will we be shot in our beds, driven to the sea, what's your impression?"

"Do you want an answer?"

"I did ask a question."

"Unlikely . . . implausible."

"Then what is plausible?"

Stuart Caldwell stirred his coffee for ten seconds, aware that no reply could please.

"I expect," he said quietly, "the British will leave in time, and North and South will patch up something in time, with or without a civil war . . . impossible to say more."

Almost inaudibly Harriet muttered: "Profound."

Glacial, the Colonel asked: "You have some solution, dear?"

"No, but I did think the Canon just now sounded peasant as Paisley without the loudmouthed charm, and I don't trust his American professor I.Q. expert, or indeed anything from that glorious civilisation."

"Mother."

"You've got a degree dear, what did they teach you at Trinity? To keep silent when people talk nonsense?"

Harriet looked down the table at her husband. Centuries of arrogance in those bloodhound eyes that stared back from that long hawk-like face drained of colour, the iron-grey head and clipped moustache fringing a heavy mouth. She looked away to the window across the lake.

The Colonel looked up at his wife who was avoiding his eyes. Last night she had fallen asleep at table. He had excused the staff and helped Milly serve dinner to eight people. Her performance this evening was a great deal more painful. Of course John Plumm was something of a bigot and a bore, but also well-meaning in his way, apart from being a very old friend. Stuart was much too sophisticated to respond to drunken petulance. Tomorrow when she half remembered what she had just said she would suffer. He felt both angry with her and sorry for her.

Harriet stood suddenly and walked with particular care towards the pantry door. In the continuing silence Alex said:

"Excellent coffee . . . excellent."

"It is," Caldwell said.

The Colonel stood and said to Canon Plumm and Caldwell: "I'm sorry."

The Canon shook his head and mumbled something. Caldwell smiled and made a small gesture. The Colonel followed Harriet. She was standing at the sink with a large whiskey looking out at the August night. The Colonel approached quietly, held her wrist, took the glass from her hand and moved to the table. She watched with anger and disbelief as he poured the whiskey back into a newly opened bottle of Haig then heard herself say:

"That was a stupid thing to do."

"You've been warned my love . . . you're killing yourself."

"I'm dead."

"Drunk, dear, and the trouble is you'll fall and crack your skull or crash the car."

"A blessed relief."

The Colonel looked at the label on the whiskey bottle and said: "Irish is cheaper than Scotch and better for making you drunk. If you get more . . ."

"A blessed relief, I said. And you will not humiliate me like this."

The Colonel watched, impassive, a seasoned politician pausing for an irrelevant heckler. Looking from the scrubbed deal table to her glazed brown eyes he said with growing edge:

"If you get more maudlin than you are now, insult guests like that, laugh hysterically at nothing, or jabber incomprehensible verse, I'll send for someone."

He had hinted before; now it had been said. She felt anger grow to a point of fury.

"Someone!"

"Qualified."

She turned her back and said to the window: "Get a medical plumber for me, Nobby, and I'll phone someone for you . . . also qualified."

There was a very long pause before the Colonel said: "What are you trying to say my love?"

"I can see through him with my eyes shut."

"Who?"

"Caldwell."

"You dislike him?"

"He makes me ill, I want him gone."

"You could have said so without all this."

The Colonel went back to the living room. Harriet leaned against the pantry sink supporting herself with both hands. The table before her seemed momentarily a raft riding on a gentle swell. She closed her eyes aware that the door leading off the pantry to the kitchen corridor had opened quietly, or had she imagined it? She opened her eyes and saw a young man with blood red hair above a corpse white face. He was pointing a pistol at her. He waved her away from the sink. More incredulous than afraid she moved as directed towards the table and thought to herself: I'm dreaming. The young man locked the door, moved across the pantry, locked another door leading to the hall, went to the sink, pulled the shutters across the window, then the curtains, and pointed towards the door leading into the living room. As she opened this green baize door she saw another young man, tall with a black beard, standing with a pistol at the far end of the room, beside him a girl with a tense narrow face, and melancholy eyes. The girl had no weapon in her hand. The man with the beard spoke.

"No hardship intended if our request is met."

The red youth walked down the long room, pulled shutters across the bay window, then the heavy tapestry curtains, ensuring that there was no gap in the middle or at either side.

The family portraits round the walls looked calmly down on the upturned faces round the hunting table, each face expressing varying degrees of incomprehension and disbelief. The Tomkin clock on the high mantel ticked evenly in the stillness that followed Leonard's cryptic statement, beech logs hissed in the Adam fire-basket. Lynam looking from face to face was startled by a sudden shock of recognition: "No . . . ! Yes . . . ? Trinity . . . ? Armstrong . . . ? Good Christ . . . !" They had shared French tutorials three years ago. She could see that the Armstrong girl could not believe the evidence of her own eyes. To Lynam she said:

"It is you?"

"Yes," Lynam said.

High in the great house they could hear shutters squealing on rusty hinges, the rasp of iron clasps, the twanging of six-inch nails being driven into doors, architraves, windows.

Leonard switched on the lights.

"How many?" the Colonel asked.

"Two more."

"How long will you keep us?"

"Tomorrow midday, unless they give us what we ask."

"And that is?"

"Three men from Long Kesh."

"And if not?"

"Bleak . . . for all of us."

Gallagher approached and whispered, nodding towards the table:

"Milord Secretary . . . he's gone . . . !"

"We'll make these do."

"Bad start."

"Good omen."

Watching them the Colonel guessed the content and spoke:

"You know that what you're attempting is not just misguided, it's plain stupid."

The red-haired youth made a brief grimace. The man with the beard, obviously the leader, returned the Colonel's stare. His left eye was sunken in its socket, both heavy-lidded above a prow-like nose, the dense beard creating a mask-like effect. Having spoken, the Colonel now felt he had to act. He stood, not quite knowing what he intended, and moved towards Leonard. With scarcely a movement of lips a voice came from the beard with emphasis:

"No further."

The scarred forefinger of his left hand was pointing rigidly. The effect was more menacing than a pistol. Some instinct advised the Colonel that this man was professional and would kill without hesitation. He paused, looked at the decanter of port on the table and said:

"You expected my son-in-law here . . . he's chairing a symposium at Queen's University. I would have thought you knew this – it was well publicised. You can't bargain with an old soldier, his family and a couple of friends – won't work. You'll have to kill us – they'll kill you – and nothing whatever will have been gained but bad propaganda for you and more business for the undertakers, and God knows they're overworked in this Province . . . Be sensible . . . you can still leave."

"Your Army is notified," Leonard said. "On its way."

"If they don't get lost about Belturbet," Gallagher muttered.

"Dear God," Canon Plumm almost whispered.

"I think," the Colonel said, "that you should know this gentleman is an American professor."

Gallagher said: "He could be an Australian kangaroo."

Leonard nodded agreement. "He's here and stays till we decide . . . otherwise, no hardship. The house will be sealed excepting the front door and hall, this room, the pantry and toilet off."

The Colonel said: "You know the house well."

"National Trust," Leonard said. "The plans are available and clear."

Harriet looked at her husband as the nailing continued above. "We're being entombed, Nobby, alive."

Milly said: "Mother, I think . . ."

"We can talk, can we not?"

"All you like," Leonard said.

"Then I think we should introduce ourselves."

In the silence that followed Leonard said: "Our names don't matter."

"Ours do . . . I am Harriet Armstrong and that is my husband Norbert, beside him is Stuart Caldwell, a Professor of military history . . . a subject indistinguishable from pornography in my view . . . I read a lot of poetry . . . Dylan Thomas mostly."

Milly said: "Mother this is not helpful."

Leonard said: "I'm quite interested."

"In mockery," Millicent said acidly.

"I said, 'Quite.' "

Harriet went on: "The Professor probably knows more about the I.R.A. than any of you people."

"I doubt it," Gallagher said.

"And this," she said, putting out her hand towards Alex, "is Alex Boyd-Crawford retired from . . . what are you retired from Alex?"

"Everything," Alex said.

"But genial courtesy and warmth . . . human warmth . . . rare in this cold world . . . and beside me this roundabout man is dear Canon Plumm, the Rector of Inver Church . . . an expert on bee-keeping." She paused and smiled before adding: "And the machinations of the Vatican . . . And my daughter Millicent, twenty-four years old . . . married . . ."

"Harriet you will stop talking now," the Colonel's voice cracked out in hard sharp command.

Harriet shrugged, picked up an empty cigarette carton, examined it, turned to Gallagher and asked: "Do you have a cigarette?"

Without answering Gallagher produced a packet with his free hand and flicked it on to the table.

"Thank you."

As Harriet lit a cigarette, Gallagher studied the six faces round the table, then moved away and began pacing the length of the room, pausing once or twice before family portraits, glancing into the great gilt mirror above the chimneypiece which framed the hostages round the table, now looking into each other's eyes like passengers aboard plane or ship when an engine bursts into flame, or a voice warns suddenly of serious emergency. The man with the beard, who was obviously the leader, seemed almost casual, talking in a low voice with the girl. The red youth seemed very tense and by far the most dangerous. Every now and then his pistol wrist gave an involuntary twitch like the tail of a caged tiger.

Watching him Lynam realised with slow horror that he would convey this tension till he had tasted blood. He wanted to kill or be killed, and she wondered if this, less manifest, was a hidden instinct in herself, in Leonard, in the McAleers. Then she saw the Colonel lean over the back of the American's chair and say something to his daughter who asked:

"Can I fetch some whiskey?"

"Where from?"

"The pantry."

Leonard nodded and said quietly to Lynam: "Go with her."

Millicent got up. Lynam followed and stood in the panelled pantry beside a Welsh dresser decked with Spode china, Wedgwood, oriental ware, and topped with an array of pewter mugs and containers. Millicent hunkered, reached into a corner cupboard and took out two bottles of Bushmills whiskey aware that Lynam was standing behind her. She straightened, turned, and said:

"When I heard your voice I knew . . . Isabel Lynam?"

"Yes."

"Impassioned at debate I remember . . . I listened then, I'll listen now."

"This is not a college debate, and I didn't know you lived here . . . unfortunate."

"You're Provisional I.R.A.?"

"Obviously."

Millicent put the two bottles on the scrubbed deal table and dropped her voice: "Those two horrors inside . . . with faces like that . . . I can see them doing anything . . . not you."

"One has three A levels and I find their faces less horrific than the painted ones round your walls."

"You'll kill me, my parents, friends, a churchman, in cold blood?"

Lynam did not answer.

"You can maim, cripple, blind the innocent . . . for what?"

"You've never been colonised, you wouldn't understand."

"I can try, if you can explain."

The unafraid manner and arrogant voice seemed patronising. She had long flaxen hair, immaculate skin, and brown searching eyes, eloquent as her mother's but less vulnerable. Lynam felt suddenly docked by a hostile witness, a self-possessed, model girl with a modelled upper-class mind. Looking straight back she said:

"I don't have to."

"You can't . . . you've had your student pub-crawls, your bedsit affairs, hitched about and got stoned, so now you're a graduate . . . work's a bore, what next . . . back-room politics with mindless killers . . . a taste of terror before you die . . . it's beyond contempt."

Lynam did not react and said after quite a pause: "You married?"

Surprised, Millicent glanced at her wedding ring: "I was to have our first child in January . . . does that mean anything to you?"

"Capricorn."

"What!?"

"Capricorn."

"I don't think you're quite human."

"Yesterday, Victoria Regina Magnifica gave five pounds for Irish famine relief and the same week five pounds to a British dog fund."

"Yesterday?"

"She's still alive . . . when you stop killing us we'll stop killing you . . . it's as simple as that."

"What have I . . . we . . . got to do with killing you?"

"Everything."

"You're not sane."

"Very, and human, and distressed about your child . . . if there's anything I can do?"

The door came in and Gallagher was suddenly standing in the pantry. He paused, looking from one girl to the other, walked between them picking up a cut-glass tumbler from the table on his way to the sink. Millicent left. Gallagher tapped off three full glasses and drank them without pause and then held the tumbler up to the light.

"Eighteenth-century Waterford; Huguenot rubbish."

He dropped the tumbler: it shattered in the teak sink.

"A Protestant cultural victory . . . nicked the Book of Kells too . . . how goes it girl?"

"Fine."

He looked at her for a moment in silence and then said: "I like you Lynam."

"You don't and it's reciprocal."

Blinking oddly Gallagher ran his tongue round his upper lip and asked: "Why?"

"Boasting your kills; sickening."

"That a fact?"

Gallagher looked at her, his eyes moving slowly from her legs up her body to her face. "Contrary bitch . . . you preach killing and puke on killers . . . two-faced . . . you're like your old man Lynam, a Republican fraud."

He moved towards the door, turned as he opened it and said: "One thing, Mise Eire nua,* a dodgy move . . ." he flicked his pistol, "and I'll be watching . . . I don't trust you."

When Gallagher had left Lynam said quietly: "Nor I, myself."

Passing the table as Caldwell poured whiskey, Gallagher said: "Enjoy it, Sir."

"I'll try," Caldwell said.

Leonard had pulled an ornate chair into the shuttered bay window, a solitary audience, aware of murmurs and movement round the table, the faces imprinted on his mind by the initial exchange. As time passed he would get to know each face in more detail, and cold action if it had to come would be that much more awful. He was aware of tension in himself as he listened to the McAleers' hammering above, and imagined the guttural roar of pigs and Saracens which would arrive from Lisnaskea within fifteen minutes or less.

Now as he saw Gallagher come padding down the room he realised that he was glad to see him. He had argued strongly with Burke against taking him on this job, pointing out that he was epileptic, and might prove unpredictable. "You'll be glad of him," Burke had said. Gallagher approached, leaned towards Leonard and said quietly:

"Heard Lynam say to the daughter 'if there's anythin' I can do.'"

"They were at college together."

Gallagher stood alongside Leonard watching the table: "Smug . . . look at them . . . we should smash something . . . make them dance on the table, face the wall with their arms out."

"Pointless Jack, relax."

"I will."

Without warning Gallagher moved from the bay window towards bookshelves on either side of the fireplace that went from floor to ceiling. He stood there for a minute or so reading titles. He then put his pistol on the high mantelpiece, took out a book and read aloud: "*The Un-finished War*, by Eric Moore Ritchie."

He opened the book and read from the fly leaf: "The drama of Anglo-German Conflict in Africa in relation to the future of the British Empire . . . eight maps, published London, 1940 . . . includes campaigns in East Africa, Cameroons and Togoland."

---

* The modern Kathleen ni Houlihan

Gallagher paused and said: "Or: who owns the Nig Nogs, their nuts and their nickel."

He put back Eric Moore Ritchie, took down another book and again read aloud: "*Pig Sticking or Hog Hunting*, by Sir Robert Baden-Powell. A complete account for sportsmen and others, published London, 1824."

Gallagher looked at the Colonel and asked: "Enoch's great-granddaddy?"

He replaced Baden-Powell and said: "Nothing in our culture to match that . . . makes you feel inferior . . . humble . . . we've a long way to go . . . we bog, we pig-in-the-parlour Irish . . . yes, Sir, a long way to go."

He picked up a nearby chair, moved towards the table and sat, placing the chair between the Colonel and Boyd-Crawford.

"Would you like to pour me a dram, Sir?"

"Of course," the Colonel said evenly.

The Colonel poured a generous measure.

"You buy Irish?"

"Northern Irish," Canon Plumm said.

"We know; they boast no natives near the mash, we have a long list of all such firms . . . I'll not discriminate . . . your good health."

Gallagher drank and said: "You're American Sir?"

"That is correct."

"Caldwell . . . Fermanagh stock . . . good planter name . . . Nixon too . . . great people . . . must make you feel proud . . . kinship with high office . . . doing a book on the troubles, Professor?"

"Research."

"Into what?"

"Ulster under Elizabeth the First."

"The Virgin Queen in Ulster?"

"She didn't come here."

"That a fact. No virgin either, was she? . . . But she could pick good butchers . . . men with big swords . . . big cannon balls . . . still does . . . nice day for killing . . . that's what the Paras said in Derry . . . Lizzie II's high-jumping men . . . kill in Irish means Church . . . cuill a wood . . . darkness and death . . . might teach you some Irish tonight . . . a few sad songs . . . we've got hundreds . . . but this war is not merry . . . it's ugly, very very ugly, and we'll keep it ugly till it's over."

Gallagher drained the rest of his whiskey and looked in silence from face to face.

"I like talking, but you don't like what I say . . . it's the silence: I can tell . . . but as the night goes on the atmosphere may improve . . . we must hope for progress towards a general understanding of the underlying tensions that gulf our ancient cultures over seven centuries . . . we've been under . . . while you were lying."

Gallagher suddenly hacked a cross on the patina of the hunting table with the bead of his pistol. "The cross and the sword: the glory of Europe."

He then placed it sideways on the table and spun it with his forefinger. As it twirled he said to Caldwell: "This is what they do in your Westerns."

It stopped with the nozzle facing Alex Boyd-Crawford: "A fossil first!"

Gallagher took the hearing-aid clipped to Alex's handkerchief pocket and using it like a microphone asked loudly: "Do you think there's any hope for peace in our time Sir?"

Alex jerked, pulling out the earpiece as Gallagher's voice exploded in his left eardrum. With a sudden movement Gallagher whipped the hearing-aid from his jacket and smashed it on the hearth.

"Deaf anyway . . . all of you . . . you'll hear and listen before we quit."

Harriet broke the silence that followed: "I think he means it Nobby."

"Every word," Gallagher said.

Impassive the Colonel turned to Leonard: "Are you supposed to be in charge?"

Leonard did not reply and kept watching till he caught Gallagher's eye. Gallagher went to him and hunkered to listen.

"They'll be here soon."

"I can't sit."

"Then move around."

The door leading to the front hall opened. Pacelli McAleer's black head appeared. He grinned and came in, followed immediately by Pascal carrying a canvas bag. Pascal smiled at Leonard.

"That's it, all nailed, wired and locked."

Pacelli looked about the magnificent room with mock awe.

"Damn it, this is a powerful place."

"It's a palace, man, a palace."

"There's beds above big as a council kitchen."

"Sleep a whole fambley."

Both stared at a full length portrait of a judge in wig and red gown, a parchment in his hand.

"Like a house'd nourish ghosts," Pascal said.

Pacelli grinned. "Every class but the Holy Ghost."

As Lynam came in from the pantry Pascal groped in the canvas bag and began issuing tear-gas masks. As Gallagher slipped one over his head, leaving it hang, he said:

"Christmas in August; thank you Santy; you're full of surprises."

Leonard pointed towards the pantry door and said: "Out there boys: three doors. Check them."

The McAleers left followed by Gallagher. As Lynam moved to join Leonard she saw the hearing-aid smashed on the hearth.

"What provoked that?"

"Jack, tense like us . . . and a bit hungover."

"The daughter's pregnant."

Leonard did not react.

"Can we let her go?"

Leonard nodded.

"Now?"

"Not yet . . . How do you feel?"

"Scarified. What now?"

Leonard looked at his watch and said: "Forces from demi-paradise."

"How long?"

"They're late."

As he spoke they heard in the distance the heavy-engined growling of Saracens, jeeps and pigs in convoy a mile off or less. Leonard stood and went to the deep recess of the doorway giving to the long hall. Lynam followed and stood beside him, her heart jumping as the growl increased to a deep-throated roar. Gallagher was back in the room sitting in the chair Leonard had left, his pistol levelled at the table.

"The Army of the Empire full of beans and bitters, I could smell them coming."

It was five minutes before the armoured wagons rolled up the long avenue to the wide front, scattering gravel, screeching to a standstill. Silence, then the sound of massive, steel-plated doors clanging shut, voices, cryptic orders, a search-light beaming through the glass panels of the tall front door. Lynam was shaking so badly she felt her legs would give. She whispered to Leonard:

"Martin."

"Yes."

It was the first time she had used his name.

"I can't."

"Can't what?"

She was in deep shadow beside him.

"Kill."

"Can you do the other?"

"I think so."

Leonard nodded and said: "On you go."

She moved from the terror of keeping still into the beam of the Army search-light. She unlocked and unbolted the front door and went out. As she walked down the wide granite steps she was aware of shadows behind the Saracens and jeeps, the search-light tilted slightly to follow her descent. Pausing at a flagged break in the stairway and shading her eyes against the militant light she flung her voice towards the dark massive shapes.

"I want to speak to the Commanding Officer."

"Over here," a Sandhurst voice from the right said.

"Here," she said, replying to the voice.

There seemed a thirty-second delay before she heard the crunching of footsteps coming towards her over gravel, then the briskness of leather boots on stone. Then he was standing before her blocking the light, khaki, chain-mail pullover, wide leather belt, black beret. Looking straight at his chest she said:

"You know who we are?"

"I can guess."

"Who we're holding?"

"The staff phoned details."

"We want Daniel Quinn, Peter McIntyre and John Fannin brought here before tomorrow noon . . . also a helicopter."

He took out a notebook and began to write. She was tempted to say, can you not remember three names. She stayed silent. As he wrote the names he said: "Top-ranking chaps?"

"Trained killers like you."

Though his face was in shadow she could see his mouth stiffen.

"If not?"

"Can't you guess?"

"You'll have to say it."

"We execute one at noon, then one every six hours."

The officer repeated the names correctly, Lynam nodded and said: "Any shock approach and it's over."

Without warning he moved from light to darkness. As she turned to go up towards the front door the search-light went off. Now, she thought, expecting a dozen soldiers to stampede past her through the door like a pack of rugby forwards. Nothing happened. She reached the door, went in, closed, locked and rebolted it and heard Leonard's voice.

"Well?"

"He wrote down the names."

"Rommel himself, what else?"

"Nothing, he listened and vanished."

"What did it feel like?"

"Being on stage."

"You did well."

Lynam felt braced, exhilarated by action and wondered how it was that she was less afraid to face guns than fire them.

"What now?"

"Watch and wait."

"Before I went out I meant what I said."

"Won't come to that."

They went into the living room.

Alex Boyd-Crawford had moved from the table. Standing separately he seemed shocked, lost. Harriet went to him: He watched her mouth, lipreading.

"Dear Alex . . . come on, sit down."

"I'm all right."

"Are you frightened?"

"Perhaps they thought I looked dangerous . . . do you think I look dangerous?"

"You look very much the bookish, kindly, broken-down landlord."

Alex looked into those eyes he knew so well. "You were pointedly rude at dinner."

"What did I say?"

"You know well what you said."

She shrugged and muttered, "All true."

He attempted a smile. "Real truth, my dear, leads to crucifixions."

Harriet did not hear. She was looking from Gallagher to Leonard:

"What do they intend?"

"Red chap wants to shoot us all, that's very clear."

Without looking at him she said:

"If anything happens you, Alex – me – any – or all of us, I want you to know how very, very dear you are to me."

"And the word you avoid?"

"You are very, very dear to me."

Gallagher now moved towards Alex Boyd-Crawford and flicked his pistol at him, indicating the pantry door. Alex got up and shuffled out. Pacelli followed, taking the canvas bag into the pantry. As the door closed Harriet said to Millicent:

"I know it's happening, but I can't quite believe it."

It was Caldwell who replied.

"People near death experience similar feelings."

Harriet knew that he had said something apt, but the sound of his voice was so repugnant that she rejected the meaning. She watched for a response in her husband's face. There was none. Caldwell went on talking.

"As a child I remember being told how Christ had been crucified . . . an Irish servant girl . . . she told it well. I was stunned and said 'They were bad men . . . they should all be killed for doing that . . .' "

She glanced at Caldwell and saw him nod towards Leonard and Lynam:

"That's how they feel, about you people . . . they've never grown up . . . dangerous deadly children."

Without quite knowing what she meant Harriet said:

"Out of the mouths of babes."

In the pantry Alex stood watching, frightened. Gallagher motioned him to sit. Pacelli groped deep in the bag, took out a small chemist's bottle and shook ten tablets onto the table. Gallagher brought a glass of water and indicated that Alex was to take the tablets. When he hesitated, Gallagher swung the pistol across his chest above his shoulder to inflict Alex, knowing that he would put both hands up protectively, an old monkey, defenceless before elemental violence. Gallagher dropped his arm as Alex picked up the tablets and swallowed them with water.

"Open your mouth."

Alex could not hear. Gallagher opened his own mouth to demonstrate.

Alex complied. Gallagher peered in, nodded, and said loudly in Alex's ear: "Keep it shut inside . . . your mouth . . . understand?"

Alex nodded.

They went back to the living room. Gallagher pointed at one of the two deep, wing-backed chairs at the fireside. Alex sat in one chair, grey, blinking at his smashed hearing-aid on the tiled hearth. The faces round the table watched, deeply concerned, questioning. After the initial exchange of looks Alex kept his head averted. Harriet moved from the table to the chair opposite. When he looked up she was asking with her eyes if he was all right. He made a small gesture with his hands, which said: "It's nothing, I'm all right." She nodded, relieved.

Gallagher winked at Leonard as he moved to the deep recess of the doorway that led to the hall. He sat in shadow watching the front door. The light from the bay window showed up the unreal pallor of his profile. Statuesque he hugged his knees, rigid, like a dog who has scented quarry and waits for it to break.

Leonard had picked up a chair and was now sitting alongside Lynam. An hour passed in total silence. The fire went low. Pascal added a few logs to the fire-basket and examined the Tomkin clock on the mantel and went back to sit beside Pacelli on the magnificent couch in buttoned grey velvet. Side by side they maintained the same fixed half-smile as though permanently in front of a camera.

Alex had fallen asleep in fifteen minutes and, fifteen minutes later, Harriet. Millicent leafed unreading through a copy of *Homes and Gardens*. The Colonel and Caldwell were well through a bottle of Bushmills. Now and then they spoke in low voices. A helicopter passed low over the house, landed somewhere on the left. When the twirling blades stopped Lynam looked at Leonard who muttered:

"Couldn't be."

Another hour passed before Lynam said:

"This is deadly."

"What?"

"Everything. I feel sick."

"Nausea?"

"Not that sort."

"Want to read?"

"Couldn't."

"Drink?"

"Yes."

"Not wise."

"What is?"

"You should eat first."

"I know."

"Can you try?"

She shook her head. Leonard went to the table and picked up a tumbler. The Colonel poured a three-finger measure. Leonard nodded thanks, topped up with water and came back with the glass to Lynam. Without looking from the doorway Gallagher said:

"Slainte."

"Slainte leat," Lynam said.

"Want some?" Leonard asked Gallagher.

Gallagher shook his head.

"That's all you're getting," Leonard said to Lynam. "You must try to eat."

She nodded. He indicated Gallagher: "He needs it more than you and he's doing without."

"I don't need bloody lectures."

Five minutes later she said: "Sorry . . . I feel odd."

"Not my idea of a night out either."

"The last."

"It's going to work, I can feel it."

"How?"

"Instinct."

From the chair Alex Boyd-Crawford muttered indistinctly:

"October . . . no growth . . . must finish picking apples before the frost comes . . . they still bear . . . old and cankered but still bear. My leaky cider press . . . no matter . . . nothing matters . . . who's right? The Secretary . . . the tribal chain gangs . . . fraudulent . . . or maybe me . . . don't know . . . know nothing."

When he began to snore Harriet went to him and did something to make him stop.

For half an hour Lynam sipped the whiskey. The ticking of the Tomkin clock became more insistent. The room seemed to lengthen slowly. Then she became aware of gradual grotesque distortion as the living flesh of each face turned grey in a fixed grimace of death. For a minute she thought she would scream as her caged heart leaped in beating terror. Normality returned.

"Can't we do something?" she asked.

Leonard thought for a moment, then winked over at Pascal and made a blowing mime with his mouth into both hands. When Pascal looked doubtful Leonard winked encouragement. Pascal took a tin whistle out of the canvas bag. When he began to play the expression on the faces of both brothers changed to one of rapt involvement, as the single note clarity carried not only its own beauty but a racial memory, evocative as the fields, battles and defeats – the music celebrated or lamented. Watching the lack of effect the music had on those round the table and aware of its impact on herself Lynam understood again why the first Elizabeth had hung Irish pipers as felons. The colour of melody neutralised the creeping terror of this ending day and the day that had to come.

The seeming naïvety of Hugh and Rosie McAleer's two sons masked, she thought, deeper roots, a culture old as pastoral Europe, clamped by history to the dead autocracy of Rome and the arrogant mess of the British Raj, themselves swamped now by the tinfoil gleam of Americana and the creeping threat of Russian paralysis, all beliefs and systems blending as old cultures died, inevitable and melancholy as the music, as the drying of tributaries with the deepening of great rivers.

At the table the talk continued in low voices, Canon Plumm turning up cards, Millicent now asleep on her arms.

"Haunting," Caldwell said.

"Noise," the Colonel said.

"Very special."

"Repetitive I thought."

"Do you know the language?" the Canon asked.

"No but . . ."

"You'd like to?"

"It's the key."

"To what?" Canon Plumm muttered. "Bingo? Chicken in the rough, non-stop reels of jig-jig trash? The great, great show with endless whining lamentations manufactured by jackeens for plough-boys and shopgirls . . . what they want . . . what they get . . . what they deserve . . . Irish culture! My idea of hell."

Caldwell smiled: "God is not a proven Protestant, Canon!"

"Damnation for me," the Canon said, "if he's Roman Catholic."

"You grow a little acid, John," the Colonel said.

"Accurate and angry," the Canon said. "Hatred, they're good at that, and killing . . . they breed good killers, poor leaders."

Almost inaudibly Caldwell muttered, "Next to love the sweetest thing is hate."

The transistorised voice of a BBC news-reader came from the doorway. They paused, listening alert. It was too faint to hear.

"All so unfair," the Colonel said. "We were never absentees, my grandfather cut rents to half and nil during the famine, mortgaged the estate to feed tenants, Catholic and Protestant, one of my cousins signed the Treaty for the Irish side, Harriet's father was related through marriage to Lloyd George . . . lunacy."

He paused looking into his whiskey. "I knew Erskine well . . . a good actor . . . in his heart of hearts he didn't believe in nationalism any more than I do."

"Did he say so?" Caldwell asked.

"I could sense it . . . it's a disease."

"Sadly," Caldwell said, "most nations suffer from it."

"The cancer is in this room and may kill us shortly."

After a minute Caldwell asked: "Could we, should we try something?"

"If you want to die *now* Stuart, yes, but I think they'll let you go."

"It didn't sound . . ."

" 'Course they will . . . doesn't do to shoot Americans . . . ancient order . . . strong subscribers."

"No special preference for humble churchmen I expect?" Canon Plumm asked.

"I doubt it John."

Gallagher's voice came from the doorway, bleak as a Derry street in January: "Pity you're not a bishop, Sir."

In a very low voice the Colonel asked: "Could he have heard?"

"Apparently," Caldwell said.

"Unnatural."

"Every way," the Canon added.

Caldwell was about to say something when the volume of Gallagher's transistor was turned to a news-reader's voice in mid-sentence.

". . . at the Armstrong Estate in County Fermanagh the Army are standing by. The kidnappers are demanding the release of three leading Provisionals from the Maze camp at Belfast. They want them brought to Inver Hall by helicopter. If this demand is not met, they say they will kill the first hostage at noon tomorrow and thereafter one every six hours. Colonel Armstrong served under General Montgomery in the African campaign and was awarded the D.S.O. Also hostage is Alexander Boyd-Crawford, member of the old Stormont Parliament for over twenty years. An American professor and a Protestant clergyman are among the six being held."

Gallagher switched off as the news-reader switched to the next topic. All awake and listening in silence except Alex. Harriet was the first to speak. To Millicent she said:

"We don't exist dear."

"I noticed," Millicent said.

"I published two poems in a school magazine over forty years ago, but I expect that's hardly newsworthy . . . but you dear are a Bachelor of Arts."

She paused, looking from face to face: "Bachelor? . . . Should it not be a Spinster of Arts . . . sounds miserable . . . dog's nice . . . who likes bitch . . . bulls are magnificent . . . cows stupid . . . boars fierce . . . sows eat their young . . . the language itself is perverse to the female . . . men only . . . we're under sentence and the BBC don't know we exist."

Harriet's voice was a great deal less slurred than earlier, but she looked haggard . . . Suddenly she asked Leonard: "What have you done to Alex?"

Leonard did not reply.

"He's a light sleeper . . . drugged him?"

Again no reply.

Harriet went to the table and held a tumbler towards the whiskey bottle. The Canon poured a measure. She held the glass under the nose of the bottle till he splashed in another finger. Millicent was again trying to sleep with her head on the table. Harriet went round and whispered to her. Millicent got up and went to the wing-backed chair. Before sitting Harriet stood looking at the McAleers with detached curiosity much as people at a zoo examine creatures they have never seen before. The McAleers looked at each other, smiled, looked back at Harriet who continued to stare, till Pascal asked:

"Can you see horns Ma'am?"

"Pardon?" Harriet asked.

Pacelli said: "My feet are cleft, but we kicked football with the best!"

"Monaghan Minors '71."

Harriet understood nothing of what they said and muttered vaguely, "Yes," shook her head, sat down and turned to Canon Plumm.

"Was I rude tonight at dinner John?"

The Canon mumbled: "No consequence."

"I'm sorry."

"Nothing . . . nothing at all."

Both the Colonel and Caldwell were aware that another apology was due. It was not forthcoming. Silence again and through it Lynam saw Millicent looking steadily into her eyes. She returned the look without hostility until Millicent turned her head and closed her eyes.

"Can't you let her go?"

"Who?"

"The daughter."

"Not yet."

Leonard took the empty glass from her hand, put it on the floor and said: "Your hands are ice cold."

"I know."

Quarter of an hour passed. Without looking at him Lynam said: "I want to make love."

Leonard did not reply till she asked: "Can we?"

"You're joking."

"Don't you want?"

It seemed to Leonard that the pitch of her voice had increased. He said: "Talk low."

"What?"

"Impossible."

She nodded towards the pantry and said: "In there."

There was a minute's silence before Leonard replied.

"Madness."

"I can't hear you."

"Insane."

"Sane . . . we're dead."

"Far from it . . . very far."

"Are you afraid?"

Leonard leaned very close to her and said: "Your voice."

"What about it?"

"It's carrying."

"Who cares?"

With a movement of his eyes Leonard indicated Gallagher.

"You might tomorrow."

"There's no tomorrow."

Leonard shrugged. The whiskey and seven hours of extreme tension had begun to tell.

"Try to sleep," he said.

She lay back in the chair and closed her eyes without answering. He was right. An absurd provocative notion which she would have welched on had he agreed. Why? To tempt him, humiliate herself, goad Gallagher, shock the atavistic McAleers, confirm the listening table in the poor opinion already held or the reflex of a sad song and the bitter knowledge of betrayal, the total certainty that this was the last night of her life. Pointless trying to disentangle. Then she was in the pantry with Leonard, the door locked and she could hear Gallagher outside whispering to the McAleers:

"The Hound of Ulster is screwing the bitch from the Pale . . . grave dereliction of duty boys . . . they should be shot both of them; I'll see to it when the job's over!" Then she saw Gallagher go up to Alex Boyd-Crawford and shoot him twice through the head. Terrified she unlocked the pantry door that led to the hall, ran down the wide flags, opened the front door and out. It was grey daylight. As she ran down the granite steps she heard glass shatter. A single shot pierced a burning pain in her womb. She fell. As she tried to get up she was kneeling facing the bay window looking into Gallagher's cold face. He was pointing his pistol directly at her. She screamed.

Leonard had such a tight grip on her wrist that it hurt. She was trembling. Everyone in the room was looking at her except Alex Boyd-Crawford who was deep asleep. Leonard said:

"It's all right."

She saw the clock on the mantel – 1:55 – and realised she had been asleep for almost an hour.

"Did I . . .?"

The faces at the table looked away, answering her unasked question. Harriet stood and moved towards the pantry door. Leonard said:

"Go with her . . . and when you come back, eat, or take a pill and sleep."

She could sense real irritation in his voice. She got up and followed the

Colonel's wife into the pantry. As the door closed Leonard motioned Pascal to stand alongside the door. The Colonel's wife had gone into the cloakroom toilet off the pantry. As she waited Lynam could hear, or imagined she could hear, retching. On the panelled wall someone had pinned recipes from newspapers and magazines. She tried to read one of them. The words had no meaning. She heard the toilet flush. The cloakroom door opened. Footsteps and the scrape of a chair and Harriet's voice saying:

"Do sit, please."

Lynam hesitated, then complied. It was a request more than an order, and she felt weak. She sat at the other end of the table facing the older woman, avoiding her eyes.

"Look at me please."

Lynam looked.

"Will you . . . they . . . shoot us all dead?"

"Depends."

"They won't do what you ask."

"They might."

Harriet shook her head.

"Nobby's not important . . . old family but not important . . . you're off target dear . . . I know a dozen houses more suitable for this operation."

There was a considerable silence before Harriet began again.

"Odd how floods, bombs, hurricanes, earthquakes happen elsewhere to others . . . never to oneself . . . I wasn't sick with fright in there, I don't care when I die provided it's quick . . . you know Milly?"

"We shared French tutorials."

"She's pregnant."

"I know."

"Told you?"

"Yes."

"Will she be sacrificed to Republican gods?"

"No."

"That's something . . . I suppose."

Harriet studied the pitted quarry tiles on the floor for thirty seconds. Her face had the stillness and depth of an El Greco portrait, hurt, haunted staring eyes which a faint sudden smile now altered to subtle knowingness as she looked up to speak.

"French?"

"Sorry?"

"You did French?"

"Yes."

"What else?"

"Irish."

"You know David Greene?"

"Yes."

"Wonderful beard."

"He's a good scholar."

"Do you like Dylan Thomas?"

"Not as much as Kavanagh."

"Really?"

Lynam tapped the table then nodded towards the dresser and said: "I prefer this to that."

Harriet did not understand.

"Which to what?"

"Scrubbed deal to a Welsh dresser."

She smiled for the first time and said: "Yes, Milly read English and French . . . but no real empathy . . . *Henry the Fifth* troubles me . . . do you like it?"

"No."

"Nor do I . . . inexcusable of Shakespeare, bad as the Old Testament . . . reeks of blood and empire . . . Nobby loves it . . . you're like a cousin of mine, Dolly Travers, incredibly like . . . dead poor Dolly, happy life . . . never married. Thought she wasn't happy but a hundred times more so than . . . I feel quite exhilarated at the idea of sudden extinction . . . Mother was accomplished . . . the piano . . . played with Paderewski in a drawing room once . . . I was a child of eight . . . And Paderewski said after it was the most beautiful rendering of a Chopin Prelude he had ever heard. Poor mother was radiant. Everyone clapped. Father was Welsh . . . shrewd at business. His money kept this place going . . . his money . . . my money . . ."

Harriet paused and studied Lynam for a moment.

"We're sister Celts, you and I . . . I can sing a little . . . though not much to sing about these days . . . Would you like to get me a glass of water . . . please."

Lynam brought the glass of water.

"After Derry I wept, you know, and Nobby was overwhelmed . . . true

. . . he's human . . . all of us . . . very human . . . so terribly sad what we do to each other don't you think? He tried to phone Frank Carrington . . . couldn't get through . . . retired Colonels in Fermanagh don't count for much . . . rather silly really holding us . . . he's liked . . . always Catholics on the staff . . . and what you're doing won't be popular with Catholics or Protestants . . . of that I'm sure . . . but you're here and that's it . . . war is a series of unfortunate blunders . . . like marriage."

She inhaled deeply on a cigarette, exhaling through her mouth and nose. She then finished the glass of water.

"That red-headed youth, such astonishing energy . . . such hatred, are you like that?"

"No."

"Do you love?"

Again Harriet asked Lynam: "Do you?"

"Do you?"

Harriet studied the floor as though she had forgotten Lynam's presence. When she began it was as though she was talking to herself.

"Once upon a time a warrior went to war. When he came back he woke half dreaming in a grey dawn distressed and crying for a comrade who had died."

She paused for ten seconds, looked up and said: "You can fight the living my dear, not the dead . . . marriage is such a cruel trap for some that they long for . . ."

She searched about her memory and found:

"That high capital where Kingly death
Keeps his pale Court in beauty and decay.

Shelley, poor boy . . . why did I tell you that?"

"We're both dead."

"Yes . . . Nobby says I'm maudlin . . . would you like some coffee? . . . I would."

"Where?"

Harriet pointed.

"In that cupboard, instant, the kettle's there . . . power point beside the sink, we keep it here . . . there's a mile of corridor to the kitchen proper . . . What happened to Maggie Reilly and the Johnstons?"

"Pardon?"

"The staff?"

"They were locked out."

"Ah! . . . Were they frighened I wonder?"

"I hope not."

"You're a feeling girl . . . I could sense that . . . Milly's cold . . . my own flesh and blood . . . sad."

Lynam moved about making the coffee.

"Your mother alive?"

"Yes."

"Father?"

"Yes."

"Family?"

"Two brothers."

"Like you?"

"Apolitical."

There was a kind of silence until Harriet broke it by asking: "What killed you?"

"Rejection."

"Always the same story . . . one thing puzzles me, I can understand those who want to kill themselves, not those who kill others . . . you look all wrong for the part . . . Nobby's professional . . . he looks right don't you think? . . . Hatred is so sad . . . personal hatred I know only too well, but to hate an entire people, race, sect or class, is so blind, so stupid, so unending, so universal, it makes one despair . . . When that red youth smashed Alex's hearing-aid I knew then it was serious."

The electric kettle began to boil. Lynam moved to switch it off.

"Will they kill Caldwell the American?"

"I doubt it."

"Politically embarrassing."

Lynam nodded.

"They're embarrassing anyway, most of them . . . he's a world authority you know . . . medieval military manoeuvres or something incredible . . . prestigious fellowship, a year's sabbatical, New England University . . . Divorce . . . said his wife was beautiful, but lacked a mind . . . I think he thinks I have no mind . . . could be right, I behave oddly at times . . . Nobby thinks he's a genius . . . met at the British Embassy in New York last

year, some military memorial thing. John Freeman introduced them . . . I
think he's illiterate – not Freeman, Caldwell."

Harriet stubbed her cigarette on an ashtray and asked: "Do you think he's
queer?"

Lynam could not answer. Harriet went on: "You can't tell nowadays . . .
nothing's certain. Has God lost interest do you think?"

"I don't believe in God."

"Nor do I . . . Are the two dark ones brothers?"

"Yes."

"Don't look quite the full shilling do they? You've put down eleven cups,
that's nice."

"Yes."

"Good idea. You don't say much . . . perhaps you dislike me?"

"No."

"I embarrass you?"

"No."

"What do you feel?"

Lynam looked into the liquid lostness of those brown unhappy eyes in
that blurred finely modelled face. In ten minutes she seemed to understand
the oblique confusion and compassion of this strange woman's mind better
than she had ever understood her own mother.

"I must know."

"Pity," Lynam said. "For all of us."

Harriet continued to stare and and the subtlety Lynam was aware of
earlier returned.

"But you're here to kill if need be."

Lynam shook her head.

"Were you forced to come?"

"I can't explain . . . sorry."

"Your hands are trembling."

"Yes."

"Are you afraid?"

"Yes."

"I fear death too . . . did you believe me when I said I didn't?"

"Not quite."

The door opened. Pascal stood smiling. Harriet stood and left the pantry.
There was silence in the long room as Lynam placed the tray of coffee on

the table. Harriet took a cup and passed the others round. Lynam supplied Pascal, Pacelli, Leonard and Gallagher. As she sat beside Leonard he said:

"You were a while out there."

"Yes."

"Talking?"

"Listening."

"Can you eat?"

As she looked at the food without interest, Pascal came over, took a silver serving spoon and put some potato and cauliflower salad on a plate. He pointed at the cold pork, tongue and underdone beef.

"No meat, Pascal . . . thanks."

"Sure?"

"Certain."

As Pascal spooned mayonnaise she glanced round at Leonard. He was staring straight ahead avoiding her eyes. Deliberately? She moved to join the brothers, Pacelli shifting on the couch, tucking his legs under tailorwise. As she ate they smiled encouragement. The food was distasteful and their concern overwhelming. It made her feel unworthy, fraudulent. As the feeling increased she stopped eating. The plate began to tremble in her hand. Pascal took it from her and pulled up a chair to screen her from the table.

"Ate a lough more Bella. The grub'll steady you."

As she began to pick at the food Pascal said: "You were a while with the ould one."

She nodded.

"Seems odd. Touched?"

"Strange," Lynam said.

"You'd know that from her talk."

In a very low voice Lynam asked: "Did I scream over there?"

"A whimper . . . nothing."

"You dropped off."

"Before that?" she asked.

The brothers looked at each other pretending not to understand. Pascal shook his head: "A dream I'd say."

"Aye, you were asleep," Pacelli explained.

She looked from one to the other gratefully and said: "You lie beautifully . . . both of you . . . Are you boys afraid?"

"Scared stiff," Pascal said. "The stomach's in knots."

"Constant fright," Pacelli added. "Natural."

"You don't show it."

"We don't let on . . . it's there."

"Keep smilin' . . . stick together."

Pacelli nodded towards the hunting table.

"You're fit to talk to those folk."

"Martin too, if he wanted."

"And Jack's afeered of nothin' in this world . . . go to hell for his friends."

"He is hell," she said.

As she looked over, Gallagher's left hand went up slowly. He tapped his left ear, then pointed upwards with his forefinger, eyes dilated, a tense listening image.

The chalk-white face turned towards Leonard in the bay window. Leonard went and hunkered close.

"Hear!?"

"Nothing."

A minute or more passed before Gallagher said: "Rats on the back roof, four or more . . . hear!"

As Leonard shook his head a slate, scrape or noise of slip came down distinctly through the house. Five seconds of utter silence followed. Leonard looked towards the McAleers and pointed at Alex Boyd-Crawford. The brothers moved as one carrying the inert body to the main hall. This took place so promptly that there was a pause before it registered that something serious had happened and was about to change everything. Leonard moved back to the bay window. Lynam sat up very straight knowing what might now occur. Muzzy from sleep Harriet stood.

"What are you . . .?"

Half stumbling, almost sleep-walking, she moved towards the door.

"What are you doing with Alex?"

Gallagher blocked the doorway and gave a small flicking movement with his left hand in much the same way as parents dismiss small children who have broken their concentration. Harriet kept coming.

"I am not afraid, and will not sit by while . . ."

Gallagher's pistol whipped across her face so quickly that those in the room saw only the effect of the impact. Suddenly she was on her knees facing the fireplace, a welt from eye to cheek-bone, blood in her mouth.

The Colonel was on his feet, veins swelling in his neck. Gallagher said, levelling at him:

"If you want."

As he spoke two pistol shots sounded in the hall. Looks of electrified horror on all faces. Gallagher motioned the Colonel to sit by pointing with his free hand.

Still on her knees, Harriet seemed to be looking for something on the floor, a denture at the leg of the hunting table. Crying, Millicent recovered these for her mother. The Colonel and Canon Plumm helped her to the couch. From the hall the sound of the bolts being withdrawn, the door opening. The search-light was switched on, then switched off as the door was closed and rebolted. The McAleers came back into the room unsmiling.

Sick, ashamed, Lynam turned her back and stood looking at the design of the tapestry curtains in the high bay window. It was swimming before her eyes. Then Leonard's voice saying to the Colonel:

"You've got one minute from now to tell them outside and get back, and they've got three to get clear . . . one more sound after, anywhere in or near the house, and we execute the next."

The Colonel went out. It was already breaking light. Under the bay window he saw Alex's prone body, a canvas bag tied over the head. The Colonel spoke with the Commanding Officer and returned at once. When he came in Millicent was placing a cushion under her mother's head. She had replaced the dentures and was holding a napkin over the gash in her mother's face.

Lynam went out to the hall. Gallagher saw her face as she passed and said: "Necessary."

She did not answer. She stood in the middle of the hall, the bulk of the armoured cars distinct through the front door. Near dawn. She could not display weakness in the room and would need time for composure to return.

"Don't stand there," Gallagher said.

She moved to the cover of the door opposite. The thing was to exclude totally the reality of nightmare that seemed to grow with the breaking light. In the other doorway Leonard was whispering with Gallagher, both checking their wristwatches, one looking up the dark stairwell, the other watching the door, both tense.

Coolfada . . . the smell of the sea, the astonishing greenness of grass that grew in lumps from the thatch, the peace of the sky and all the cats named after saints and townlands. People came to the house every evening because her grandmother had the cure for shingles. Once she was allowed to sit on the creepie and watch. The old woman placed twigs in the glowing turf, withdrew them glowing and went round a woman's stricken face half an inch from the skin saying prayers in Irish. One summer's day, a neighbour man came with a mongrel terrier. When he was inside the terrier chased and caught a white kitten and crushed it with a snap. She ran with it into her grandmother, screaming, warm blood on her hands. Her grandmother wrapped the kitten in brown paper, washed her hands and went out to the potato patch. As she buried it, she said:

"Some dogs kill cats, some men kill other men . . . the sea, hunger, disorder, old age, aye and a broken heart, night brings day brings night . . . death comes . . . don't cry love, it's life."

The one image of Coolfada that she had wanted to forget had jerked back now with sickening vividness. The blood was on her hands now as it had been twenty years ago. If Coolfada conjured images of blood and death, there was no refuge in memory. Her eyes were closed. She did not see Leonard cross the hall. She heard him say:

"You'll have to come back . . . deadly out here."

When she looked he thumbed at the wide stairwell leading up into the darkness of the house.

"Did he have to be so brutal?"

"She's all right . . . sitting up."

Leonard waited. Lynam ran the back of her hand up both cheeks to ensure that they were dry and went back to the living room. Gallagher had moved the two chairs from the bay window and now swung back the heavy curtains. He unclasped the shutters. As he folded them back Pascal switched off the lights. A dim light filled the room. Millicent stood, her body shaking, as she said directly to Gallagher:

"Bastard, sickly cowardly murdering bastard."

Suddenly she turned to Lynam.

"Are these your friends? A one-eyed dummy, two imbeciles and a sadist . . . ! My Christ, you're sick . . . ! All of you . . . sick!!"

The effect on Gallagher was almost physical. For ten seconds he could scarcely speak with fury. The first words coming in a whisper: "Stuffed bitch . . . your mind's feeble as your tongue."

Suddenly he shouted: "Why are we sick? Come on, answer. Why?! Let's hear, any, all of you . . . come on . . . why?! Answer . . . you know it . . . you are it."

In the silence that followed Leonard said quietly to the Colonel: "Your wife was foolhardy Sir. Lucky she's alive."

"That's arguable," Harriet muttered.

"I would advise you," Leonard said, "to warn your daughter that she has no licence to insult . . . that, for the time being, is our privilege."

The Colonel did not look at Leonard as he asked: "Is this how you treat prisoners . . . wage war?"

Before Leonard could respond Gallagher cut in, his face rigid with hatred: "You talk of war and prisoners? You!"

He flicked his pistol.

"When we look for common rights the way you got your empire, all your lackeys in the Press and Commons yap; hang them, hang them, hang them. Mother of Parliaments? A fat knacker's wife who's flayed half the bloody world . . . and you think the world is with you? Such shits they say . . . such lying bullying hypocrites . . . with your mock monarchy and zoo-keeping dukes and public schools, all stiff upper prick and regiments of back-street rats and buggering Horatios, you have deported, degraded, starved and tortured us and still do . . . and no apology and never will . . . but smirk and snigger at stupid Paddy, dirty Paddy,

Ugly superstitious Paddy,

Paddy drop-out, Paddy drunk

Paddy half-wit, Paddy Punk."

Gallagher moved round the table as the words came savaging from his mouth. He paused at the end of the sideboard beneath an oil painting of a First World War Brigadier. Suddenly he elbowed a magnificent oriental soup tureen. It went sliding, spinning, down the long sideboard, scattering ornamental plates and silver before it shattered to the floor. With a back whip of his pistol he tore the face of the Brigadier.

"You smash us for seven hundred years, you haven't quit yet and you wonder why we hate you . . . 'hate' is a nothing word for what we feel."

The Colonel looked from Gallagher's livid face to the torn portrait and the smashed ware. A spitting mini-Hitler . . . pointless to argue with such hysterical hatred. As he thought this he heard himself say coldly:

"That was an Irishman leading other Irishmen."

"To free small nations! . . . don't make me vomit."

Gallagher returned to the doorway. Pascal and Leonard took up screened positions at the edge of the window. Pacelli sat at the far end of the room near the pantry door. Lynam sat in the corner alongside the Sheraton table near Leonard.

A quarter of an hour passed in silence. Nothing but the ticking of the clock and the Gothic screech of a peacock. Harriet stood. Sound of smaller birds, the first signs of light. She knew this from innumerable dawns. She walked to the bay window, saw Alex's prone body, then looked away to the lake beyond the half circle of military wagons. Grey, utterly still, mist hung, autumnal as though waiting and aware of the coming winter. There were a few faint stars very high, and faint tinctures of pink and red. She had seen a painting once in someone's house all grey and black and although she knew something awful had happened, and that something more awful was impending, she forced herself to say:

"Daybreak . . . Sunday . . . reminds me of a painting I saw in someone's house. We sleep when the world's most beautiful."

"I wouldn't stand there," Gallagher said.

"Will you smash me again if I do?"

"Dangerous," Leonard said.

"Dangerous?"

Harriet looked with incredulity at the pistols and smiled: "Quite a sense of humour . . . I like that."

She turned from the window and looked towards the corner. Lynam was glad of the grey, half light. Harriet quoted: "*L'aurore grelottante en robe rose et verte*. How are you?"

"How are you?" Lynam asked, scarcely audible.

Harriet's voice wobbled as she said: "Alive . . . but lacking a dear friend."

She went back to the table and sat close to the wing-backed chair occupied by Millicent who said: "I wouldn't talk to them."

Harriet stared at the dead ashes in the grate and spoke with unexpected edge: "Alex was dragged out and shot dead while two military gentlemen sat by."

"Mother, please."

"Doing nothing . . . there are times when one must do something regardless of military handbooks and personal safety."

Caldwell said, very quietly: "You don't seem to . . ."

"I understand precisely what's going on, and what's likely to occur."

In the silence that followed Millicent covered her face and kept it covered while she cried. Harriet put a hand on her daughter's head and looked over at Lynam. When the effect of the crying and Harriet's eyes became unbearable Lynam stood and whispered to Leonard:

"For Christ's sake Martin."

Without looking at Lynam, or back at the table, Leonard said: "She can go . . . and the American."

From the doorway Gallagher frowned and shook his head. Leonard shrugged much as to say "they're going anyway." There was a silence before they adjusted to what had been said.

"Now?" the Colonel asked.

"Yes."

Millicent stood. When she had kissed her father Harriet held her face for a moment, looking as though trying to read or recall something. Very gently, visibly moved, she kissed her daughter's forehead as a mother kisses the head of a very small child. In silence Caldwell shook hands in turn with the Colonel and Canon Plumm. Harriet had walked to the corner, her back to the table. Caldwell approached to make his farewell. She took his hand without turning to look at his face.

Gallagher stood to let them into the hall, followed them to the front door, opened it, relocking and rebolting when they were gone.

From where he stood Leonard could see them go down the granite staircase, across the half circle of gravel and out of sight behind the armoured wagons. Harriet came back to the table and lit a cigarette. The Colonel moved to the fireplace and stood looking at the Tomkin clock as though it contained some secret. The hands read 5:55. Canon Plumm, despite his fleshy face and bulky frame, seemed greyer, older, more exhausted than either the Colonel or his wife, as though he now fully realised that his calling would count for nothing in this ruthless double siege.

Gallagher went towards the pantry. Pascal moved to take his place in the doorway. Above the wood across the dark water the mist fell away leaving one bright star adrift in a metallic sky. Morning star. Lynam approached Leonard. Looking out and up she was aware of a numbness that swamped the nightmare hours and the coming fear. She wanted to pray but had forgotten how to begin or who to pray to . . . Lord have mercy, Christ have mercy.

"Remember Benediction?"

Leonard nodded and said:

"I used to sit and look at someone's back waiting for the priest to say 'Morning star' . . . That I understood, nothing else."

"Pagan at heart."

Silence.

"It's quiet."

"Very."

"Did it affect you?"

"What?"

"The crying?"

"What do you think?"

"I think you must be very strong or very cold."

Leonard shrugged slightly and indicated Pascal in the doorway.

"They're strong . . . they've got God on their side, the Mammy and Pearse's ghost."

"Gallagher . . . he's terrifying."

Leonard did not answer and she said: "Psychopathic."

"I can't judge . . . I'm here . . . so are you."

"Why?"

Leonard shook his head as though the effort of answering such a complex question was impossible. A tired priest of violence, she thought, who had ceased to believe in the Creed. As he looked at her now she got a sense of something else; enigmatic, obscure, almost frightening.

"You are annoyed?"

"No."

"By what I said."

"No."

"Last night, you're still angry?"

Again he shook his head. She remembered how he had said Gallagher would not waste words when it came to killing. Gallagher's racial and political bitterness were genuine. He was a natural mechanism of terror and disorder. He did not, never would, want peace and harmony. When it ended, and if the Leonards had control, they would despatch him. She realised now that Leonard's silence was more sinister, more frightening than Gallagher's savage outbursts. His surface warmth and ease masked an inner detachment, clinical, ice-cold. For the first time she felt utterly alone.

She looked back from the window. The Canon had his elbows on the table, eyes closed, supporting his head with his hands. The Colonel's wife was again in the wing-backed chair, the Colonel sitting alongside her. He was holding one of her hands in both of his. Lynam turned away, aware that she was intruding on something very personal. Harriet could sense emotion in her husband's voice as he said now:

"Always separate."

She thought before replying.

"Very . . . I understand."

"I did say at the time and since that if ever . . ." He paused.

"You proved less than husband and lover?"

The Colonel nodded and said: "You were free."

"Free?"

"Yes."

"I died that morning as a woman . . . you do understand that?"

Tears from the blood-hound eyes came down each side of his nose, disappearing in the grey, clipped moustache as he began to speak again unevenly.

"I was . . . am . . . abject . . . can say only . . . that despite . . . my very deepest truest love for you . . ." He shook his head. "No words."

"Beyond words . . . I loved my illusion of you Nobby."

"If we must die, can we die friends."

"Well said."

"You don't mock?"

Harriet shook her head.

"Friendship is better than love . . . much better."

Again, as she had kissed her daughter, she now kissed her husband on the forehead, as humans kiss their beloved dead.

The pantry door opened. Gallagher came padding quietly down the long room. He had washed his face, damped and combed his hair and seemed, Lynam thought, alert, unafraid, almost celebratory. As he approached he said:

"Reading my face . . . what's written there Lynam? Thug? Criminal?"

The repulsion she had felt watching him come down the room must have been evident. Gallagher smiled and asked: "Can we kiss?"

"Cut it Jack."

"I am Ireland. She loves me, she should show it."

Cunning logic to shame and establish her in brutal collusion before watching eyes from the table and wing-backed chair. Leonard had warned, and kept his back to her now as the warning stood roosting in smiling blackmail. She caught Pascal's and then Pacelli's eye. If she refused and it caused Gallagher to explode it would throw Leonard and the brothers on a tight-rope. Leonard glanced at her and his expression read, "It's nothing, do it and be done with it." As she hesitated, Gallagher said, for her ears only:

"You wanted to screw with him four hours back."

His voice normal he said again: "A kiss . . . no more."

As he neared she felt her stomach revulse. When their lips touched he caught her chin, inserting his tongue, his eyes open, staring. When it was over she felt defiled as though she had been kissed by a grinning corpse. She wanted to scream and claw with her nails at the mocking face. With a tremendous effort she controlled the churning in her stomach and kept her expression impassive. Emotionless, Leonard asked:

"Coffee? Can you make some?"

Lynam went straight to the pantry, aware of Harriet's watching eyes as she walked. She stood trembling at the teak sink and rinsed her mouth out. "Why am I trembling?" she thought. "Death might be three hours away, less." It was unlike her that self-control could be shattered by a sick Judas kiss, unreal that she should react soul and body with such revulsion. Intuitively she could sense an otherness in that kiss, something coming, hidden; what? Gallagher, none of them could tell what would happen before or at midday. Filling the kettle it seemed to her that the woman she had both liked and pitied last night now seemed enormously enviable. The victims had a dignity. She had joined with executioners, the army of the damned. As she thought this she knew the thought was treason. Waiting for the kettle to boil, Lynam took out the pistol and looked at it without the repulsion she had felt the evening before.

At the window Leonard asked: "Did you have to do that?"

"She's soft, snivelling at the first whiff of action."

"That didn't help."

"I'm inhuman, a mindless killer, she said it, meant it . . . what's she? . . . a hysterical, gutless, middle-class yacker . . . and what's Burke at, sending her?"

"Good question."

"She could wreck it."

Leonard shook his head.

"I won't let her," Gallagher said.

Leonard felt the impact of this jostle. He did not respond. Gallagher would never lead. He had the racial defect to a marked degree; too personal. It coloured his every word and act. Deliberateness was professional and although he had an ulcer from worry, slept badly and doubted much, Leonard knew that he was professional and said now:

"Leave her be, Jack, she'll learn."

A BBC station wagon came up the avenue, bounced onto the lawn and drove behind the half circle of Army wagons. Well in view, two men got up on the roof of the station wagon, mounted a tripod camera and faced it towards the house.

"The eyes of the world," Gallagher said.

Leonard nodded. Gallagher looked at his watch; it was 9:45.

"If the boys aren't here by twelve?"

"We go ahead."

"We?"

Again Leonard knew what Gallagher was implying. Apart from five kills in action, he had executed, with cold efficiency, a Belfastman found guilty of treason. Now he presumed Leonard would ask him to execute the old man lying drugged under the bay window, half suggesting that he would use his position as leader to deputise the ugly work.

"I'll do that," Leonard said.

"You will?"

Leonard nodded. Gallagher seemed surprised.

"Whatever you say Commandant."

It was whatever he said and Gallagher would have to see unmistakably that he meant and did what he said. Three words prompted by an oblique question. He was now committed to action which he knew he could and would do against the instinct which prompted avoidance.

Canon Plumm was alerted by the sound of the arriving station wagon. He looked at the time and then went to the Colonel and said something. The Colonel nodded and pointed towards a row of bookshelves. The Canon read the titles for a while, then took down a book and leafed through it for five minutes. Lynam came in with coffee and passed it around. As they sipped coffee the Canon said:

"Sunday: I'd like to give a brief reading, do you mind?"

"Fine," Leonard said.

The Canon sat at the head of the table, the Colonel on one side, Harriet on the other. He put on spectacles, cleared his throat and read:

"A heavy yoke is upon the children of Adam, from the day of their coming out of their mother's womb, until the day of their burial into the mother of all. Fear not the sentence of death. Remember what things have been before and what follow after. This sentence is from the Lord on all flesh. The time of death matters not, nor the place, nor the manner. Therefore be ready, strive for high ideals. Be yourself. Do not feign affection, neither be cynical or without love for in the face of all disenchantment it is perennial as the grass. Nurture strength of spirit to shield you in sudden misfortune."

The Canon paused before going on.

"In war and peace victims are many. Do not distress yourself with imaginings. Many fears are born of fatigue and loneliness. You are a child of the universe, no less than the trees and the stars; you have a right to be here, and whether or not it is clear to you the universe is unfolding as it should. Therefore be at peace with God whatever you conceive him to be. In the noise of life keep peace with your soul. With all its sham, drudgery, its conflicts and broken dreams . . . the world is still beautiful."

In the stillness that followed the reading Gallagher said distinctly: "Introibo ad altare Dei."

Leonard responded almost inaudibly: "Ad Deum, qui laetificat juventutem meam."

Harriet had not come across this excerpt. Moved, she looked first at her husband, then at Canon Plumm and said:

"Very fitting . . . thank you Canon."

The Canon closed the book of selected Sunday readings, considered for a moment, then stood and walked towards Leonard and Gallagher. Without looking at either he said:

"I want you . . . all of you to understand that while I abhor your methods profoundly and dislike your politics, I hold no hatred in my heart." He paused. "I have often thought and said . . . things . . . unbecoming a man of God . . . we are what we are because of history."

Gallagher scratched his chin with the muzzle of his pistol and said: "History can be altered."

Canon Plumm did not respond. He held out his hand towards Leonard. Leonard had to change his pistol from his right hand to his left hand in order to shake hands. Gallagher hesitated before following suit. As the Canon moved towards the McAleers and Lynam, Gallagher said quietly to Leonard:

"Plumm velvet, his ticket to heaven . . ."

Leonard did not reply. As the Canon sat after this the Colonel said: "I would like to identify myself with what Canon Plumm just read and said."

There was quite a silence before Leonard spoke.

"You understand, Sir, that we are at war."

All waited for Leonard to elaborate. He did not. It was Gallagher who added without looking round: "You know what war means: or should."

Outside, Caldwell stood beside the British officer who was in radio contact. Twice he said: "I understand."

When he put down the military phone he shook his head. Caldwell looked away to the lake, looked at his watch and said: "They'll let them be slaughtered?"

"They have masks . . . four pistols and three point blank targets . . . lunacy to go in."

The August sun was now high over lake and forest flooding the long room with glorious light. Leonard stood at the edge of the window and watched Alex's prone figure, and the camera on the roof of the station wagon. There was a light wind blowing across the water. The Tomkin clock ticked with unrelenting steadiness towards twelve. His heart slowed as he prepared for deliberate action. The three faces at the table were fixed in expressions of frozen fear and resignation. Gallagher was looking at Leonard intently. As the clock began to strike the McAleers stood. Lynam sat in the corner her face blank. Total silence as the last gong of the Tomkin clock faded. Leonard stepped back so that his shooting arm would not be visible. Holding his shooting wrist with his left hand he fired two shots towards the canvas covered head, pausing between each shot. After the first shot the body had twitched. It was now still. Gallagher nodded faintly. Lynam noticed a slight tremor in Leonard's hand as he inserted two fresh bullets, her mind empty as though some mechanism had excluded the brutality of fact. The McAleers blessed themselves. The faces at the table registered total incomprehension. It was the Colonel who asked:

"What? . . . Why did you fire?"

No one replied.

Lynam became aware of movement and looked up. Harriet was standing in the window. Lynam could not see her face, but could tell from her back that she was crying. When the effect of this soundless anguish became too much Lynam went to the lavatory. She stood staring blankly at the Delft bowl with its throne-like mahogany seating. She was there quite a while, teeth and fists clenched against the rigours of trembling when the door creaked open. Gallagher. She recognised his jeans and desert boots. She did not look up and felt nothing. When he said without inflection, "You all right Lynam?" she kicked the door shut with both feet. Gradually she began to feel normal, blood running in arteries and with it warmth returning.

As she returned to the room only the McAleers smiled. She sat separately watching the afternoon shadow edge across the wide bleached floorboards in the bay window. The silence and purity of light, and the tension of stillness became so oppressive that she stood. As she did, a megaphoned voice bombarded the house:

"A word requested with Colonel Armstrong at the front door."

She saw Leonard nod immediately at the Colonel. She went to the window. Standing behind Leonard she could see out and down. With a dull nausea she saw what had distressed Harriet; Boyd-Crawford curled in the grass, an abandoned foetus wrapped in tweed and hessian. The officer said about three sentences. As the Colonel came back, Leonard went to meet him.

Lynam watched them walk to the other end of the hall. Twice they paused, neither looking at the other. The Colonel then moved away and stood looking up through the banisters at an Italian landscape hanging on the panelled wall of the wide, slow-raked stairs, waiting. For what seemed like minutes Leonard stood rooted, staring at centuries of wear on the flagged floor. Was he going to consult? It was clear that what had been suggested or threatened was unexpected. He glanced up, caught her unmoving eyes and almost immediately looked away and approached the Colonel. From the way they spoke, turned about and listened intently, she had no doubt that some form of compromise had been agreed. She could sense Gallagher alongside her, alert, listening. Without looking at him she said:

"Can you hear?"

"He knows what he's at."

"Do you?"

There was quite a pause before Gallagher asked:

"Do I what?"

"Know what he's at?"

"We don't matter."

An acid comment occurred. She let it go. No time left now for anything but the pervasive and increasing fear. What was agreed?

She had heard, or imagined she had heard, the word "disarming" and saw Leonard nod. She stood back now as they crossed the hall, the Colonel in front. She kept looking in Leonard's face. Again she got the impression that he deliberately avoided her eyes. He said as he followed the Colonel into the room: "They're bringing them."

The McAleers laughed.

"Powerful."

"Good man Martin."

"He was right all along."

"He always is."

Gallagher smiled watchfully. Lynam's expression like Gallagher's was questioning. There was no triumph in Leonard's voice as he announced the release, and he seemed even bleaker as he said:

"I might take a drink now."

The Colonel poured. Leonard took the whiskey, walked away and stood by himself at the fireplace. As Gallagher moved towards him Leonard said with sudden sharpness:

"Keep watch all of you."

Gallagher kept looking at Leonard with a suspicion verging on menace. With reluctance he went back as ordered to the doorway. They took up their positions again. Lynam could not catch Leonard's eye. After five minutes she came over to him.

"They're bringing them?"

"Yes."

"When?"

"Soon. An hour, maybe less."

"Why did they wait till now? . . . So stupid . . ."

Leonard shrugged.

"It's a trick," she said.

"If it is, we go ahead as planned."

Both Harriet and Canon Plumm were questioning the Colonel with their eyes. He would not be drawn other than saying:

"I think it's all right."

"Thank God," Canon Plumm said.

Leonard finished his whiskey and poured another. He had made up his mind, but the more he thought about it, the more doubtful he became as he visualised its execution. For three years his life had been one unnerving choice. He had grown accustomed to hard decisions, but this one involved very cold thinking. The killing of the first victim compromised his position. He left his second whiskey untouched on the mantel beside the clock: 12:30. The helicopter, unless they planned shock action in the meantime, should arrive at 2. He felt suddenly very tired. He went to the couch and lay down and closed his eyes. An hour passed. Then he heard Gallagher's voice at his ear.

"The snag, Martin."

He looked at Gallagher. There was no way of lying to that cold ungiving face, always a move ahead.

"We'll have to wait."

"The snag?"

"We must wait."

"You're lying."

"Tired."

"Not that kind."

"Careful Jack."

"They don't do things that way, I want to know."

Leonard looked at Lynam. He knew that, like Gallagher, she could sense something unforeseen, unexpected. There was no way he could tell them.

"I won't be pushed Jack."

When Gallagher accepted that Leonard would not be forced to speak he began to move. Lenoard watched him obey then gave a silent whistle. Gallagher came back and bent towards Leonard who whispered. Gallagher straightened. For quite a while he stood thinking. Finally he nodded and glanced at Lynam with a look almost akin to compassion. As she saw this look a feeling of doom crept about her heart. What had been said? Was Gallagher privy to it? If so why was she excluded?

"There was a deal," she said.

Leonard nodded.

"What?"

"Presently."

The Colonel looked up from a book called *Beautiful Flowering Shrubs*, by G. Clarke Nuttal, opened at chapter XVIII, "The Evergreen Rhododendrons."

He had read the same paragraph three times without comprehension. He now turned the pages, looking at splendid colour illustrations. Now and then he showed a plate to his wife who nodded and said: "Exquisite" or "Beautiful." Canon Plumm continued with the *Selected Sunday Readings*. Now and then he pointed out a passage to Harriet who read, smoking continuously.

At ten past two they all heard the helicopter approaching. As it dropped to silence Leonard got up, nodding towards the Colonel. In the hall Leonard said:

"If they're here we take two of you as far as the helicopter."

"Disarming?"

"When you come back."

The Colonel went down behind the armoured wagons and was back in less than a minute. As he came in the door he said to Leonard:

"They're here."

Leonard went into the room and walked towards Lynam. He picked up her handbag, took out the pistol and put it in his back pocket. Baffled, half understanding, she watched as he approached Pascal and whispered. Pascal handed his pistol to Leonard. He then approached Pacelli, who also handed him his pistol. Leonard then handed one of the pistols to Gallagher.

"What are you doing?" Lynam asked.

Leonard did not reply. He walked to the Adam fireplace and stood under the great gilt mirror. Gallagher moved from the window towards the far end of the room and stood where everyone was well in focus. Leonard had obviously prepared and picked his words with great care, speaking now in such a low voice that all had to strain to catch what he said.

"The offer was nothing or . . . three for three . . ." He paused. "The men being released you know about . . . their value . . . I had to choose . . . I've chosen."

Lynam listened unbelieving as the spare words branded her accessory to murder, condemned her to the brutality and living death of a prison compound. Leonard was looking at Pascal and Pacelli as he said:

"I'm sorry boys . . . Your mother will be cared."

He turned to Lynam. What he had intended saying now seemed inadequate. Suddenly behind those hooded eyes she saw meanness, cowardice and treachery. Before he could speak she said:

"Picked yourself! . . . My God you're a coward."

She was on her feet, trembling so much she could scarcely speak. She nodded at Gallagher.

"Picked . . . him . . . before me?"

"He does what he does better than you."

He stopped himself from adding: "And so do they."

Her voice was shrill as she said: "Psychopathic and you know it."

"Then so am I . . . I won't judge and I've decided . . . I'm sorry."

"You're not . . . The captain and the first mate leaving the crew to sink; they'll write ballads about you Commandant when you're court-martialled . . . Coward and Leonard will rhyme well enough."

The words stung. What she said now had occurred to Leonard again and again in the two-hour wait. He was certain that Burke and the military council would approve but regret his decision. Two bomb technicians and a suspect propagandist were nothing like the force, drive and dedication of the three men released. And he had to decide that Gallagher and himself were the most useful of the five. Enemies would whisper what she had just called him now, the only word that shames a soldier. The fact that he had killed before witnesses and cameras excluded the possibility of a chivalrous offer to stay. If one of the brothers had killed he would have chosen him to go. One way or another Lynam would have been left. Gallagher's voice came from the corner.

"This is not a cruise where captains drown with honour, it's war; he commands . . . you obey . . . that's it." Less harshly he said: "If you prize your life that much, you go, I'll stay. That goes for the boys too."

Leonard was about to intervene when Pascal and Pacelli said simultaneously:

"I'll go by Martin."

"Me too, Martin's right."

Gallagher asked:

"Well?"

"You mean it?"

"I mean it."

Were nice guys bastards, and bastards noble? Still unbelieving she looked from Leonard to Gallagher. Was he bluffing? She had only to say yes. As she looked she realised that Gallagher's offer was contemptuous. He was flaunting his prowess as a killer against her troubled conscience and humanity. Far from Carton country he was turning the screw with cruel psychological cunning, daring her to choose herself before him. To accept his offer would be vastly more ignominious than the grim, fast-looming alternative. She felt now that every word, step and sequence had led inevitably to this moment of terror and rejection. Very quietly she said:

"I prefer gaol to either of you."

"That," Gallagher said, "is no surprise."

There was a noise of footsteps on gravel. Leonard went to the side of the bay window: Caldwell again on his way to the house. To the Colonel, Leonard said:

"We take you and the Canon."

Gallagher embraced both Pascal and Pacelli. From where he stood he directed his voice towards Lynam and said:

"Slán."

She did not answer.

When Leonard had shaken hands with the brothers he looked at Lynam. As he approached her she said:

"His offer was an insult . . . I'd rather be dead than see you rule."

Leonard thought his thoughts. He did not express them. With his unaltering voice he said:

"I know."

As he turned to go, Gallagher took him aside. Sensing what he would say Leonard said: "She didn't mean that."

"She said it . . . all she knows Martin . . . who, why, when, what . . . they'll get it . . . we can't leave her!"

"The offer is three for three."

As Gallagher pondered the reality Leonard said: "I've had two hours to think: this is the only way."

"I'll stay for one of the boys."

"You'll not."

"I want to Martin."

"Bomb technicians are two a penny . . . you're needed."

"We're soldiers . . . we should . . . we can't leave them, Martin . . . not both."

"When I move, move with me; ready?"

For ten seconds it seemed to Leonard that Gallagher would not obey. Without looking at him he asked again: "Ready?"

"Ready," Gallagher said.

Leonard motioned the Colonel and Canon Plumm to the hall. Gallagher made a pushing away movement with his free hand towards the brothers, a gesture of defeat and farewell. In response the McAleers stood and saluted. Leonard acknowledged the salute bleakly and followed. As they went Lynam sat lost, her back to the window. Gradually she became aware first of Harriet's eyes, then voice saying:

> "A tale lamentable of things ill done
> For the Living Dead: no comfort from the sun."

As Harriet left the room Pascal and Pacelli approached, both smiling unnaturally. She stared into their faces.

"They'll brutalise . . . torture us."

"Don't think on it, love," Pascal said.

"Bounce of the ball," Pacelli added.

"Some must suffer."

"We'll laugh five years from now."

"Aye to be sure."

"Show them you're not afeered Bella."

"Stand, you're a soldier."

"Put on bravery . . . face them with us."

As she stood between them they kissed her as they had kissed her the evening before.

Harriet watched from the door as three camera crews filmed the four walking across the front of the Tudor house towards the waiting helicopter. When they were out of sight she went to Alex, knelt at his head and uncovered the face. The two bullets had entered his skull within the hairline leaving his face unmarked. She pulled off her shoe and propped it under his chin to close his mouth, shutting his eyes with her thumbs, aware of soldiers running across the gravel towards the steps. They ran past her into the house. Then a British officer was beside her on one knee holding her arm:

"Mrs. Armstrong."

"Yes."

"We'll attend to that."

"I can manage . . . a friend . . . a dear, dear friend, so kind, a human being, do you understand?"

"Of course."

"A human being."

She shook her head. Alex's face blurred.

"I think you should come inside."

The officer was exerting gentle pressure on her arm.

"No . . . I . . . perfectly all right."

From her knees she saw the McAleers and Lynam come through the front door escorted by soldiers. As Lynam slowed to say something she was pushed roughly onwards by soldiers. Harriet bowed her head and wept. The helicopter rose from the side of the house, its blade whirling in the afternoon sun, a monstrous insect heading south across the quiet lake, meadow and forest.

When she looked up, the Colonel and the Canon were being interviewed by television reporters. Caldwell stood behind the camera crews watching. A reporter and a camera man with a hand-held camera approached the steps. The officer stood up and waved them away. They kept coming and he said:

"Please gentlemen, please . . . later."

Harriet saw them coming, stood and said: "I don't mind, provided they don't show Alex like that."

They were three yards away now. The camera began to whirr.

"What do you want to know? Surely it's clear!"

The reporter said: "I understand you were brutally beaten, Mrs. Armstrong."

Harriet shook her head.

"Your face is bruised."

"Nothing."

"What is your feeling now?"

"My feeling? . . . about what?"

The reporter hesitated, unsure. She waited till he asked: "A few minutes ago you were at death's door."

Harriet nodded. "Yes . . . well . . . my feeling."

She paused, apparently unable to go on. The officer shook his head motioning the reporter to cut the interview.

"No, no I can answer . . . my feeling at the moment is one of . . . desolation . . . of unutterable despair . . . that is my feeling now . . . despair . . . but look around you."

Harriet looked out over the massive shapes of war and the uniforms below, to the long lake, the great forest beyond and up into the August sun, the blinding sky.

"Look about you."

Her face fell apart as she said: "The world is still beautiful."

She nodded trying to smile and said again:

"Beautiful."

The Orphan

WHEN THE HARD HUNGER reached us the Mother went half cracked blamin' Dada for near everythin', the landlord, the agent, the pig dyin', the leaky thatch, even the blight itself. Once when the run-off from the dungheap overflowed to the well she accused it made our Micilín sick. The truth is far different I'd say. It was her cuffin' and scoldin', then smotherin' the wee cratur with kisses, did some of the harm. Sadder again, Dada stood by. The man was too weakly to face up to her and then he couldn't look at us hungry, and the worse things got the worse she got, tongued and tongued and tongued. Betimes there were screechin' matches so awful me and Grace my twin sister put our two fingers in our two ears and ran away from the house and hid down in the sheugh that divides our ten acres from Noel Callaghan's land.

The Mother was all outshow and pride. What would the priest and the neighbours think of her two daughters were near hoors out dancin' and gallivantin' like mad heifers in heat and half the parish half dead from hunger? It was nothin' to her we were young and wanted our bit of life away from misery. She cared mostly for Micilín, God help him. He was forever coughin'. She kept him in a bag skirt to fool the fairies, but sure the fairies could see him at the back door holdin' his wee man to make his pee. Every bit of love and special care in our house went into that sick boy. She slept with him above in the cockloft over the byre.

One night when we came in late Dada was sittin' alone on the settle bed in the kitchen sayin' the same thing over and over. He was fair drunk I suppose. He said there was no way we'd get through the winter alive without a spud kind and every bird and beast about the place long gone. We'd be better off without him. There would be that much more to eat for the rest of us. Grace cried and begged him not to leave. I was upset too, but mostly stayed quiet.

He kept shakin' his head. He was a countryman's tailor but people had long since quit liftin' the latch. Like every other trade there was no money, only the promise of money. At fairs and gatherin's he was often, he said, at a loss. Men would order a swallow-tailed coat maybe, or britches, or a workin' waistcoat, and never come back to the lodgin's he worked out of. Then the Mother would say,

—That's your story, Tom Brady!

Then she'd tackle in to say he drank the money.

—What customer'd pay for clothes so illmade a monkey wouldn't wear them for fear of bein' laughed at!

Or she'd shout at him other times,

—You'll not shame me before the whole country!

No matter what any of us done we were shamin' her before the whole country! No one ever told her "the whole country" doesn't know or care if you're alive or dead; no one in the country gives an ass's fart for anyone only themselves, and any halfwit could tell you that, and the same halfwit could tell you there's not a family in all Ireland hasn't some shame to hang its head about.

God knows me and Grace didn't want to think it but Dada was a poor enough tailor. When he come to this townland of Drumlanna twenty years back the Mother was long past thirty.

By all accounts they were happy enough in the early years with a bit of land and the tailorin'. It was she calved and milked the cow, cut and footed the turf, put in and dug out the spuds, but when the blight came and rotted them in the ground the cow had to be sold. Then the fowl were eaten and when the hard hunger came she'd scream at him,

—You have a wife and three childer to feed now, Tom Brady. Have you no shame to be gulpin' and pissin' the most of it in a ditch! It's horsewhipped you should be, you and drunkards like you!

Then he'd leave the house for days. When he'd come back we could tell he was drinkin' from his dead eyes and senseless talk. Thing is, he could measure, cut and sew, but he was careless or maybe the drink would put a tremble in his fingers and that made a *prácás* of the work he was at. When a customer was tryin' on we could see it was wrong and if that happened he'd give the garment a tug or twist and say there was poor give in the cloth.

—It'll warm into your body, he'd say.

What put the Mother astray in the head was the way he mostly wouldn't talk back. When she tongued he just stood there and looked at the floor.

Not long before he left us for good Lord Clonroy sent for him. The Viceroy Lord Clarendon had arrived at Eden Hall with a bolt of Donegal tweed under his arm. He wanted a pair of shootin' britches made. Dada brought the cloth home and worked all day and all night and terrible nervous he was because the great man was left-handed and left-handed men are hung opposite to right-handed men so everythin' had to be made the other way about.

When he brought the britches to Eden Hall they were all at dinner, full of wine and good humour. The Viceroy went into another room and came back in wearin' the britches. No one said a thing at first. Then Lord Clonroy said,

—I'll tell you what you've done, Brady. You've made a bags of the Viceroy's britches!

They all thought that was so funny they near laughed themselves sick except the Viceroy. This is where me and Grace differ. She had tears in her eyes on account of the way Dada was shamed, took his hand, kissed it and said,

—That was terrible for you, Dada.

I was filled with so much anger I wanted to hit him and walk out of the house. That kind of self sorry whinge makes me sick to my stomach. Small wonder he loved Grace more than he loved me and maybe that made me jealous a track, but not all that much. The truth is I loved her too much to be mad jealous.

Anyway he went on with his story. In the middle of all the laughin' the Viceroy crossed the room, took Dada's arm and went out to the great hall. He asked him how many childer he had, were there grandparents in the house? Had we any spuds at all, and what other food was there in the house or garden? And how was it with our neighbours? Dada told him the hard hunger was on us, that all our neighbours were the same as us.

—The people, your honour, are starvin', and that's the truth.

The Viceroy repeated that in Irish, put his hand up to his mouth and made a wee hummin' noise. Then he took a golden guinea out of his purse and pressed it on Dada.

—No, no, your Lordship, Dada said, that's a ransom for bad made britches.

—The britches, the Viceroy said, are grand.

—The man's a born gentleman, Dada said, every inch of him. I'd follow him to hell if he gave me the nod.

The Mother we all thought deep asleep above in the cockloft with Micilín. She must have heard 'cause all of a sudden she spoke,

—It's the like of that fine born gentleman has made a hell out of this whole island.

We stared up at her. You could see Dada didn't understand till she said,

—And it's the like of you, Tom Brady, has made a hell out of this house with your booze and your blether. Let you show your dotin' daughters now what's left of the great lord's hansel.

The Mother's temper is worse than any storm. He had no choice. He had sixteen shillings and a few pence left, enough to feed us all for a month. He had drunk near a week's food and though we loved him we all felt angry and ashamed about this. The Mother had come down from the cockloft. We watched her countin' the money. She went over then to where Dada was sittin' on the settle bed, put her head down sideways and shouted into his face five or six times,

—Fool, fool, fool, fool, fool, fool!

Each time it was like she'd slapped him with her open hand across the face and then she was half-gulpin', half-chokin' as she cried out,

—We'll all starve to death here, Tom Brady, because I married a fool.

That was the night he left and never come back, no message, nothin'. And when I think now of the differ between that man, our father, and that woman, our mother, I have to say Grace was more like him. She couldn't stand up for herself. She was soft. She'd cry over a sick kitten or a dead chicken or a silly story. I was well able to cry myself but I'd near die before I'd let anyone see me. But I pray God I won't end up like the Mother. I heard Dada mutter once,

—It's not hunger'll kill that woman, it's pride!

No matter how hungry we were she'd always have bought soap in the house or if there was no money she'd make it herself.

—Water costs nothin', she'd say, and by God you girls'll keep your bodies clean and your souls pure as long as you're in my care.

She smelled of carbolic herself and made sure we did too. It was out to the turfshed every mornin', summer and winter, with the tin jug and basin, teeth first with soot, then strip down while she watched to make sure we'd wash neck, ears, back passage and up between our legs, and there was stuff in that soap went up into you like a bee sting. Then dry yourself with a hessian bag and, the only good thing, it gave us a chance to see what the other looked like because no one could tell us apart. What I saw, Grace saw. Eyes and hair black as sloes above a heron's neck, shapely legs goin' up to her lovepurse and the rise of her bottom, and a heather dye you'd swear round her brown nipples, and all her skin as white as her teeth.

—Why does she put us through that washin' "torture"? Grace asked once.

—Because we smell young and natural, I said. She hates that. Snig off our rosebuds if she had her way and tell us the Devil put them in there to make us sin.

When I'd say the like she'd laugh, bite her lip and say,

—God forgive you, Rosh.

I was the first born and had a hard time comin' into the world or so I was often told. Maybe that's what made me harder than Grace in my head and heart or so I imagine but none of that matters anymore. Dada left that night after she shouted "fool" at him so wicked vicious, and hardly a day passes or a night but I think of him. How or where did he die? Who buried him? Where? Ditch, bog or mountain place? Did he throw himself in a deep river or the sea like so many? If that's what fell out I'll have to think of him as gone to God's light or the Devil's dark or is he maybe alive somewhere up about Dundalk or Dublin? They say the hunger's as bad in the towns as the country and anyway who'd employ a poor tailor only the poor and the poor have nothin'. He's dead I think with a million others.

When the Mother found him gone the next day it wasn't tears came out of her two eyes but bad temper out of her mouth.

—A rotten match my own father made for me with Tom Brady. What good's my stone thatched cabin and ten acres with a poor breed of man drunk in the chimbley corner, a class of coward runs out on his whole family when trouble comes.

Then because she had no man to cut with her tongue she grigged us about every other thing we did or said. So we kept away from the house every chance we got. And why not! Weren't we young girls out for a bit of life and who could blame us with death every other day in every other townland? At night we'd lie close and talk and giggle about the boys and the kind of them, who was good for a coort, and who was shy, and who we'd let and how far we'd let them. Then one night Grace asked me,

—Did ever you let a fella proper?

—Close enough, I said.

—I let Jimmy Ned O'Hara.

—You did not, Grace!

—God help I did.

—You're mad in the head.

—I know.

—Why?

—He cried, Rosh.

—What!

—Cried, wept and gulped like a babby.

—For why?

—For me to let him in. Said he'd die if I said no.

—Well isn't Jimmy Ned the quare cute one! I'd say you're not the first lassie he's cried for!

—I know.

Then she started in to cry to herself, so I put my two arms around her and kissed away her fright. Then I lay awake long after she'd gone to sleep. I couldn't take in what she'd told me about herself and Jimmy Ned. She was ahead of me in the biggest thing happens to a girl. She was a woman now even if the way it happened was silly enough. I couldn't take it in rightly. I looked and looked at her face asleep. Not the smallest change, but it was a woman's face I was lookin' at and I thought I can't be such a nice creature to have jealous thoughts about the person I love most in the world and who loves me even more than she loves herself. From the time we were wee things I could see nothin' in that face but admiration. She was fierce proud of me. I'd hear her boastin' about me to others, how I could run and jump and wrestle and best any boy my own size.

It never seemed to come into her head that me bein' better at everythin' cast her into a kind of shade. She loved bein' my sister and I had to admit to myself she had more nature, more heart, more kindness and goodness, more gentleness and warmth than me, and then I became so upset thinkin' about how much better she was than me at everythin' that mattered that I began to be sorry for myself. She woke up, put her two arms around me and said,

—Roisin, Roisin, don't you be sorry for me, I'll be alright, I'll be alright.

I couldn't tell her it wasn't for her I was cryin' but for myself, and that made me all the more miserable.

As luck would have it she was far from alright. Life began to waken in her belly from the crybaby boy, and one mornin' after the stirabout, when she left in a hurry to get sick, didn't the Mother see her and know right off. Then there was a screechin' match to end all screechin' matches. She took Grace up to the cockloft by the ear, put a cow's chain round her neck and closed it tight with a blacksmith's pincers. Then she nailed the end of the chain to the roofbeam with nails as big as the ones they used on Christ and kept her up there with a bowl and a bucket. We were too young and too frightened to know what to do. With Dada long gone, no money, nothin' in the house but ten days of stirabout, nothin' in our fields but cabbage stumps and nothin' but a cock's step between us and the poorhouse I began to wonder what I could do to get money in my fist to feed us all.

Lord Clonroy had a twenty-acre turnip field over the estate wall that marched Drumlanna, our wee garden of a farm. The turnips were long since dug by squads of men to feed sheep and bullocks. Twice the Mother let me out to cross the wall and glean at night. Each time I came back with a bag of crow-pecked, half-frosted roots. The Mother fried them with a little pig fat. They were so delicious they made our heads light. Each time in the black dark I could hear the German wolfdogs over a mile away up at the big house. They were kept in a special yard alongside the prize cattle and sheep penned in every night for fear the gangs of Ribbonmen would slash their tendons. The third time out I got braver. There was a moon and I went a long way from the estate wall out into the middle of the field. I was hokin' and gatherin' rightly when I heard first the chains and then the growlin' of wolfdogs. They must have smelled me and for a few seconds of terror my heart stopped entirely. I could hear a henchman shoutin',

—Gwon, gwon, gettim, boy, gettim!

I knew that Wishy Mulligan's throat was ripped out by those dogs. Then I was runnin' as I'd never run in my life and was over that wall a brave few minutes before the dogs came howlin' up to where I'd crossed. The fright was bad but the loss of the turnips was worse. The Mother had to hear all and said she'd have near died of shame if one of her daughters was caught clawin' like a starved rat in the dark of an empty landlord's turnip field.

Not long after this, Mervyn Johnston, the warden of the ten townlands, came to visit us, a Protestant gentleman with over a hundred acres. He spoke Irish like us and most people said he was kindly and helpful, but for the Mother the word "Protestant" meant he had cloven feet and horns.

—You can't see them but they're there.

So when he said he thought he could place one of us in the scullery of the big house, if that would be any help, the Mother said,

—You can send your own daughter for a scullion, Mr. Johnston, you'll not get mine.

And even with that said to his face he answered quiet,

—If you change your mind, Mam, just let me know.

Not get mine! Hers to give! Body and soul! Does the mad, proud woman of Drumlanna own her two daughters and her sick son?

—Oh, she didn't mean it that way, Grace said.

—How then so did she mean it? What does that chain round your neck mean?

And of course she had no answer to that. From the time we were small I could always talk her into a knot she couldn't unknot except with a protest.

—God you're a fright, Roisin.

—And I'll stay one if it keeps us alive, I said.

It was the night I had to race from the turnip field that I lay awake thinkin' how from the age of twelve I could run faster than any other girl or boy I knew, but what good was runnin' to get bread? Then it came to me that gentry will pay money to see boxin' matches, and wager money on hounds, cocks and coursin' hares, and at the field day sports Lord Clonroy would give prize money for runnin' and jumpin' but that was only one day in the year when you could show your paces. It was that spake, "Show your paces," that gave me a mad idea. At horse fairs the seller always had to show the paces of the horse he was sellin', and watchin' this I used to think, I could run as fast as that horse, faster, and then I thought how every other day there were grand visitors to Eden Hall would have fat purses of money. I could run alongside the carriage no matter how fast it went. They'd see me and think, "She'll tire, she can't go on." Then after half a mile they'd have to look at me and if they had any breedin' they'd throw me out a coin or maybe somethin' from a hamper or maybe a rug I could pawn. But if I got nothin' I'd lost nothin' and I hadn't begged. So I watched my chance, climbed the wall a good bit down from the gatekeeper's lodge where Ivan Dowler lived. As luck would have it, I saw a carriage a long way off. That gave me time to get down and run to a bend of the avenue where I stood behind one of the great lime trees that marched on either side all the way up to the big house.

When the carriage came level I began to run ahead of the horses. The coachman Clancy let a roar at me to get to hell out of the way. I obeyed him, moved to the side and let the coach draw alongside. He roared again,

—Get off the earth!

I paid no heed, knowing well that whoever was inside the coach must see me now and wonder what I was at, a girl of seventeen runnin' as easy as a runnin' dog. I was careful not to turn my head and look into the carriage but I heard a young man's voice say,

—Faster, Clancy.

I still didn't look but I increased my pace to keep up with the slow gallop of the horses knowin' I could go ahead of them if I wanted. Then I heard three more words from the same voice,

—The whip, Clancy.

—To her or the horses, Master?

—The horses, man, the horses!

I was sorry then for the way the knotted thongs cut the poor creatures. I could see foam at their mouths and smell the sweet smell of horse sweat. I was still runnin' easy enough, and plenty left.

The big house was still over half a mile away. At a downhill stretch the carriage drew level. From the corner of my eye I could see three young men and two young ladies inside. I knew one of the young men was Mathew, Lord Clonroy's only son. He leaned out the window and made a gesture with his hand which meant, "Go away." I paid no heed, then heard him shout above the clatter of wheels and hooves,

—You'll burst your lungs, girl, go home!

At that very moment I felt blood on my thighs and knew what had happened. Then something caught my foot. I fell down on my face. I knew they had all seen me fall but if they did they saw me get up as quick. I was still level but now my nose was bloody. I was half glad of that because maybe they'd only see that and not the other. Inside in myself I felt I was like a child who'd fallen and can't get breath because the hurt is so painful. I was tempted to stop but I must have that pride my mother has.

I'll keep runnin', I thought, till someone throws out somethin'. Just when it was hardest with the big house and the lake in view I heard a coin sing on the stone of the avenue. Then another. Then another. Then another. Then another. Five sixpences. Enough to buy two weeks' India meal. I stopped. The carriage drew away. My hands, in truth my whole body, were tremblin'. There was a taste of blood and sweat in my mouth. I went straight off the avenue into a copse of oak trees and sat on the ground. I realised then I could hardly breathe.

When it got easier I was cryin'. I cried a brave bit while I wiped my nose and thighs with moss and tried to think why I was whingein' like a two-year-old. Hadn't I two full shillin's and sixpence in the linin' of my shift? Maybe it was the relief of knowin' we could hold off from the poorhouse a while longer and I hadn't held out my hand to whine like a beggar. I'd run proud with my head up, but I'd fallen. Dear Jesus, I'd fallen on my mouth and nose and maybe it was that fall and the knowledge of what was happenin' below under the eyes of high bred young men and women. Through my patched rags they must have seen the bareness of poverty. Was that what caused them to drop out the biteens of silver?

I burned with shame thinkin' of this. Would I, could I, do the same again if I had to, two weeks from now? I was thinkin' these thoughts when I saw Ivan Dowler, the gatelodge keeper, the worst breed of henchman, come into the oak copse carryin' his whitethorn stick. He had frog eyes and the low hung lip of a bully.

Did someone tell him how I'd raced the carriage and braved Clancy's whip? I'm not sure what come over me, maybe hundreds of years of bein' wronged, but somewhere from my lungs I screamed at him so loud it near frightened me as much as him. Then I let another and another till the screamin' became more like the howlin' of a trapped creature through clenched teeth. I could see that he had stopped and could hear him growl,

—Quit, quit that. Quit!

Then of a sudden I was gone.

How long I was lyin' there I've no notion. I know only I was chilled through and through when I woke and so stiff I could scarce move. Did that landlord's brute come up and stare, then walk away and leave me there like a creel of rubbish? As I sat up I heard a foxbitch give her wee sharp bark and I thought if she can feed and rear her litter with all the world agin' her, why can't I take care for my mad, proud mother, my pregnant sister and my sick brother? I can.

The first stars were about the sky when I got home and the Mother waitin' for me like black thunder till I took the five sixpences from the hem of my shift. She looked into the cup of my hand and her face was two faces, one lit up because we'd eat, the other with a twist on her mouth which said,

—You begged, daughter?

—I ran.

—You what!

—I ran.

—Liar!

—I ran against Lord Clonroy's carriage. I never spoke, I never looked, I ran and they dropped out silver. .

She seemed too stunned to understand and muttered,

—That's beggary.

She was so desperate she asked no more, snatched the silver and went to Dermody's for meal and fat. I went up to Grace in the cockloft. She had the white face of a half-starved girl with a child growin' in her belly. We were all like ghosts but she was by far the poorest and whitest of ghosts. I put my two arms around her and every bit of me loved every bit of her and I kept sayin' how I loved her and how she'd be alright and how her babby would be alright and maybe someway I'd get the money and we'd have a new life in America. All the roads of Ireland, I said, were full of the poor of Ireland walkin' to the ports. In America there would be no Kings or Queens, no agents or landlords, no bailiffs or house tumblers. We'd be welcomed by our own people into a new world. There would be food and clothes, singin' and dancin', proper work and proper wages in a country where we'd be all free at last.

I knew in my heart of hearts that none of this was true, not lies, but not true. Even so, I kept sayin' it again and again and again. Then she had to know how I got the money and when I told her my story I could see her eyes gettin' bigger and bigger and her mouth openin' in wonder.

—Gawdy! If I fell down that way I'd stay down.

She was speakin' the truth about herself, but sittin' on that bag of rushes with that chain around her neck I knew the round of her belly was a chain could never be loosened except by death, and again I began to badmouth the Mother even though that always upset her.

—She loves us, Roisin.

I pointed at the chain and asked,

—Is that love?

—She's sick with worry over the head of everythin'.

—She's mad with pride, or just plain mad.

Again Grace looked away for a while and then said,

—It was me that sinned, Rosh. Me, not her.

I made no answer to that silliness. The Mother was either mouthin' prayers or usin' a tongue would cut you in two. I knew Rosh half believed what she preached, that Holy God had sent down the blight and the hard hunger to punish us for all our sins of impurity.

—Three Hail Marys, she'd say, for this, that and the other, every other half hour of the night or day and we'd have to answer,

—Holy Mary, Mother of God, pray for us sinners now and at the hour of our death.

Night and day it's sinners and death. Death the last word in that prayer. Every time death, death, death, death, death, death, death, death, death, death. Ten deaths with every decade. Thousands everywhere now, in every townland of every barony of every province, sick from sin, Godstruck unto death. And thousands of poor halfwits and unlucky girls like Grace locked up, tied or chained in lofts, sheds or sties, hidin' their shame from God and the neighbours. Jesus, God, are You as cruel as that? Are You?

—Holy, holy, holy, Lord God of hosts, heaven and earth are full of Thy glory.

When the time come for the babby to be born the Mother gagged Grace for fear she'd cry out with the pains and the neighbours would hear. I was kept out. I stood in the dark listenin' and cryin'.

No midwife. The babby was a day and a night comin' into the world and when I heard its wee cry I couldn't think how it would be suckled in a house with a grandmother hated it, so I did a mad thing, God help me. I ran away from our house to John Joseph Duffy. I crossed four townlands in the dark till I reached the lock-keeper's cottage. I tapped on his window and told him the way things were above in Drumlanna and that I wanted us to be man and woman that night. And we were, in the cabin of a barge called "The Rose of Mooncoyne." Three times that night we cried out together and I don't know to this day why it had to be that night and that way, and I don't know now if he's alive or dead or taken up with another or sendin' the passage money he promised in a letter he sent on his way to America.

It was near daylight when I got back to Drumlanna to hear a terrible story. God help me, I can't hardly let into my head what dark things were done after I left. It's all between God and my poor mother in the idiot ward of the poorhouse.

Grace was stretched dead as any dead thing you'd see in a ditch or a bog. It was a great flood of bleeding did it. I saw after where the blood dripped down through the cockloft to the group of the byre below.

—The babby, she said, was dead born. It made no shape to breathe at all, only a wee gurgle.

—Was it a boy or a girl? I asked.

—What matters that to you? You weren't here wherever you were. It's dead. When I'm at myself you'll answer to me where you were till this hour.

—Where is the wee thing buried?

—It's with God.

And she went straight to Micilín in the settle bed where he was coughin' like a sick cat. When they were both asleep I went up and cried my eyes dry beside Grace. I thought of the way we'd walk together, my arm around her neck and her arm around my waist, and all the silly talk we made and all the laughin' and betimes the cryin', about everythin' and nothin', and I knew lookin' at her I'd never love any creature in the world the way I loved my sister.

When I was fit to cry no more I went out to look for where the *bábóg* was buried. I wasn't long in findin' it. I could see where she'd prised up a flagstone in the byre. I did the same and there was a Lisnaskea butter box and inside the box the babby with a terrible red ring on its neck from the rope its grandmother used to put it out of the world forever. A wee girl it was, and I can't tell you why that made it worse, but it did.

It was rage then I felt for this woman would sicken you with her moanin' and her prayers and her rosaries, her saints, pishogues and fairies. She had murdered her own flesh and blood and I was her daughter, the daughter of a murderer, and her so proud of her kin, the grand Daly blood she had in her veins compared to the poor, thin Brady blood in Dada's veins. It's true he got drunk betimes but if he did he told us funny stories, showed us card tricks, never hit or cuffed us the way she did, and never a bad word out of his mouth about anybody, not even the landlords.

—And sure maybe they have their own troubles, he'd say, and people would look at him as if he was mad.

Aloud in that byre I said,

—Dada, she's murdered your granddaughter. You're well out of it.

It was midday before the priest, Brendan Galligan, came on his horse with his top hat and his horsewhip. He said the settle bed should be sold to buy a cheap coffin. Then he said his few prayers and sprinkled holy water on Grace and the way that woman bleated after him, Father this, Father that, and Father the other, and the whole carry on of her, you'd swear Jesus Christ Himself was in the house and not one word about chains and cocklofts and buckets and chokin' a babby to death. Then he turned to me,

—A sad day this but it must be said, both you girls have disgraced our parish, one worse than the other. This death is a judgement of God on your mad capers.

—Oh God help us, said the Mother, but it's the truth you've spoken, Father.

I kept my mouth shut and he went on,

—The whole country knows about your dancin' and what you get up to in barns and ditches. You've put a lot of decent young men astray in the head and the whole country half starved. It's wicked beyond words. I'm certain sure it was the burden of shame drove your poor father out of his own house.

I stared down at my two bare feet and made not one word of an answer.

—Have you nothin' to say for yourself, girl?

Then I looked at his grand shiny boots, and the shine of good feedin' on his face and the proud stance of him, and the belly on him like there were twins in it at least, and wondered the way any girl would was he all shrivelled up in there or hung like a stallion ass. Then I looked straight into his two eyes and I thought for a minute he'd hit me with his horsewhip, but he took a big breath and said,

—It's to God you'll have to answer, girl, God, not me.

He was hardly out the door when the Mother slapped me hard across the face and if she did I slapped her back so quick and sudden she fell back against the crook of the hearth and I said to her,

—True as God, woman, if you hit me again I'll kill you dead because it's dead you should be.

And I picked up the pincers she'd used to close the cow-chain on Grace's neck.

—God and His holy Mother, protect me, says she, what have I done to deserve this?

—What have you not done? You know well what you've done. You're the Devil's own now.

She knew I knew but not a word was said. When it came to the layin' out of Grace I was in such a fury of grief I wouldn't let her near. I sent for

John Joseph. As he took her down the ladder from the cockloft with one arm her head was restin' on his shoulder the way I'd often seen her at a dance, that sudden lift and laugh as merry as a child's, and I could hardly see what I was at because it's myself I was layin' out and washin' for the last time and I remembered how elders often talked of the dead as bein' "peaceful."

—At peace, they'd say, at rest, happy now.

But Grace's face was a way I'd never seen it, her soft mouth a hard line across her clamped teeth. Rage? For youth and beauty cheated? For what? Pride.

It fair sickened me watchin' the Mother after the keenin' was over and the grave filled bendin' her head to neighbours, all of them lettin' on to know nothin' and knowin' or guessin' everythin'.

—She's gone to Jesus.

—Cratur's with God's Mother now.

—She's an angel with angels.

And a dose of other holy sayin's put me mad angry or maybe it was the way the Mother muttered back,

—Aye, she's happy now in heaven surely.

I wanted to shout out like a whiplash through all the whisperin',

—She was chained to a roofbeam, she was terrified and she died a cruel, bloody death, and that carbolic-smellin' woman with the pious face choked and buried her wee babby. She was in hell, my lovely, gentle sister, and is she now in heaven with Jesus? And if Jesus knew the carry on in our house why could He not shift Himself to help her? And for a bad minute I thought I'd shout out,

—It's a clip on the ear Jesus wants to waken Him up!

But I held my tongue, thank God.

The Mother was never in her right mind from that day out. If she heard the squeal of an owl or rabbit, the shriek of a swallow, or a hound howlin' at night, she'd think it was the babby she heard and start in to cry and wander the country prayin' and ravin' about two angels were lost and how she'd earn hell if they weren't found. It was the warden, Mervyn Johnston, found her naked in the bog of Scart, her whole body scrabbed by thorns and briars.

There's a shed here for mad women in the grounds of the poorhouse. That's where they put her. I saw her there just the once. I won't ever see her again. Leastways I don't want to. I thought I hated her but when I saw her in that ward I don't know what I felt. She was still clean, on clean straw, but surrounded by filth and smell, her only company the gibberin' and laughin' of mad women night and day.

Her eyes were blank but her lips were movin'. Hail Mary, Holy Mary. Where did all those Hail Marys lead in the end but down the darkest road of all? Once for the smallest second I thought she twigged who I was but when I tried to look into her eyes she swivelled them off. I tried again. She did the same and then I saw the tell-tale tears and thought, she knows or half knows, remembers or half remembers, somethin' of that terrible night, and I knelt and took her hands and kissed them. Oh God, I kissed those hands and heard myself sayin',

—I can't forgive you, Mother, ever, you must know that.

She looked at me proper then for the first time, covered her face, no sound, but I could see her body shakin'. Some mad pauper woman started in to howl like a hound. Another joined her. That's how I left her in the hell she made for herself. That's when I saw her last and it's the last time I'll ever see her or less we meet in heaven, if God forgives her.

That left me and Micilín half alive and half dead in an empty house with hardly a crumb between the two of us.

A short time after this Mister Johnston came back to talk about the Mother and see how we were faring. He knew no neighbours could help out. We were all in the one boat and it goin' down.

When he saw Micilín out on the street in daylight I could tell from the way he blinked that things were bad. He sent for Doctor O'Grady, who took me aside and said,

—The caudie has typhus, he's not long for this world.

I had to lean against the cabin wall when I heard this.

—You can't nurse him or go near him or you'll not be long after him.

Then he looked into the byre and showed me where Micilín was to lie on a bed of rushes near enough to where the *bábóg* was buried. I was to lock the door tight and seal it with blue clay and give him his stirabout and water on a shovel through the small windy, then close the windy tight and keep well away from infection.

—A dog would die of loneliness from the like of that, I said.

The only answer he made was to nod and say,

—When he dies it would be best to leave him in there and burn the byre.

I carried him out and laid him on rushes in the corner of the byre like I was told. He pleaded with me to get back into the cabin. I was sick with grief and pity but what could I do?

He never took a mouthful of stirabout or a porringer of water off the shovel, just sobbed, curled up and stopped breathin'. Neighbours came then with sticks and creels of turf to make sure the byre was well burned. For three nights and three days it burned, and I wept bitter tears because all belongin' to me were now gone. I was an orphan like thousands and thousands the country over. Then Mister Johnston called again and out of his pocket he took a red book of tickets with numbers on them. He wrote my name on one and gave it to me.

—What's this for? I asked.

—The workhouse, Roisin, it's your only hope.

I looked at the red ticket in my hand with my name and number on it. At first I couldn't speak. When I was fit to I said,

—Hereabouts, Mister Johnston, people call this the death ticket. I'd rather die here where I was born.

He looked away for a while and then said,

—There's tumblin' talk.

—Is there?

—I heard them in the barracks, a squad from Mayo, and I've seen the list, Drumlanna's on it, next Thursday.

My heart and insides were suddenly tumblin' in terror. I'd seen the Callaghans, my cousins, evicted in the mouth of Christmas last year, five of them, the door smashed down, and what choice had they then but the workhouse or the killin' winter? They were carted off to the poorhouse, three of them now dead. I'd seen the tumblers at work, men from another county evicted themselves and now tumblin' out their own kin into cruel December. One jumps up and saws the roofbeam, the others throw up grapple hooks, and the roof is down in minutes. We saw the Constabulary sittin' on horseback watchin' with muskets and truncheons. Terror, fright and howlin' to break the hardest heart.

I looked again at the red ticket and he saw me lookin'.

—You've some kind of a chance in the workhouse, girl. Stay here and you've none.

I thanked him and said, no, I'd rather take to the fields and roads than go to the poorhouse.

—You're making a big mistake, he said.

He must have gone to Reggie Murphy, the workhouse master, who came out himself to persuade me. I'd never seen the man, but I'd heard tell a lot about him. With a name like that I was mad curious to know was he a Protestant or one of us. I found out soon enough. He'd no time for any class of religion. When he said a word or two in English it sounded the way the English talk but his Irish is without fault, a big easy man with a deep voice, well set up and for all the world like a bishop or gentry. He came on a horse but wore no hat. His clothes were the clothes of a fine gentleman. He's got bluey eyes like you'd see in a tinker's piebald, and the crinkly hair of a mountainy man.

They all say hereabouts he's a bad lad. If he takes a notion of some girl or woman he'll buy her passage if she opens her legs for him. 'Tis said he ships paupers to America and the landlords pay him well for that and they say he has land leased from evicted paupers for next nothin' and fine bullocks fattenin' on it and a sty of pigs not far from the poorhouse. So! Hasn't every doctor, priest, merchant and auctioneer his own bit of land and sty of pigs? Sure what have the landlords behind their stone walls only a wee kingdom of birds and beasts, of fields and gardens? Isn't that how we all stay alive, the bit of land and the bit to eat?

When I told him my story a sort of mist came into his eyes and I thought to myself he can't be as bad as they all say. I'd prefer him a lot to the likes of Father Brendan Galligan with his bad temper and his threats of hell. He said he could find me fair to middlin' sleepin' quarters. I'd be off the stone floor. I'd be workin' in the kitchen. I'd bring his meals to his room. If I proved useful I might get some paid work. He then put his hands on my neck and felt my glands, made me open my mouth and looked down my throat. I felt like a filly at a horse fair. When he was at this I could see him lookin' down through my poor patched smock and I knew well what was in his head. A while back I'd have said, "It's bad manners to stare at a girl like that" but I just said,

—I'll take the red ticket.

And that's what has me in this place. But I'll fight, I'll do anythin' to stay alive and, with luck, I'll get my hands on five golden guineas and get away to America, because no place in the world could be worse than this except hell itself, and no girl ever had to be shamed like me. But then look how fear of shame tumbled the Mother into hell, and anyway I knew well what to expect when I said,

—I'll take the red ticket.

The Master

HOW CAN I BEGIN TO explain what I scarcely understand myself? And how should I address you? My Dearest Anne Marie? That's too formal. My Dearest Sister? Not much better. Dear Annie? That's what I called you long ago in Calcutta where our father, Willie Murphy, was batman to General Lord Clonroy. We were the fourth generation of Murphys to be employed by that landed, Fermanagh family.

There were only the two of us: me (Lonan) and yourself. Father sometimes called you Mary Ann for a tease. Anne Marie, he said, was much too uppity for a batman's daughter and I have no idea what notion or fashion possessed them to brand me with Reginald as a second name.

I can still hear those bugles at dawn and the flapping of a flag the night I woke screaming about vultures in the quadrangle. Was that a forewarning? And always the smell of otherness from the surrounding streets. Do you remember the blind beggars, maimed children and mothers suckling infants at the barracks gates? Hungry looking and begging. Once, in the care of a servant on some errand, we saw a pack of dogs feasting on a bloated body thrown up by the river.

Is it not strange now with service bred in me how I can write that word "servant" so easily? But then even batmen can hire house servants in India. She couldn't have been too responsible when she allowed us to stare like that at human degradation. And who would have thought such horror could ever visit this ancient island of ours so thronged with saints, so especially beloved of God Himself and His Blessèd Mother? Or so we've always been led to believe.

Small wonder we crept from our beds to Mother's bed for the comfort of whisperings in Irish in the cradle of her arms, the joy of her storytelling, and the way she'd laugh and kiss us turn about. She was love and protection we thought could never end. But it did, when an army doctor said quietly to Father,

—I'm afraid, Willie, it's more serious than sunstroke. Your poor wife has meningitis.

Then that night of vomiting, and she was gone. Sometimes I think of her across all that vastness of land and sea at the other end of the earth, lying in a military graveyard with no kin of her own to visit and talk kindly. Aboardship on the way back Father got so sick we weren't allowed to see him in sick bay and, when he died of dehydration, that knowledge was kept from you. They buried him at sea. That I did not witness but have dreamt of it a thousand times. Was it the grief of that double loss that's made me cold seeming to common compassion, indifferent almost to the dying I have to accommodate almost daily in this union of death?

I was eight at the time and too stricken to weep. You were three or four and kept asking,

—Lolo, when will we see Dada? When will Mama come back from heaven?

Finally I had to use that saddest of sad words,

—Never.

I can still see your eyes at Granard as Aunt Bridie carried you from coach to ass and cart without the smallest warning that we were to be parted. That transfer was so brutal seeming, so unexpected, that I've no memory of what our aunt looked like. All I remember is being alone and your calling out my pet name again and again.

—Lolo, Lolo, Lolo.

Afterwards I wept enough to do me a lifetime. That's thirty years ago now and during all that time I don't think I cried once till that black afternoon and the days following Lady's Day, the twenty-fifth of March. This memoir is intended to mark that date. It's an apology, Annie, part confession and part explanation for why I behaved as I did. A late and useless apology, but I'd like you to understand why I've become what I've become. In truth, I'm loath to recall and set down detail, but I'll try. Like all such accounts I may steer off truth by recalling everything but the one thing that overwhelmed me that afternoon and still does two weeks later.

After the wrench of Granard they brought me on here to Fermanagh where I was fostered out to people called Ferguson. Fostered or adopted? I'm not sure which, but there must be a difference. Sam and Hannah Ferguson of Derrylester. They had a valley farm in a sheltered townland under the Bragan mountains. It looked down on a twelve-acre lake. There was a crown of mature beech near the house and rows of tall hardwoods in the well-kept ditches. Decent, south-facing land it was, marched by a modest river, and a decent, childless Presbyterian couple they were. I was fond enough of them growing up though they never encouraged me to visit you on my way to or from school in Kilkenny. In truth I was neither dissuaded nor encouraged, but difficulties were implied. The coach would have to make a detour or I would have to overnight in Granard. A bit young for that on my own. Perhaps when I was older. From an early age you learn to read the hints and nods, the smiles and silences of what will, or will not, be approved.

And, although I thought of you from time to time, I still kept away long after I was free to travel. Would we recognise each other I wondered? What would we have in common? Blood, of course, but would you remember anything that far back? I knew I'd be welcomed as family, knew also that that can have drawbacks. Requests, I suspected, would follow: a pig, a cow, a dowry, something for someone's confirmation, fares to America, Australia. I'm as selfish as the next fellow, my life ahead. I knew indirectly that you were hired out in some midland town – Ferbane, Athlone, Mullingar – that you'd married, had a child. Your husband, I was told, had emigrated. Someday, I thought, I'll find out where you are and call. Maybe. My only kin, although that girl I shipped off swore she was carrying to me. How can a man be sure? Life is hard on females when they're trapped that way unless, of course, they set the trap themselves and pay the price of such deception.

The Brady girl was gone when I awoke this morning. I'll tell you about her as I go along. She'll be back shortly with my breakfast. Once or twice she's hinted about what happened that afternoon. She knows better than to refer to it openly. I still can't think about it without emotion, let alone talk about it, to her, to anyone.

—A raving beauty, the Matron, Norma Butler, described her the day I brought her in. It was Mervyn Johnston, our local field warden, who first drew attention to her.

—She's in a bad way, Mister Murphy, an orphan you might say, and won't listen to me. You'll have to see her for yourself.

I went out to the townland of Drumlanna and found her sitting among the ruins of a tumbled cottage. I was startled when I saw her.

No mere flower on a dungheap. There was something out of the ordinary about her expression and manner. At first she said no to the red ticket. I felt the glands on her neck, looked down her throat. No sign of disease. I persuaded her then to change her mind, explaining there were things I could arrange as Master that would make life more bearable. Let me be honest now and say it was the brute in me that made me so persuasive, made it hard not to stare, to imagine that body under those pitiable rags. When she said yes, I offered her a seat behind me as far as the town, told her she'd have to dismount and walk from the outskirts to the poorhouse itself. It wouldn't be seemly for the Master to be seen bringing in a female pauper on horseback. I was surprised when she refused the offer with a headshake.

—Then walk on, girl, I said.

For three miles I watched her walking, her gait graceful as that of a trained dancer. Compared with most country girls she trod the road like a racehorse. Once or twice I tried talking. Each time she pretended not to understand. Then I saw tears on her face and remembered what it was like to be deep in grief, homeless and alone in the world, as we were once, at the mercy of strangers. The rest of the journey passed in silence.

I put her to childminding in the female children's ward. When not with me in this room she sleeps on a stretcher near the oven in the bake-house. It's warm and not as sickly foul as the female dormitory or the idiot ward where her mother's lodged. She brings my meals to this room, cleans it out every day, and the pantry off, and the boardroom next door when the Board of Guardians are due to meet.

A raving beauty now seems an odd description for a girl who opens her legs more readily than she opens her mouth, though, when she does speak, it's to ask pointed questions. She must have crept away quietly in the half-light this morning. Prefers not to be seen coming and going to the Master's room.

—But you bring my meals here, I said, it's part of your work.

—Not at night, she said.

I thought about this for a while.

—Is there talk?

No answer but, once, deep asleep, I heard her mutter.

—Jealous cunts.

So I woke her and asked,

—Who's jealous?

She pretended not to understand. I told her what she said, using the blunt word she'd used to startle her into response.

—And why would anyone be jealous?

—That's my question.

She responded with a shrug and a stare from those green, cat-brazen eyes. Silly to ask. Who wants me, who wants me not? Vain and silly. Clean well-water, the leftovers of fresh bread, the cuttings of cheese and meat scraps she gets from my table. That's what she wants; that's what brings her to this bed. Not me. Hunger.

When she first arrived I showed her the fifty-gallon water barrel I draw from a mountain spring near Derravarragh. Fortnightly. I told her to drink nothing else. Ever. It's a granite landscape up there. The water's like crystal with a kind of bluey tinge. I watch her drinking it from a glass, and she watches me watching with those knowing eyes. It's like being watched by a wild animal. Sometimes when I give her butter, bread and honey, she trembles while eating. A little colour comes into her face, but the manner is unafraid, insolent almost in one so young. Clearly her looks promote envy and, as you must know, girls endowed that way tend to have high notions of their worth.

She was here two full weeks before I touched her. When I did, she looked at me for what seemed like a minute or longer, until I was obliged to ask,

—Do you object?

—How can I?

—By saying no!

To this she made no answer but continued staring in silence which I read as consent. She seldom talks before, during, or after congress. More disconcerting, she utters no sound, no hint or moan of pleasure. Oddly, as I became familiar with her body the less I seemed to know her mind and began to wonder was there any mind worth knowing. Then one night out of nowhere she surprised me by asking,

—Do you have kin?

—Not that I know.

In the silence that followed I knew that reply was half true, half false.

—Are you Catholic or Protestant?

—Neither.

—You're not Christian so?

—I was baptised Catholic, I said, but expect nothing from this world or the next.

—So what made your mother put a name like Reggie on you?

I was unready for these sudden questions. Even less did I care for the blunt way they were asked.

—My kin, creed or name is no affair of yours, girl, I said.

She was silent for a while, then shrugged faintly.

—The priest Galligan says you have a sister, married out of Granard.

—Does he now?

—He does, so he does.

—A knowing man is the Reverend Galligan! I said.

—It's what he told me.

—I'm sure he did.

Clever little thing, I thought. She knew I'd be angered by the idea of Galligan nosing into my life. Clearly he'd got word from some long-eared cleric in Longford. A holy finger in every pie, they have, and more than a finger, if truth be told, which they seldom tell but damn little they don't know about the ups and downs in towns and townlands, the streets and cities of this saintly island, and what they don't hear in confession gets whispered and altered elsewhere, at crossroads and schoolyards, in parochial parlours and sacristies.

—She bragged it herself, Father.

—True as God, your Reverence.

—Not a dog in the street but has it.

—Every ass in the bog knows it for fact.

—May I be struck dead if I'm tellin' a word of a lie.

Or maybe she heard it from Hanratty, the sub-master here, an Armagh sacristan's son, an ex-seminarian with a big head and mock priesty voice, creeping about the boys' dormitory at night, listening at doors and windows. A seminal man in league with the clergy, spying, scheming and informing. Bred in him. My Lord-ing Old Clonroy at the beginning and end of every sentence. Told me once he'd lost his vocation at Maynooth after two years.

—In bed, I asked him, or in a sheugh? Well, Ratty, I greet him each morning. How many dead? What's the count?

He pretends to enjoy black banter but loathes me, thank God. I can tell from his fixed smile and the way he never looks me in the eye. Nonetheless I'd prefer him to the priest Galligan, by a rat's whisker. It was that sly reference to your existence and to your poverty that angered me, made me snap back,

—If there is a hell there's more priests than whores in it, and I am Sir to you, girl! What else about Galligan?

—Have you mortal sins on your soul? he asked me. Is the man Murphy using you?

—Did you tell him to go to hell?

—It's bad luck to curse a priest – *Sir*.

—Did you tell him you were using "the man Murphy"?

—I don't have a foodpress – Sir.

—So?

—I want to stay alive, Sir.

—Then go to the dayroom and pick oakum. You don't have to come here. What else?

—He said you were a landlord's lackey, Sir, a traitor to Ireland, and would surely burn in the lowest pit of hell.

Those words were like a stomach punch. I tried not to show how they struck home.

—That fella's a traitor to common sense, and make no mistake, girl, I'm Master here. If he lifts a finger to you or an eyebrow to me, it's out on his arse he'll go. You can tell him that if you want.

Sudden anger had made me deaf to her next question which I had to make her repeat.

—I asked you, Sir, was he lying about your sister?

—Trying to make trouble.

I then heard myself say,

—She was an infant when we were parted.

I could see her thinking behind those green eyes that looked directly into mine and began to wish she'd stayed as silent as she appeared to be when she first came here.

—That was a cruel thing they did, Sir.

—They had no choice, maybe.

—And no sight of her since? Your own sister?

I then realised this was more than country cuteness. Here was a little vixen playing off one man against another, prying deep into privacy but, worse again, playing the hypocrite and thinking I wouldn't or couldn't twig it.

—You don't visit your mother in the idiot ward, I said. She's dying, you do know that?

Her response was to look away for a moment and then find another question deliberately meant to irritate. I didn't bother answering and tried to tell myself I was in no way bothered by her. Certainly not my conscience.

I've no guilt about what happens in this bed, or this room, because the more I see of death every day the more I crave congress every night. Most likely she hates me for having to come here at all, and there's something in me that dislikes her coming, but when those arms are around my neck it's like that whispering mouth in Calcutta long ago. More and more now I try to discourage it from talking but she manages most times to slip in an enquiry about passage money, knowing well I can arrange it with Clonroy. I explain each time. A "free" five pounds steerage ticket to America could be a death warrant. Cramped, stifling, shift-filthy conditions and wretched food would sicken a dog. She doesn't believe or only half believes me.

—What does it cost to go cabin?

—Twenty pounds, a great deal of money, and you bring your own food and water, and you need another twenty for when you get there.

—I can work for that, Sir. If you'd loan me I'll send it back.

—You want me to loan you forty pounds!

She stared at me and made no answer, so I said,

—A girl like you? Alone? In New York? Boston? Put it out of your head.

—Why?

—The dock rats'd get you for a brothel.

—I'm a hoor you think, Sir?

—They'd make you one.

—Have you not done that, Sir?

—Your choice, girl, and mind your tongue!

Next day I didn't go to the foodpress when she was drinking water. The day after that she was a track more mannerly, like a dog that sees you reaching for the cane; biddable, but not cowering.

Once, after intimacy, I heard her mutter,

—You don't own me.

I said I had no wish to own or dominate, and asked her to explain. She refused, but did say at another time,

—The Mother thought she owned us. That was her mistake.

Of course the dream they all dream is America, America, America. Paradise! Happiness! Freedom! Abundance! Meantime, the nightmare is here and now and being awake to the other bodies lodged in this house, half alive and otherwise. Who in God's name or the Devil's would want to own them? All boding time till abide with me. Yours, hers, mine and theirs. Grave matter. That's what I'm master of. Till my time is up! Must be one of the most unenviable posts in the history of the world thus far. They called Christ "Master" long ago but I'm a long way from Him and in sore need of a few miracles. Like all of us I'd like to ask Him some questions about man- and womankind, about why He made us and the world the way it is, and how and when He means to end it? Or why if He means to end it did He bother making it at all? And the billions of stars and beyond? What purpose? How can anyone look about the world and believe in a God? How can anyone look about the world and not believe in a God? Is it some cruel game He's playing up there? Lep at the stars and break your neck?

When I got up this morning I went to the admittance book to check when she came in. There it was in Hanratty's elaborate hand:

February the third 1848
Brady, Roisin/Female/Age 17, RC/Not disabled/Very
clean/Townland of Drumlanna/Tenant of Eden Hall
Estate/House tumbled.

Underneath I'd scribbled,

Mother confined to idiot ward. Only kin.

Like me, one frail tie she can't wait to untie.

Last night we had to close the gates forcibly. About two dozen were locked out. Most of them slept under the canal bridge. Earlier, from the window, I could see some stirring, others still. Dead still. They'll be carted later to the open pit behind the turfshed along with the ones found in ditches and sheughs and the poor wretches the Council fish out of the canal from time to time, all of them consigned to perpetual light or darkness with their neighbours from a hundred townlands. Galway and Scarriff have just been closed by the treasury. Over-spending, they say, and every pauper who could walk was shown the road to everlasting. This place has become a kind of Public School for the impoverished. Their only lesson? How to die, and I am death's headmaster. Soon we'll have to open another pit. Most masters don't like using paupers for the pit digging. I never had qualms that way until recently. Hired labour, being costly, meant less money to buy food and every circular from the Castle used the word "rationalise" at least three times. It was the priest Galligan who protested,

—Unseemly, he said, to have the dead burying the dead.

I shrugged him off by saying,

—Kings or paupers, I said, we all dispose of each other, this way, when the time comes. And priests? Does it matter how?

I could see him looking with disbelief.

But I must tell you that many things I considered ridiculous then now appear to me in a very different and painful light. Certainly I'll ask for voluntary teams to do the digging from now on, if I decide to stay on.

Did I tell you that, a month back in the Phoenix Park, the Viceroy looked at me and asked,

—Who are you, Sir?

I told him but thought to myself, who in hell is he? For that matter who is anybody, in heaven or in hell? When our parents christened me Lonan Reginald Murphy in Calcutta they'd no notion I'd say of calling me Reggie which I quickly became, for obvious reasons. Clonroy's name is Bob Skinner and the Viceroy who laid the first stone at Maynooth was a man called Pratt. More fitting, we now have an English ex-general in charge of Poor Law relief, food for the starving, and he's called Sir Edward Pine Coffin! A decent man they say but the Dickens of a name, with quarter of a million in poorhouses, up on three millions or more starving and Christ knows how many wandering the roads or packed into coffin ships, one in five dumped at sea. I've a thousand in this place built for six hundred. None of them can afford a shroud let alone a coffin.

> Rattle my bones over the stones,
> I'm a poor pauper nobody owns.
> Where am I going, where am I bound?
> Naked and lonely into the ground.

No, sister, I'm not being cynical. I'm trying to be candid about brutal facts. As Master here I admit paupers. That's my work. From entry to exit, public ward to burial pit. Eighty-seven last week. Lurgan was unluckier; they had ninety-eight. It's what we Masters are paid for, processing paupers, and better paid than a postmaster or stationmaster, but they don't have to traffic with dysentery, cholera, typhus, or be present when we sign in families and then segregate them, husband from wife, parents from children, or listen to the crying and keening I'd almost ceased to hear, the way people who live near rookeries no longer hear the rooks. But I do see a lot of them go mad with grief which I now understand in a deeper way.

In truth I'm cangled to grief for fifty pounds a year and it's not enough. Six of us, workhouse Masters that is, died this past twelve months, along with nine priests, two chaplains, seven doctors, all in the line of duty. Typhus mostly. They haven't a pup's notion how it spreads.

I know. In fact I'm certain. It's the water contaminated by corpses. You can smell it. Yes, it is a dangerous occupation, but I've emigrated dead paupers from time to time and collected a small bonus for the extra bookwork involved! Nothing criminal, you must understand. I'm trying to be candid. I'm no saint, sister, as you'll have gathered, but I'm far from the worst which would leave me about the same as the rest of man- and womankind.

Yesterday two weeks back was Saint Patrick's feast day. It came in mild. Galligan said Mass in the men's yard with my permission. Segregation was strictly enforced, as always. Chaos otherwise, mothers with suckling infants excepted, though mostly they're suckling at nothing. All trooping out to kneel like ghosts in the March sunlight. Afterwards two paupers with a tin whistle and a squeezebox wheezed out a few melodies, Tom Moore's weepy parlour stuff, dreams that never were, nor ever will be. Then all sang feebly, Galligan leading loudly,

—Hail glorious, Saint Patrick, dear saint of our isle,

On us, thy poor children, bestow a sweet smile.

Stringer, our chaplain, kept his poor Protestants apart in the main hall, hymning their way to heaven. Wilson's bakery donated a thousand sweet fingers to mark the day. One each at noon. Amid the fast a pauper's feast. Fingers of death. Three died during Mass. The able-bodied carried them away to the dead cart and eternity.

If you think the conveying of these details a little cold let me give you an item or two from my Complaints Book. Here's the kind of thing I've had to write up again and again:

COMPLAINT

The Roman Catholic priest, Brendan Galligan, objects forcefully to the Church of Ireland chaplain, Norman Stringer, deliberately reading the Bible in the school house with Papist children present.

MASTER'S RULING

Catholic children to be removed during Bible readings.

COMPLAINT

The Protestant chaplain, Norman Stringer, protests angrily that the priest Galligan brings in and distributes "bagfuls of rosaries, medals, trinkets and other such trumpery to Protestant children during school hours."

MASTER'S RULING

The priest Galligan must desist from this practice.

And these fellows call themselves apostles of Christ. Holy men? Holy God, Holy hell! Stupid, stupid, stupid men! And I'm obliged to nod to both but you'll pardon me, sister, when I tell you that I fart as I nod, when possible, because I don't give a pauper's shite about the breed or creed of either. I'm fairly sure they see me as evil but, God knows, I'm nowhere near as devious as such masters of promise and pretence.

The Brady girl came back with my breakfast as I began to set down this confession. I ate a little without appetite, gave her some bread and a decent hunk of cheese from the foodpress. She looked at me with something close to disbelief, ate both quickly and gulped down two glasses of water. She then muttered thank you so quietly it might have been a curse. As she left the Kilkenny dream came back with sudden clarity. I was in that middle classroom in the catacombs of St. Paul's, as old Darling barked out his obsession with words:

—*Phytophthora infestans?*

—Come on, boys. *Phytophthora infestans*, Murphy? What does it mean?

—I don't know, Sir.

—With a name like yours! *Phytophthora infestans* is a blight, Murphy, and here in Ireland at the peak of our Empire it has brought famine, poverty and death on a scale more harrowing than the worst areas of Calcutta. This island, always a backdoor nuisance to the greater island, is now a scarecrow in a foul rickyard, a rotting corpse in an empty larder caused, you must surely know, by the arrival of this blight, this disease of the common spud or Murphies. The word itself derives from the Anglo-Saxon *blican*, a lightning strike, or possibly from the Middle German *blichen*, to grow pale, to decay, to die. Thus the word has become synonymous with, Murphy? With?

—Death, Sir!

Like most dreams, illogical nonsense. Famine? How could it be? In a country exporting food on every tide? Certainly there was no blight, famine or starvation when I was at St. Paul's apart from the blight of loneliness. They allowed me out for Instruction and Confession every Saturday.

On Sundays I went to Mass in the town, emancipated! We were all emancipated by then, we Irish Roman Catholics. Whatever army benefit there was went on my schooling. You got nothing, Annie, but the coach fare from Cobh to Granard and a midland bog. Sometimes I envied the remoteness of a life like that. I was a curiosity. Being the only Papist was a challenge to bullies, three in particular who couldn't leave me be.

—Tell us, Spud, is it true you Papes believe Jesus Christ is in a wafer, blood and bone?

I held my tongue.

—Do you eat him guts and all?

I held my tongue.

—Do rascally priests feel you people up at Confession?

I held my tongue.

—Did *your* man ever try that on you?

At which I blurted,

—You silly shits, go bugger each other!

They tackled me then but I was strong, still am, and not being gentle born I fought back with teeth, boots and nails. Two of them were bruised and scrabbed, the third badly enough bitten for the infirmary. They never tackled me again, even though I'd mutter "Silly shits" any time they were near.

It was during that first Christmas holiday I realised my reports were sent both to Eden Hall and Derrylester. Old Clonroy sent for me. When I arrived I could see he had a copy of my report, and if his face was serious his manner was benign.

—Under *Conduct and Behaviour* it says here, "Inclined to brutal tactics. Unprovoked. One boy treated in the infirmary. Two others badly marked. Recurrence may mean expulsion." This has your headmaster's signature. What was it about, boy?

—My religion, my Lord, was being mocked.

—Not worth fighting over, he said. Most religion is make-believe, most mockery envy. You should have ignored both.

When I'd finished at Kilkenny, he sent for me again.

—So! You've started well. Not the top, but close enough. Very good. But what are we going to do with you now, eh? Soldiering? Like your father? Best regiments in the world are Irish. It's one thing we're damned good at here, fighting! No? Law? I could get you apprenticed. No? Then you tell me what's in your head.

I said I loved Derrylester, house and farm. I'd become attached to the Fergusons and I liked farming.

—The idea of it, perhaps. Farming, he went on to say, was hard enough at the best of times. Hereabouts with our Irish hackers and poisoners it can be a bloody nightmare, fortress farming, and don't forget we're all slightly mad in this country. Inbreeding mostly, and religious nonsense.

The kettle calling the pot black. Dust and disorder seemed more offensive to him than death. Last time he was here he barked out,

—When were those windows cleaned, Murphy? A new building and you can hardly see through the windows! Surely you can delegate some paupers for the job.

Most paupers, I explained, were too weak to climb ladders, let alone clean windows.

Barracks life since he was twenty, all that marching and killing for Queen and Empire has him half crazy like most old soldiers. Unpolished boots more likely to keep him wakeful than some poor sapper's death. Or paupers. Nor did I like to suggest that as a farmer I'd be viewed differently from the titled descendant of a Cromwellian settler with twenty thousand acres of confiscated land. Derrylester was a modest holding not likely to inspire the envy or hatred that seemed to cling like arrogance or a bad odour to the owners of big estates. Nor did I want to tell him what old Sam Ferguson had said to me once, his eyes full of tears,

—You're more to me than a son, you must know that.

I do know he meant it. There were a hundred freehold acres at Derrylester of well fenced, well laid-out fields, a sound, cut stone house, yards and barns, an orchard garden, half a mile of trout river, a ten-acre lake, an artesian well eighty feet deep in the flagged dairy and a herd of fifty shorthorn cattle, roans, reds and blues, that took prizes for milk and beef wherever they were shown. It was near paradise, to my mind.

Naturally I stayed on and worked as an unpaid steward, eighteen years of hard work, the neverending watch for thieving and idling of tenant workers, and dairymaids! They could be lively but I wasn't free for that kind of freedom. I had to be circumspect about how I paid myself and about private matters. Still have to be. Along with the mixed farming we kept a hunt pack. Fallen animals for miles about were dumped in the yard to feed hounds. Dear God, that deathly smell of bloated beasts in high summer. Even in winter it lingered in my clothes and hair, a mix of dogshit, entrails and rotting flesh.

Every now and then a plague of rats had to be poisoned. No one would or could flay those carcasses but me. The old man was too arthritic so I accustomed my stomach to the fact and smell of animal death. What made others retch instantly was nothing to me, the perfect apprenticeship for my work as Master of this poorhouse, workhouse, union, call it what you like. What's in a name?

A great deal, I was soon to learn. Too late. The old man's nephew, Richard, wrote from Australia once a year. He had no other kin. I was shown the letters, no sense of a special bond, but Sam replied. Naturally I didn't see his replies but hoped, presumed, I was to inherit. Meantime, in truth, I liked the work, and I loved the place, and so stayed on happily enough.

I can narrow down my love for that farm to one day, and one field, the lake meadow, with its great single beech in the middle. During that midsummer's day under a glorious sun with ten Fermanagh men, I scythed down a hundred and fifty rucks. There was still light when we quit the field near midnight. Two rainless weeks later it was stacked and thatched in the haggard and, because engendering is proscribed in heaven, the smell of green hay, I remember thinking, must be what they use up there to engender happiness. Some day, I imagined, I'd be master of the earth, water and sky over Derrylester, without the snarling of dogs or the odour of dead animals, mowing grass under a summer sun or feeding green scented hay in midwinter, till kingdom come.

It was not to be. When he died, the house and garden were willed to the old lady for her lifetime and, thereafter, everything – land, lock, stock and barrel – to his nephew, Richard.

I couldn't think or speak for days. They thought I was heartbroken about the old man passing on. Gradually I began to understand. Blood goes deep. It tells. And names do matter. Ours, Murphy, is like a brand here in Ulster, and even though I was moulded and educated to their likeness I was bred from the conquered tribe. Stupidly I'd ignored what I'd heard them mulling over in their hot whiskies.

—Aye, you can rear the wild thing, Sam, and ye think ye know it, but some day it'll growl and tear your throat out! The identical same with Taigs. Keep an eye, keep your distance, keep them out.

That, I knew, was an article of faith with the more ignorant type of Presbyterian and, while I was certain old Ferguson was not such a one, I should have realised I wasn't blood. Like it or not, I was a Taig.

In his will he referred to my "good education and good head to use it. He will better himself in the world. I have no doubt of this. I leave him three hundred guineas and, as a token of my special affection, the silver embossed snuff box willed me by my father, Alex."

Not mean, but to buy and stock even a modest farm it was less than a pittance. My life was half gone. I'd bided my time for a dream, for nothing. I almost kicked the snuff box into a boghole, changed my mind and pawned it at Enniskillen for one guinea and, fond as I was of old Hannah Ferguson, I left suddenly. Since then I expect nothing from anyone, take what's my due and more if it's safe. The thing nearest to my heart was suddenly gone, like our mother and father, in thirteen words. It was like death again: "To my nephew, Richard Ferguson, I leave the farmlands and house at Derrylester."

I heard nothing further as the attorney droned on, itemising bequests. So names do matter, blood does tell and some hurts never heal.

That disappointment clenched my heart against expectation of any kind and a heart clenched, Annie, becomes a cold thing. It has to. It would seem now that I am rummaging about for excuses, for exoneration. Whether or not, I am trying to be candid and most abjectly begging your forgiveness. In truth these past few years I've become unkind, not just dead to feeling, unkind. It was, I decided, the only way to function in this world. Never again would I allow life to betray me as it had. To hurt me. You will think now, sister, that I'm straying far from you in this account. Let me beg your patience a little longer while I tell you why I agreed to become Master of this place, what that means, and how that must affect and alter, not only me, but any man in my position. Or woman. Above all, why I greeted you as I did.

That hard blow, the will, came sometime late in March of 1843. At Eden Hall they'd heard about it and my sudden leavetaking. Old Clonroy sent for me. He was as I always found him, oblique, kindly and a little odd. I thought he was referring indirectly to the will when he said,

—You'll find life a lot easier without expectations of any kind.

Two years later, when Eden Hall went on the market, I realised he was thinking about himself when he said that, being the last of the line and betrayed in a way by kin, his only son, Mathew. Three hundred years of continuity discontinued, but all of that's another story. Why he sent for me was to tell me that his neighbour and friend, Mr. Shirley, a direct descendant of the Earl of Essex and owner of Castle Fea, a whole barony of south Monaghan which ran to near seventy thousand acres, had just engaged a new land agent, an Englishman called Stuart Trench. Would I care to act as sub-agent and translator?

The money offered was tempting. It had to be. It was a time when landlords and their agents were being assassinated or half beaten to death all over Ireland. I didn't want the job but without training for other work I was in no position to refuse. Three days later, April the third, I found myself alongside Trench outside the agent's house in the main street of Carrick-macross. He was only a week in the country but I'd been with him for three days, got to know him a little. I liked him, though I kept wanting to stop him and say, "It's not England here, Sir, nor Scotland, nor Wales. It's as different as France or Spain." He was listening, not hearing, but being a clever man I felt he'd learn quickly.

That morning outside the agent's house he was standing on a table to make sure he could be heard, and a commanding voice and manner he had; very sure of himself. I was on a chair beside him to interpret for that south Monaghan crowd, a huge, ragged mass of hungry humans as far as we could see, and a cold, hasky day it was. Showers of sleet and rain. There was something in excess of ten thousand, the Constabulary said afterwards.

What I had to convey from Trench speaking for his new master was bad news. There was, I had to shout out, a vast amount of rent owing. The estate was in real danger of bankruptcy. There could be no question whatsoever of forgoing or reducing rent. He also talked of "appropriate action in the event of non-payment" which I could only translate as "bad news for the house," a euphemism for eviction. This went through the crowd like a growl, followed by a deathly silence, till a voice shouted out in both tongues,

—Down on your knees, boys, we'll ask him again on our knees.

And that huge crowd were suddenly bareheaded on their knees in a silence so absolute you could hear the daws racketing in the town chimneys.

I had seen the kneeling before and knew it to be a form of abjection both sinister and threatening. Trench was startled.

—What's going on? he asked through the side of his mouth.

—What you see, I whispered. Abject supplication.

I could tell he was more irritated than afraid or, if afraid, he didn't show it. He seemed almost unaware of the menace.

—Any suggestions?

—I'd promise them something.

Maybe it was the urgency of my whisper that made him say aloud,

—I'm damned if I will!

Was that sidemouth whisper overheard? Or was it Trench's unafraid mutter and shrug? I don't know but suddenly, without warning, the table upended, he was grabbed and disappeared. There followed a frenzy of milling and shouting so turbulent, so enraged and hysterical, that I couldn't see him being stripped, punched, beaten and kicked, because he didn't call out.

I knew roughly where he was and was trying to get to him when suddenly I saw him, almost naked and upright, both arms pinned against a cartwheel, a crowd of men round him with cudgels, screeching into his face in a language that needed no interpreter.

I don't think I've ever been so frightened in my life, not so much for myself as for what I feared was about to happen. Maybe it was sudden fear that gave me the strength to jostle my way towards him, shouting out,

—The man's new. Give him a chance. Don't, men, don't. He's a stranger!

Or it might have been when I shouted out,

—For Jesus' sake, don't murder the man, lads, don't do it, they'll hang you!

Maybe it was the words "murder" and "hang" that caused a lull because suddenly I was at his side and he had voice and courage enough to shout out,

—I will do everything in my power to persuade Mister Shirley of the strength of your feelings and ask him to reconsider the justice of your case.

This I translated as,

—Listen, lads, he knows your troubles, but he needs your patience and good nature to sort things out. Will ye give the man a chance?

At which some voice shouted out,

—God bless you, Stuart Trench.

And as quick as the kneeling crowd turned ugly the standing crowd now began to cheer and shout down blessings on his head.

I worked with Trench for a learning year. He was still arrogant but a great deal more circumspect. He convinced Mister Shirley that emigrating tenant paupers to America at five pounds a head was cheaper than keeping them in the poorhouse at four pounds a year. By buying passage he'd be free of the swarming cottiers, squatters and ditch beggars who couldn't pay rent and were, in any case, half starving because of the blight. He would benefit, they would benefit. The scheme was a huge success till the black tide of sea burials came floating back to haunt every family in the country.

Meantime Lord Lansdowne had heard of the scheme and written Shirley. Could he recommend someone to emigrate three thousand tenants from his estate in Kenmare in the County of Kerry? I was approached and said why not. I knew the system, the pay was better, the climate milder, the people more colourful than the dour tidy Scots-English I'd grown up amongst, and they were clamouring for tickets. So down I went, and for two years bank drafts of four hundred pounds arrived regularly. I shipped between two and three hundred tenants a week from Kenmare to Queenstown on foot. It was like an ancient cattle drive but not as easy. The road was filled with men, women and children, singing and laughing, clowning and arguing along with their pigs, goats, fowl, donkeys, creels and carts, all of them elated and heartbroken because this was a farewell forever to the garden of spuds, to hearth and hovel, to mountain and bog, to Mother Ireland herself. So they all kept shouting up in tears and waving to the poor scarecrows hoeing in turnip fields.

—We're on our way to Amerikay!

And the poor scarecrows would wave back. The dead waving farewell to the dead.

If the weather was against us we'd have to overnight. That was always trouble. The appetite for porter being insatiable leads on to fighting and shouting and wandering and no end of rounding up. With only three paid henchmen this caused serious delays. Unlike Ulster folk, these Kerry people were without a word of English. Most of them had never been more than a mile or so outside their own townlands. They were the same people Saint Patrick had preached to in the fifth century, noisy, good humoured, unpredictable, and the young ones now far from the prying eyes of neighbours were none too particular about their conduct, much of which I could see from horseback. In their own heads, I suppose, they were bound for the excitements of another world, a great adventure, not knowing that one in five would indeed end up in another world, ocean deep.

Last year, of the two hundred and twenty thousand emigrated, forty thousand died on the way or on arrival. It was nothing like that when I was down there but I became uneasy as newspapers began writing of "Extermination," "Bloodletting" and "Innocents consigned to the deep," and described me as "An Ulster turncoat, the cruel whipmaster of Lansdowne's death riders." So you will understand that when a letter came from Eden Hall telling me about a new workhouse on the outskirts of the town I moved quickly. Being Master of a workhouse up here seemed both safer and more attractive than being a death rider in Kerry. I knew also that the position itself tends to inspire a kind of awe akin to gentry or clergy.

I have to confess that I wasn't indifferent to that. Also, I was glad to be back in my own province where I'd once been happy at Derrylester although, any time I passed it, I could see slates missing and great patches of nettles flowering in the orchard garden. Hannah Ferguson had died when I was away and the land, now rented out to cattle dealers and jobbers, was already reverting to ragwort and rushes.

Have I already told you that some time in February of this year the Viceroy, Clarendon, requested a delegation of a dozen masters, three from each province, to discuss the increased death rate in almost all of the hundred and fifty poorhouses? I travelled up with John Wynne of Carrickmacross who was very much in the news at the time. At some point I said the workhouse system itself was causing the increase. Clarendon had already asked my name but glanced down at his notes to make sure.

—Mister Murphy? You're not serious?

—I'm certain, I said. It's putrefaction from burial pits leaking into workhouse wells, infecting staff and paupers. Our pit's at the march of our twelve acres but I wouldn't drink the water.

—Your paupers drink it?

—They have no choice, nor have we. With a thousand souls, we must pump water.

—What solution would you suggest, Sir?

—I'd burn the corpses.

This caused quite a silence till John Wynne said,

—My Lord, I'm inclined to agree with Mister Murphy. Cremation is a more cleansing process, my Lord.

Clarendon knew John Wynne. A while back some peeping squint of a squireen had seen him "at it" in a ditch with a pauper girl and written to Dublin Castle about the shock this vision had caused to what he called his "moral sensibility." All hell then broke over Wynne's head. He was the Devil incarnate using his position to seduce poor dying pauper girls. The poor girls were dying to seduce him for anything going, extra food rations, passage money or shenanigans for the sake of shenanigans.

I know. He ended up in the House of Lords defending himself and was acquitted, but then they'd respond well to him over there. He's a bit craven about position and titles, My Lord–ing Clarendon at the beginning and end of every sentence, and Clarendon is a very Patrician gentleman, but he farts, shits and copulates like any other man and he's afraid of the Catholic Church.

—The Church of Rome, he said, will not discuss cremation. I will not antagonise them. We have more than enough on our hands, gentlemen.

—But when families die of typhus, I said, the hovel's burned over them and the clergy sprinkle ashes. That's cremation surely? Why pretend it's not?

—I cannot answer for the Church of Rome, Clarendon muttered.

To which I almost added, An institution run by hypocrites for idiots.

I held my tongue but let me say now that, as a practising hypocrite, I'm moderately gifted. My position here obliges me to give out morning and evening prayers and grace before meals.

—Bless us, O Lord, and these Thy gifts which of Thy bounty we are about to receive.

If I had my way I'd consign most holy men to the idiot wards but then the paupers would be desolate. They cling to them, hang on every word. Heaven's next door, over the hill, upstairs, round the corner, destination of the destitute. Naked, diseased, raving, filthy and skeletal, they go straight to the arms of Jesus and Mary! It's alms we need from Jesus and Mary to clothe the naked and feed the hungry.

—The poor you have always with you. Me you have not.

Quare big notions You had of Yourself. Jesus, God of love. Small wonder they crucified You!

Annie, I'm sorry if such notions offend you, but anger, as you made so clear to me, is a comrade to grief and all day I've been penning this confession to explain both. I've been to the press just now and poured the tumbler of whiskey that numbs before it worsens. Twice during the day the

Brady girl has tapped on the door asking if I wanted to eat in the staff room or here. I've no appetite whatever and tell her what I've been telling her every day, that I'm still unwell, but on the mend. Not true. Time may be a healer for the body. For the soul, in my case, it's no cure. In truth, to my mind, it can sicken even more.

It's dusk now, near dark again, and there's the Angelus ringing high over the clatter and murmur coming up from the paupers' dining hall. Some-where – it must be from the female sleeping quarters – I can hear an infant crying and crying and crying and it wrings my heart. I don't know why. Or perhaps I do because every hour of this long day I've been aware of the coming night, the night of ending. The night of Lady's Day.

Let me tell you that from daybreak it's threatened rain from a sky as black as the Bangor blues on the roof of the admissions block. It held off somehow, and somehow I've been holding out against that word "admis-sions," much like the children's game where "yes" or "no" is the forbidden word but no child ever wins. Nor can I when that word comes into my head.

I'll pour another tumbler and tonight, instead of evicting memory, I'll try to explain. And there's another word, explain, explain, explain! How many times have I used it when in my heart of hearts I know there is no explanation that deserves forgiveness? None. But I have tried to grapple with some few details of what we call life with all the honesty I can muster, and maybe that deserves a morsel of mitigation. Does it not? Bless me, Mother, Father, Creator, Lord Jesus, Allah, Buddah, Somebody, Nobody, Anybody. Bless me, bless me, bless me, for I have sinned and am sorrowful. My sister, Annie, bless me and forgive me. Can you hear me? I am talking to you and no one else and let me not grow mawkish nor evasive when the whiskey throngs, nor unafraid to admit right off that soft-sounding word "admissions," nor to tell you what it signifies. Let me say it aloud,

—Admissions.

Workhouse admissions. Work. Not pleasant but it becomes routine like all work. Families mostly, starving of course, must agree to sign over all rights to land and property. Before we can admit them they must prove destitu-tion, and then walk away forever from neighbour and village, field and well, hearth and home.

We supply the documents proving poverty. They line up and I question them. Name, townland, religion, landlord and so on. Then I make sure they understand that the house they have just left will be tumbled, levelled back into the landscape. Mostly they're too weak and sick to take this in. A clerk writes down details. They make their mark. I sign them in and pass them on to the medical officer, O'Grady.

The doctor before him, Ambrose O'Donnell, was hopeless. We all agreed about that. He was either in, or on the edge of, tears most of the time. And a big strong Donegal fella he was. Caused great upset. He couldn't stomach the process and had to go. As he was leaving he told me he'd rather be a pauper than an admitting officer and I remember thinking at the time, this man is quite mad; certainly he's weak, foolish, unbalanced. I now think the very opposite.

When the physical condition is decided by O'Grady, segregation takes place. Men, women, boys, girls, proceed to separate quarters where they remain separate till they sign out, which is, in many cases, lights out. It can be noisy. The orderlies, most of them able-bodied paupers, are there to protect me and the admitting staff from outlandish behaviour, hysterical kneeling, shrieking and begging, the throwing of arms around our legs.

Hanratty's good at calming them and the Matron, Norma Butler. They take them aside and talk quietly. If they're unhappy about segregation, then they're free to go. There's no obligation to come in. They have of course nowhere to go so they say their goodbyes and are led to the washhouses and from there to the dayrooms, workrooms, yards, schoolhouse, fever shed, idiot ward, or often straight to the dying rooms where, during this last year, they mostly end.

That morning of the twenty-fifth of March, admissions were going quietly. Generally they're so desolate they've no energy for making scenes, but halfway down the line I noticed a woman, wild-eyed and standing out. She was holding a child by the hand, both emaciated, the child in a bag skirt wearing a man's cap so I couldn't tell its gender.

She was looking at me very directly. I kept avoiding her eyes but I could sense them staring in that way you can and thought, do I know her maybe from somewhere? Maybe even slept with her long ago, back in the Derrylester days? No. Surely I'd remember that. But she was familiar in some way. I knew I knew her and was thinking this when she broke line and began walking towards me dragging the child and ignoring the orderly who seemed unsure about what to do. As she approached she called out in a kind of broken voice,

—Lolo!

Oh Christ of Calcutta, that one word, a pet name from long ago, should be like a sword twist in the bowels, an invisible bullet to stop my heart like nothing I'd ever known. My breathing shallowed and I suppose my mouth fell open. She called again louder,

—Lolo!

Only one person in the world knew that pet name. As a little one, Annie, you couldn't get your mouth round my first name, Lonan, so beyond all doubt the frightened, haggard, approaching face I knew was yours, beyond doubt, and the child staring up from familiar eyes was, recognisably, my nephew, or niece. The orderly was watching me for a sign. Unnerved, I looked away to the clerk's ledger and said what I say to every pauper,

—Name?

To which she said again,

—Lolo, it's me, Annie.

—Townland?

—Your sister, Annie, Anne Marie, remember! Look at me, Lolo!

I was aware I'd lost control, could sense a curious silence, staff and paupers watching to see what would happen next.

My eyes were filling but I kept staring at the ledger, stupidly. Then I heard you shouting as though in a dream,

—For Jesus' sake, Lolo, look at me, you're my brother! I'm your sister!

I should have said something loving and familial but what came out of my mouth, may God forgive me, was,

—All female paupers are my sisters. Take your place in the line.

I glanced from the ledger to your face and saw the disbelief in your eyes as you twisted away with a kind of wail, wrenching the child after you and heading for the main gates, half running, half stumbling, stopping once briefly to gulp out curses. A lot of them I only half heard, but I did hear clearly,

—Brother bollocks, landlords' lickarse. May the Devil blight your prick and God send you and your childer, and theirs, to rot in leperland!

They taught you to curse well down in Granard. As they echoed and re-echoed round the yard I was thinking I couldn't admit you to the squalor of a pauper's ward, separate you from your child. That was unthinkable! Into my room, or get you a cabin somewhere? Perhaps. I don't know. I'm not sure what went through my head but I knew I'd rejected you, and now you ask me why? Embarrassment and sudden anger at being trapped? Exposed? Caught off guard as you shouted out "brother" like that, using your sex to gain advantage? A breed of blackmail? But these thoughts I knew were poor cover for the guilt that was shortly to overwhelm me, and still does.

I am not poor but I'd refused a sibling help and shelter, lest my position as Master be called into question, when in truth I'm as crooked and partial as any man. Somewhere in that clenched heart I knew as you stumbled away that I'd made the mistake of a lifetime. I wanted to shout after you but had no voice, wanted to follow but my legs were trembly, and anyway I saw the priest Galligan running to stop you, his buttocks wobbling, and even through my chaos of mind I saw that his arse wobbled in much the same way as his jowls when he talked. When he'd caught up with you at the entrance gates I'd found my voice and said to the clerk and orderlies,

—Continue admitting.

As though nothing had happened!

But I could see you at the gates with Galligan, shaking your head and wiping away tears, and then suddenly you were gone and Galligan was walking back. I watched him approaching with a kind of cold anger. I'd never before seen him chase a pauper family. Why mine? He was trespassing. He came very close to my ear and whispered,

—I tried my best. All she would say was, I'll trouble him no more.

To which I said,

—Thank you, Sir. I'll find her and mind her when we're finished here.

He stared at me for a long moment. I returned his stare till he nodded and joined the rest of the staff.

Admissions complete, I told a pauper orderly to saddle my horse but I began with a mistake no countryman should ever make when stock go missing. Instead of looking near and close I went far and wide, away down the south road to where I thought you'd be heading for. Granard. No sign. I lost hours. It was near dark when I got back, lights in the dormer windows, the heavy gates of the workhouse closed.

Something unseen, something more than dread began circling round me as I started out to look again, this time closer. How, tell me, do you find starvelings in the starving dark? So many places to look for locked out paupers. I tried them all, under the canal bridge, the eaves of the canal stores, the eaves of the butteryard, the hollow of the round tower, the Norman fort, the old graveyard with its table tombs which gave some shelter. I searched them all, calling aloud, the echo of your name coming back from long ago. Annie, Annie, Annie. I had no name for your child and said to myself that night,

—I'll find them tomorrow.

And, as I said this, the circling thing crept into my soul and I knew with certainty that you and your child were dead and that I had let ye die.

How can we know such things beforehand? Not fear, merely, or dread, but *know*. When the knock came at daybreak it was Hanratty wearing his most lugubrious face and manner. Before he spoke I said,

—Just tell me where they were found.

He did. I got through that day somehow. Cassidy, the town undertaker, said,

—They'd be best boxed together.

I agreed. Your child was a boy. I buried you according to the rite of the Catholic Church of which I am a lost member, Father Brendan Galligan officiating. Not knowing your married name nor the name for your boy he asked me what I thought about Patrick as a name.

—None better, I said, and I have to say now that his few words about "Annie and Patrick" being "at one in life, death, and now finally at peace, thanks be to God" filled me with a grief I had not thought possible. Like drowning, I imagine. Let me admit, confess, in addition, that he was genuinely kind. Everyone, staff, paupers, townspeople, all kindly, kinder than I deserve. I began to see, to understand as never before that we are all kin, all of a kind, all humankind. Too late.

Maybe when the heart's unkind as mine is we make enemies where we long for friends. Worst of all, I'd closed the door on my own, had missed your life and, stupidly, your death. That night I joined the chorus of grieving paupers in this place and for the first time in thirty years howled like a dog, sobbed, wept, got lost in grief, and when that was done I found I was looking at what I'd become.

Things in life I'd shrugged off as nothing now seemed monstrous. I was the Devil manifest, my soul leprous, and, leaving God aside where he lives in silence, I knew I'd have to suffer before I could forgive myself. I began to see clearly that I was trained to be alien amongst my own people. No excuses any more. I would have to make reparation.

Two days ago I asked the porter to bring me the rags of a dead pauper. I have them here in a cupboard. They smell. I asked for them because my first instinct was to lay aside the clothes of authority and whatever I possess, put on the discards of the poor, and walk to Granard and enter the poorhouse there, as a pauper. Every night I decide on this. Every morning I decide otherwise.

Too easy, in any case. I have been Master here for three years and here I must admit myself under Hanratty, as Master. That would be fitting. That would be punishment. That word again, "admit," like a knife.

And now it all comes flowing back. Oh God, let me not think on how they ended. The hurt and loneliness. When I saw you, Annie, you lay in death like a curled forefinger. Cradling your dead child. Thumb into forefinger. Thus.

Oh Mama, Dada, why did you leave us? Oh my poor sister, my poor people, forgive me, and may God almighty forgive me. Jesus, mercy; Mary, help.

The Landlord

Bonaparte. The Tuileries. Grandiose Imperial desk. Hardly a glance:
—Who are you?
—General Lord Clonroy.
—Where's the title from?
—It's a blend of Irish and French, Sire. My grandmother was French.
—Meaning what?
—The king's meadow.
—And your seat?
—Fermanagh. South Ulster.
—Ah!
—At one time I was the youngest General in the English Army.
—Serving where?
—India. With Field Marshal Gough.
—The Limerick clown?
—And with the other Irish *clown*. At Waterloo!
That made him look up, the astonishing eyes full of sullen anger. I returned the stare till he muttered,
—You didn't win.
—On the contrary, we did.
—Wellington's hated by his peers and public. I'm still adored. Will be till history ends.
He then stood, turned his back, lifted a haunch and farted like a schoolboy.
Is there no antidote for this dreaming nonsense? A petty landlord from Corsica makes himself "Emperor"! Farts in my face. "Adored"? Sees himself as a God. Like the Caesars? Dream or no dream I called him "Sire." Shameful.

2 April 1848

Murphy still locked in his room. The Brady girl says he eats almost nothing. Tried talking through the door. Sounds unbalanced. Muttered about entering the poorhouse as a pauper. I pretended not to hear that. Told him I'd have behaved as he did, with firmness and courtesy. How else could he have guessed she was his sister, being a child herself when he saw her last? They say she screeched, ballyragged, cursed and left in a great huff because he asked her to stay in line. Terrible the way she was found with her child next morning. Deeply grieved since then.

Close to a fortnight now. Mourning out of all proportion. As Master for two years now how many has he buried? Thought he'd be impervious to the empire of death.

3 April 1848

Post brought a circular from Leslie. Odd fellow. Suspect crowd politically. Every way. Mad dogs or crazy dons? High Church or atheist? More books than cattle in their keep. Our crowd military and pastoral. Did nothing about it at the time. Is that as suspect? Not much I could do.

> Castle Leslie,
>   Glaslough,
>   Co Monaghan
>   31 March 1848

Open letter to all the considerable landowners in the Baronies of South Ulster

This morning we were wakened by a voice crying out "Mercy, mercy, mercy," followed by keening on the front lawn. The workhouse at Kilnaleck, closed for lack of funds, leaving a straggle of paupers with nowhere to go. They arrived here before dawn, starving, cold and wretched beyond description. When we looked down the men were kneeling, the women and children standing or lying; amongst them, a young girl holding a dead infant towards our window.

Some of you may have read Carlyle's piece:

—Ireland is like a half-starved rat that crosses the path of an elephant. What must the elephant do? Squelch it, by heavens, squelch it!

We are long accustomed to being called "The idiot daughter" by the other Island, but what creature other than a preachy, servile Scot could pen such a sentence, at such a time? It is now clear that Westminster will continue to cut funding. Our absentees don't know or care, so those of us who reside must act now. Here at Glaslough we have been using a mix of boiled turnips and India meal for hungry tenants, beggars and stray paupers. It is not appetising but is sustaining.

I know all the objections but common humanity and selfish interest suggest that common sense must be laid aside until this crisis is over. If we allow the poorest of the poor to die on our doorsteps we will never be forgiven. The result will be a death knell for the landed class, not just here in South Ulster, but all over Ireland.

—Leslie

P.S. Heard Mathew was over at Gilmartin's. Our giddy girls say he's "the most breathtaking creature" they've ever laid eyes on! Is he still with you? Still mad Republican? And how are you both? The above is doomsday rhetoric but I believe it. It's an age since we've seen either your good self or "Poor Knoggins." We must rectify that soon.

It was Leslie first called her "Poor Knoggins." Ironic clownerie that stuck. She rather likes it. Showed her the above after dinner. Watched her read. Affected by paupers crying out and dead infant. Then asked,

—How many is he talking about? Hundreds? Thousands? Strolling or lying about on our front lawn? Drinking raw poteen? Where will they shelter? In our barns? Stables? They'll burn them! And will they work? Will they stay forever? Surely they'll steal and vandalise everything, then murder us in our beds! That's what they're doing everywhere. Must we commit suicide because they're too lazy to provide for themselves? I will not agree to a soup kitchen in our courtyard, Robert, and, if you do, I'm leaving. Immediately.

Field Marshal Knoggs piping. Must I follow?

4 APRIL 1848

Nothing equals what we loved as children. We didn't know then how all things begin and end, like a tale, a shower of rain, a star, a life. Early April sun on the garden walls. Astonishing. Worth being alive to see. To walk and look. Why do we weep at beauty? The skull behind? Lost happiness? The coming dark? Nothing to fear from nothingness, is there? This island should be Europe's garden, not its graveyard. More and more reminds me of India. Swarming humanity, famine and filth, palaces and pigsties, a wretched Eden more garrisoned, troubled and troublesome than all India. Here I was born though, grew up and, despite famine, horror and hatred, it's where I'd choose to die and be buried. Unlikely now.

6 April 1848

Called at the poorhouse again. Murphy still hiding away. Sounds less unhinged. Put my head into the yard privies on the way out. Even a thousand paupers shat there today they shouldn't smell so foul. Crap pits could have been built over barrows for dragging straight to the fields. Romans doing that before Christ, the Chinese before that. Wilkinson's fault. Wretched, puffed up architect.

—Clearing them out'll give them something to do, he said.

Shoddy jobwork. No imagination. I implied as much last time he was here.

—Would you like a paupers' billiard hall, my Lord? A ballroom? A few tennis courts? A croquet lawn perhaps?

Touchy man. Went on to say the first poorhouses in England were designed as houses of terror, and that John Russell, the PM himself, had admired "the humane and frugal grace" of his plans.

—It would be difficult, I said, to imagine anything more frugal. I could have added "Or more inhuman."

He noted that. Swilling down my claret, apropos of nothing he said,

—What ruins most landscapes from here to Moscow are these brute erections with their balls up on gatepillars shouting: "Behold me, little people! See my big windows, my big doors, my ice-house, my artificial lake!" Makes for bad architecture and worse politics!

After quite a silence I asked,

—Would you include Versailles?

—In particular Versailles.

—Its gardens?

—Worse again.

What gardens, I asked, did he most admire?

—Any cottier's vegetable patch, anywhere.

Tin-made spouting. Middle-class jealousy. What the French revolution was mostly about. Won't eat with me again. His plans used all over Ireland. The outskirts of every other town. Grim bastilles of despair. Imagines himself a radical reformer. An obtuse idiot. Could have, but didn't, return rudeness for rudeness.

10 APRIL 1848

Murphy opened his door today. A hollow-eyed ghost. Still not eating much. Drinking a lot, I'd guess. Slow speech and the stricken look.

—More fitting, I said, to drink yourself to death at my age than yours!

No response. Hinted the poorhouse was disorderly without him. Hanratty a sort of mock-priest creeping about, a telltale with no authority. An irritant to board and paupers.

—That fellow couldn't run a hen run, I said.

No response. Went on to tell him we were alike with a sister apiece. Mine, Judy, the older by four years. As youngsters she'd pinch and punch for no reason, then smother me with kisses and beg me not to tell. This I thought the female way, till one day she taunted,

—You'll be a Lord, my Lord, when you grow up! You'll get a whole barony because of your little bits!

Then grabbed my testicles and squeezed till I screamed.

Yet again I didn't tell. "Just a lark," she said. Sensing her dislike, I'd disliked her in return. From then on began to hate her and continued hating till I could hit back. End of ear-twisting and bullying. You don't forget such things, though I did promote her husband, young Gillespie. Arrogant ass. Disobeyed Wellington and got himself court-martialled.

Murphy listening. No effect. I went further. Pointed through his window towards the canal.

—If she was drowning in that lock I'd be tempted to walk away!

Still no response. Irrational grief. Didn't want to put it blunt as that so asked him,

—What are you in mourning for? A three-year-old child or a strange woman who cursed you?

Finally he looked at me with something akin to hatred. The longer I live the less I understand the human heart. My own included.

12 April 1848

The *Times* today. Two figures, one fact.

1780: Population of Ireland. Two and a half millions.

1845: Population of Ireland. Nine millions plus!

Some seven million tenants at will. And who squeezes the rent from these poor creatures? Agents! Middle-class middle-men, gombeen men, all prospering, all mostly Irish! And the emergent Church of Rome now building like beavers all over the island. Free labour and farthings of the poor. Every Chapel on a higher site than the Protestant Church. Nearer My God to Thee? Elevated thinking!

The Galligan priest's a surly rascal. Knows something or pretends to. Long ago I'd have flogged the half smile off his face or marched him into an ambush. Or thought about it!

14 April 1848

Stood at the bedroom window a long time this morning. Again a low mist on the lake, thorn ditches a glory of white. Fields of thriving cattle and sheep as far as I could see. Land of green and plenty. Brairds of winter oats and wheat, squads of men with spades, slipes and horses. Drain digging and barrowing of stones. Pastoral peace. Or seeming? Work till dark this time of year. For whom, now? All ending soon.

Draft for July edition of the *Farmer's Gazette* came yesterday. Hid letter till now. Heartbreak to read and look out on what must go. My approval for the following requested. Eyes filling as I read:

DAY OF SALE FIXED
Fermanagh Barony on the market.
W. W. Simpson has the honour to announce by
order of the noble proprietor, at the Royal Hotel
Belfast on Wed 7th of July at 11 a.m. sharp, the
sale of Eden Hall Estate comprising circa 20,000
Irish acres including the townlands of Drumbofin,
Burdautien, Cooldarra.

And on it went naming, mapping, describing. Know every bush and tree, ditch and sheugh, lake and river bend. The shape of every field, forest and meadow. Can't believe they're printed out. For sale. End of everything. How do I walk a hundred townlands, my heart breaking? Who'll buy? Whose eyes see what I see when I waken to the light of this morning's wonder? A Belfast cattle shipper? A Dublin corn merchant? A builder from Cork? My heart stops at the thought. Neighbours will see it with a chill and think, Well, it's not us yet!

And when they gather next they'll say,

—See old Clonroy's in the *Gazette*?

—Surprising! Wife has no end of money, they say!

Won't care much. Leslie maybe. Likes me well enough. Says we think alike. We don't. O'Connell and native politics! A parliament of cattle dealers and bank clerks, ruled by a rookery of priests plotting our downfall! Squabbling over who'll rule a mess of beggars! No. No. No. I'd prefer Birmingham to that! Talked to me once about our rights here being suspect.

—Nothing here when we arrived, I said, but bush, bog and plain.

—And the native Irish! he said.

—We drained bogs and marshes, made roads. What's suspect about building mills and manor houses, towns and villages? We civilised it. I refuse to be guilty about that.

He smiled. Swift lodged there. And O'Connell.

Given half a chance he'd patronise the Pope.

16 April 1848

Murphy out and about again. Almost genial in his morose way. Very out of character showed me lines from *The Nation* written by some poet who died young.

> "I have seen death strike so fast
> That churchyards could not hold
> The bright-eyed and the bold.
> I must be very, very old,
> A very old, man."

He watched me reading and said,

—That's how I feel.

Clearly not himself yet. Can't tell anyone how I feel about selling. Not merely old, but desolate betimes. Tells me the third burial pit's near full. Two and a half thousand dying every week now from Malin to Dingle. Workhouse figures only. God alone knows how many more unrecorded, unburied out through the islands, mountains and bogs. Last year he was all for burning our dead in the grounds, out of sight of the paupers. Corpses fouling the water. Could be right. Galligan, for the Roman Church, said wrong. A desecration. Some claptrap about resurrection of the body. Too inane to argue over.

Parsee "towers of silence" near Bombay. There they put their dead high up on grids. Chimney stacks of the dead. Vultures then flopping out of the mangos, circling around and up, to feast. I watched, appalled. Their bones picked clean in the sun. We choose slow rot in the earth, rats and worms nesting in our bowels. No great choices. All the one.

18 APRIL 1848

What is wrong? Who's to blame? What to do? All newspapers, gazettes and journals, wheeling out these questions every other day. *Times* quoting the silly Wilde woman's whining doggerel:

> "A ghastly spectral army, before the great God we'll stand
> And arraign ye as our murderers, the spoilers of our land."

Crazy. I know the answer in a word, or two. Daren't print for fear of being shrieked down by the patriot press. *Improvidence. Congenital improvidence.*

Devil-me-care, happy-go-lucky children. Next week's a hundred years off. When they get money every farthing's gulped in shebeens and pissed out in sheughs. Raving lunatics then, reciting and bellowing out dismal ballads about lost battles, dispossession, and glorious Celtic past! Drunken and shifty living in shit with pigs and fowl! Christ alone knows the swarming incest rife in those wretched hovels! How otherwise? Blame us for that too? Of course.

What about Rome? Manufacturing and baptising hundreds of thousands of impoverished wretches. The whole family caboodle in the image and likeness of God! Catholic clergy plays a wily part in general disaffection. Preach against rebellion. Skilled at saying one thing means the other. Galligan, a sample. Curate at Strokestown before here. His PP, McDermott, likened young Mahon to Oliver Cromwell, knowing full well most Irishmen would kill each other for honour of killing Cromwell. Exit Denis Mahon with a bullet in his head, as decent a reforming landowner as ever drew breath. Murdered with Rome's blessing.

Then all the back somersaulting in aftermath. Condemnation and denial. The handwashing of guilt in crocodile tears. Unholy terrors. Know their capers inside out. Seamus Shillelagh, the skull basher, shakes his ruggy head.

—A bad doin', your honour, to be sure.

If they fear "the smile of an Englishman," let all of English blood beware the Hibernian headshake.

20 April 1848

Edmund Spenser, poet to the Virgin Queen. A great Irish hater. Small wonder. His children burned one night by Irish rebels. Kilcolman Castle. Surviving grandson flirted with Popery. Lands escheated by Cromwell. Banished to Connaught despite plea by Lord Deputy. Dot's nightmare. Hates it when I used Irish with Mathew.

—It sounds rude, it is rude!

In Russia, I said, landowners and serfs speak the same language. A bond. Like one great family. Revolution most unlikely there. Dangerous to be alienated by language as we are here.

She stared blinking and asked,

—What language did the Sans Culottes speak? Chinese?

—Went on to talk about a Seigneur Memmay of Quincey. Knowing the great chateaus were burning all over France he invited the whole countryside to a banquet. Laid on barrels of wine and gunpowder. Blew them and his chateau to kingdom come and disappeared. An ugly parable, I said. Did *she* admire Seigneur Memmay?

—He stole a march on the enemy. Thought as a soldier, you'd admire that!

22 April 1848

Stringer, our Church of Ireland man, eavesdropped on Galligan's preaching. Wrote out what he overheard.

> *Life has conquered, the wind has blown away*
> *Alexander, Caesar and all their power and sway,*
> *Tara and Troy have made no longer stay.*
> *Maybe the English too will have their day.*

Then a long, unchristian diatribe which ended,

> *Brothers and sisters in Christ, Spain got shut of the Moors after fourteen hundred*
> *years. The English are only here six and their time's near done. Soon you'll look*
> *down from above on an Ireland that once again belongs to us, free of English, free*
> *of landlords, free of agents, free of bailiffs, free of house tumblers. Our day will*
> *come.*

Will it? If a pauper myself sitting with no hope, on a bench in an Ulster poorhouse, mid-nineteenth century, waiting for death, that would, I suppose, lift my spirits a little. Our day will come! Will it?

—All men are born equal and everywhere in chains!

Yah! The same Rousseau ran off and left his wife and five children "in chains." Penniless. A bloody rascal – like Bonaparte, like most "heroes."

23 April 1848

Whatever the cause, famine has prowled this island since God knows when, and will, till kingdom come. April to August. "The hungry months." Half a million starving more or less every year. Now with blight it's multitudinous, a nation of diseased scarecrows, swarming on centuries of beggary. Out of the townlands into the towns, cities and villages, down from the mountains to crowd out ports and seashores. Beggars huddled and huddles of beggars, all ages and stages. What happens when you see incurable beggary year in, year out? Indifference? Can't admit to that!

24 APRIL 1848

Went to attic bin to check on last year's diary. There *he* was, exactly one year back, 24 APRIL 1847. The giant, genius of "Freedom"! Great Saviour of the world!

—With the stroke of a pen, he said, I will end all famines. As gifted as a hundred gifted men but a monumental hypocrite. Curious to re-read now what I dreamt a year ago.

Pissing into his cocked hat on horseback. Laughing at gravediggers deep in Russia. Dead Frenchmen piled in heaps. Death no laughing matter I told him. Asked him had he no shame. He shrugged and said,

—I'm trying to make a new world. You're starving the old one to death.

As he galloped off I shouted after him,

—Emperor, my arse! You're a relic, man, a relic!

Damn nearly wet the bed. Too much port? Ageing bladder more like. Seventy-two next week. Old. No way out of that but one. Why "relic"?

Read on as far as the midsummer entries, now called BLACK '47. Worse than plague. Indescribable. Every other day the odour of blight mentioned. *Phytophthora infestans.* Death smell. Death knell, more like. All over. Terrible reports. Every province. Towns, townlands, villages, cities and seashores. All heading for the ports and America. God help them. Will He? Will America? Can anyone? Poorhouses a wretched answer.

Last year's brief entry for

21 JUNE 1847

Poor Law rates long overdue. Dorothy paid. Festus Daly on the lawn. Croquet.

The start of an unlucky history, in those thirteen words. Bank had said no to second mortgage. Dot helped out. Lump sums fatten her account from Birmingham and elsewhere. As chairman and biggest landowner all starving poor lodged in new poorhouse to my account. Six hundred and eighty-seven paupers last year at four pounds per annum, per pauper. Can't be done. Has me near pauperised. Irish Squireen's refusing to pay. As RM I have no choice.

—Festus Daly on the lawn. Croquet!

Grotesque memory! *Humanitas infestans*. Who was Saint Festus? Yet another Irish "saint" topping up the provender of Hibernian sanctity. Face like an axe, voice like a rasp. "Festy Waterloo" they call him hereabouts. Sounds quaint. Not so quaint with his wooden leg and Basque beret. Tenant in a rough, mountainy area. Bragan country. A Bonaparte veteran. Composite of everything that's worst or "best" in the Irish character. Depending on viewpoint. On losing side at Waterloo. Walked drunk onto the croquet lawn that evening. Challenged me!

—Gun or sword, Skinner, I'll bate you with aither.

"Escorted" off he got, shouting out,

—I'm better bred than you, Skinner, a better soldier and a proper Irishman, and you mind that!

I said I'd bear it in mind. Farcical request before thirty guests. In every barony of Ireland they're descended from Kings or High Kings. You can see that at a glance! All thought it, "Very Irish, immensely amusing."

Shirley of Castle Fea begged me to mimic the accent and manner. I refused. Could have, with the Irish I've had since childhood.

—Learn every inflection, son, my father said. More practical than going about armed to the teeth with bodyguards you can't trust.

Shrewd advice. Hard to kill a man who can curse, sing, dance and tell jokes in the language. But came back an ex-general, peer and landlord. Embellishments not popular here. Not hated though, the way Leitrim is, or Lansdowne, but I do keep German shepherds. Dot keeps wolfhounds. Great, silly brutes wolfing down bones and offal. Obscene, these famine days, with no wolves left to hunt. My German shepherds a must for night watches, and my steel shutters and gun room with its cast iron door. A necessity. Siege clobber of caste.

I'm a soldier. I know men, especially Irishmen. I didn't think Daly amusing.

—Dangit, and the landlord's the quare bad lad, so he is. He's the boy I'd hang, so I would!

And he would. Cut my throat or put a bullet in my brain without a shrug. Something not sane in those bulging eyes, something not sane about the whole race. Belligerent, resentful, capricious, treacherous. Uncivil citizens.

Worse servants, with the odd exception. The Murphys with us here two hundred years. His father my batman in Calcutta, more friend than servant. Died aboard ship on the way home. Saddest of sad events. Saved my life once, his own at risk. That's more than loyalty.

Read on looking for second tangle with Festus. Found it painful reading.

GALE DAY, SEPTEMBER 1847

Agent's office. Daly came in sober, wearing his Basque beret. As he put his rent on the nail Sammy Agnew said,

—Bare your head, Daly, in Lord Clonroy's presence!

—He's gettin' his rent. Why should he view my head?

Agnew then snatched at Daly's beret, who caught his arm and twisted it up till his face gouged onto the rent table. He then put his backside over Agnew's mouth and said,

—You can view up there any time you like, Sammy!

Jerked his peg leg up at me, he added,

—You too, Mister Skinner!

I could have ended it there by saying,

—Let him wear his beret, Sammy. I don't want to "view" his head or his arse!

I pulled the bellcord for Dowler and Bailey. From the landing window saw Daly being thrown out, held, punched and kicked on the ground. His wooden leg came off. He grabbed it and pointed up at Agnew mouthing savagely. Seldom seen such hatred in a human face. Should have stopped it. Or tried to. I was angry. A mistake.

30 SEPTEMBER 1847

History lesson for poor student. Act of Union. The Britannic Islands. 1800. John Bull bulling his rebellious daughter. Outraged by her defiance and hatred. Violates her even more. Like it or not, it seems like that. No mean violater myself!

31 DECEMBER 1847

Sammy Agnew found this morning hanging from an apple tree. Agent's garden. What a year's end! Hard to imagine anything more savage. Whole house, village and barony deeply shocked. Signed with Daly's brutal signature. Pock marks from his peg leg under the apple tree. A bright, glorious winter's day. Made it somehow more grotesque. Nightmare again. Bonaparte pointing and smiling.

7 MARCH 1848

Day of sale fixed.
Fermanagh Barony on the market.
W. W. Simpson has the honour etc.
Wed 7th of July at noon.
The noble proprietor.

A Belfast salesroom. Four months from now. Days falling off one by one. The hand bids one by one. Then the hammer like a guillotine. The end.

Nathaniel Skinner came here land-hungry 1612. From English/Scottish borderlands. Old Irish scattered. His blood abiding in me beside this lake. Same walled garden, same apple trees, oldest in Ulster. Our own church and graveyard. No wish to be buried elsewhere.

Attachment to place means little to Dot. Seems unaware of what it means to me. Indifferent almost. At the start though, spent lavishly. Re-roofed house and stables, built a water tower, new entrances. Miles of enclosing wall. Gave employment. Also gained her deeds to house, grounds and gardens. Entitlement to change the name. First dwelling here was in townland of Drumbofin. Ancient placename.

—What does it mean, Robert, Drumbofin?

—The ridge of the white cow, I said, and the O sounds like the O in low.

—What it means is more ridiculous than how it sounds!

I protested. A necklace of townlands connected to estate. I named some, explained their meaning. Tamlaght, Rathclough, Inishglora, Mullinamuck, Gola, Drumlanna, Largy, Tubberlucas.

She didn't like any of them and opted for Eden Hall. Very Birmingham to my ears, I said. She took exception to that.

—Eden, she said, is paradise, and paradise is from the Arabic, meaning a walled garden. I'd prefer that to places called after cows, pigs, or goats, or wells!

—What objection, I asked, did she have to Oxford or Tunbridge Wells?

—They don't sound spineless.

No arguing with fixed prejudice. Well educated but understands very little. Or very differently. None of it matters now. If it ever did.

8 MARCH 1848

Daly had foolproof alibi. Got off. Predictably. By law, now, three Catholics on every jury a legal obligation. Unless all three witnessed him string up Sammy Agnew they'd never find against. That makes nine agents and six landlords assassinated this past twelve months. Nobody got for them. With huge police force and standing army big as India's the Dalys are still at large all over Ireland. Rebellion and famine hand in hand. Heard Leitrim mutter his drunken solution at Dartry:

—Bloody Irish, bloody awful. Let them starve!

17 MARCH 1848

Looked up "Skinner" in Johnson. "A flayer of beasts, scum of pools, pelt or hide of animals." Also he gives thickskin, thinskin and scarfskin. Quotes Shakespeare:

> "Authority, though it err like others,
> Has yet a kind of medicine in itself,
> That skins the vice o' th' top."

The big monkey steals the big banana. Bonaparte marched into Switzerland. Gobbled their gold. The world secretly applauded. Wretched Swiss Bankers. Theft canonised by Crown and Church and State the world over. Father toyed with notion of deed polling Skinner to Scarfe. Act of Union bribe netted a peerage. Tittle, tittle, tattle, title and, hey presto, look ye, poor Skinner's glorified to Clonroy!

And thanks be to God for that, Lady Clonroy said. Growing up Dot Knoggs was bad enough. To be Mrs. Bob Skinner would have been insupportable. Formerly Dorothy Knoggs, only child of Sir George Knoggs, Gin Distiller, Birmingham. Very much her father's daughter. He trundled down streets with a barrow. Ended up with a distillery. Flung so much loot at the Tories they dubbed him Sir George. Early on, when we came back from India, she said,

—If you can't make this property pay, Robert, we should sell and go to Birmingham.

I can't make it pay, but *we* should sell it and go somewhere like Eden Place, Daddy George's mock baronial edifice. Talks now of ending her days in like setting. More dignity in a Bath lodging house. Let me not think on it!

20 MARCH 1848

Famine if anything worse than this time last year.

The improvidence of my neighbour, Johnson says, must not make me inhuman.

Of course not. Who are mine? Leslie and Shirley? Wyndham and Farnham? Erne, Leitrim and Enniskillen? With quarter of a million acres between us! And out there, beyond our walls, out of sight, but never out of mind, that swarming otherness, that Irishness, their hatred fuelled by disease, famine and death. Out there is hell. In here, where I live, is heaven! Is it? Life with Field Marshal Knoggs! Did mutter once, as a general the lives of thousands in my care. Tinkered on two continents with arms and discipline, training and logistics, strategy, purveying, budgeting, medical field-care and some other details. She laughed.

—Your underlings did *that* for you, Robert!

—Odd they should make me a general?

—Because you look and sound like somebody.

Thanked her for commending my phonics and physiognomy. Irony lost on her. Like anyone with purse strings. Tends to the capricious. Brutal worldly truth. A man of meagre banking account is a man of little or no account. So dance to her jig, me Lord, and be happy you're not a bare-arsed pauper starving in a poorhouse. Murphy's mad solution. Become a pauper myself! In a way I am. Pauperised.

21 MARCH 1848

The word "underling" squatting in my brain since yesterday. Sees me as a hollow vessel, does she? Does it matter at my age? As others see us? Valid both ways. The Ball in Calcutta where wives of high ranking officers refused place in a booked carriage to young Captain's wife who fell ill. Rank cruelty.

Dot sided with senior ladies. Bitches conscious of station and lacking all dignity. Was appalled and said so. Argument then. As a ginmonger's daughter she would naturally, I said, be grander in manner and mind than a Duchess.

Greatly resented. Suddenly got silly and went, "Law Di Daw, Law Di Daw!" like a Birmingham street urchin.

—And where did the noble Skinners hail from? she asked. Skinning dead animals in a shambles?

Still rankles twenty years on. And still comes up.

23 MARCH 1848

Bonaparte back again to mock my sleep? Greed and grandeur? Far from grand when he's off his horse. Fat, dumpy fellow with small feet walking the shore of a tiny island. Billy goats bleating at him. The Upper Lough? Wearing dancing pumps, a greatcoat and silly hat. Talking to himself. Staring out at the water through a telescope. His "Empire" cut to nothing. When he turned to look at me it was *my* baggy bloodhound eyes I was looking into. Me, is he? All men?

—I know men, he said, and Jesus Christ was no man!

Who then was He? Is He? The Man God not of this world, friend to whores and halfwits, corpse raiser, water walker, promiser of a kingdom no one's ever seen. Thy kingdom come?

Mine's earmarked for the *Farmer's Gazette*. July. That much is certain.

27 MARCH 1848

Leitrim evicted a cottier refused to salute his horses clopping down through his village. All must grovel when he passes in person. Being a lord and landowner not enough. Bonaparte made the Pope grovel, forced a pen-stroke through six hundred years of inquisition. A genius for good as well as self glory. Leitrim an untalented bully. Insane, degenerate.

28 MARCH 1848

A large rat near the poorhouse bakery. Pushed his way through a cracked flag. Fat, sick and wet. I stood very still, staring. He was so close, so unafraid, I could see him blinking, nose and whiskers twitching in my direction.

—Don't blink at me, brother, I said quietly. I'm no pauper, not on your menu yet!

When he didn't move I shouted,

—Run, rat, run! Back to the burial pit! You can feast there for a hundred years! And keep away from the living, Sir, the half living, and half dying!

Nobody about. Odd, a bit, shouting out like that in a poorhouse yard? Thought I'd be unaffected, but watching him squeeze down through that crack, tail slithering after, gave me a sudden shiver. And dry mouth. Yet another premonition of mortality? What else? Death now a constant companion. Partly what brought me back. No longer hiding up a tree or round a bend. Alongside peering from a rathole. Best be on friendly terms when it turns to blink.

—You are welcome, Sir? Madam? Rat? I've been expecting you. May I ask where we're going?

30 MARCH 1848

Clarendon with us again en route to Belfast. Unassuming and kind. Affects everyone. Asked to see kitchen staff to thank in person. Dot says more likely wanted to see if it was clean as Viceregal Lodge! First time I've been below stairs in God knows when. He's more interested in landscape and woodland than wheels and spokes of politics.

I pointed out conifers, hardwoods and block plantings to echo battle lines at Waterloo. Hugely interested. Or pretended. Told me John Russell treated him last year like a sub-post office clerk at Number 10. Behaved as though rebellion and famine here had little to do with London. Then snapped suddenly,

—I'm sorry if your Irish landlords and agents are being shot like hares, Clarendon, but I can't pretend to be shocked. Our people here aren't evicting whole villages into the jaws of winter. Migrating by the hundred thousand! Our big-hearted friends in America are now closing their ports. They can! We can't! From now on we'll let your Irish landlords support the paupers they evict, not the British treasury.

—Then you'll bankrupt them, Prime Minister, almost all.

—Probably, Russell said. Deservedly. Was there ever a more hated class?

Deservedly! I know we're mostly despised over there and certainly hated here but I'm no villain. I've no secret wish to evict, hang, starve or transport the poorest of the poor which some are accusing us of. Nor did I know the Tories had disowned us as a class.

1 APRIL 1848

Since Clarendon's visit the message from Russell hasn't left my head.

—We'll make your Irish landlords pay!

A litany of five words in my head, awake or asleep.

—I am pauperised by paupers, I am pauperised by paupers, I am pauperised by paupers.

5 APRIL 1848

Inclined to count things. Words, steps, chimneys, hayrucks, turfclamps, paupers. Counted seven magpies this morning on the front lawn. What tale hasn't been told? Doubtful if anything in this world, this island, this family, could surprise me now.

7 April 1848

Stringer preached a long sermon. Church cold. The "Son of Man" paraded for endless edification. God knows how many times he uttered it. Silly wording. Son of Man. Son of a child-bearing male? Keep females out. Not so easy when it comes to procreation. Does he believe the pious nonsense he preaches? Does anyone? Certainly doesn't practise. Not a word to his daughter Norma since she married Fitzpatrick, the Papish corn merchant.

8 April 1848

One full year into the famine and things seem worse. How to cure poverty? By feeding? Insane! By ignoring? Heartless. Teach them to provide for themselves. If they refuse they're digging their graves. If we feed them we're digging ours. Like other landowners, if they forgo their plots I pay passage to America, to anywhere. For years I told my cottiers God created a hundred vegetables for us to live on. Surely you can grow enough to feed yourselves and your families. How do they answer? They fall on their knees and whine,

—We have no brains, your honour, to grow vegetables like gentlefolk. Only the praties, your honour.

> *Prátaí i maidi*
> *Prátaí san ló*
> *Agus ma éiríghim san oíche*
> *Prátaí a geobhainn.*

Christ in heaven what's to be done with such people?

Last year I bought seeds. Turnip, mangold, carrot, cabbage, and kale, cauliflower, parsnip and leeks. I translated the instructions. How to sow, thin, weed, mulch, water, routine horticultural stuff. A child of five could do it, then saw what they tried or didn't! A mess of weeds in lazy beds!

—Bad seeds, your honour, a poor strike, your honour! The slugs ate them, your honour! I lost them, your honour! The crows ate them, your honour.

The pigeons, rabbits, squirrels, daws, magpies, rats and mice, all regiments of the vermin world converging on one pratie plot! And who's to blame?

The landlords of Ireland! Convenient to have a bogeyman to flog for everything that goes wrong in life!

9 APRIL 1848

Called today on the curate, Galligan. Old PP in the corner. Glared at me in silence. McKenna. Looks quite mad. Smell of bacon and cabbage. Slated foursquare house like strong farmer's. God's earthy agents. Pigs grunting out the back. Glossy bullocks on front pasture. Oil portraits of Bishop of Rome and Clogher between gilt-framed Madonna, eyes rolling upwards, hands over virginal quiver, feet crushing serpent's head. Obscene effect.

Can't see what's in front of them. More ways than one. Explained the merits of vegetable varieties, how you must be diligent and work. Can't put tiny seeds in the ground and forget like "praties." Would they talk about this at Sunday Mass? With the hungry months now upon us a matter of grave urgency for cottiers to grow alternatives. Blight bad as last year.

They listened, with reserve. "Perfidious Albion"? Am I? Fatheads! How could vegetable growing be a landlord's trap? Thundering every other Sunday, both of them, about God's "punishment" for being natural. Coupling in ditches mostly. Marry at sixteen. Ten years later, enormous families living in starving squalor! They're the bogeymen with their pigs and bullocks, their black suits and dog collars.

11 APRIL 1848

High Court in Dublin today. Daly got his hands on Daniel O'Connell. God knows how. Unlucky to have Judge Liam O'Hanrahan presiding. Cold eye, colder smile. Ruled there was no law obliging a man to bare his head while paying rent. O'Connell played to gallery. Festus described as "A noble warrior maimed in cause of liberty"! I was derided as "Lord Hatsoff, a neighbour Lord of the Lord who likes his horses to be saluted"! Uproarious laughter. Reprimanded for "Domineering behaviour." Fined a shilling and costs. O'Connell's fee, fifty guineas! The patriot press no doubt will be vindictive and jubilant.

13 April 1848

Chaired third last meeting of Poorhouse Guardians. When advertisement appears it must close. Said nothing. Murphy quiet. Deferential to Galligan. Surprising. His view of Romishness more jaundiced than mine. After the meeting Galligan caught my sleeve, closed boardroom door. Did I know the Bradys of Drumlanna? Impossible not to. The orphan girl walks like a ballet dancer, her mother a sister of Festus Daly's. Same mad eyes. Confined to idiot ward like a trapped hare. Murdered her granddaughter, they say.

—They're tenants of mine, I said. Drumlanna's the next townland.

—Ex-tenants, he said. Evicted. Their house was tumbled and burned.

—Because of typhus. Mister Murphy went out of his way to place them here.

—Murphy, he said, was using the girl, and may again.

—In what way? I asked.

—The only way a man in his position can.

—Did she complain?

—No.

—Confess, perhaps?

He reacted very sharply to this. Overstepped the mark? Insulting implication? Sacred seal. All sins go straight from his ear to God's. Shrewd information dodge. Of course I knew the Bradys. Father's bloodshot eyes and trembling hands. Shouldn't have asked him to tailor breeks for Clarendon. Probably gave them away to the first bare-arsed beggar he met.

15 April 1848

Mathew arrived this evening with young Dixon and the two Gilmartin girls. Both redheads. Gigglers both. The younger full-breasted as a springing heifer. Leaning forward at table to show them off. A freckled beauty. There was talk about some child running alongside the carriage on last visit. I wasn't here. Mathew's tone cool and accusing. Dot didn't know. Or pretended. Greek meets Greek. His cold temper a match for her blazing one. He hasn't changed. Dismissive about almost everything.

Seems I sleepwalked into the blue bedroom where the younger girl was sleeping. Tried to get in beside her. A lot of crying out and hysteria. The whole house up, staff running with cudgels and candles. No sign of Mathew or young Dixon. Wherever they were. I made matters worse by saying,

—Do excuse me. Thought this was an army-licensed brothel.

Dot very cross. No memory of anything. Refused to believe it till I was shown my slippers in the blue room. More and more inclined to stray by night. By day as well. Is the head going? Searching for something? My grave? Lost youth? Virgin breasts? Pray God I die before Birmingham. What a lucky exit that would be. At seventy-three.

17 April 1848

Very glad to be shut of young Dixon's staring hero-worship. Hanging on Mathew's every word. Do those girls or Dot have the faintest notion? He got me alone in the kitchen garden. Told me he'd been accepted for a Jesuit seminary in Spain. Somewhere near Zaragosa. Convert to Church of Rome. Kept my face like a boot. Asked me not to tell his mother. Yet. No great surprise. Always inclined to playacting and dressing up. Prep school a hotbed for that inclination. Most graduate to females. Clearly he didn't. Conversion to Rome I did not expect. Jesuits will love him till they catch him out. Unless they're at the same caper themselves and turn the blind eye like Nelson. Like I had to, in the army.

19 April 1848

Up very late drinking port with Mathew. Not by choice. Spiky conversation.

—No famine here, he said. Plenty of food. Ports should be closed and people fed.

—How? I asked. Who'd pay?

By way of answer he shrugged and said,

—It's what Bonaparte would have done.

During a silence I got the draft advertisement for the *Farmer's Gazette*. Foolish. He read it without expression of interest or regret and said,

—Just as well. We're not wanted here.

—Perhaps we're needed?

—For what?

—To run the country.

—You think?

—I do.

—The way we're running it now?

Stared at me the way the slightly drunk do. Each word as it came slowly out seemed framed.

—They might just manage without us.

His patrimony and half a millennium of rule dumped with half a dozen words. Indifference more hurtful than contempt. I can hide what I feel. May even have smiled. Have always known he wanted no link with pastoral life. Later in the night he said,

—Military people are mostly bullies dressed up to kill.

—Like Bonaparte?

—Yes, like Bonaparte.

—And he'd close the ports, would he?

—Yes, he would.

Preachy and contradictory. The Roman Church will suit him well. I stood. Went to bed without another word.

27 APRIL 1848

How to convey Mathew's intentions to Dot. She keeps him supplied with money. Has never said this, but I know it. She'll be baffled, angry.

—But Rome is evil, she'll say.

Far from Christ, I'll agree, and remind her about "England's hallowed walls founded on King Henry's balls." Our Church here the poor eunuch over the water. Would God bother His celestial arse with either? Or with Rome, Constantinople, Avignon or a hundred other variations? Christianity as much to do with Christ as a pack of dogs snarling over their own vomit. Won't say that, though. A believing person, Dot. Or pretends. So am I!

28 APRIL 1848

Mathew in my head night and day. His defection makes selling easier. No heir now but Judy's stupid boy. Prefer to sell on. Three months left.

29 April 1848

Yet another tangle with Festus. Came in the form of a blackmail letter delivered by a stableboy. Said he'd found it in a manger. It was addressed to *"The Skinners, father and son."*

I opened it. We read together. I glanced once at Mathew's face as I read. It was chalky white.

"First and last warning to Mathew Skinner bugger be gone a week from this day we have heerd tell of your bad carry on a stableboy complained you did a bugger on him and was afeard to say no to a gentleman the likes of you it was a bad thing you done to that poor boy and not a dam thing can put it right when it come to our ears we lit on a cure from the old days and a sure one it is a red hot poker goes in to the buggers arse hole he lets out one shout and its his last its a proper cure."

I said nothing. He said nothing. I read his silence the only way I could. Thieving, gambling, whoring or passional murder I could have stomached. Not shaming the house by fouling innocence. Watch out for men who preach at you, including your own family! Especially your own family!

Dear God, what a reversal of shame. The radical hater of military bullies turns out to be a hypocrite. How could it be otherwise with Rousseau and Bonaparte as exemplars? Believe no one absolutely, ever. Trust no one absolutely, ever. Query everything. Bear in mind what's true today is false tomorrow and vice versa till the next Ice Age or kingdom dumb. Grow your carrots, mind your corner, and expect nothing much from this life or the next.

30 April 1848

Mathew left this morning. We embraced in the hall. It was cold. The embrace. Will I see him again, in this world? Doubtful. Do I want to? Doubtful. Must be heartbreak in that but can't feel it. Yet. Dot went out to wave him off. Wondered why I didn't. I made some reply, not sure what.

—Is Mathew in trouble of some sort? she asked. In debt?

To which I muttered,

—I wish he was.

—Has it to do with the history of this wretched island?

—It *is* the history, I said, of this wretched island.

The house seemed like a prison, all that careful building, the accumulation of centuries, tumbling now like a house of cards. I went out for air. Stayed out. No appetite, no wish to return to the house. Walked till dusk alongside the enclosing walls screening off what I'd no stomach to look at, hovels like rotten teeth in a green mouth, a silent countryside without cattle, sheep or fowl. Turfsmoke a reminder of whole families starving at the hearth. Am I deserting these fields, this house where I was born, this island I once so deeply loved, the speech I dreamt in as a child? And the people? I can ask the question now. Was there love ever, anywhere, at any time between the dispossessed and those who dispossessed?

At evening yard bell, saw squads of workers and horses heading back for the stables. Wanted badly to get outside the walls, revisit forbidden fields, townlands and river stretches where I'd played out of bounds before the walls went up. Dangerous now. Knew I couldn't leave by the front or back entrance without being seen. Had a key to a small access gate, opened it and let myself out. Must have been walking a long time looking at places where I'd been happy. Stopped to listen to a murmur down by Gola where the river forks. Had swum there often as a cub with local lads, Jimmy the Goat, Fisty McDonagh, Nosey O'Hara and Farty Boyle. All dead now but Farty. I then realised it wasn't water I was hearing but the murmur of people. Wasn't sure what to expect. A council of Ribbonmen armed with cudgels and cleavers? Festus Daly binding them with oaths and orders? A night-wandering landlord a banquet to such a crew!

In the mood I was in I didn't care. I would greet death like an old friend. Was it a wake perhaps? People too frightened now of cholera and typhus to attend wakes. Everywhere the dead buried secretly or left to nature in remote bogs or mountain areas.

Keeping to the shadow of the ditch I came to a small garden level with a cottage chimney. Could see down through a screen of thorn hedge to the street. I knew at once I was witnessing an "American wake," a common thing these days in every other townland of the island.

Under a moon tattered with clouds the people looked spectral. Famished ghosts more than humans. Saw a young man moving through them, shaking hands with neighbours, embracing relations, lifting and kissing children. Then saw him whisper something to a young girl who left the gathering and stood below me under the garden bank. Out of sight, but I could hear her emotion as the mother held on to the son calling him her "*bábóg*," kissing his hands and eyes and begging him not to go. The professional keeners then began a lament for "The Dead Traveller," an archaic rigmarole praising his noble deeds, his prowess of body, his beauty of soul. Near the end of this, as though at the bidding of a hidden master of ceremonies, the crowd drew back to form a circle leaving two men alone in the middle. It now became clear that these two were father and son, clear too that they could find neither words nor actions to match what they felt at that moment, until the father spoke,

—Face me now, son, in a step, for likely as not, it's the last step we'll take in this world together.

As I watched them, hands at their sides in the rigid folk manner, heads up, boots thumping the dirt street, eyes locked on each other's face, I saw that many in the circle were unable to keep watching and had to turn away and, remembering then my own son and how we had parted and how I would soon be leaving here forever, I, myself, was obliged to turn away and, although no stranger to mortality and grief, it seemed to me that never until that moment had I fully understood the suffering of these people my own family had lived amongst for so long, and never before had I witnessed anything so affecting, so full of heartbreak, as that awkward, final dance of farewell.

The Mother

REACH ME DOWN comfort, O Virgin most powerful. Cover me with sleep and sleep and sleep till my eyes open at the feet of Christ.

Hail Mary, full of grace. Hail Grace, full of O'Hara, Pat O'Hara's Jimmy Ned up on my wee innocent.

—Don't let them near your hidey place, I warned them girls, 'cause there's men walkin' the world ready to slip in and strut off braggin' into black pongers.

The angel of the Lord declared, so he did. And more. And she was conceived, so she was. And the word was made flesh. A mystery, that's for certain. Yes. And thon's her bell. The Angelus, is it? House of gold. Near dark or light? Which?

Dead bell more like. Never quits here, nor the squeal of that deadcart. Jesus, who for? Me, Mary Josephine Brady, née Daly? And where am I? Why let on, when I know full well? Chained in with barrels of piss and shit and a go of cracked Bridies is where I am, a shambles shed of howls is where I am, a screamin' hell is where I am, the idiot ward of a poorhouse is where I am, and serve me right, may God in His mercy forgive me, and Mary, His Blessèd Mother, and all the saints in heaven. It's punishment, so it is. And what was it we done on You, Lord, made You punish us that way, blight our praties, turn Your head away, then turn it back to watch us starve and sicken, go mad and die? Our poor sins, was it? What harm did they do You? What harm? May God forgive me, a sinner, to throw contrary questions at the face of Glory.

Thy will be done.

Thy will be done.

Thy will be done.

Was it Your will that bitter blow in March broke my heart beyond all mendin', took my Grace, warped my Roisin's heart, made my foolish husband lave, and left me nothin' of home and happiness but this poor cracked thing I am, in this foul purgatory? Is that the price You'd have me pay, Lord, for a few stumbles? Or have I more to pay? Has the Landlord of Heaven a harder heart than Skinner of Drumbofin? Is there nothin' from this day out only death and burials, burials, burials?

Ah my love, my love, my Roisin Dubh, you wronged me, daughter.

I renounce the world, the flesh and the Devil.

I renounce the world, the flesh and the Devil.

I renounce the world, the flesh and the Devil.

Full of Grace and Roisin I was one time, twin beauties, and the Devil knows how. I warned them day in day out, so I did. God knows I did. Any night they'd creep in late from wake or dance I'd shout at them,

—Is it a pair of hoors I have for daughters? Go out wash yerselves, ye dirty clarts, ye have me shamed before the whole country. Have ye neither a titter of wit nor track of dacency?

Wore out I was tellin' them how your sins wing back to find you out in the old meadows, poor frighted crakes, runnin' and hidin' from the hook of God, and there's no half-wise body in the world but knows that for the truth. They paid no heed. No heed. No heed. And did she cry, the cratur, when the blood come, God help her, and when her monthly didn't I lost the head and got her by the ear and chained her above like a pedlar's monkey, well hid from the eyes of Maggie Scarlett and her like.

I did. So I did.

So I did.

So I did. God forgive me.

—No Mama, no Mama, please Mama, please!

Grace, disgrace.

Grace, disgrace.

Grace, disgrace.

I tongued and tongued her in mad tempers for givin' in to a fly article the like of O'Hara. My Roisin was too wide to be caught that way but I'd a nose for her capers, away with the boys behind the boar's shack where the young ones pair off, aye, let them do it on her belly or her bum, too choosy to let them in, silly wee ditch hoors the two of them, no wit and half the country famished. Oh Christ forgive me. It's got in sin they were, them girls; aye, troth they were, but such beauties naked or dressed forninst the like of Maggie Scarlett's lumps. Small wonder she's jealous.

Like swans, my two. Take the sight from your eyes, so they would. Gone now both. Under the earth, and over the sea. Oh the head was half gone or full gone that time they brought me here and tied me down.

A mistake I made, to be sure, a mistake, and aren't we all wise after blunders, and don't we all blunder on, and swear never again, and on we go again all forgot, or do any of us know what we're at when nature's hot or the head's bothered? Do we? Who was it chained my girleen up like a stray goat? Me? Asha who else, woman? Don't cod yourself when you know rightly it was yourself. Me, myself, the bespoke tailor's wife. Bespoke? Brady, is it? A sham article couldn't sew a shroud on a ghost?

Now my Dada, John Daly, was a proper man with a proper grip on God and the Devil on account of Canon McKenna with his fancy Leinster Irish couldn't twig the Kerry boys' confessions, them squads of travellin' chancers diggin' turnips for Lord Skinner. Put him on a chair in a dark sacristy and made him face away from the Kerrymen and translate their sins. Bound him over to secrecy.

"Holy John" the neighbours called him from that day out. "Holy John" of Drumlanna and the people travelled from the Bragans and farther out to ask his blessin' or get the cure for this or that and then he got the name of a man whose touch could make a barren woman hold and that made him cross.

—No, no, no, no, no, no, no, no, and the more he no-ed the more they'd fall to their knees and beg and in the end he'd put his two hands on their heads and pray to the Virgin Mother and they got their babbies, the most of them.

Now there's a mystery. Fierce holy, he was, and strict with it.

—If you girls don't quit that I'll redden your arses!

For a fit of the giggles only, at the Rosary. And more than a growl it was. He meant it. We quit our giggles quick, so we did. No man for empty threats. Forever traipsin' to clergy with backdoor tattle.

"Blessèd John Bollox of Drumlanna!" That's what Festus called him, the only one of the boys ever to face up to him and hit back. Two of a kind, only Festus grew to hate him, his own father. We all loved Mama, red-eyed in turfsmoke and clabber, stooped all her days over pots till she tumbled into her grave at fifty like most poor weemen in the world. Where are you now, Mama, with your bad cough? Can you hear me? And Granny Maguire? And Granny's Granny and her Granny and her Granny and all the Grannies of a hundred thousand winters away back to the blind start of the world? Up in heaven, are ye all? God help yeer ghosts, wherever ye are. Poor weemen, their vennel of tears dried up in the latter end. In their poor graves with their lost babbies. Me with them soon. At peace. My Roisin's gone, the wee bitch. How could she accuse the way she did? Greedy for the nipple she was, right off. The other wee thing had to be coaxed to suck. And they grew that way, hard and soft, open and closed, warm and cauld, one tagged for life, the other for death. Aye.

Body of Christ. Communion soon from Galligan, the priest of God.

—The settle bed'll buy a coffin to bury her proper, he said. The chape one with the lath and cardboard bottom I got from MacManus in Chapel Street. 'Twas Maggie Scarlett's grunt I heard at the graveside.

—She'll have her arse through that in a week.

Cross-eyed auld sow across from me here suckin' on her broken pipe. Never look in her eye or let on I hear her jibes.

—That Murphy fella has your other daughter bowlegged, Brady. Take care she doesn't end up potbellied like the others!

That class of spite's aisy shrugged off, but when your own blood stares from hooded eyes accusin', that's a heartscald.

—Can you hear me, Mama? I can talk kindly with you any time I want. Queenie Donnelly you were, before you married.

Queen of Angels.

Queen of Patriarchs.

Queen of Prophets.

Queen of Apostles.

Queen of Martyrs.

Queen of Confessors.

Queen of Virgins.

Queen of all Saints.

Queen conceived without original sin.

—How were we conceived, Mama, with you below in the settle bed and Dada above in the cockloft?

—Hands on from Holy John, Festus said.

Or maybe seven more Immaculate Conceptions, and we childer were shocked and laughed but didn't Nora Tom blurt this round the pot of spuds? Dada cut an ash-plant and lashed Festus till he wasn't fit to scream and locked him in the byre for a week on cold stirabout and water. He come out like a ghost. After that he held his tongue. Couldn't get away from Drumlanna quick enough. All the boys left one by one. Festus for Scotland, then France; Michael and Joe for Amerikay. The three girls married hereabouts, bar me, Mary Josephine.

—The big hallion of a lassie, spit of the father, everyone said.

It was Sadie put about what was overheerd in Caffrey's shebeen.

—Imagine slavin' out all day with Holy John and then the Rosary and litanies at night and, after that, gettin' up on big Mary Joe! Any man fit for thon'd need to be part saint, part hoe boy, and part billy goat!

Cruel and true. There was no pad tramped to our door by young fellas lookin' to join with me at Drumlanna. Any man wanted me and the ten acres knew he'd have to live in and work out with the half priest, Holy John. They kept well away. Every now and then there was a new babby for Cissie, Sadie or Nora Tom. He must've heard me one night cryin' quiet after a christenin' I didn't go to. I couldn't. It was Sadie's fourth and her not twenty-two.

—What ails ye, daughter? he called down from the cockloft. I was too choked up to answer.

—You want your own babby? Am I right?

I was so shamed he twigged this I quit the cryin' of a sudden.

—You're far too good for any man, he said. But I'll find you one.

—I don't want that, Dada, I said. Please. I don't want that. I'd as lief lie my lone.

—You'll do what I say, daughter, quit the cryin' now, say your prayers and go to sleep.

I always done what he said. I prayed.

"From growth to age, from age to death,
Be Thy two arms here, oh Christ about me."

Got stiff as he aged. The hinches. I did the outside work. He kept the kitchen and often, when I come down from mouldin' spuds on the bracken hill or up from the gut field mindin' geese or in from turnin' hay beyont in the church field, he'd tell me who'd come and gone and what news there was in the world. Them were happy times, happy, happy times. Just the two of us and not a cross word nor a dumb patch between us, ever.

Oh Jesus, the heartbreak in this place now to mind such happiness, our own ass to bring home turf before the days grew chill, and the way we'd fall on our knees at night to thank the Maker of stars for this world and its wonders. Aye God, You were good to us then, when I was a girsha, so You were, praise be, in them days before the blight, before that time I scrubbed for the Mercys at Bellaney. Twelve I was and worse nor here it was, them long corridors hung with bishops and holy pictures so lonely I'd count fields in my head could be reckoned from our street at Drumlanna where you'd see sheep and goats and donkeys and hear childer in townlands as far off as Ballagh that I walked to once under the stars drunk with wonder at the sky and, anyway, I knew worse had befallen others than skivvyin' a year for nuns, up at five on my knees scrubbin' in the kitchen or emptyin' their chamberpots and them on their knees prayin' and prayin' great wheens of prayer for the souls of sinners and all the pagans in the world lost to God's mercy, and the time I cried out when it scalded me to pee and Reverend Mother come close with her witherdy face.

—Were you at yourself, girl?

—What, Mother?

—Don't pretend.

—I've no notion what—

—Immodestly? Tell the truth.

—I was not.

—If that's a lie and your bladder bursts it'll be a judgement of God.

How could she accuse that way so sure of herself? Pretend is what they were at, kinder to yard cats nor me, clackin' away to God in their heads like magpies or whisperin' in corners till they're buried separate in God's acre, brides of Christ till they bed down with God Almighty Himself, God help Him. And there goes the Devil makin' me badmind the holy nuns, may God forgive me, but them were happy times forby that one year, happy, happy times till the travellin' tailor called.

—A well-spoken wee fella, Dada said, name of Brady. Thomas Brady. Measured me for a workin' waistcoat. Well fit to read and write, a man with a trade and a share of Latin. He'll be back soon with the waistcoat tailored.

I guessed right off. The match was made and a bad match it was. When Brady come back with the waistcoat it buttoned crooked. Small worry that. But with legs on him like a donkey's foal and no arse worth a mention, that was cause for worry. God help me, I thought, the minute I saw him, do I have to breed with this cratur? Itself is he fit to breed? From the start his trade kept him away, mostly at fairs, or in a tailor's workshop up about Dundalk. Always the smell of whiskey off him when he come back. And the poor mouth. And the excuses. And no money ever.

It was Maggie Scarlett said once,

—Course the like of a travellin' tailor could have weemen here and there.

And, in my own head I thought, Well, if he has, he's left no scatter of childer behind 'cause all he ever planted in me in ten years was one sick caudie, wee Micilín, God help him.

Poor Dada, poor Dada! Them silly girls never quit with their Poor Dada.

Betimes I was near tempted to tell them the way they were planted. A knifegrinder from Kildysart it was. Not a day passes but I think of him. A tall man he was, with good teeth and them heavy-lidded eyes and the soft way they talk down there. Mid-July. Duskus. 1831.

—Have you anythin' needs to be honed, Mam? says he.

—I have, says I. A pair of scissors.

—I can touch them up nicely for you, says he.

—Come in a while, says I. I'm alone in this place.

May God forgive the night I had in the feathers with the knifegrinder. I lost track of who he was and who I was in a fog so blind I didn't give a donkey's howl if they heard me ten townlands away. And when he left at first light and I went down to wash in Callaghan's pool I knew for certain life inside me had begun. Two lives he planted. Never asked him his name. Wild carry on. The Devil was in me that night. He knows his business.

Dada went walkin' to Lough Derg after I married Brady. To shrive his soul and give me a time alone with the bridegroom, God help him.

That first night in the feathers I lay back and laughed at him when he was at his best. Any woman would. The next night, knowin' rightly how the sisters giggled 'bout bein' near split in two by their men, I quit the laughin', opened my legs wide, and said,

—Would you, for God's sake, look at what you're at, man!

You'd swear he was starin' into the mouth of hell with them rabbity eyes.

—What are you afeard of? I asked.

Useless wee shagger, a mickey on him like a thimble and, worse again, a thirst on him for whiskey like an empty still! And the more I'd tongued 'bout how useless he was the more I'd hear them girls whisper,

—Poor Dada. Poor Dada.

And I'd say each time,

—Small loss he's gone, girls, small loss.

Guardian of Virgins. Pray for me.

Pillar of families. Pray for me.

Queen of Confessors. Pray for me.

Never did confess how they were got to a single soul, nor what we were at long ago, half asleep in the straw, tops and tails, boys and girls, and you never knew whose foot was between your legs till the thrill was over and then it was one of the boys with your foot against his thing till it got wet and no one made a sound, may God forgive us, or let on it was goin' on till I asked one day,

—Is it right, this carry on with the feet? What would the clergy make of it? Would the Virgin Mary be at the like?

—Maybe she had no brothers, Cissie said, very shy of herself.

—Clergy have no notion of the like, Sadie said, wicked cross, they're not fit to understand, and you quit this talk, Mary Joe, there's no call for it.

I knew rightly why she wanted the talk to quit. When I was small she'd get me to feel her nipples when her breasts were swellin' pointy. I done this for her and other capers I'd as lief not think or talk about. And why would I? I'm not one for tattle and anyway I'd my own sins to think about, then and now.

Poor Cissie ended up married to the great brute Noel Callaghan. She must be up in heaven now with her three wee girls as sure as Noel's down in hell, and it was our Dada, Holy John, who sent him there, 'cause after a fair at Lisbellaw didn't the same Noel bring home the wida woman from Grencha, Aggie Halpin, a breed of half hoor, the two of them astray in the head from drink. Cissie was too afeard to face them but in dread of what her wee girls might hear or see she got out a windy and come down to our house with her story.

—Go back quick, says Dada, before you're missed, and he carried her story on to Canon McKenna who carried it on to Sergeant Reilly and the two of them lit in on Noel stretched above on the hearth with Halpin astride him wrigglin' hard to plaze him for sixpence.

—Is it your arse in the air now, Jezebel? shouts the Canon givin' her buttocks a woeful lash with his whip.

She screamed and fell off Callaghan and started to crawl for a corner. He follied, whippin' her and shoutin',

—If it's hell you're after, woman, it's hell you'll get from me, bad cess to your filthy trade. I'll name you from the altar, so I will, you blight, you poison, you family polluter, you foul thing in a clean parish! And when she had welts on her as thick as your finger he turned to Callaghan and roared,

—Let that be a lesson to you, Noel Callaghan!

Aye, that's the way of it in this world. It's the men that matter. Two butter balls and a squirty, Father, Son and Holy Ghost. They get off most times with a shout, when the woman gets bate like an ass, 'cause they were hardly out the door when it was Cissie's turn for torture. The brave Noel got her ear till she cringed to her knees.

—Where were you, woman, when I called for me supper? Dancin' over the fields, was it? To whinge off your mouth to the Church and the Law? Was it? And did ya dar' inform on me, ya cunt, ya never give me a manchild yet!

And he took the plough reins from the top of the dresser and every time he lashed Cissie about the kitchen he'd roar time about,

—Where's the Church now? Where's the Law now?

When she come down to our house next day scorched from the plough reins, Mama and we girls cried as she told her story, how Wee Tess was deaf in one ear from a cuff, and how there was always one of her girls bruised or worse, and that was only the half of it 'cause there was other carry on couldn't be spoke of, and the truth is they were all in livin' terror of Noel and most days God sent she said she'd rather be dead and out of it entirely with the angels and saints in heaven. She'd suffered enough. She'd her purgatory done twice over in this world. And who could say other than that?

When Cissie was gone Dada stood listenin' at the half-door as the boys got fierce angry about Callaghan's villainy. We girls joined in and were all noisy at this when he spoke up.

—Quit the talk now, he said. Callaghan's dead.

We all looked at him, his jaw set like a blacksmith's vice. I saw Mama and the girls go white and I'm sure I did too. The three boys were blinkin' hard. No one offered to spake. We all knew he meant what he said.

It was two weeks before Callaghan was fished out of a boghole off our laneway. Dada helped carry his coffin and shovel him under and the Canon preached a sermon 'bout the evils of drink and the mercy of Christ. Poor Noel he said was in trouble with the first and in sore need of the second but most neighbours said,

—It's a wonder to God he lasted so long, the same Noel, but a half miracle for Cissie and her girls now he's gone.

Near the latter end of his life I asked him straight out how Callaghan met his death. He looked at me a brave while before he spoke.

—He was the bad thief, daughter. Christ turned away from the bad thief.
So did I.

I knew God told Dada what he must do betimes but to hear it said straight
out was a chill to the heart. I accuse he confessed to the clergy, a holy man to
be sure, and, true, I'd a great love for him but maybe a greater fear on
account of his strictness. A hard judge of men and weemen, but harder again
of himself.

—May God forgive me, he said one day, my head's full of nothin' but bad
notions.

And the tears come into his eyes, a thing you'd hardly ever see. I asked
him how a Christian man as good livin' could be so troubled, and he said,

—The Devil at night, daughter. He poisons the head.

—There's no sin in dreams, I said. Sure the Pope himself has nature like
us. He must dream like us, surely to God.

—True enough, he said, only betimes you'd be hard put to know when
you're awake and when you're asleep.

That was when I minded a dream wouldn't leave me be, no matter how I
prayed or who I prayed to. I tried the Virgin herself, then Brigid, then
Monica, and none of them were fit to banish the dream. When I was asleep,
down he'd come from the cockloft into the settle bed and I'd take his piesel
in my two hands and when I put it inside me it took the breath from me and
when we were done he'd crawl out to the street and howl up at the stars like
a dog, beggin' God Almighty to forgive him. Then I'd wake in a wet fright
to hear him snorin' above and thank God it was a dream only. Even so, I
wouldn't be myself all next day.

Maybe it was the like of that had him annoyed. The Devil's a crafty villain
and maybe in black dark he planted the same in Dada's head. Who can say?
It could never be talked about.

—Bless me, Dada, for I have sinned. My soul's cangled to the Devil on
account of—

—What, daughter?

—God knows.

—Tell me.

—I can't.

—Holy God knows all.

—Tell me.

—I can't.

—Then you can't be forgive.

—You're not God, Dada.

—That's where you're wrong.

—You're not God, Dada.

—That's where you're wrong.

—You're astray in the head to think you're God.

—The head's more your trouble than mine.

—Got dead, he was, on the road near Pettigo on his way back from that island in Lough Derg where they say it's all circles of Rosaries and rain prayed out over stones in a great red lake, all his sins in the lap of God, and not a one to brag his holiness, or mark his grave, only grass and docks and nettles to redden the arses of angels maybe giggled at the wrong time. Holy John.

No odds much where a body lies in the latter end. Is it? Grave or pit, boneyard or the bottom of the sea. All the one till the trumpet sounds.

May God forgive him just the same for what he done to Noel Callaghan. Bad and all as Noel was he got no chance to make his peace with God, and I've a daughter thinks I done the same to her sister's babby, cold-hearted wee cutty she turned out to be. Did she hear talk maybe 'bout how Dada tipped Callaghan into a boghole? The whole country knew Festus strung up Sammy Agnew like a fox, and if that was father and son then, maybe, she'd think me well fit to block out the life of a wee innocent. And may be the same badness is in her too. Said she'd kill me and meant it, so she did, and when I shaped to tell her different times she screamed back at me, her two fingers in her two ears. I quit tryin'. I wasn't goin' to beg a hearin' from my own blood. I'm proud too. And that one time she come here and kissed my hands I thought, I'll tell her now. I couldn't. Not with that look in her face and now she'll never hear what was in my head to say.

I was half cracked with grief that time, daughter, but no murderer. I chained up your sister's shame to hide it 'cause I'm cangled to shame myself, chained her in fright and sorrow with mad-eyed hunger and death starin' into every other cabin. I'll not deny what I done but give me a second chance I'd have marched her round the neighbours all and bared her belly to the sun and shouted out,

—Look, my daughter Grace is full of life. God's work, and God is good, is He not? God'll mind us. God'll send down food from heaven. God is kinder surely than Murphy, the Master of this poorhouse, is He not? Is He?

Sadie it was first brought news of that Murphy fella to Drumlanna, that time she was bonded out to Fergusons. Full of him she was, the workin' boy steward, a skelp of Lord Skinner's, some said, but whatever he was she'd fair sicken you talkin' 'bout the lovely voice of him, and oh the laugh of him, and oh the jokes of him, and oh the way he could sit a horse, and oh the way he could talk aisy with gentry or country folk and how all the byre girls were wet for him. She was that much of a dose I asked her once,

—Were you wet for him, Sadie, did he sit on you?

—Ya jealous lump, she said. Whatever he done with me he wouldn'a done with you. No man with an eye in his head'd bother with a hallion like you.

And straight back to her face I said,

—One cunt's as good as another in the dark.

Oh she fair screamed out her temper and scrabbed my face with her nails and we never spoke aisy from that day till she married nor for long after, nor her childer to mine, and me closer to her growin' up than any of the others. Not a secret between us. And now she's buried in the ocean deep, the half of her childer down there with her. God, how I loved her long ago! May Christ have mercy on her soul at the bottom of the sea. It's far she is now from byre kisses and the larks of Bragan. Oh Jesus, why do we human families torture other the way we do? A silly grig from me, a bad tempered scrab from her, and then the long bitterness. Oh Sadie, if you came to me now smilin' from the bottom of the sea I'd throw my two arms round you and cry hot tears for all them years we lost hatin' other over the head of nothin'. Better again, if my Roisin come back for five minutes and listened to my story and believed it I'd die happy. Stood across from me at Grace's grave, so she did, and when the first shovel dundered on the boards that near stopped my heart with grief I looked up and saw her face all glares and stares forninst me. Hatred, or near enough, writ all over it. My own daughter. Neighbours I half knew gave me more comfort.

Oh my love, my love, my Roisin Dubh, wherever you're gone remember me kindly,

I'd walk the dew beside you, or the bitter desert
In hopes I might merit a smile of your love.
Fragrant branch of mine, give me word, let me hope,
O choicest flower of Ireland, my Roisin Dubh.
Have pity on your poor mother and may the Mother of God have pity on

the fruit of my womb, my dead daughter Grace, and the dead-born fruit of her womb. Ask your Son to forgive her, and me, your disgraced servant, Mary Josephine, all our sins.

God help me, God help me, God help me.

Out of the depths I have cried unto thee, O Lord.

Lord, hear my voice, because with Thee, Lord, there is mercy, with Thee there is plentiful redemption. With Thee there is forgiveness. Aye, but hunger too!

The pity was I didn't die in the briars of Scart that time I was crazed. Die and be done with it. What had we to live for, the most of us? Not a bite in the house bar England's charity, the stirabout of India meal. A dose of the skitters, they sent us, gravel and shite, and their great ships sailin' from our ports half foundered with food from every townland of Ireland to feed their murderin' armies at the four ends of the earth. May they suffer some day for what they done to us. And where was Tom Brady, the bespoke tailor, left us in our time of need? Piss blind in Dundalk.

—Small loss he's gone, girls, I said every time. Small loss. I'd as lief we'd all starve and be ghosts ourselves as see aither of you plump at Drumbofin! Scullions to Bob Skinner, Lord Clonroy, is it? Ride whatever's handy, them gentry, high or low, man or woman, boy or girl, calf or nanny goat, up and in and jiggle away till their wee fit's over. May the Devil fuck them! Oh God, forgive my tongue but may He double fuck them down to hell, and his hired brutes skewered us for rent of land was ours, that tumbled us into the jaws of winter when the praties failed, that left us without sow or cow, calf or clucking hen, that tipped my flax-wheel and my stool, my poor pillows of meadowsweet, like dead things into a sheugh, whose flunkeys cut my nightlines set for jack pikes in the lough at Tirnahinch, that took the sleep from me, and the hope from me, and my house from me, and my family from me, and my wits from me, that robbed me of the sweet mint from the hill of Corduff, that left me naked in the bog of Scart astray in the head and chewin' on bitter sorrel. Oh Christ the Judge, there's no forgivin' the like, none now, or ever more, Amen.

Ah my love, my love, my Roisin Dubh, if you'd come to me you'd have heard the way it was that night and no one in it only myself in a blind of terror, that night you ran away when the babby was caught at the shoulders for hours and dead for hours, and I callin' every minute on God above to help me before I dragged it from her body by its neck and then the great bloodfall and me on my knees watchin' the life go out of my own poor cratur, dyin', dyin' like a candle, before my eyes.

And after that in deep sleep I seen her free herself from the chain and run down through the night with her babby to Callaghan's pool and heerd her voice and her wee thing cryin' out in the black dark. Near broke my heart 'cause she'd nothin' in her belly, and how could she have milk in her breasts to feed the babby, and I was runnin' and runnin' and shoutin',

—They'll die, they'll die, they'll drown theirselves, my daughter, oh my daughter, my poor, poor daughter, don't do it, Grace, for the love of God, and the Blessèd Virgin, don't do it. And another voice in my head was sayin',

—They'll come to no harm, no harm at all, God'll mind them.

Aye, surely, but the Devil's know'd my story and where do you look for two lost angels in the dark when that's what you're up agin'? And I was sarchin' and sarchin' in sheughs and vennels all thorn scrabbed, tore and bloody, with no notion in the world they were dead. Gone now, Grace and her wee blue-faced bundle, dead, gone, buried and forgot! Forgot? No mercy then or now. I was in hell that night that last time you come here and I sarchin' for words to begin my story when you said of a sudden,

—May God forgive you, Mama, I never will.

And walked away from here with your bag and your boat ticket, and that Murphy man locked the door and me screamin' and screamin' out through the windy,

—Don't lave me here to die, daughter, for the love of Jesus Christ, have pity on your poor mother. Don't lave me.

And you walked on across that big yard through ghosty paupers, out and away through them big gates, forever and ever. And never once looked back.

Virgin most merciful, I'll die alone in this place now and, if that's how my story ends, be with me at the end. And be with me now through this day. Help sweeten my thoughts and soften my tongue. Give me back the old, rounded days of nature long ago when we had the black cow with the white nose and the garden of lumpers every year on the south hill under Carn, and I watchin' Dada dig them in or shovel them out and bag more than enough to feed us all, and the odd beggar too, and the scatter of hens, and a pig betimes, and oaten bread from the cut of oats, and every year come early May, bright or hasky, we'd be off to the red bog of Bragan to save turf and